MELODY DAWN

A MELODY DAWN VAMP

MELODY DAWN

by Frank Lauria

Rothco Press • Los Angeles, California

Published by
Rothco Press
8033 West Sunset Blvd., Ste. 1022
West Hollywood, CA 90046

Copyright © 2015 by Frank Lauria

Cover design by Rob Cohen

This book is a work of fiction. Names, characters, places and incidents are products of the author's imagination or are used fictitiously. Any resemblance to actual events or locales or persons, living or dead, is entirely coincidental.

All rights reserved.

No part of this book may be reproduced, or stored in a retrieval system, or transmitted in any form or by any means, electronic, mechanical, photocopying, recording, or otherwise, without written permission of the publisher. For information regarding permission, write to Rothco Press, Attention: Permissions Department, 8033 West Sunset Blvd., Ste. 1022, West Hollywood, CA 90046

Rothco Press is a division of Over Easy Media Inc.

ISBN: 978-1-941519-72-1

Electronic ISBN: 978-1-941519-73-8

For Keith Deutsch; publisher, poet, and pulp hero

Book One

Stealthily the dark haunts round
And, When the lamp goes, without sound
At a swifter bound
Than the swiftest hound.
Arrives, and all else is drowned...

                Edward Thomas, Out In the Dark

Chapter 1

Les Hensen considered himself an excellent wheel man. His partner Dave Chin thought otherwise. But Chin knew it was Henson's turn to drive so when the attendant mistakenly handed him the key he tossed it over the hood.

Hensen snatched it in mid-air and held it aloft. "*Yes*," he said under his breath.

Dave settled inside the black Chevy Malibu they'd drawn for this assignment. "You're frisky this morning."

"And hungry."

Les punched their destination on the GPS, "You ready for a real Southern breakfast?"

Chin turned on the AC. "I'm ready for anything that includes strong coffee. So dude—now that we're alone—what the hell are we doing here in Dixie?"

"Far as I know we find out when we get there."

"Seriously, partner, they must have told you more than that."

"Only that it's a breakfast meeting."

"Real southern breakfast my butt," Dave grumbled, "probably some franchise fry stand in a local mall. I already have a bum stomach from the flight."

Both agents were based in New York and had flown out separately to Louis Armstrong Airport in New Orleans. They proceeded to Lafayette, booked rooms at separate motels and only met for the first time at the gas station where they got the Malibu. The cover story was they were picking up the newly serviced car for their boss.

That was as much as Dave knew. Given the fact that he and Les had often worked together in the past, all this secrecy on the part of the Bureau seemed ominous. The FBI division in New Orleans had a satellite office in Lafayette. They could have been briefed and issued a vehicle right there.

"I don't like this Les. Why us?"

Les grinned. "Because we're the best. Top Guns... Maverick and Goose."

"Didn't Goose die in the end?"

"Lighten up buddy. All this hide and seek crap means one thing: big case, big budget, big bump in pay grade."

"That's three things. Why are you so damn bouncy anyway? Did you get lucky last night?"

Hensen's expression became guarded. At forty five he was older than Chin by ten years and lately had become increasingly concerned with promotions, pensions, and covering his ass. A one night stand while on the job was highly frowned upon by the Bureau. Dave understood his reluctance. Still he was disappointed that Les hadn't learned to trust him.

Les was senior agent on one of Dave's first cases. He had shown remarkable patience with his rookie partner and taught him well. He was also an asset under fire. Their second case involved a bank robber who had them pinned down in a small cellar where they thought he was hiding. Instead the suspect slipped around the outside and started spitting quick bursts from his AK47 through the slanted wooden door, chopping it apart. Both of them found cover at opposite ends of the dark room but the bullets continued to ricochet like steel golf balls even after the firing stopped.

So when Les rolled an empty can across the floor drawing another burst Dave cursed him. Abruptly the firing jerked to a halt and Dave heard a metallic clicking.

Without hesitation Les marched right up to the shattered door and shot the bastard while he was reloading.

Since then, Dave felt secure that his partner had his back.

As if reading his mind Les gave him a sly smile,

"Yeah, you might say I got lucky. This lady was no lady. Technically I was off duty," he added, "we haven't been briefed yet."

"I'll put that in my report, "Dave said with heavy sarcasm, making sure he got the point. "This lady have a name?"

Lost in reverie Les stared straight ahead at the two lane road that wound beneath a canopy of low hanging vegetation. Except for the receding blond hair that accentuated the craggy angles in his face, the only other signs of aging were the hard creases edging his deep-set blue eyes. At six-one, one hundred ninety five, Les was quite fit, a distance runner, martial artist, top marksman and a crummy driver.

"Whoa boy…" Dave muttered.

Les swerved. The tires pounded the encroaching roots of a gnarled magnolia tree but he avoided the trunk. "What the hell," Les said indignantly, "somebody should report *that*."

Dave didn't answer. He had been there before. Les had a tendency to lose focus while behind the wheel.

"So?" he said instead.

"So… what?"

"The girl, the lady—details homey, details—like her name."

"Melody," he rolled the word.

"That it?"

"One name's enough for a double-double."

"Double-double?"

"Ten for looks, ten in the sack—perfect. I'm ready to roll this morning."

Dave wasn't ready. He had left a pregnant wife and three-year-old girl back in Manhattan and always had trouble sleeping after a flight. He hoped there was time for coffee before their top-secret briefing. No doubt someone from Division would be there to take names and numbers. It was always the same with covert operations. If they failed they went on the shit list. If they succeeded it went unnoticed.

"How do you figure this is so high-profile?" Dave asked. "Might be another interstate drug cartel."

Les shrugged. "After twenty plus years my educated nose can smell it. I'm betting terrorists, ISIS shit."

"Again, why us? We've been working fraud, kidnap, bank robbery, meth labs... we know squat about terrorists."

"A bad guy is a bad guy."

"Where did you get that—a fortune cookie?"

To Dave's relief the site chosen for the briefing was a small mom and pop eatery named Shorty's Café. Despite the early hour he felt his shirt sticking to his skin as soon as they left the air-conditioned Malibu. Inside the café, two wooden ceiling fans made the humidity bearable if not better.

They had arrived ahead of schedule and Dave ordered coffee right away. The waitress came back with a pot and he ordered breakfast. Halfway through his eggs and grits two men entered. They walked directly to their table and sat down.

Like Dave and Les they were dressed in shirts and jeans. One of them sported a black baseball cap with the gold fleur-de-lis logo of the New Orleans Saints. The other man had short black hair and a sunburned neck. Both wore shades.

"Glad you boys could make it," the baseball cap said, as if they had a choice.

Les gestured at his plate with his fork. "Food here is worth the drive. I'm Hensen..."

The baseball cap lowered his voice. "We know who you are. I'm Lake, deputy director Louisiana Division. This is director Matt Easton from our local shop in Lafayette," he said in a deep southern drawl. He spoke in a measured cadence as if delivering a sotto voce sermon.

Dave smiled warily. Les nodded and continued eating his French toast.

When Lake removed his sunglasses Dave saw the sagging skin around his pale blue eyes. His sallow expression suggested deep sorrow laced with contempt, like a priest weary of human corruption. Or a hanging judge, Dave thought

The waitress arrived and Lake and Easton ordered cheese omelets and coffee. Lake waited for her to leave before he spoke.

"Reason you're down here is because you come from outside the division."

Les stopped eating. "You have a leak?" he said after a moment.

"We don't know. We're counting on you boys to find out."

"How many people know we're here?" Dave asked.

Easton spoke for the first time. "Good question. Right now it's just me and Virgil."

Dave and Les looked at each other.

"Who's Virgil?" Les said.

Slightly embarrassed Lake raised his hand.

Although the only other patron was sitting on the other side of the cafe, both he and Easton acted as if they were being watched. Their manner was furtive, and they kept their voices low.

"Look I've got the files and photographs in the car," Easton said. "We can discuss it outside, after breakfast."

The biscuits were delicious and Dave managed to squeeze in a third coffee before breakfast was cut short. He and Les exchanged glances on their way outside but said nothing. Each knew what the other was thinking.

These guys seemed scared shitless.

Outside it was getting hotter. Lake had parked at the end of the small lot next to the café, backing the Lexus into the space so that when he popped the trunk the raised top shielded them from view. Dave and Les stood on either side of Easton as he reached into a backpack and took out a fat file. He opened the file inside the trunk and spread out the contents. Printed reports on one side, photographs on the other.

"This file is highly sensitive," Lake said his tone far less genial than it had been inside the café. "Lose it and it will be your ass, clear?"

Dave nodded, Les shrugged.

"You can peruse the official reports and statements at your leisure. I'll give you the short version now." He took a deep breath.

"Damn it's getting hot," he murmured, then went on. "Two months ago an undercover cop from Lafayette, Ron Delcie, went missing during a drug surveillance operation. A team of two detectives was assigned to locate Delcie. A week later Delcie's body turned up in New Iberia, but the two detectives disappeared. The Lafayette police commissioner appealed to director Easton here and he sent a pair of field agents to investigate."

Les scratched his ear. "Don't say they're missing too,"

"Oh we know where they are alright." Easton handed them some photographs. "They're in the New Orleans morgue. Bodies were found in a cemetery three days ago, their throats ripped out and their hearts and livers gone."

After looking at the grisly photographs Dave struggled to keep his breakfast down. He regretted the extra biscuits and coffee.

"Here's the kicker boys," Lake said laconically, "the same thing happened to Detective Delcie: throat, heart, liver. See, at first we thought it was scavengers, because the body was found in a bayou—until they found our agents."

"Let me get this clear. One undercover cop and two FBI field agents have been murdered and mutilated, and there are two more detectives missing—correct?" Dave said.

"Yes sadly, that is correct, Lake said.

Easton stepped closer. "I feel personally responsible for Ken Larkin and Sid Fairman."

The director of the Lafayette division was shorter than Dave with the broad shoulders and thick neck of a wrestler or gymnast. His cold grey eyes made it clear he wanted blood.

Dave met his gaze. "And there's a possibility someone inside the bureau fingered them?"

Easton glanced at Lake.

"We can't overlook any possibility." Lake said smoothly.

Dave ignored him, eyes locked on Easton. "What makes you think it's possible?"

"My agents were completely anonymous," Easton said, "the local police did not know they had been deployed. So if there was a leak it had to come from my unit."

Deployed, unit; Dave noted the tendency toward military terminology unlike Lake's laconic southern gentry style.

"This might take a while, us being from New York," he said casually but Lake caught his drift.

The deputy director nodded. "It's a mixed blessing, We are in need of invisible agents. We also need a multi ethnic team. Detective Delcie received intel about heroin shipments and had staked out a bar called Minny's. Local Vietnamese shrimpers frequent the establishment."

Dave shrugged. "Just for the record I'm Chinese."

"Whatever," Lake said, "Minny's is as good a place as any to start."

"How about the cemetery in New Orleans?" Les put in.

Both Lake and Easton seemed annoyed by the question. "It's always best to follow procedure and start at the beginning," Easton said patiently.

"Seems to me getting briefed in a parking lot is far from procedure," Les pointed out, "we'll need access to forensics, DNA lab, data base, body armor…"

Easton handed him a card. "This is my private email and the password. Go there, write a message, but do not send it. Repeat, do not send it. Instead save it in the Draft box. Whatever you men require will be provided I'll check the box often. You do the same. I'll expect daily reports of course."

"We'll also need cash," Les said, "credit cards are no good in the street."

Beaming like a kindly benefactor, Lake reached down and lifted a thick envelope halfway from the backpack then put it back. "We thought of that. You'll find twelve thousand US dollars in there."

Easton began gathering the file, "Any questions gentleman?"

"Yes," Les said, "when's the next shuttle back to Earth?"

+ + +

Les had a way of getting them off on the wrong foot, Dave thought, but in this case he was justified. They didn't speak as they watched Lake and Easton drive off in a silver Lexus with tinted windows.

Easton's backpack slung over one shoulder Dave walked slowly to the Malibu, aware of the crunch of pecan shells under his feet and the oppressive heat wilting his clothes.

"What the hell was that?" he said when they were in the car.

"Didn't you hear?" Les said, starting the engine "We've just been briefed."

For a few minutes they were silent. "Where are we going?" Dave said finally.

"New Orleans."

"Why?"

"I have reasons."

"We need to go over this file before we do anything."

"Problem is Dave we have one file and live in two hotels."

"So we take turns…"

"What we need to do is find a nice cool cocktail lounge where we can go over this thing together."

"Nothing is open. It's barely nine a.m."

Les gave him a mischievous glance. "By the time we get to New Orleans everything will be open."

"That the only reason we're going?"

"It figures that whatever agents Larkin and Fairman found at Minny's led them to New Orleans."

Dave nodded. "Makes sense."

"And it will definitely piss Easton off."

"Excellent reason. I think the guy is former military."

"You think?"

"His choice of words and that mail drop he gave us."

"What about the drop?"

"It's the same technique General Petraeus used to contact his lady friend."

"Sure didn't work for him." Les said, referring to the scandal that forced the Director of the CIA to retire.

"All things considered, that educated nose of yours couldn't smell meat in a butcher shop."

Les didn't answer as he turned toward route 10.

"Know what I smell now?" he said, going through a stop sign.

"Enlighten me."

"A goddamn setup." Les said, accelerating. "If we can't clean up their mess but live, we get the bad mark. If we end up like our predecessors, they'll just order two more like us."

"What happened to Maverick and Goose, top guns...?"

"Ultimately we're hired muscle, expendable assets."

"That briefing made you a philosopher," Dave yawned. He pulled down the windshield visor and leaned back. "Wake me when we get to New Orleans."

He closed his eyes but couldn't sleep.

The first thing he saw when he reopened his eyes were the insects spattered across the windshield. Although an hour shy of noon the juke joints were open. Les selected a gloomy lounge in the French Quarter that was empty of customers and they took a booth far from the bar. Les went for drinks while Dave opened the file and arranged the reports in chronological order. He left the crime photos face down on the Formica table.

There were two headshots of the missing detectives, Ryan Morgan and Norman Damon. Morgan seemed much younger than his partner, with long blonde hair and a boyish smile. Damon was heavy set and dour. And they both had vanished.

Les came back with two tall green drinks.

"Absinthe," he said, setting the glasses down.

Engrossed in his task Dave sipped his drink It had an odd taste, like anise or licorice.

"What did you say this is?"

"Absinthe, we're in the French Quarter, right?"

Dave shrugged and took another sip. It was cold and went down easy. "Nothing unusual in the police reports, take a look," He shoved the papers across the table, "I'll go over Easton's reports."

Halfway down his drink Dave realized he was feeling too good.

"Absinthe?" he said.

Les grinned. "Hundred and twenty proof."

"Christ, we need to stay frosty on this."

"Easy, I've got us covered. Did you notice the name of the cemetery where they found the bodies?"

"Yeah, St. Louis I think."

"St. Louis *number one,*" Les corrected.

"Okay one, so?"

"So it's right nearby. We can check it out."

"Not right now. Let's just stay put while I sober up and try to sort out a few things."

Les leaned back in the booth. "No hurry buddy.'

Four or five customers had wandered into the lounge and were scattered across the bar, their backs to the booth. Someone had fed the jukebox and the low twang of a blues guitar pulsed through the cool, half-lit room. It was something like being on an island, Dave thought. He was reminded of the lyric to a song called *Lush Life*: '...*where one relaxes on the axis of the wheel of life, to get the feel of life.*' Billy Strayhorn was only seventeen when he wrote it. Where did he get all that experience?

Then another question popped into his head.

"Who assigned you this case?"

Les looked at him with surprise.

"Beaumont, like our last one. Why..?"

"Pat Kramer sent me out here."

"Assistant Director Kramer?"

Dave nodded. The blues tune ended and another song began but Dave was no longer paying attention,

"This stinks Les," he said.

"We already know that."

"It's worse than we thought. This isn't local anymore. This goes all the way up."

"You're saying these murdered agents aren't the issue here?"

"Exactly."

"Then what is?"

"Whatever it is we're the sacrificial lambs."

Les took a deep breath "And you think all this because we were assigned by different people?"

"Deniability," Dave said firmly, "has to be."

"Deniability?" Les shook his head, "how about plain old *bureaucracy*?"

When Dave remained silent he went on. "Look we agree that we're being set up by Lake and Easton to cover their local garbage," Les said with a hint of condescension, "but I don't think this goes to Virginia or even New York."

Dave didn't answer. Sure, it was an intuitive leap but he had learned to trust his instinct. Although Les's attitude pissed him off, he also knew his partner was being reasonable. "Guess you think I'm paranoid," he said finally.

"Hell no," Les said, leaning closer, "it's the Green Goddess talking."

"What are *you* talking about?"

"Your drink old buddy. Real absinthe was illegal until recently. Back in the day all the French impressionists drank it. They say it drove a lot of them crazy."

Dave groaned, gathered up the file and shoved it into the backpack.

"Fuck it. Let's go check out this cemetery."

Located in the Treme district, St Louis Cemetery Number One was surrounded by grey stone walls that separated it from the passing traffic and rows of warehouses nearby. From the outside it looked like a demolition site but Dave acknowledged he was a tad obsessive about neatness. It had been the source of some contention between himself and Les in the past and he learned to let it go. The world was a messy place.

Certainly the venerable resting place was no different. In fact it had taken messy to a new level. When Dave entered it seemed he'd landed on a planet with its own geometric laws. The tombs were crammed together in no discernible order and were mostly in various states of disrepair, ranging from tattered glory to toppling grandeur. Some tombs leaned as if tipsy, others seemed slumped in resignation at the fact that they housed the dead.

They walked slowly through the maze of raised stone coffins protected by dirty white angels, mausoleums crouched behind rusty gates and sepulchers that were scratched with strange symbols. A few looked like grand cathedrals and mosques but most resembled lost temples, decayed and moss covered.

It was lunchtime so the tourists were somewhere downing *po' boys* and cold beer. Reluctantly, Dave reached into the backpack for the crime scene photos in an effort to locate the exact spot where the agents had been found. He tried not to look at the mutilated bodies and focused on the tombs that framed their remains.

"See anything looks like this?" he said, passing the photos to Les.

His partner seemed equally reluctant to accept the pictures. Les held them at arm's length as if offended by the horrific evidence of human evil. "Those weird X's on that one in the back there?"

"Yeah, I see it."

"Look for that one."

"Maybe we should split."

Les gave him a thumb's up and they turned in different directions.

The inner paths were a maze and many of the tombs had graffiti. A few were marked with X's but not the right kind. One or two had shrine-like offerings before them: cheap beads, small flasks of liquor, cigarettes, brightly colored flowers.

Dave tried to visualize the marked sepulcher in the picture with little success. He hated crime scene photos, hated the carelessly grotesque angles of the limbs, the victims' rigid grimaces, their wide-eyed stares into the abyss. The images reduced their humanity to a surreal form of pornography. Try as he might Dave couldn't keep those images out of his dreams once they had invaded his consciousness, which is why he had problems with background details... and sleeping.

A few yards ahead he saw a brick wall housing rows of burial vaults stacked one above the other. The wall was known as an 'oven-vault' for the arched, brick oven shapes of the burial sites but all Dave knew was that he was nowhere near the spot he was looking for.

Three men were seated on the ground, their backs leaning against the burial wall. One of them, a rangy white man with black tattoos covering his arms passed a bottle to his companion, a burly biker type wearing a leather vest over a grimy red T shirt. There was a knife in a scabbard at his belt. The third was very thin with greasy black hair and bulging dark eyes that fixed Dave with a blurry glare.

Drinking in the cemetery was probably legal in a city that sold daiquiris at drive-thrus Dave reflected, pausing to get his bearings. It crossed his mind to ask the transients if they had seen anything. From their appearance he guessed they slept in the cemetery.

However he knew from experience he'd get nothing but evasions, lies and pit bull hostility. He started back the way he came when he heard something.

"Hey laundry boy, you lost? No speekee 'melican?"

Just keep walking, he told himself. Dave was six feet even and tipped in at two hundred pounds. His wide shoulders and broad chest tapered down to narrow hips and long, muscular legs kept in trim with weights and basketball three times a week. However at the moment he was very hot, tired, and had serious matters on his mind. Then he had a better idea. Maybe these junkyard dogs could be flipped to his advantage.

"Bye bye, gook," the biker called.

Dave paused.

"Awww, he no likee" the tattooed white guy said even before Dave turned.

He was slowly getting to his feet, grinning in anticipation as Dave weighed his options.

Les was out of the game and the area was deserted. His Glock 9 was in an ankle holster and a Cobra spring loaded police baton was nestled at the small of his back. There was also still time to run.

The three men moved slowly towards him, spreading out slightly. The skinny man's jaw was knotted and his mouth twitched like a rodent. Meth, Dave thought

He saw the burly man's drop his hand to his knife but he wasn't concerned about him. It was the rangy one with the prison tats he had to watch. Those hard, lean guys with long arms were all sharp elbows and knees in a fight, sneaky fast and vicious.

He let the men come closer before reaching under his shirt. Hand on the rubber grip of his baton Dave raised his other hand.

"You guys are making a mistake."

"No you makee plenty mistake gook," the rangy man said, roughly pushing Dave back a step.

But Dave had anticipated the move and visualized his response. He took two steps back, a half step to the side and lashed out.

Dave whipped the Cobra's weighted head free and snapped it across the man's nose, breaking it. In the same motion he slashed the steel ball back against the burly man's ear who dropped to his knees like a stunned bull. The meth freak started to run.

Dave ignored the fugitive. In his state he was useless anyway. He pushed the steel head of the baton against a nearby tombstone and retracted it. After replacing the Cobra in the holder at the small of his back he reached down to unsnap his ankle holster. Glock in hand he took his badge and ID from his breast pocket.

"Look at me," he barked.

He brandished his credentials before their gaping eyes. "You have just committed assault with a deadly weapon on a federal agent. If you move I will shoot you. My guess is you boy have sheets—maybe even on parole or probation."

He paused for effect. "Oops, guess you fucked up. Now you have to go back inside—and when you get out… you go back inside again. The assault charge carries five to seven minimum. But I'm sure you have good lawyers, smart guys like you."

"Hey man we were just bustin' your chops," the burly man whined, "had a little too much booze is all."

The tattooed man remained silent, glaring sullenly at Dave from above the hand covering his bloody nose.

The whole encounter has taken less than a minute but Dave's shirt was soaked with sweat.

Les came running up behind them. "Whoa what's up?"

"These guys tried to assault me," Dave said calmly, "and oh, come to think of it they used racial slurs."

Les nodded. "Hate crime, federal offense. Five to ten." One thing about Les, he caught on fast.

"Get up," Dave told the burly man,

Still wobbly he got to his feet.

Dave looked at his partner. "You think maybe that knife on his belt could be the weapon that killed those agents?"

"High probability," Les said, deadpan. "Place the weapon on the ground."

"Oh man no," the burly man groaned, gingerly unsheathing his knife and dropping it, "you can't hang that freaky shit on me. Weren't no knife did that."

"Show us where it happened."

"What?"

"You heard me, where they found the bodies, take us there."

Suddenly the tattooed man looked up. "Don't tell them shit."

The burly man glanced fearfully at him and ducked his head.

"Hey," Les said, "I think you and me need a little walk." He roughly pulled the tattooed man to his feet.

"Okay, here's how it works," Dave said, once the tattooed man was out of earshot, "You show me where they found the bodies and maybe I'll drop the hate crime beef. You fuck with me and you get the full Monte, maybe even a murder charge. Understand what I'm saying?"

The burly man nodded.

"What do they call you?"

"Shake."

"Okay Shake let's go."

Actually they had been close. However the exact spot was in an area if front of three tombs that formed a cul de sac and in the center was the tomb marked with Xs that they had been looking for.

"How do you know this is the place they were found?"

"C'mon man, there were cops all over here, it was taped off, dogs… the whole nine."

"And you and your crew live here." It wasn't a question.

"Not exactly. I mean yeah we crash sometimes. *But around here?* Never."

"Why not here?"

"Shit don't you know man? That there is Marie Laveau's grave."

"Who?"

"The Voodoo mama, high priestess, curses and shit."

"So you think this place is cursed?"

"Maybe. All I know is people show up here to worship the Voodoo queen of New Orleans. Ask anybody man—hell the tour guides will tell you that much."

"Okay so where exactly were you the night the men were killed?"

"Across there, where them new tombs are. There's an open fence gate, I can hunker down back there, nobody can see."

"But you heard something didn't you?" It was a shot in the dark but what the hell.

Shake looked at the ground. "Hey man can I set down? My head's still ringin' from that fuckin' blackjack you got."

"Yeah, squat. So you heard something?"

The big bellied man painfully bent, put one hand on the ground then slowly lowered himself until he was sitting. He wrapped his arms around his knees and began rocking.

"Tell me what you heard Shake or this is going bad for you."

When Shake lifted his head he looked like a child with a beard. "Okay, okay, but you can't let on to Serb."

"The other guy with you?"

"The guy you whacked on the nose."

"Okay deal. "What did you hear?"

Still rocking Shake half closed his eyes. "I heard them runnin' at first, ground was poundin' know what I'm sayin'? So I got deep in a corner,"

"Them? You mean you heard them before?"

Shake took a deep breath and put a hand to his swollen ear.

Dave waited patiently, sensing he was close to something that wasn't in the files.

"Yeah, three four nights this last month. Every time something bad happens. My buddy Monte disappeared first night they came runnin' through. Ain't seen him since."

"The night those men were killed. You heard people running and what else?"

The burly man lowered his eyes. "Maybe it was a scream, more like a howl. Next day there was cops everywhere. We had to crash at a fuckin' shelter."

"Sorry for the inconvenience. One more time, these people you heard running, you say they worship at this tomb?"

"Naw man, I don't think so. This pack is different."

"Pack? You mean like a gang?"

"They ain't no gang, more like a pack of animals. Look man that's all I got. I showed you the place. How about cuttin' me some slack?" Shake tried to get to his feet. It was a major effort.

Dave stayed firm. "One more and I'll cut you loose. Why are you worried about Serb. What's he got to do with this?"

"Nothin.' He's just a little crazy is all. Don't like cops, don't like nobody."

"What was it he didn't want you to say?" Dave persisted.

Shake took a deep breath and it came spilling out in a fearful whisper. "He ain't afraid of the pack. One night he went runnin off himself, tryin' to find 'em. Came back smellin' like a shit eatin' dog. Almost made me sick. Look man if you go back and ask him about this he'll know I said somethin.'"

Dave nodded. "I hear you Shake. Okay you can go. But my advice—find a new friend."

As Shake waddled away Dave remembered. "Hold it Shake, better leave the knife here."

"Aww man this is New Orleans. I need something' to defend myself. They got twelve-year-olds with UZIs out there."

"Then a knife isn't much use is it? Lose it and get lost Shake."

Reluctantly he dropped the knife on the ground and hurried off before Dave could think of something else. Dave always carried a few plastic baggies in his packet for just these occasions. He'd have the knife tested for prints and possible DNA.

As he bent to collect the knife he noticed something else. It looked like a dirty fingernail half buried in the ground.. After carefully bagging the knife Dave picked up a twig and pried the tiny object free.

Actually it was indeed a fingernail but it wasn't really tiny, more like a claw that came to a broken point. He bagged the object and circled Marie Laveau's tomb before returning to their other suspect. The problem was, tourists were trickling into the cemetery and questioning a perp in public was highly frowned upon by the Bureau.

He didn't spot Les at first, then he saw his partner had pulled Serb beside a tall white statue of a Roman cherub with a laurel wreath on its head. Les had Serb by one arm. The perp glared at Dave. His nose was swollen and there were black circles around his eyes.

"He give you a name?" Dave asked. It was partially to protect his snitch and partially to check if the information matched.

"Says they call him Serb."

"He from Serbia? Did you check his ID?"

"Says his wallet was stolen. He reported it,"

"Probation or parole?"

"Parole. Robbery beef."

"Two to one there's an assault in there too. Isn't that right Serb? I think you're going back inside. Get medical treatment for your nose."

The coiled hostility in Serb's body melted. His shoulders and chest slumped inward as if beaten. "Alright look, I'll tell you what I know. But it ain't much. Everybody was somewhere else or hiding."

Les looked at Dave. "Hiding from what?"

"This strange gang comes bustin' through here every so often and people end up hurt... bad. One dude lost an arm."

"What kind of gang, Latino, Black, Asian...?" Les prompted.

"I never saw one. They're like shadows or somethin. You hear 'em comin' and they're gone."

Dave looked at Les. "You believe this?"

"Maybe."

Serb's attention was on something behind him. "You know you dudes are abusing my civil rights with this shit. Take me in or I'll start yellin' for a lawyer."

Dave tilted his head and saw a group of tourists approaching.

"Hey, let's cut this one loose," Les said smoothly, "I don't need the paperwork."

"Your call," Dave said, eying Serb. The man's white skin was crawling with black swastikas, six pointed stars, SS lightning bolts, and a large Gothic cross with a crucified Jesus. This guy is way wrong, Dave thought but an arrest would blow everything.

"Come on," Les said, playing his part, "I'm hungry bro."

"Yeah, yeah sure, let the bastard walk." Dave turned and headed back to the area where the bodies were found.

Les caught up to him in a few minutes but by then Marie Laveau's tomb was circled by people taking pictures, their smart phones lifted in salute to the queen of darkness.

"This the spot?" Les asked

"Yeah. Seems this is also the tomb of Marie…" Dave hesitated.

"…Laveau," Les said, "strange they were found here. What did you get from the fat guy?"

"That would be Shake. His story checks out with Serb's except for one major difference."

"How so?"

"Shake calls it a *pack*, not a gang. Says a pack runs through here, like animals."

"The man's brain is fried," Les snorted, "We're in the middle of New Orleans. All they have around here are gangsters and alligators."

"I also bagged some evidence."

"Like what?"

"Lets get a beer and go over it."

On their way to find a bar, Dave stopped off to buy a fresh shirt. The one he was wearing was drenched. Les decided to do the same. Dave chose a red checked cotton and Les a pale blue button down. They wore their dry new shirts, putting their wet ones in a shopping bag. Dave got a second shopping bag to carry the evidence. The knife made an uncomfortable bulge in his pocket and threatened to stab him when he sat in the car.

They spotted a neon showgirl winking at them a block from the clothing store so they left the car and walked over, carrying their bags. The temperature dropped twenty degrees when they entered. The place was named Fats and was a dimly lit, version of their previous stop except for the industrial strength air conditioning. Fats served food and had an outdoor veranda that was deserted. Opting for better light and more privacy they went outside and took a table beneath a multi colored umbrella.

Les ordered beers and poor boy sandwiches on their way outside and a perky blonde waitress arrived soon after with four bottles of Dixie beer and two frosted glasses.

"Specialty of the house," she said proudly, setting the glasses down, "your food be right out."

Les raised his glass. "Nice work partner. You shook something loose back there."

"You were pretty good yourself. But I hated letting Serb walk. He gave it up way too easy. The creep was just buying time so he could pull his civil rights act in front of an audience."

Les nodded. "He was a hardass alright. Hardly gave me his name. What did you hit him with anyway?"

"The Cobra. Bastard called me a gook and pushed me with intent." The cold glass felt good against his mouth and the beer tasted like honey.

"Intent against a federal agent is good for three years," Les said.

"Only nobody is supposed to know we're here."

"They do now." Les refilled his glass. "So where's our evidence?"

Dave showed him the knife first. "It's a real long shot but we can run the prints at least. Something we can't do with Serb."

The waitress appeared with their sandwiches and Dave replaced the knife in his shopping bag.

Les gave her his megawatt smile. "I could eat that all by myself. How about another round of beers?"

Dave raised two fingers. "Two this time around, he's driving."

The waitress gave Les a sidewise smile. "I bet he could drive just fine."

"I love your confidence in me darlin' but you better make it two. We have all night to party."

Giggling she hurried back inside.

"Can't help yourself," Dave said. "God's gift to the female species." He took a big bite of his sandwich.

Les leaned back and drained his glass. With the sun on his blonde hair and his loud Hawaiian shirt he looked like a surfer in a beer commercial. "So is that all we got? The knife and a half-assed story about a pack of animals?"

"Not quite, I found this too." Dave handed him the baggie with the strange claw-like fragment.

"Could be anything," Les said after close examination. He tossed the baggie on the table. "Do you know how many people visit that Voodoo tomb every day? The crime scene is totally contaminated."

Dave ate his sandwich and chewed reflectively. "Could be an angle there. Choosing a kill zone that's useless to forensics. Two agents here, another one in the bayou…"

"Okay, we have a smart killer."

"Or a gang of killers. Both those creeps agree a group was running through the cemetery that night."

Les grinned as the waitress emerged with two beers and two fresh frosted glasses. "See it pays to be charming partner. You need to loosen up. We are in the Big Easy now."

"I'll take that under advisement," Dave said, "ask your lady friend for the check."

The waitress seemed disappointed by their departure but Les gave her a nice big tip courtesy of the Bureau. It had cooled a bit and they walked slowly back to the car enjoying the light breeze. Dark clouds were gathering in the distance and there was an occasional flicker of heat lightning.

"Where to now, big daddy?" Dave said.

Before he could answer a smiling figure lurched in front of them. He was a hard fifty with matted blonde hair and a faced webbed with deep lines. His bare chest was concave and he was drunk as well as shirtless. His bleary blue eyes seemed exhausted but he pulled himself up as they neared.

Can you gentlemen spare some change for a veteran?"

Les shrugged and gave him a few dollars.

The man saluted. "Bless you sir—semper fi."

Les paused. "Marine?"

The man pointed to a faded tattoo on his ropey grey forearm. "Gung ho all the way."

"Where did you do boot camp?"

The man squinted as if trying to remember.

"Paris Island," he said finally."

Les reached into the shopping bag and handed him his damp shirt.

"Me too. You're out of uniform."

Back inside the car Dave gave Les a disbelieving grin. "Why didn't you give him my shirt too?"

"You're not a marine."

"Fine. So where to now? Hotel I hope."

"Back to Lafayette it is."

"We can meet later. Maybe check out Iberia,"

"You can check out Iberia tonight. I will be investigating Melody. Anyway you fit in better."

Dave bristled. "I'm Chinese not Vietnamese and you are now officially on the case." He said it slowly and quietly. This wasn't like Les. He was always professional. Not by the book but never careless.

"Relax buddy, it's me," Les said. "Yes I will drop in on Melody but I'll be asking questions here and there."

"Two conditions. One, you tell me where you're meeting her. Two, you don't take her to your room. We're deep cover."

"We're in deep shit," Les said, "are you sending the knife for prints?"

It was a clumsy diversion. "May as well find out now if general Easton's message system works," Dave said, "hey, let's back up a sec. Where did you say you were meeting Melody?"

Les frowned and looked away but Dave knew he'd tell him. "It's a joint called Styx," he said finally.

"Like the band?"
"Like the river."
"Classy."
"Do not be casting aspersions on the woman I lust."

+ + +

As soon as Dave arrived at his motel he opened his laptop and contacted Easton. He saw from the business card that the director's first name was Matthew. Dave left his request in the draft box, took off his clothes and dropped on the bed.

He awoke two hours later feeling groggy and far from rested. He checked his watch and saw it was a good time to call home.

"Jen?"

"Oh, I'm glad you called early. How was your flight?"

"The usual, you feeling okay?"

"Yeah, I'm good but Robin's a handful. She misses you."

Jennifer was in her fifth month and their daughter Robin, accustomed to being Princess Chin, felt threatened.

"She doesn't have her daddy to do her bidding," Jennifer said. She was teasing but everybody knew Dave had a weakness for his daughter.

"Did you eat?"

"I had lunch."

"Linda called. She and Rick want to have dinner soon."

"Right now I'm in limbo. Sorry Jen."

"Be nice to have a little fun before I'm too far gone."

"When I get back we'll go to a Broadway musical."

"I'm recording this."

"Word. You pick the show. Where's Robin?"

"In bed waiting for me to read her a story. Want to say goodnight?"

"Sure."

During the long pause Dave could dimly hear Jennifer's voice. Robin's response was muted.

"Daddy?"

"It's me, honey."

"When are you coming home?"

"Pretty soon. How was school today?"

"Okay. Here's mommy. Goodnight daddy."

Before he could answer she was gone.

"Guess that's a long conversation for a three-year-old."

"She wants her story." Jennifer said

"You okay, Jen?"

"We all just want you home soon."

"This shouldn't take long," Dave said. "Go read to Robin. I love you."

"Me too."

A long shower failed to ease his guilt at lying to Jennifer. This bizarre case might take months to untangle. They had no resources or back-up. And their quarry liked to murder cops and cut out their organs. *Who was the prey here?* Dave brooded. Wrapped in a towel he unpacked his flight bag.

+ + +

Les had hung his new shirt near the air conditioner while he showered and it felt cold when he put it on. He checked himself in the mirror, patting his belly. Starting now no more than two beers a day.

As he got himself ready he realized he was anxious to see Melody again.

Like Dave he carried a Glock in an ankle holster and a Cobra at the small of his back. He also carried a short combat knife on his left ankle, a habit he acquired in the Marines.

He scanned the mirror again. *Good to go.*

The Styx was in an urban area a short taxi ride from his motel. Les had found the club—and Melody—quite by chance while looking for a drink his first night in Lafayette. He liked dimly lit joints and the Styx was a perfect spot to wind down.

He took a seat at the bar and scanned the room, reflexively taking in the exits, patrons and staff. There were about a dozen candle-lit tables around an empty stage. Three booths along each wall; the bar itself was backlit in blue. Not yet ten p.m. the place was sparsely populated. Dr. John sang softly on the overhead speaker.

Got here too early like a damn schoolboy, Les thought ruefully. He ordered a vodka tonic and tried to compose himself. He hadn't felt this way for a long time.

Mid life crisis, he told himself, you don't even know where she was born. A woman that beautiful must have a past, She looked to be on the edge of thirty but who knew these days. What's she doing in this dive anyway?

Rational arguments failed to dissuade him. The moment he had locked on Melody's crystal green eyes their connection was clear, powerful and inevitable.

He ordered blackened shrimp and corn biscuits as a hedge against drinking too much and managed to nurse his vodka until the food was served.

The shrimp were excellent and the biscuits warm and moist. He definitely had an affinity for Louisiana cuisine Les thought, and Louisiana ladies. He signaled for another round.

The barman nodded, "Vodka?"

"Make it absinthe." Les hadn't told Dave but Melody had introduced him to her favorite drink. Just sip it slow, he cautioned, Melody will want one as soon as she gets here.

Fifteen minutes later he wasn't sure she'd ever get there. They had gone to her apartment and he left before dawn with only a fleeting assurance they'd meet again that night. He wasn't even sure he could locate her place again.

His emotions swung between disappointment and anger at himself for assuming she wanted to see him again.

The barman performed the ritual. He poured the absinthe over a spoon holding a sugar cube then added water.

Les watched the glass turn emerald green then took a long swallow. It was deceptively sweet. Aware it hit him hard the night before he drank some water and reached for the pack of Camels he'd bought at the convenience store next to the motel. Dave didn't have to worry about him bringing Melody back to a seedy dump like the Royal Court motel, Les mused. Only thing royal about it was the purple sheets.

He still hadn't really slept there. When he did he hoped there were no bedbugs.

The food had been a good idea. The absinthe spread warmly across his stomach and up his spine. He was starting to relax. Wondering if smoking was allowed he put a cigarette to his mouth. The barman answered his question by giving him a light. Les nodded thanks then remembered something.

"A pal of mine called Ron told me about this place. Have you seen him? Ron Delcie…"

It was the name of the Lafayette detective they had fished out of the bayou. A long shot but at least he could tell Dave he tried.

The barman, hefty and genial, resembled a bohemian Saint Nick as he scratched his braided white beard.

"Can't say I know anybody by that name. Know lots of my regulars by sight but it gets real busy here after ten."

He was right. Deserted when he sat down the booths had filled up. A number of couples were seated near the stage and the bus boys and waiters were moving between tables. Doctor John had given way to Ray Charles and the energy in the room was rising. Then he saw her.

Her smile stilled his breath. Les watched her drift down the stairs and hurry to his side.

"I was half worried you might not be here." Melody said, her warm against his ear. Her low voice dissolved into her musky lavender scent.

"Here I am," Les said thickly, unable to keep the emotion out of his voice.

"Here you go,"

Les turned and saw the barman pouring water into an absinthe for Melody.

The barman nodded. "I know my people by what they drink."

Melody lifted her glass.. "You certainly do Victor." She turned to Les. "Are you okay?"

"You're pretty well known here," Les said, keeping his tone light.

"I should be," Melody said.

The overhead music cut off and a slender male with long dark hair mounted the stage carrying a guitar. He sat down on a chair and plugged his guitar into an amplifier. Without any preamble he began playing smooth jazz chords.

It was as if the entire club just had a massage. The loud chatter was muted by the guitar's easy rhythms.

"Why is it you're so famous here?" Les said quietly.

Melody put her glass next to his and kissed him lightly on the cheek.

"I'll be back soon."

Confused, Les watched her weave through the tables on her way to the stage accompanied by a smattering of applause.

The guitar player seemed surprised to see her standing beside him but recovered immediately. "Ladies and gentleman Melody Dawn," he announced, then passed his mike to her.

She said something and he began to play the familiar chords of *Yesterday*.

It was a simple song but the way Melody's smoky voice bent the notes it became a hymn to human faith and loss with a twist of blues. Les was half awed by her presence on the tiny stage. Someone had turned on the spotlight, shadowing her green eyes and high cheekbones. A black mini skirt set off her long alabaster smooth legs and lustrous black hair framed the delicately sculpted contours of her face.

The audience watched in total silence then broke out in enthusiastic applause, unwilling to let her leave the stage. Melody accommodated with an edgy jazz version of *The Beat Goes On*, then handed the mike back to the guitar player. "It's actually my day off, see you all Friday," she said before moving back to the bar amid a fresh wave of applause.

"Are we clear now?" she said when she rejoined him.

"Crystal," Les said, slightly embarrassed.

"How about you, any hidden talents I don't know about?"

Les grinned. "Lots."

"Married?"

"Never had the pleasure, how about you?"

Melody leaned closer. "The bar has ears. Finish your drink and take me home."

Her scent was intoxicating. Les swallowed his absinthe a bit faster than he intended and followed her to the door.

Outside it was warm and quiet "Now then," she said, taking his arm, "ask me anything you like."

+ + +

Dave left his motel room reluctantly. Driving alone to a strange town in Bayou country on a fact-finding tour was not a great idea. He brought along the backpack containing the file, having no good spot to stash it in his motel room. He also took his laptop. Just a drive by and back home before midnight, he told himself, punching his destination in the GPS.

New Iberia was quite different than Lafayette, an island fishing community both for profit and sport. As he expected many of the shrimp boat workers were Vietnamese. He didn't speak the language but he knew they were clannish and wary of strangers, especially Chinese strangers.

His first stop was a bar called Nick's that served food. Dave had a leisurely meal of crab gumbo and rice topped off with strong Vietnamese coffee. The food was delicious and as his coffee dripped slowly into a glass he had time to scan the room.

Nick's was an airy dive with overhead fans and a bamboo motif. Blues music wailed from speakers on either side of the liquor display. There were a trio of Vietnamese at one table and a couple at another. The male was young with shaggy blond hair and a plaid western shirt. His date was a slim Vietnamese girl. Dave didn't understand what was being said but it was clear the boys at the other table did not approve of the couple.

Dave hoped there wouldn't be trouble.

Two men playing pool in the rear glanced over from time to time. From their dress and sunburned skin Dave guessed they were fisherman. A short bald man with a diamond stud in one ear sat at the far end of the bar conferring with the Asian barmaid. Dave figured him for the owner. He too was keeping an eye on the Vietnamese trio.

The blond man seemed oblivious but his companion was clearly uncomfortable.

Dave sipped his coffee. He was supposed to be undercover, invisible, he reminded, it wasn't his affair.

The girl said something to her companion and he looked at the trio for the first time.

The men smirked and continued their banter. Dave saw the blond man's neck redden. The pot was hot and in another minute it would boil over.

Maybe it was the coffee. Dave sighed, picked up the check and stood. On his way to the bar he paused at the young couple's table. "Aren't you Tim O'Hara, quarterback for Austin High?"

The blond man stared at Dave. "What?"

"Austin High Texas, you were quarterback right?"

Dave looked over at the trio. They were staring too.

"This guy was one tough player," he said and walked to the bar.

When Dave went to pay the bald man took the bill and tore it in two. "One the house," he said.

Up close he was much bigger with wide shoulders and a chest that stretched the buttons on his crisp white shirt. He was smiling but his hard blue eyes were appraising him.

Dave returned the smile. "Thanks, the food is first rate. But why the comp?"

The man tilted his head toward the young couple.

They were leaving. The trio taunting them looked disappointed but made no move to follow. "Nice move."

Dave shrugged. "Just trying to break the tension."

"I'm Nick Casio, I own the joint and you saved me at least two thousand dollars in breakage. Not to mention the wear and tear on my delicate persona. Time for a drink?"

Dave smiled in spite of himself. "Thanks, name's Dave. I'm new around here." He took a stool and noticed the Vietnamese trio staring at him, as were the pool players. In fact an older couple in a corner booth, were the only people in the place not staring at him.

"What's your pleasure suh?" Nick asked.

"What are you drinking?"

"Small batch bourbon a friend of mine brews up."

"I'm in.".

Nick turned to the barmaid. "Sam darlin' fix this gentleman a bayou bourbon. Then go give those bad boys a nice fat check."

When the drink came Dave raised his glass. "To my host."

"To you suh," Nick said, "and to my lovely associate."

Dave noticed everyone's attention had turned from him and was now focused on Sam as she moved to the trio at the table, long legs easing gracefully between chairs.

The bourbon was smooth with a long fuse. It warmed his throat and chest before gently exploding in his belly. The tension in his neck and shoulders evaporated.

In contrast Sam's errand wasn't going that well. One of the men said something in what Dave assumed was Vietnamese and he saw Sam's body stiffen.

Nick saw it too. "Shit. And here I thought this was going to be a nice quiet night." He drained his glass and stood up.

He was taller than he looked when seated, with most of his weight in his upper body.

Shit, Dave echoed silently, pausing long enough for another sip before he slipped off his stool.

The Vietnamese man was standing now. He made an obscene gesture and his companions laughed.

They stopped laughing when Nick brushed Sam aside and without any preamble grasped the man who made the gesture firmly by the throat.

"Apologize."

The man took a wild swing but Nick held him at arm's length as if inspecting a necktie.

"Apologize please," he said voice flat and calm.

One of the man's companions hopped to his feet and threw a punch that nearly hit Sam but Dave's arm got in the way.

Dave blocked the blow and shoved the man back into his chair tipping it over. The man rolled and tried to sit up. Dave lifted a warning finger and he stayed on the floor. Dave looked at his companion who sat motionless.

'I ah... ahpologize."

Dave glanced back. Nick was smiling but the man in his vise like grip had turned dark red. "I didn't hear you." Nick said.

"Apologize... sorry... apologize." He almost collapsed when Nick released him. He stood bent over, one hand on a chair gasping for breath.

Dave turned and was surprised to see Sam smiling at him. For the first time he noticed that she was a stunner. He smiled back.

Nick pointed at the man who remained seated. "Kindly settle your bill and escort your friends out."

The man nodded, fumbling for his wallet.

Dave returned to his drink, skin crawling with adrenaline.

He drained his glass in one swallow then sat back and settled himself. Nick had moved behind the bar and poured three large snifters of cognac from a crystal decanter on the top shelf. Dave turned. Sam had taken the stool next to his. Totally unsettling, he thought, again noting her extraordinary beauty, part Asian and part Venus.

She was still smiling at him. "Thank you," she said, her throaty voice oddly formal.

"Exactly what did those shrimpers say to you sweetheart?" Nick said. "You know I don't speak much Vietnamese."

Her smile wavered but she directed her answer at Dave.

"He called me a mongrel whore."

As if on cue the trio filed silently out the door.

Nick raised his snifter to Dave. "Here's to stand up men."

Dave sipped his cognac, letting it burn off the energy snapping at his nerves. He took a deep breath and felt his muscles relax. It was excellent cognac.

Nick smiled and refreshed his snifter. "Aged seventy five years," he said, regarding the crystal bottle fondly.

"At this rate, I may not make it that far."

Sam snorted. "You'll live to be a hundred and fifty."

She winked at Dave. "Too stubborn to die."

"So Dave tell me," Nick said. "What brings you to our tranquil bayou?"

Dave was ready for the question. He'd put together a cover story on the way from the motel. "I flew in from New York to scout locations for an independent film."

Nick grinned. "Is that right? Hear that Sam? Dave is gonna make us movie stars."

"Just a low budget horror film, nothing fancy." The cognac had started a glowing fire in his belly and he wondered if he should leave while he could still drive.

"As a matter of fact, it looks like I'm going to go back empty."

"Why on earth would you do that?" Nick said with an expansive wave of his hand. "The eminent author Mr. James Lee Burke, himself- has found this area- *especially* New Iberia-a ripe location. Even shot a couple of movies based on his fine works."

Dave shook his head. "It's not exactly the location proper. I was supposed to hook up with a police detective to act as a technical advisor and facilitator."

Nick laughed. "Oh there's a lot of facilitating down here that's sure."

"Problem is the guy disappeared on me. I can't reach him on his phone or at his office?"

"His office? You mean the police station?"

Dave drained his glass, taking his time. "Yes"

We are a relatively tight knit community here."

Dave shrugged. "Actually he's from Lafayette. Ryan Morgan. Young dude, Blonde hair."

Nick and Sam exchanged a glance. "I know him, Sam said from behind the bar. "I see him now and then at Minny's."

"Yes I know who you mean." Nick said. "Tell you what Dave, it's a tad late now but why don't you drop by tomorrow afternoon and Sam will run you over to Minny's. The proprietor is Vietnamese and she speaks the language."

"That's very kind of you Nick but I don't want to impose."

"It's no imposition," Sam said, "I look forward to it. Say about four—right here."

Feeling pleased with his night's work Dave stood at the doorway breathing in the thick scent of the tropical night. It's a good cover story, he told himself. And a long ride with Sam could prove instructive. The thought invoked a pang of guilt—and caution. She was beautiful enough to be trouble.

He had parked nearby and slightly tipsy, fumbled for his key. For some reason the air seemed heavy and foul. He heard a scuffling sound behind him and his instincts kicked in. He could either pull his piece or get into his car, a few feet away. He did both, one hand pointing the electronic key as the other drew the Glock. The Malibu's headlights blinked and Dave flung the door open. He scrambled inside, locked the car and jabbed the key into the ignition. He missed the first time and forced himself to focus. As the key slid in something thumped the trunk hard. The engine rumbled to life and he was tempted to back up and shoot it out.

Oh no, Dave told himself. A showdown with a gang of Vietnamese hoods hell-bent on revenge would be a flat out disaster. Instead he gunned the car out of the parking area. Screeching onto the road he glanced in his rear view and saw three or four figures sprinting after the car. When they flashed past the dim exit light Dave glimpsed long dark hair and bearded faces that seemed contorted. Dave pressed the accelerator but the two-lane blacktop was sharply curved and very dark and the car fishtailed forcing him to slow down.

When he looked in the mirror the shadowed figures were still coming.

Incredibly they were *gaining*.

Dave pushed it from thirty five to forty and the car skidded scraping a tree. One of the gang lunged forward and was actually slapping at the rear fender before Dave hit a straight stretch and floored it.

At forty seven his pursuers dropped back. But even when Dave was able to drive at sixty he kept checking his rear view mirror. The lazy glow he had carried away from Nick's had congealed to a frozen block of adrenalin. On reaching his motel he couldn't quite recall how he got there.

Chapter 3

A shivering boom of thunder woke Dave Chin. It was five minutes short of six a.m and the raindrops drumming against the window were oddly reassuring. He dug hs head into the warm pillow and remained there listening until he dozed off again. A half-hour later he opened his eyes. It was then the memory flooded back. He half believed what he had seen last night.
Who were those guys? He asked no one in particular.
How drunk was I? Was his next question as his head throbbed at the effort it took to sit up. You need to slow down, he told himself, two fights in one day is way too many.
And dial the drinking way down.
While in the shower Dave remembered the file. He has neglected to remove it from its hiding place under the spare. A brief wave of paranoia hurried him into a bathrobe. He toweled off and dressed quickly.
It was drizzling when he went outside. To his relief the file was there intact.
But the Malibu was a mess.
There was a long scrape where he had fishtailed into a tree and—most disturbing—deep gashes on the trunk and rear door that raked the metal like claw marks.
Dave sighed. For the next five years, Les will be crowing about what a superior driver he is. As for the scratches, he'd think about that over breakfast.
A local diner served up fluffy grits, eggs and Cajun sausage but it was the coffee that was memorable. By his third cup he still hadn't made up his mind. He did leave Nick's pretty well buzzed. In the dark like that he might have misjudged who was after him. And how fast they were going. As for the scratches, they could have been done with a hand rake or some fisherman's hook.

He called Les who didn't answer. Les was scheduled for a nine a.m. pick up and it was barely seven-fifteen so Dave walked back to the motel, the file clutched against his chest like a football.

He stopped in the parking lot to take photographs of the damaged car with his iPhone, then went inside and got ready for his rendezvous with Sam.

By eight thirty he had completed his preparations which included sending the car damage photos to his private account. Problem was, Les still didn't answer his phone.

Dave decided to drive over to his motel and park at a discreet distance. Sure enough within ten minutes a cab pulled to the curb and Les got out.

Les looked disheveled but when he heard Dave's horn he responded with a nod and walked slowly to the car.

He peered inside and gave Dave a bleary smile. "Twenty minutes and I'll be ready to roll," Dave shrugged. They really had nowhere to go before his appointment with Sam.

"No problem partner," he said with resignation, "but keep your damn phone on."

+ + +

Les heard the reproach in Dave's voice. And he had no defense. He was acting like an unprofessional asshole, which directly impacted his partner and could possibly get him killed.

You better man up, he told his unshaven reflection in the bathroom mirror. A shower, fresh clothes and two aspirin patched his self-esteem. But he had a sinking feeling when he saw the condition of the car. Something had happened while he was in heaven with Melody.

"What's up with the body work buddy?" he said as he got into the Malibu, "I thought you were in for the night."

"Assumption is the mother of all fuck ups," Dave said.

"Steven Segal movie right?"

"This ain't no movie Les."

Let's get some coffee and talk," Les said quietly.

+ + +

Les's emotions careened from guilt to disbelief to awe as Dave recounted the night's events. He knew his partner was not prone to exaggeration which lent credence to the part about being chased down by guys who could run forty miles an hour, and made deep scratch marks on the Malibu. But tracing the missing cop back to Minny's was brilliant work. *First night out and he hits a home run* Les thought with a twinge of envy.

"Look Dave," he said slowly, "about the phone. It won't happen again."

"I know," Dave said, face impassive. "What's up with this babe? She's got you way off your game."

Les looked out the window. "You got that right partner. Tell you what, I'll arrange for car repair and drop off our evidence bag. You rent a car and keep your rendezvous in New Iberia. When you're done give me a call."

"Sound's like a plan," Dave said, somewhat relieved.

+ + +

The rental was a good idea, Dave decided as he neared New Iberia driving a red Ford Taurus. The damaged Malibu would make him a target in the small community.

Like a red car won't Dave thought ruefully. He tried to focus on his meeting with Sam.

Make no mistake he felt conflicted. Her help might provide a breakthrough in this case. However he couldn't deny the fact that she was beautiful. Which somehow made him feel guilty. *It's the Jimmy Carter syndrome*, he told himself, *you lust in your heart.* Then he thought of Robin, which brought him back to reality. He was here to find out what happened to detective Morgan. Sam was a professional asset no more no less.

His resolve crumbled when he entered Nick's and saw her waiting at the bar. Sam was wearing a faded purple T-shirt that read LSU in yellow, cut down Levi shorts and flip-flops. A yellow visor shaded her eyes but the lower part of her face broke into a wide smile when he entered.

"You're on time," she said, "for sure you're not from round here."

He tried not to grin. "Film business runs on schedules."

"Good luck with that in New Iberia." She hopped off the stool. "A beer for the road?"

"Maybe when we get there."

She ducked behind the bar for her bag and for the first time Dave noticed the white haired bartender watching them.

Sam noticed too. "Lenny this is Dave. I'm going to help him scout locations for a film."

Lenny's flinty squint eased a notch and he nodded.

"When Nick comes in tell him we need bourbon. I swear he drinks it all himself." She swung the bag over her shoulder and looked at Dave. "Your car or mine?"

They took hers, an '84 Caddy Biarritz convertible.

The vintage Caddy, lovely Sam, it all fit his Hollywood cover story Dave mused. taking in the scenery. Certainly there were lots of places to shoot a film: flat, monotonous marsh lands, moody bayous, rickety docks, patchwork general stores, proud mansions shaded by weathered cypress trees, weary shacks, rusted bridges and worn out fishing boats. All of it set back in time.

To stay in character as a location scout Dave dutifully took pictures with his phone.

"How long have you been doing this?"

"A few years. Mostly horror films."

He glanced over. Sam's flowing black hair was backlit by a golden sun and her haloed profile seemed like an ivory cameo. Playfully he snapped her picture. She threw her hand up. "Don't," she said laughing. "I'm a mess."

Dave turned to shoot an old gas station, unwilling to get too close. Or even have too much fun. It reminded him of his father who was suspicious of any form of fun. Maybe dad had the right idea after all.

"We're almost there."

He looked up uncertain of what she meant until he saw the sign. Painted in large red letters across the side of a long, low building was the name *Minny's*.

He felt relieved. Now he could focus on the real job at hand.

Sam parked and led the way inside. Dave ambled behind her trying to stay in character as an advance member of a film crew.

+ + +

Les was on the case.

He had delivered the evidence bag to the designated drop and taken the Malibu to a local body shop for repairs. They gave him a loaner, an '05 Dodge Charger with new racing tires. Rather than wait for Dave he decided to drive back to New Orleans. He needed to stay busy to keep his head straight. And his mind off Melody.

Of course he was kidding himself. Strange, Les thought, here he was a bachelor, feeling guilty about a hot liaison. *Guess I'm married to the Bureau* he decided. *And I am my partner's keeper.*

He enumerated all the reasons to play it by the book but in the end it all came down to the same thing.

Melody Dawn.

It made him angry. He knew better than to get involved with a lady who used drugs and even worse, induced him to join her. Or was it seduced.

Man up, he told himself, *you made the choice.*

It had been a memorable night fueled by absinthe, cocaine, and opium that left him drained, and ashamed that he had let his partner down. Dave deserved better.

When he reached New Orleans he pulled into a small motel and took a room. He paid cash and the clerk didn't ask for ID.

There was a bar a few doors down where he got a poor boy sandwich to go. The room was standard low rent, twin beds facing a TV. He switched it on, found a basketball game, ate his poor boy, and fell asleep.

The sun was going down when he woke up. He rolled out of bed, stretched, did his sit ups, pushups, then jumped into the shower.

The nap had been a good idea, he felt great. While dressing he considered his options. Maybe another tour of the cemetery now that he was familiar with the layout. That was it for the options.

Big city, few assets.

The TV was still on. The basketball game had given way to the nightly news. Les decided to go out. He always left the TV on in motels to discourage burglars. He stopped at the door, did an about face, marched to the TV and turned up the volume.

"Both victims were homeless but any other connection between them is unclear. Although their bodies were found in separate areas police say some aspects of these murders are similar. One unnamed source claims both men were mutilated."

The newscaster's expression went from somber to cheery. *"Good weather ahead. Full details after this."*

Les stared at the screen as the news cut to a car commercial. After a few moments he went out for coffee. He decided to walk and bought two newspapers along the way. He stopped at a small café, ordered some beignets with his coffee and began going through the papers for something on the murders on the chance they'd been covered in depth.

The Times-Picayune made it the lead story in their crime section The Advocate had a photo of one of the victims.

Les squinted and looked harder.

It was the scumbag Dave had rousted in the cemetery.

Shake.

He had shorter hair and looked a lot cleaner but Les recognized the cherubic features behind the beard.

The paper said his name was Harold Dewey. Les drank his coffee and googled the coroner's office on his mobile.

The New Orleans Forensic Center was located on Martin Luther King Jr. Boulevard. When Les entered the run down building he found that the Coroner's office was actually an old funeral home. The place had been partially damaged by Katrina and due to the limited space bodies were stored in refrigerated trucks behind the building.

Les flashed his FBI credentials and had little trouble gaining access to the murdered man's corpse. His guide was a middle aged black nurse who examined his ID impassively from behind her computer. She heaved a great sigh, pushed her considerable bulk erect then signaled him to follow her.

"Y'all the second visitor from the FBI today," she said, as if this was yet another burden she had to bear. The nurse, whose nameplate bore the name Belle led the way to a rear door. There were three large trucks parked behind the building.

"They run out of space," Nurse Belle grumbled, "so we got to keep the remains out here in these 'frigerated trucks."

Remains was the right word. Harold Dewey's torso had been literally torn apart like a paper bag spilling its contents. His neck too had been ripped—not cut—open as if some animal had bitten off a chunk. Aware that Nurse Belle was watching, Les kept his face blank and briskly took pictures with his phone ignoring the beignets and coffee churning in his belly.

"Autopsy pictures in the file," Belle said, "your friend wanted to take it, I told him hell no." She glowered as if expecting an argument.

Les smiled. "He's not my friend Belle They found two bodies last night, is that right?"

"More like five last night. Only two messed up like this though."

"Can I look at the other victim?"

"Over here."

When Belle lifted the rubber sheet Les averted his eyes and hid behind his phone camera, buying a moment to steel himself. If possible the second body was even more cruelly mutilated. In addition to the ragged craters in his chest, and neck, half his face was gone. Judging from the defensive wounds on his arms and shins he had fought the attacker.

Les lowered his phone.

He recognized the faded tattoo on the man's forearm. The familiar eagle, globe and anchor of the U.S. Marines.

"Could I see those autopsy files now?" He said, breath fogging in the frigid air of the makeshift morgue.

Belle took him back to the Coroner's Office. She rummaged through a packed cabinet and fished out two file jackets held together by rubber bands. Belle handed him the files and returned to her desk.

"Did you get pictures of the crime scene, where the bodies were found?"

Belle didn't look up from her computer. "They in there."

Les found a chair and went through the files. In both cases heart and liver were listed missing. The crime scene photo of the Marine, Horace Devaux startled him. Then he remembered. He had given Horace the shirt he was wearing when he died. The blood stains looked like tie-dye.

Les jotted down the locations were both bodies had been found and returned the files to Nurse Belle.

"Thanks, this helps," he said, and meant it.

What were the odds? They encounter two separate men during the course of an investigation who turn up dead in the very same manner as the killings they're trying to solve.

Forget coincidence Les thought walking out into the sweltering air. This was way too close for comfort. Not to mention what happened to Dave last night. Now he totally believed his partner. He also had the uncomfortable feeling they were being stalked. He decided to get some food and a much-needed beer.

He found a small dive in the French Quarter and ordered a shrimp salad and a Dixie—definitely no gumbo after his gruesome visit to the coroner.

The spicy salad and cold beer relaxed him a bit and he sifted through his options. Finally he sent Dave a cryptic text, "2 more in NO". His partner would know what he meant.

Les planned to stick around town for a few hours. Maybe he could get a line on the other dirtbag in that cemetery. The one who was still alive. The lanky snake called Serb.

+ + +

Dave Chin hated to admit it but he was enjoying himself. He was something of a film buff and had no problem playing location scout for an independent horror movie. However it was Sam's company that provided the real glamour.

Not that Minny's was glamorous. It was a larger, somewhat shabbier version of Nick's with a long ho bar lined with pocked red leather, tables strewn around a scuffed wood floor, pool tables in the rear, and a stage area with speakers and a sound board.

The stage was bare but a jukebox pumped out a steady mix of blues and country western and the bar was doing a brisk business.

Sam introduced him to Carson the bartender, a rangy, sun reddened blond man with a toothy grin.

"Good meetin' you Dave. You in mighty fine company. What can I get you Sam honey?"

Dave noticed his hair was bleached and his teeth capped. When Carson leaned on the bar he saw the black lightning tattoos on both forearms.

"Two drafts please," Sam said, "I'm as dry as sand. I'm hungry too." She smiled at Dave, "You like shrimp?"

Dave smiled back. "I do now."

They shared a huge plate of grilled shrimp laced with Louisiana's finest hot spices and a long, cold beer.

"So what's your favorite movie?" Sam said playfully.

"Depends."

"On what?"

"Drama, comedy, musical, western, noir…"

"Noir, French. Like me. Half anyway."

"That's easy. *Casablanca*, hands down."

"Anybody could say that."

"How about *Force Of Evil*?"

She cocked her head and Dave guessed she'd practiced that move before. But he knew she had never heard of the film.

"You're too young," he said but she took it as a challenge.

"Okay," she snapped," best western."

Dave sighed. Was it Asian women he thought, or all women? "*Unforgiven*."

"That's easy too."

"How about *Tombstone*?

She laughed. "How about another draft?" And then, just to prove she knew her stuff she leaned closer and whispered "I'm your huckleberry."

Dave's reserve melted a notch.

Carson arrived with fresh beers. 'So what brings you to these parts Dave? He grinned, showing his perfect teeth. "You a fisherman?"

"Not really. I'm a film scout. They're thinking of shooting a movie down here."

"No shit?"

"No shit," Dave said.

"That's gonna be great."

"Only thing, there's a problem."

Carson leaned on the bar, hands flat. It was then Dave noticed the black polished fingernails.

"Like what kind of problem?"

Dave sipped his beer. "The guy who's supposed to facilitate the deal is MIA. Can't locate him."

"Who is this dude?"

"Name's Morgan, Ryan Morgan. He's a…"

"He's a cop," Carson finished, nodding his head. Yeah sure, he comes round these parts a lot. Haven't seen him for a month of Sundays. Hell Sam you know him."

"Sure do. He hangs at Nick's from time to time. That's why we stopped by. Is Minny here?"

Carson inclined his head. "In the office."

"Be right back okay?" Sam hopped off the bar stool and walked to an open door between the bar and the pool tables.

Carson regarded Dave thoughtfully. "So what's Morgan gonna do on your movie?"

"Help get permits and police cooperation mainly."

Carson nodded. "Grease the wheels so to speak."

"Mainly, yeah." Dave shrugged. "I suppose that makes the world go round."

The lankly bartender started moving to serve a new patron.

"Well you came to the right place. This here is the wheel grease capitol of America."

Dave idly studied Carson while he waited for Sam. The bartender was tall and lean and his drawl was more western than Cajun. Despite the heat he wore a long sleeved blue shirt partially rolled up above his wrists. The shirt was open to his muscle ribbed stomach and Davis guessed he had been an athlete.

The black fingernail polish ruled out construction work.

He saw Sam coming back escorted by an Asian woman who might have been Sam's mother or older sister. Her beautiful features were made even more striking by the way she carried herself, naturally regal and all female. Dave hadn't smoked for three years but he had a sudden yen for a cigarette.

Miss Minny Free, this is David Chin," Sam said, her manner formal.

Dave composed himself and bowed his head slightly. "My honor Miss Free."

"Please call me Minny," she said, "how may I help you David?"

"Perhaps Samantha explained," he said, "I was supposed to meet a man who could help me expedite the groundwork for a film shoot. His name is Ryan Morgan and he's known to be one of your customers."

"Yes of course. He comes in from time to time, very polite, never makes trouble. Perhaps you could try the police department in Lafayette. I believe Mr. Morgan is a detective." She clasped her hands as if that ended the matter.

She was right, Dave knew it would be useless to persist and could arouse suspicion.

"Well thank you Minny, I appreciate it."

She smiled. "Don't forget us when you make your movie."

"Guess we should make our way back to Nick's," Dave said when the lovely Asian proprietor had gone. "I have to get back to Lafayette and check in with the producers."

Sam made a face. "So soon?"

"We can take the scenic route back. I need to shoot more locations." Dave was impressed with how easily he lied.

It took longer to get back to Nick's than it had to go to Minny's. Sam turned up the radio and took a few back roads to show Dave some of her favorite places.

They stopped at Mama Lupe's Bait Shop and Apothecary, located at the edge of a precarious dock where Dave bought a small glass vial filled with healing herbs at Sam's urging. Then she took him to a secluded juke joint where a blues musician named Harley David played guitar for an audience of three including the bartender. The sun was setting when they returned and Nick was waiting anxiously.

"Darlin' we know it doesn't take that long to go to Minny's," he said eyeing Dave suspiciously. "I've been covering the bar for you."

Sam sniffed. "About time you did some work."

Nick winked at Dave. Then his manner became confidential. "I've been asking a few people here and there. They say Morgan hasn't been seen for a couple weeks."

"What are you going to do?" Sam asked.

"Guess I'll try to recruit another cop in Lafayette to help us out."

Nick nodded. "Good thinking. You hungry? We're serving something extra special this evening Zydeco snapper with rice and red beans. Nothing like it."

He was right. Dave cooled the spicy dish with a frosty beer and finished with sweet Vietnamese coffee for dessert."

Nick joined him for coffee. It was early but the tables were filled with diners and drinkers. Dave realized it was an after-work crowd.

Nick seemed to read his thoughts. "Shrimpers, oilmen, construction, they all come in here," he said with a touch of pride.

"Good food, that's for sure."

Nick leaned closer and lowered his voice. "You okay last night? When you left I thought I heard tires screeching and something banging."

"I banged up my fender pulling out," Dave said, "nothing serious."

Nick nodded. "That's why you rented that red job."

Nothing much gets past him Dave noted, on his guard. He decided to turn the conversation. "I did see a bunch of weirdoes hanging out in the lot."

"Long hair, beards?"

"That's them."

Nick slapped his palm on the table. "First thing tomorrow I'm going to install a bank of security cameras around the lot. Every time I go out there they've vanished. But lots of my patrons report the same thing. They haven't made any trouble yet but it's just a matter of time." Nick's demeanor had quickly changed from gracious to indignant.

"Cameras are a good idea," Dave said, taking out his wallet.

"Forget about it," Nick said, sounding like Al Pacino.

"C'mon Nick," Dave protested, "I can't keep eating here for free."

Nick waved his protest aside. "Very few stand up guys in this world," he said, "and Sam likes you. Not many people have that distinction."

Nick also insisted on walking Dave to his car. "Make sure you get out without banging your fender."

Sam pouted. "Don't forget to come back."

The parking lot was deserted and while driving back to Lafayette Dave's mind kept drifting back to Sam.

When he reached the motel he saw the text and immediately called Les.

His damned phone didn't answer.

Chapter 4

Les started in the French Quarter and eventually found his way to Jackson Square. Located in front of St. Louis Cathedral the area around the grassy square was a haven for portrait artists, street musicians, souvenir stands, T-shirt peddlers and layabouts of various persuasion. A knot of skinheads occupied one bench, some young drunks were sprawled on another. A coven of Goths flocked like blackbirds near a female blues singer while in between it all strolled the tourists.

Perfect, Les thought, sooner or later Serb was bound to show up here. To provide a bit of cover he purchased a black baseball cap emblazoned with the words Mardi Gras and a pair of mirrored sunglasses.

On his second turn around the square he found a vacant bench and lounged for an hour.

No Serb.

Les decided to get something to eat and come back. After downing a beignet he returned to the square with a container of coffee and a pack of Camels. The benches were crowded so he leaned against a fence rail and sipped his coffee. He had only had one beer all day so he treated himself to a cigarette. Dave called it Les Logic.

He thought about Melody and shoved the memory aside. No booze, no Melody. He was not about to let his partner down again.

Then he spotted him.

Les recognized the man's black tattoos and the distinctive new bandage across his nose where Dave had whacked him. Serb was weaving a bit and walking slowly. He probably scored some pain killers at the ER Les speculated. But the man's eyes were alert, looking for potential victims among the unsuspecting tourists. He bumped into one older woman wearing a pink hat, excused himself profusely and moved away quickly.

Too quickly.

Just a moment ago Serb was floating. Even as it dawned that Serb had boosted the woman's wallet Les moved.

He wasn't hard to catch. Les felt like a street cop making a petty crime collar when he grabbed Serb's arm and yanked him to a stop. He lifted his sunglasses. "Remember me Serb? My partner gave you that nose job. So hand me the wallet and I won't strip search you right here in front your homeys."

"Shit." Serb said calmly. "You again." He reached under his shirt.

Les tightened his grip. "Easy."

With mock humility Serb handed Les a thick pink wallet.

Les walked him back to a souvenir vendor where the woman with the pink hat stood anxiously rummaging through her handbag.

"Did you lose this ma'am?"

The woman gaped at the wallet then at him. "Thank you. Did I drop it?" Then she recognized Serb. "Oh my… did he…?"

Les smiled. "Glad to be of service ma'am,"

"Wait," she cried out as he started to move away.

Les turned and saw she was lifting her smart phone.

"This will be fabulous on Face book."

Les ducked his head and hustled Serb away.

"Where we goin?" Serb demanded. "You got no more evidence."

"This isn't about jacking old women Serb. It's about why you killed your ol' buddy Stash."

Serb was unfazed by the accusation. "Do I look like a fucking cannibal?"

"You look like you'd eat your mother." Les squeezed his arm harder. He had strong hands. Serb winced but he didn't crack.

"Where you takin' me?" he demanded. "This is kidnappin'… false arrest." His voice started to rise until Les whipped out his

Cobra and let the lead weight at the end of the spring snap out inches from his face.

"Another word and I flatten your nose like a postage stamp."

Serb fell silent and Les relaxed his grip. "Let's go someplace quiet and talk."

Still holding Serb's arm he walked him over to the Cathedral. Dramatic lighting enhanced the church's magnificent pointed spires. The effect gave the structure the other worldly quality of a gleaming Disney castle with three mysterious towers.

Serb kept quiet but he remained defiant. Les found an unoccupied bench and sat him down. He put the Cobra away and lit a cigarette. He saw Serb watching him hungrily and shook one loose from the pack.

"Smoke?"

Warily, Serb reached for the cigarette.

Les gave him a light. "Now I know you know exactly what happened to Stash. He told us that you sometimes ran with this pack haunting the cemetery."

"Stash was a pussy-assed punk."

"Don't you know it's not nice to speak ill of the dead? This is going to turn out two ways. At best you'll have to go back to the ER for patching up. At worst you'll end up at the County Jail ER. So about this pack, who are they?"

"All I know is that mostly they're at the cemetery. I crash there. Once in a while I see them but I don't run with them."

Les put his foot up on the bench and casually drew the Glock from his ankle holster.

"Suppose we go to the cemetery and take a look. You can show me where you saw them last."

It was a short walk to St. Louis Cemetery #1.

As they neared the brick walls Serb became visibly nervous. "If we go inside like this they'll know."

Les Paused. "What do you mean like this?"

"Like you're bustin' me."

"How would they know?"

"They know everything."

Les looked at him. The street lights gave Serb's pinched features a strange intensity.

"Tell me more."

"I don't know any more. These people ain't normal."

"How many are there?"

"Four, maybe more. I never got a good look. Nobody does until…"

"Until what?"

"Until they rip out your guts."

"Empty your pockets."

"Come on, man…"

"Now. Or you empty them in jail. Last time you said you lost your ID. You better have found it or I'll take your prints." Les leaned closer. "And I'm guessing you have lots to hide."

Tight-lipped, Serb fished out a couple of ID cards bound by a rubber band. One was a Texas driver's license the other a Costco photo ID. Serb's legal name was Ernst Bauer. After recording the information of the driver's license on his iPhone Les returned the cards.

Then he took the Cobra from the small of his back and put the Glock in its place. He slipped the Cobra halfway up his sleeve. "There. No gun, no bust, just a couple of guys on the town."

Les steered Serb to a nearby liquor store and bought a pint of Jim Beam.

"Okay, we're good to go." Les said. "Now let's check out the boneyard."

"Man you're gonna get us killed. You don't know what you're dealin' with."

"You're right Ernst I don't know but you're going to help me learn. Hey it's your choice. If you want to take the jail option I'll drop you off right now. We can spend a few hours in the interrogation room getting to know each other."

Serb's narrow shoulders sagged in resignation.

How about a drink first?"

Les unscrewed the top and passed the bottle to him. "Here's to Stash dumb as horseshit." Serb took a long pull of whiskey. "We're all next."

"Nice sentiment," Les said, taking the bottle.

Serb led Les to a service gate that was unlocked.

Although just a few feet from the street, the burial ground inside the walls was a thousand years away. Many of the mausoleums and vaults had candlelight offerings that cast flickering shadows across the tombs.

Once inside they moved slowly through the darkness. Serb was tense. He stopped and peered into the gloom. "Hey man let's back off. Somethin's not right."

Les unscrewed the top of the pint bottle. "Have another drink."

Serb took a long slug of bourbon. "Fuck you."

Les took the bottle and replaced the cap. "Show me where you saw them last."

For a few minutes they walked quietly between the darkened tombs. A few feet ahead a circle of candles on the ground illuminated their path and they quickened their pace.

Then Serb stopped. Les peered beyond the candlelight. Something seemed to move in the shadows. He listened. Nothing.

"There," Serb hissed, "behind the big dome. Sometimes they meet there."

The mausoleum was in the shape of a domed temple with winged angels at either side. It blocked out the nearby candlelight and Les stepped into pitch blackness.

"How about a drink?"

As Les passed him the bottle his phone began to vibrate. It was Dave. In the dim glow of the screen he saw Serb put the bottle to his mouth. The man's eyes blazed fiercely.

A flash of hot pain jolted his skull from ear to jaw. Les stumbled against an iron fence and held on, dazed for a few chaotic seconds. When the ringing in his skull subsided, Les realized that

Serb had cold cocked him with the pint bottle while he was occupied with Dave's call. He looked around wildly.

Serb was long gone.

And he had lost his phone.

Through his panic he felt the ground beneath his feet begin to rumble.

Chapter 5

Melody was not taking rejection well.

When Victor saw her signal for her third drink in twenty minutes he pretended to be busy with another customer.

Finally he caught the anger flaring in her eyes and ambled over.

"Are you trying to ignore me?" she asked sharply.

"Trying," he admitted, "you're hitting it too hard."

"So now you…"

He leaned across the bar. It was early and the club's few patrons were on the other end of the bar. Still he kept his voice low and level. "If you had taken care of this right away we'd all be happy."

"I didn't know he was a fed. That could complicate our situation."

Victor stroked the red beaded braid in his white beard. "But you saw him again. That's not like you."

"I'm terminally bored Victor. I need a little amusement. And I like him. He is so much fun to corrupt."

"You're drunk Melody. You need to end it tonight."

"You don't get it darling. He's not coming tonight."

Victor's genial façade hardened. "How do you know that?"

She rolled her eyes. "Don't be naïve."

"Perhaps you're losing your touch."

"Perhaps."

"Your indifference could jeopardize everything. Do you have a death wish?"

"Yes, actually."

"Well, I don't, my dear and if you don't make this right there are ways…"

"Yes, yes, I know all the ways. How do I love thee, let me count the ways."

"Romantic poetry? You are getting soft. What happened to Rimbaud and Yeats?"

"What happened to my damned drink?" Her voice was subdued but Victor heard the threat edging her tone and moved off to fetch her absinthe. Melody could be extremely dangerous when crossed.

Victor made a big show of observing the traditions as he poured her drink through the requisite sugar cube.

Melody lifted her glass. "Thank you darling. Don't worry he'll be back sooner or later."

"And meanwhile?"

Her green eyes fixed on his over the rim of her glass. "I'll select someone for the short term. Does that make you feel better?"

Victor's tight-lipped expression relaxed to that of a genial barman.

"Much better thank you. But drink that slowly."

Melody did him one better. She retired to the ladies room. Due to the early hour it was empty. She locked herself in the large handicapped stall. She took a small hand mirror from her bag and placed it on the shelf. She took out a small glass bottle and tapped a tiny mound of white powder onto the mirror. Then she carefully slid the mirror's handle out revealing a six-inch blade. Using the knife she pecked out two neat lines which she snorted through a short straw. Thus fortified she returned to the bar and her absinthe.

One of the nice things about cocaine Melody reflected, is that you can drink all night and not get sloppy

More patrons started to drift into the club. Melody recognized four or five regulars but there was an ample selection of new faces. Melody averted her eyes from the door knowing it was useless. There would be no surprises tonight… for her.

Still, she couldn't help wondering. By tonight he should have been begging to see her. *Maybe that's what attracted me* she mused, *a sense of inner strength*. So rare these days.

She sipped her drink slowly, mood shifting from wounded pride to predatory anticipation. Now fully alert she scanned the room carefully. Her attention settled on two men at the far end of the bar. They were seated a few stools apart, both handsome in different ways. One was vain, eyeing all the ladies, constantly checking his reflection. He was engaged in conversation with a cheap blond who shared his fascination with the mirror behind the bar.

The other was reflective. He sat brooding over his drink occasionally lifting his head and studying the crowd. He seemed to be absorbing their secrets—or hiding from them. Might be an artist. Might be a gangster Melody speculated.

The man in the mirror was some sort of flashy player, maybe gambling or used cars. No contest Melody decided, the flashy one was the mark.

Soon the pick-up artist tired of the cheap blond and his roving eye came to rest on her.

She glanced up, locked on his gaze then turned away. Moments later when she shyly looked over her glass he was still staring.

Melody felt a quickening in her veins. This was the turning point. She looked away. Minutes later she saw Victor nod in her direction and knew the game was on. The mark had taken the bait. And in true mark fashion thought he was the aggressor.

"May I buy you a drink lovely lady?" The mark asked.

Melody looked up and smiled demurely. "That would be nice."

Victor arrived on cue. "Would you like something over here?"

"Another bourbon and whatever the lady is having."

The order solidified the mark's move from the other end of the bar. In the corner of her eye she could see the cheap blond glaring at her.

"I'm Larry."

"Melody."

He flashed the smile that launched a thousand fluttering hearts. When he ran a hand through his long hair she saw the showy emerald ring on his finger.

"Melody, maybe we can make some sweet music tonight."

She groaned inwardly, having heard some variation for what seemed centuries.

Fortunately Victor returned with the drinks.

"You like absinthe." Larry said as Victor poured her drink through the requisite sugar cube. "Tastes too much like licorice for me."

"You might say I grew up drinking it."

"I thought it was illegal until a few years ago."

She smiled. "I lived in Prague."

He cocked his head, giving his handsome features a boyish cast. He had dark piercing eyes, an aquiline nose and perfect white teeth. His mouth had an arrogant curl but she could see his confidence had been dented. Americans were only dimly aware of Europe

"It's in Czechoslovakia."

Larry's eyes flicked to the mirror. "I'm from Georgia. We drink bourbon."

"So what do you do Larry?'

He leaned closer. "I make people happy."

She sipped her drink thoughtfully. "That covers a wide territory."

Larry grinned. "That's what I do—cover a lot of territory. I'm a pilot."

Melody looked impressed. "Airliners?"

"Mostly small planes, sometimes private jets."

"Really. And you make people happy by taking them where they want to go?" Her tone suggested it was akin to driving a cab.

Again he took the bait. "Hey—I make them happy by bringing souvenirs from my trips."

"And where might these trips take you Larry?"

"Resorts mainly. Jamaica, St Thomas, Cartagena…"

For a drug courier Larry wasn't very discreet Melody noted, but she continued to play innocent.

"Sounds glamorous."

"It is—just like you." He leaned closer. "How about we continue the conversation back at my place."

"What's wrong with right here?"

"I can show you some of the souvenirs from my last flight."

"You mean like wood carvings and woven baskets?"

He chuckled. "More like exotic party favors. You like to party?"

"Love it but I'm wary of strangers."

He gave her a searching look straight out of a silent movie. "I'm no stranger. Knew it the second I saw you. Something connected with me."

Melody nodded. *Naturally it's all about you* she thought, but played along. "Can't deny that but I don't even know your full name."

"Larry Edwards, at your service. The bartender is running my credit card if that makes you feel better."

Victor has already run your name, address, financial history and criminal record Melody noted.

"You never know these days," she said.

He shook his head in amusement, eyes retuning to the mirror. "It's up to you Melody. I'm moving on."

She gave him a slow smile and took her purse from the bar. "Then let's move."

Larry drove a silver Corvette, very fast.

"I have a rule," Melody said, "never commit a misdemeanor on your way to committing a felony."

"What's that mean?"

"You get stopped for speeding they may decide to search."

"So? I'm cool. Never carry in the car."

"But I am carrying. It could ruin our evening."

He slowed down immediately. "Smart lady,"

Melody relaxed. She didn't need police attention or a fender bender. It was bad enough they were seen together at the Styx.

+ + +

Larry's apartment was an extension of his Corvette: chrome and leather furniture, chrome track lights, gaudy acrylic abstract art better suited to decorate airports and a black leather bar with chrome studs.

He picked up a remote and the brash sound of pop music filtered through the room.

"Make yourself at home." He went behind the bar, produced a small glass jar filled with white powder and began tapping out lines.

"Sorry, there's no absinthe but I'll guarantee that whatever you're carrying ain't nearly as pure as this."

"Purity," she repeated, joining him at the bar, "isn't that we're all longing for?"

"Not in your case."

Got that right Larry she thought inhaling a line through the rolled up hundred he provided. He was also right about the coke. It was excellent. It went up her nostrils like air, expanding her senses.

"Some champagne?" He pulled a bottle from the fridge behind him.

Crystal wine, crystal flutes, Larry liked his luxuries but she wasn't going to be part of his collection.

Quite the opposite.

"I love what you've done to this place," she said.

It wasn't long before he made his move. Another line another wine and his arms were around her, his busy hands caressing her thighs. Her already amplified senses shifted to another level. Suddenly every cell in her body yawned with relentless desire, rushing toward a single, raw need. The sour scent of his skin, his lungs heart and hips pumping against hers ignited an ancient hunger. Their lips and tongues intertwined fiercely until Melody pulled back, heaved a deep breath... and struck. Her extended canines pierced his jugular and she felt a voluptuous rush of ecstasy convulse her body as hot blood steamed though her parched flesh.

+ + +

Melody went over the place before Victor arrived. A casual search turned up a couple of ounces of cocaine, a nine-millimeter Beretta, and fifty two thousand dollars in cash. She kept the coke and gave Victor two thousand dollars and the Beretta. He seemed suspicious but knew better than to argue. What he wanted could not be bought with money.

"Did you make the call?"

"They're on the way. Are you sure he's alive?"

Melody felt a tinge of embarrassment. She hadn't realized how famished she was. Her restraint with Les had left her vulnerable. Hunger had eroded her control.

Fortunately the cocaine helped keep parts of her brain alert and she stopped short of draining him. However the mark was left in a less than desirable state. Larry was semi-conscious and couldn't walk. He would have to be carried to his car. Victor could handle it but it would make them conspicuous.

Melody took the keys to Larry's Corvette and went outside. The night air was warm and moist. The complex was composed of semi-detached condos and she could see lights in some nearby windows.

The car was parked in the driveway. Melody checked the visor and found a remote. She pressed the red button and the garage door slid open.

She drove the car inside and shut the garage door behind her.

Victor was still upstairs, wrestling with Larry's limp body. "Think you could transfuse some of your blood to wake him up a bit?" he said though gritted teeth.

"You know better than that," she snapped, "that might turn him. Now pick him up under the shoulders and drag him into the garage."

Wheezing Victor did as he was told, grateful Melody hadn't noticed the flashy emerald ring he'd taken from Larry's finger.

+ + +

Melody had noticed the ring. It confirmed her suspicion that Victor had gone through the place while she was in the garage.

She drove the Corvette with Larry in the passenger seat, belted in. Victor followed in his Caddy.

Melody pulled into the meeting place—a parking lot behind a darkened grocery market—ahead of schedule. She left the car and stood in the shadows behind a dumpster. A few minutes later Victor's Caddy stopped across the street. Everything was in place.

Precisely on time her client's car rolled slowly into view, its headlights dark. With her superb night vision Melody could see there were three people inside. She speed dialed Victor, alerting him. Then she pressed her client's number.

"Yes?" he said calmly. His voice carried a faint southern drawl.

"Stop your car or risk being shot."

The car stopped. "Are you crazy? You know me."

"I know you violated our agreement. Two not three."

"Melody dear, don't you trust me?"

"Come alone. Tell your friends to drive away."

There was a pause. "Only for you."

A heavyset shambling figure got out of the car and watched it drive off before he walked slowly to the parking lot. When he neared the Corvette she called out in a hushed tone.

"Far enough."

"Why all this now?"

"Because you broke your word."

"I apologize. It won't happen again."

"Next time I'll consider it an act of aggression."
"Aggression? Come on, I need you."
"You have my fee?"
"Yes."
"Put it on top of the car."

Melody saw his eyes narrow, peering through the shadows for some sign of hidden danger. Finally he sighed heavily and put a thick envelope on the top of the Corvette, "You're so dramatic my dear. I presume you have my goods?"

Melody stepped out of the shadows, took the envelope and tossed the car keys on the hood.

"Your goods are inside. Prime specimen as specified. And you get to keep the car. Now go, and don't turn on your lights until you get down the block. Understand?"

"Perfectly. I trust I'll see you at the usual time in two weeks?"

"I'll call with new arrangements."

"I look forward to it," the man said. He folded his portly body into the low car with some effort.

Still in the shadows Melody watched him drive off with Larry then called Victor. A few moments later the Caddy pulled up in front of the lot.

As they drove Melody counted out three thousand from her thirty thousand dollar fee and gave it to Victor. The rest she put in her shoulder bag along with Larry's fifty thousand and the coke.

"Not bad for a night's work," Victor gloated, "too bad you had to give up the Corvette."

"Might be traced."

Victor prattled on, buoyed by their success. "Makes three this month."

"Who's counting?" she said absently, bored now.

"You said when we dispose of six or seven you would…" His voice trailed off.

"Would what, Victor?"

"…turn me."

Melody glared at him. Still angry at her client's transgression she focused her full fury on Victor.

He felt it before she spoke. He gripped the wheel and stared straight ahead but her eyes burned into his peripheral vision.

"If and when I decide to turn you it will be because you deserve it. Not because you've racked up mileage points. Be thankful I just don't have you for dinner."

Her fierce whisper smothered his euphoria and he didn't speak the rest of the way.

Which suited Melody perfectly, who remained wrapped in her dark, unutterable dreams.

Chapter 6

Naked fear propelled Les headlong into a narrow crevice between tomb and statue. He clawed at his leg holster and found the Glock as the galloping footsteps pounded closer. Back pressed the wall of the tomb he lifted his body, trying to cover both exposed sides of his fragile fortress.

They were very close. Their foul stench pervaded the moist air like toxic gas.

He heard hoarse breathing and saw a group of shadows loom up on his right. Without hesitation he yanked the trigger. The quick flash illuminated hairy, bestial faces contorted with rage and surprise. Before he could fire again they were gone. He could hear their receding footsteps. Their stink hung in the air as he carefully left the crude shelter, outstretched gun sweeping the area.

His hand was shaking. He lowered his Glock and started to call Dave. That's when he realized his phone was gone. He'd lost it somewhere after Serb hit him.

Cursing he slowly circled the darkened area, his feet scuffing at the dirt. A pair of votive candles on a nearby grave afforded dim light but the glass containers were too hot to handle. He peeled his wet shirt from one arm and wrapped the damp cloth around his hand. Small candle aloft he continued to drag his feet across the ground while he searched between the shadowed tombs.

His foot brushed against something soft. Les swung the light down. It was a leg.

The leg belonged to what was left of Serb after he'd been torn open from belly to chest. Les was willing to bet his body was a few vital organs short.

A low buzz drew his attention. It was his phone.

In the midst of his frantic search the candle went out.

Seconds later the phone stopped buzzing but by that time he had a fix on its general location.

When he finally found it he took a few deep breaths and started to call Dave.

Then something jabbed his instincts and he switched on the phone's flashlight.

Reluctantly he went back to where he had found the mutilated body. After a quick scan under strong light Les realized he'd made a mistake.

The dead man was skinny and marked with tattoos.

But he definitely was not Serb.

+ + +

Les met Dave in a small bar on the outskirts of Lafayette. He ordered a double bourbon as soon as her sat down. "First drink of the day and I fucking earned it." he announced.

Dave took him at his word. He drank his beer and listened to Les tell him what he had encountered in New Orleans.

"Three more bodies and they nearly nailed you." Dave shook his head. "I had a play date by comparison."

He looked at Les. "Who are these guys?"

Les drained his glass and signaled for another.

"They're not guys. More like Beasts R Us. Maybe I was confused but… I don't think so."

"Hey, I remember what they did to my Malibu. Which reminds me. We pick it up at the body shop tomorrow noon."

Les smiled. "I drive this time."

"Just for that you pay for the drinks. So what do we report tonight?"

"We have established cover and are tracing the missing cop in New Iberia."

"Nothing about New Orleans?"

Les shook his head. "Not right now."

Dave sat back and signaled to the waitress. They were silent as she approached their booth.

"Another beer and bourbon?"

"Make it two bourbons," Dave said.

Les watched her depart. "What's the problem?"

"I'm thinking about your suggestion."

"I've been thinking about it too." Les said.

Dave examined his empty beer bottle. "We need to cover our ass here. We'll be held accountable for everything we post."

Les suddenly felt tired. "Exactly why we don't mention New Orleans. Two attacks: One directly on you, one too damned close on me. Do you believe in coincidence? Have a drink and think about that."

"Now you're paranoid," Dave said.

Les didn't reply. When their drinks arrived Dave drank slowly letting the bourbon burn through the beer haze.

"And why were we warned off New Orleans anyway?" Les asked quietly. "This hasn't smelled right from the jump."

Dave raised his glass. "Big budget, big bump in pay grade you said,"

"Think about it. You saw what those guys did. Was that a random attack?"

"I don't know. I told you, I got into a scuffle earlier. Could have been payback."

"Banged the car pretty good, unless you scratched the back fender yourself."

Dave sighed. "Funny. Okay tonight I omit your side trip in the report. But tomorrow we both go to New Orleans."

+ + +

Despite a slight hangover Dave woke up feeling a lot better about Les.

His partner had uncovered significant links to the murdered field agents. And found evidence to back up his story. Hopefully his fling with Melody seemed over. His next thought was of Sam. Immediately he felt guilty. He pushed that aside and called Jennifer.

The conversation with his family left Dave determined to stay alert. People were getting massacred out there.

But he wasn't quite ready to conclude he and Les were specific targets. His partner could be paranoid.

The met for a late breakfast at a café near the repair garage. A good night's sleep had done wonders for Les. "Doubt if we'll locate Serb at the usual places," he said, head bent over his grits and bacon. "The bastard probably set me up last night."

"We can nose around the cemetery. See if anything turns up."

"Sure… whatever" It was clear Les wasn't anxious to return.

They decided to give New Orleans a once over then drive back to New Iberia. Dave would introduce Les as one of the producers of the film. It was a solid plan.

At half past twelve Les drove his loaner to the garage. The mechanic, a rangy young man sporting a wispy red goatee shook his head apologetically.

"It'll be a few hours yet. Come back at six this evenin."

Les shrugged. "Okay to keep the Charger?"

"Sure thing. Oh by the way, he added as they started to leave. "What do you want me to do with this?"

He took a metallic box from the pocket of his overalls.

"How do you mean?"

"It was inside your rear door," the mechanic told him.

Les looked at Dave who shook his head.

"What is it?" he muttered, turning it over in his hand.

The mechanic seemed surprised. "It's a Viper… you know a wireless recorder. Picks up conversation through the radio speakers. You can get them on the internet."

"I'll take it with me," Les said calmly, "see you at six,"

"Do you believe me now?" Les said as they drove off. He tossed the box to Dave. "They've been bugging us."

Dave examined the device. "I'm a believer in hard evidence. Okay at the moment we have a neutral vehicle. Only way they can track us is through our smart phones." Les slapped the steering wheel in frustration. "Probably got us on the screen right now."

"Probably not," Dave said calmly. "When we get to New Orleans we'll park the car, stash the phones and buy a couple of prepaid cells."

Les smiled. "Smart and simple. Like us." He stepped on the accelerator.

Dave's doubts continued to simmer and he kept sorting through the evidence they'd gathered. By the time they arrived in New Orleans he had reached a number of conclusions.

"We are stuck between deep shit and sure death," he half whispered as they waited for lunch in a small restaurant booth.

"Been sayin'" Les said.

"Obviously the leak placed the bug in our car. Probably the same guy who got our agents killed."

"Easton. Who else?"

"Virgil?"

Les shrugged. "Maybe."

"And we are being targeted by some beast boys who run in a pack and rip organs from their victims."

Dave paused as the waiter arrived with their order. Shrimp salad for him, shrimp gumbo for Les. Both of them were drinking iced tea.

"You were saying beast boys," Les prompted digging into his food.

"Whatever the hell they are, they're killers. Thing is, we haven't mentioned them in our reports."

Les snorted. "Sure, try mentioning our perps are 'beast boys' and the Bureau will recommend us for psycho leave."

"Which leaves us swinging without a net."

"Undercover is like that."

"What about you're missing lead?"

"Serb? He'll be tough to find after last night. But he's all we've got."

Les gave the parking valet a twenty and left the car at the restaurant while they scoured the area on foot. They covered Jackson Square then walked to the cemetery only to find police had blocked the gates. It was still a crime scene. Two TV vans were parked nearby.

"That takes care of that idea," Les said. "We'll have to drive back tomorrow."

"Wait a second." Dave scanned the street on both sides. "These guys, this pack, run through the graveyard right?"

"Yeah so?"

"So they have to run *out* again. This is a busy area. They'd need to find cover before they're seen." Dave gestured at a warehouse complex two blocks away.

"Like over there."

"Long way to go without somebody spotting them."

"Fast as I saw them run they could make it in ninety seconds."

Les nodded. "Seeing as how the boneyard is closed, why not?"

There was activity around the warehouses. Dave and Les had to weave around forklifts and trucks moving in and out of the loading platforms. The complex consisted of sixteen warehouses of various size. At least ten were open for business. It was noisy, it was hot and it was chaotic.

They wandered aimlessly about the area but it was clear there was no hope of finding physical evidence. The workers were normal guys going about their business. The heavy traffic obliterated any sign of the previous night's activity. If in fact there was any at all.

"It was a long shot," Les said, "but a good one."

Dave headed to a deserted area. "These are all shut down."

"Sea food." Les pointed to a sign on a nearby building. "They do business early in the morning."

Dave moved closer. "Make's sense. But look at this."

"Knight's Sea Food," Les read aloud, "Gulf Road, New Iberia."

"What, you think there's a connection?"

"Maybe. Why not?"

"Well since New Iberia is a fishing region, I'd say half these warehouses are based in New Iberia."

Les was almost right. Of the seven seafood companies that maintained warehouses, three were based in New Iberia. He dutifully noted each company name: Knights Seafood, the Fresh Catch, and Clete's Sea Feast.

Knights occupied the largest building and Fresh Catch a relatively small warehouse in one corner behind Clete's.

"Now that we know somebody's bugging us we have to check these out on a neutral computer," Les said.

Dave nodded and started back to the car. "Let's take care of hardware on our way to New Iberia. I'll drive."

"Why are we going there?"

"Dinner, what else?" Dave said over his shoulder.

+ + +

It was a bit more than just dinner.

They had stopped in a mall outside Lafayette and purchased prepaid phones. Dave found a used Mac pro laptop in a pawnshop that had all the software he needed. Les chose a Toshiba for back up. From there they went to New Iberia.

Dave drove to Nick's and introduced Les as the producer on the film he was scouting.

Les had to agree the food was excellent but he could see it wasn't the only reason Dave chose to have dinner there.

Sam, the lady behind the bar was a knockout.

It was a side of Dave he hadn't seen before. The polite but unbending FBI agent became flirtatious around Sam. It wasn't obvious but Les could tell.

He wondered if Sam could tell too. Probably she did Les decided, women know these things.

For the first time that day he thought of Melody. It wasn't a good idea. A swirl of lust clogged his thoughts like a sandstorm.

"Is this your first film?" Les looked up and saw Sam smiling at him. It was a nice smile. Dave was smiling too but he was tense, afraid Les would blow their cover."

"If this happens it will be my first feature. I've been an assistant on a few documentaries."

"Like wild life and stuff? I love those shows."

"Actually, more military."

"Oh?" Nick said. "What sort of military films?" Nick said. "I'm most interested."

They had finished dinner and were having a drink with Sam and the proprietor Nick.

Les gave Nick an appraising glance. He could see their host was tough and sharp under his flamboyant exterior.

"I did a film for military and law enforcement promoting Glock pistols."

"A most admirable firearm. I take it that is the weapon you carry in your ankle holster."

Nick gave Les an apologetic smile. "Your trouser leg is riding up."

Les calmly straightened it "Yes, it is a Glock. I heard it's a good idea to have protection in Louisiana."

"Quite wise suh. Our inhabitants are very short tempered. I attribute it to the spicy food."

Although still early the restaurant was crowded as was the bar. Sam and Nick worked well as a team, alternately serving drinks and waiting on tables. Sam left to take care of a table and Nick slipped behind the bar. "I insist you gentlemen join me in sampling a fine cognac." The bald, muscular man worked smoothly, producing a bottle from a lower cabinet and pouring the contents into three snifters. "I keep a shotgun back here myself," he confided, "and a baseball bat. Fortunately I've only had one occasion to use the bat."

The cognac was excellent but Les was wary of Nick's hospitality. The discovery of the listening device had compounded his natural paranoia—and alerted his trained instincts. Obviously

Nick was a player of some sort but what bar owner in Louisiana wasn't? It went with the territory.

"Did you find any locations yet?" Sam asked.

Dave glanced at Les. "Sure, there's lots of possibilities."

"Right now it's a matter of financing," Les said. "We'll send the pictures Dave took back to the coast." He noticed both Dave and Sam smiled. "We were also hoping to find a new contact."

Nick frowned. "Oh yes, Morgan. Who did you speak to at the Lafayette P.D.?"

"No one yet. Why?"

"Because Detective Hank Orsini is dining with us tonight." Nick tilted his head toward a table in the corner where a large man in a wrinkled white suit sat with a pretty blond girl at least half his age.

"Would you like an introduction?"

Les shook his head. "Thanks but it's a bad time. I don't like to intrude."

"Timing is everything," Nick said. He moved off to serve drinks to some new arrivals.

Les glanced at Dave but his partner was distracted by something Sam was saying.

When Sam left Les tapped Dave on the bicep. "Did you get that?"

"You mean timing?" Dave leaned closer. "Sam was giving me some gossip on Orsini."

"Don't look his way."

"Apology accepted."

"A stunner like Sam could churn a man's brain that's all."

"You should know."

"What about Orsini?"

"Likes young girls, lousy tipper… Get back in character."

Les looked up and saw Nick coming towards them with Orsini in tow.

The detective slowly navigated his sizable paunch between tables, his jowly face set in a scowl.

"Dave and Les, I'd like you to meet Detective Orsini," Nick said.

Orsini solemnly shook hands. "Call me Hank. Nick tells me you were lookin' to hook up with Ryan Morgan."

"Yes, do you know him?" Dave asked.

"For sure. He works on my floor in Lafayette. That's mainly homicide but we catch all kinds of cases."

"Do you know where we can find him?"

With some effort Orsini settled on a barstool. "No sir I do not. Seems he went undercover and never surfaced. Nick would you pour me some of that fine brandy these gentlemen are drinking."

"Cognac," Nick corrected. "What about your lady friend?"

"Send over a bourbon and a Dr. Pepper and tell her I'll be back presently. I just wanted to meet your friends. We've had a fair amount of movie and TV people pass through lately."

"The scenery is spectacular," Les said.

"And we can keep the budget in line," Dave added.

"Always a prime consideration," Orsini said gravely. He picked up the snifter Nick gave him and drained it in one large gulp.

Nick rolled his eyes. "Hank you drink fine cognac like it's tequila."

When Orsini smiled his eyes became slits behind his florid jowls. "I'm a simple country boy of simple tastes. I'd better get back to Judy Belle there. She's startin' to squirm." He took a business card from his pocket and gave it to Les. "Give me a call and I'll try to help you get your movie over here."

He rolled off the stool with surprising agility and ambled back to his table.

Les and Dave looked at each other, then at Nick.

"Is he for real?" Les said under his breath.

Nick refilled their snifters. "Real as taxes. Hank there knows everything that goes on in this part of the state."

"Thanks for the introduction," Dave said.

"Thank Sam. It—was her idea."

"I just thought it would help." Sam said airily and went off to wait a table.

Nick winked at Dave. "She just wants to keep you around."

"Be careful partner," Les said quietly as they walked outside, "she's lovely, you're married and it looks like it's getting personal. From one who's been there, go easy."

Dave felt his ears redden. "She's an asset okay? And a damned good one. Now we can get one foot in the door of the Lafayette PD," He paused and took a deep breath. "So don't lose that card."

Les had also stopped but he didn't seem to be listening.

The night air was misted with insects and the scent of stagnant water and night blooming flowers. But another odor hung over the lot.

Smell that?"

Dave sniffed the air and caught it, a foul animal stench. He looked around. The parking lot was deserted and poorly lit. He had been too busy fending off Les to pay attention to his surroundings. After his last encounter in this lot he should have known better.

He drew the Glock from his ankle holster.

Les was already armed. "I know that stink," he whispered, "last night."

How far is the car?"

"Too far. Maybe we should go back inside."

They took a few careful steps towards the restaurant, outstretched weapons sweeping the area.

A shadow moved.

A tree rustled.

Then the shadows rose up like a howling tornado.

Les fired first, two quick shots. The bullets caught one figure in mid-air. Dave followed with a three round burst. In the fleeting light he saw a tall, wild-haired man, eyes shining blankly, mouth twisted in a bestial snarl, both hands lifted as if to ward off the bullets as he dove directly at Dave.

Instinctively Dave ducked. He felt a sharp blow as something jolted his shoulder with brutal force toppling him to the ground.

Suddenly, the lot was silent and empty.

"Dave, you okay?"

He looked up and saw Les staring at him with grave concern.

"I think so. Why?"

"You're bleeding."

"Hey!" someone shouted in the distance.

Les reached down and grabbed Dave's wrist with his free hand. "We've got company. Stay in character."

As Les pulled him to his feet Dave felt pain throb through his arm. He looked down and saw it was streaming blood.

Les picked Dave's gun from the ground. "Put this away he whispered, "I'll talk."

"Hey, what's up out here? We heard gunfire."

Dazed, Dave fumbled with his ankle holster. He looked up and saw Nick coming quickly towards them holding a shotgun

"What the hell happened?"

"Some creeps tried to mug us." Les said, "Dave's hurt. He's bleeding."

"Emergency hospital is close by." Nick told him, "I'll take you there."

Les waved him off. "You lead the way. No sense getting your seats bloody."

It took less than ten minutes to reach the small emergency ward. Les had made a crude bandage with his T-shirt and Dave seemed conscious and alert.

Along the way Les reminded him to stick to the cover story.

"Visiting film people who'd been mugged. You know the drill. Hell, you're the guy who came up with it.

Dave didn't answer.

"You feel alright?"

"No. This is the third time they've come at us."

"I could swear I hit one of them in the chest."

"Maybe I hit one too. He was right in front of me."

Les nodded in sympathy. "Then they fucking disappear."

Up ahead the blinking red directional on Nick's Mustang signaled they had arrived at the emergency ward.

A few people were waiting but when the nurse on duty saw Dave's wound she hustled him inside to see a doctor.

Nick sat with Les who was crashing from the adrenaline rush of the intense skirmish.

"I should have brought the cognac," Nick said after a while.

"The way I feel right now I need a transfusion."

"Lucky you were armed. Even so they managed to slash Dave."

"I thought I hit one of them but they ran."

"Just as well. Otherwise you'd be talking to the police."

"Good point Nick. Did you see anything when you came out?"

"A few minutes after you left, I heard gunfire. By the time I got there you were helping Dave off the ground."

"Dave told me some guys went after him the other night."

"I've ordered surveillance cameras and lights for that lot. Problem is the land behind my restaurant is wild territory. Bayou for miles. We're at the edge of the world."

It's not quite the Amazon jungle Les thought but he remained silent. Whatever attacked them wasn't civilized that was certain.

He was beginning to get worried when the nurse finally appeared and motioned to him.

"Are you Les?"

"Yes."

"You can come in. Not you sir," she added as Nick tried to follow.

Les silently thanked her.

He found Dave in a screened cubicle. He was sitting up shirtless while the doctor applied antiseptic to a pair of long red gashes on his shoulder that had been stitched. He hadn't realized it was that bad.

"How is he doctor?"

The physician's nameplate read Naipur and he spoke with a slight Indian accent. "I numbed his arm for the stitches and gave him some pain killers. He'll need help getting home. He said you were attacked—by an animal or something?"

"Human… or something."

Doctor Naipur gave a snorting laugh but Les was deadly serious.

Chapter 7

"So where the fuck do you think he is?"

Don Benito's tone made Cozy squirm inwardly. He prayed it didn't show.

"Larry's apartment is empty, no sign of the merch or the money. His Corvette is gone. We're checking everything from airports to Craig's List for the car."

The Don slapped his hand on the desk. "Don't use the fucking computer."

Cozy maintained a deadpan expression.

"A figure of speech Don Benito. But because of my daughter I do have a computer and a cell phone."

The Don shrugged and waved his hand as if giving him a Papal dispensation.

"As for our missing associate, he's a pilot. So he might be anywhere."

Benito sighed heavily. "I can't use *might be*. He owes me money and goods. Do you understand?"

"Perfectly Don Benito."

"You know the bastard right?"

"I'm his contact."

"He a friend, you have a drink?"

"Straight business, in and out. He's a ladies man, has too much action around him for me. I keep a low profile."

Benito nodded approval of Cozy's discretion. However he was far from satisfied He had been a soccer player in his native town of Bari and still carried his huge bulk with athletic grace. Age had not dimmed his legendary temper and at seventy he was still a man to fear. Cozy couldn't help remembering what the Don had reputedly did to an associate called Vince who had been arrested with a large shipment of heroin and was about to make a deal with the DEA. Don Benito had paid the Vince's sizable bond and sprung him. A few days later the Don invited him to dinner at Antoine's where he insisted Vince eat a huge meal. Over dinner he questioned Vince about the arrest. What Vince didn't know was that the Don had a man inside the DEA that was feeding him information. Two days later they found Vince's charred body in the burnt out skeleton of his car. He had been locked inside the trunk and the car set on fire. Vince was burned alive.

Don Benito fixed Cozy with a cool, half-lidded stare.

"You recommended him right?"

Cozy pressed his palms together. "With all due respect I did *not* recommend that guy for anything."

"Who did?"

"Uh I believe it was your daughter."

Benito's jaw knotted and the veins in his temple swelled.

"Maybe you believe I'm stupid."

Cozy knew his life was over."

The Don spread his huge hands. "What can I do? I'm too soft when it comes to Nadia. My wife used to complain I spoiled her… you have a daughter, you understand."

Relieved to be off the hook Cozy nodded vigorously.

"But when it comes to business I'm a piece if granite.'

Like a tombstone Cozy thought unhappily.

"And that money belongs to my family. So I'm telling you now—find this rat bastard who stole from my family."

Cozy left the Don's mansion with an acid stomach.

Fortunately he hadn't recommended Larry, however as his contact he was responsible.

The problem was it didn't make sense. Larry made fifty grand in a single run as a courier. He also had access to wholesale drugs. Why risk pissing off Don Benito?

Driving to New Orleans Cozy recalled the story of why the Don had to flee Italy. Apparently the goalie on his hometown soccer team had been throwing games so Benito found out where the goalie was meeting his fixer and killed them both with his bare hands. He was secretly hailed as a hero and a senator from his region helped facilitate his escape to America. Cozy knew that if he came up empty his position was in serious jeopardy. This was a test. Everything the Don did was a test. Old school, never forgets a favor —or a mistake. At best he would lose status which made him expendable, Cozy brooded. Either way he would end up whacked if he didn't find Larry.

Richard 'Cozy' Costanza lived in a three unit terraced building near the French Quarter that he owned along with a few other properties. One of those properties was a bar called Cana two blocks from his home. He parked his black Mercedes S in the garage and walked to the bar. Usually he enjoyed the stroll but his brain was steaming like an overheated engine.

His crew was already in the back office when he arrived. He had called Jason and told him to alert the other three.

As soon as he entered he pulled Jason aside.

"Get me everything you can find on Larry Edwards. Here's his address. He drives a silver corvette and he's a pilot. And while you're on the computer check if he flew out of here. Flight plans are a matter of record."

The skinny twenty-year-old frowned. "Could be tough hacking in."

Cozy patted his cheek. "That's why you get the big bucks."

Jason left without another word. A big reason he liked the kid, no drama, all business, very smart. Of course he had to hip Jason up. The kid was a tech genius but he dressed like a hobo and ate like a five-year-old. Cozy had to buy him some unwrinkled clothes: good jeans, fresh shirts, even a sports jacket. He started taking Jason to fine restaurants and taught him basic table manners. Now Jason could hold his own in the world outside his computers.

"Say Cozy, why we here?"

The man who spoke was Sal Paneforte, his enforcer and debt collector. Sal was an ex heavy weight boxer whose battered mug was enough to scare his debtors into paying

"I'm glad you asked Sal," Cozy said as he joined them at the table, "because this is a collection problem. Our courier Larry Edwards skipped off with fifty grand of the old man's money. The guy is a pilot, so check the local airports. Look for a silver Corvette. He's a pussy hound, likes to go to the clubs."

"I met the guy one time," Sal rumbled, "conceited asshole."

"So this guy owes money," Anthony Falconi said impatiently. "Where do I fit in?"

"He took two bottles of the old man's 30-year-old scotch."

Scotch was their code for heroin Tequila for cocaine and wine for marijuana. Falconi was in charge of drug distribution.

"Ask around if anybody is trying to auction them off." Cozy said. "Something like that is bound to cause a ripple."

Falconi rubbed his pointed jaw. "I'll make inquiries."

Cozy turned to the third man at the table. Franny Five Angels handled gambling and prostitution from his strip joint in the quarter.

"You know this guy right?"

Franny lifted his palms. "We had drinks once or twice. Like you said he's a real pussy hound. I had to tell him not to do blow at my club. But he lives over by Lafayette right?"

"We've been to his condo. Nothing. Doesn't answer his phone."

"I'll check down south," Franny said, "if he steps in a skin joint anywhere I'll hear about it."

Cozy sat back. "Then it's settled. All of you work your territory and we'll find him. The old man is taking this personally so stay on it."

Cozy needed a drink himself but he didn't want whiskey on his breath when he came home and kissed his daughter.

Gina was seven. She had been four when his wife died. Denise was never an enthusiastic mother and he raised Gina with the help of his mother.

Mama Costanza, lived on the second floor and his apartment was on the top floor. The bottom flat was his office but lately Gina made it a playroom. It was a good arrangement for everybody and the Don approved.

Cozy went directly to his mother's place.

As he came up the stairs he could smell the cooking.

Entering her apartment was like stepping into another era. Straight back chairs, lace doilies on the sofa, large fringed lampshades, and a formal dining room table where Gina sat doing her homework. Behind her a Verdi opera played on the radio.

"Daddy's home," Gina cried and ran to jump in his arms.

For a moment Cozy's problems melted into a warm fuzzy glow.

"You're late. I'm going to ruin dinner."

"Sorry mom I had to meet the old man."

"You shouldn't call him that. It's disrespectful."

"That's in case somebody's listening Ma."

She lifted her hands in resignation. "Va Bene. I'm always wrong. Let's eat."

"I have to go out tonight, business."

"Well now you sit down and eat. I made rigatoni."

"I love rigatoni," Gina said.

Cozy sat beside her. "Me too, baby."

"I got an A in art class today."

"Art," Mama said, carrying a big bowl of pasta from the kitchen, "they should teach girls practical things like sewing."

Gina rolled her eyes.

"Ma, these rigatoni are delicious." Cozy winked at Gina. It was useless to explain. His mother lived in a world long gone.

He read Gina a story after dinner while she was getting ready for bed. The hours he spent with Gina every day were precious to him.

After Gina went to bed he showered and changed clothes. Checking himself in the mirror he still looked as fit as the two years he played college football. At six feet, one hundred ninety pounds he could still dash fifty yards to chase down the ball. He compensated for a receding hairline with a short ponytail that complimented his blunt cheekbones and thick jaw. He'd been told the thin scar that cut through his eyebrow made him look mysterious. His dark eyes surveyed the figure in white linen trousers and a dark blue blazer, satisfied with what they saw.

Later as Cozy drove to his other apartment that he shared with his mistress, he felt a twinge of regret that Gina didn't have a young mother.

He still didn't understand why his wife Denise wanted to divorce him and take partial custody. She knew he would never allow his daughter to go through all that.

Denise didn't care as long as she could manipulate him using Gina. What kind of mother was that?

Even though it was years in the past, intense anger rippled through his thoughts.

Almost as intense as the day he killed her.

CHAPTER 8

Dave awoke late.

It was already eight a.m. He was due to meet Les at nine. And he felt like crap.

His sleep had been disrupted by a vivid nightmare in which he was being chased by a fearful being but his legs moved slowly as if through a snow drift. He tried to speak but all that came out was an unintelligible growl. He work up in a cold sweat and realized he had been yelling. When he sat up his shoulder began to throb.

A shower helped and sunlight dispersed the dregs of his unhappy dreams. Stretching seemed to relieve the stiffness in his wounded arm. He dressed quickly looking forward to coffee.

T-Coons café had become their favorite spot for breakfast. It featured Zydeco cooking and everything was homemade. Dave ordered a sausage and cheese omelet, which surprised Les.

"When did you give up your sensible diet?"

"Last night. What the hell are these things? They're fast, ugly and rabid like a pack of…"

"Wolves?"

"I was going to say junk yard dogs. Wolves have a leader. These guys seem disorganized."

"And they don't like guns. I could swear I hit one of them," Les added. "Didn't seem to slow him down. Gone, *poof*, like that."

"We could go back and check for blood."

"Worth a try."

"Okay we'll leave directly from here. Nick's will likely be closed this early. You drive. I need to use the computer."

They stopped at a large drug store for plastic surgical gloves, cotton swaps and baggies then headed for New Iberia. Dave remained silently intent on his laptop for most of the trip.

"What are you looking for?"

"I'm checking local public records for the owners of those warehouses in New Orleans."

"Any luck?"

"Getting close."

"Mind if I turn on the radio?"

"Yes."

Les tried to enjoy the scenery but his mind kept going back to the murderous pack out there. Dave was right they are incredibly fast and definitely ugly.

More like Hyenas than wolves. No way they could elude detection on the street unless they had an escape hatch.

"Son of a…" Dave looked up. "Clete's Sea Feast is owned by Minny Free."

"You know her?"

"Sam introduced me. She also owns Minny's ."

"What about the others?"

"Coming right up. The proprietor of Knights is someone called Wellington Swan."

They were nearing New Iberia when Dave let out a low whistle.

"What?"

"Fresh Catch is owned by our new friend Nick… Nick Casio."

"Makes sense to wholesale fish if you own a restaurant." Les offered.

"We'll see."

Les slowly pulled into the empty parking lot next to Nick's Bar. As expected the place hadn't yet opened.

Retracing their steps from the bar, they stopped in the area where they had been attacked.

"They came out from behind those trees I think," Les said.

"I think you're right. They left the same way."

The two agents carefully circled the area for traces of the previous night's attack. They found shell casings but little else until they widened their circle to the edge of the tree line.

Dave spotted something familiar. A curved yellow brown nail or claw similar to the one they found in the cemetery in New Orleans.

He held it up to show Les. "Remember this?"

"Have they come back with results on the first one?"

"Nothing. Our evidence is going down a black hole."

"Wait, don't move." Les got down on one knee and took the knife from the sheath on his lower leg. There was a large dark patch and several smaller ones that looked like liquid had pooled and dried. Like blood would.

"What do you think?"

Dave crouched beside him. "If you hit him this must be the spatter."

Les started scraping samples off the asphalt and the dirt near the trees. He placed the samples in separate baggies. "If that is blood, the trail leads over there."

"Let's find out what's in the bayou," Les said. But as he got to his feet Dave was already edging past the tree line.

It was like stepping into your standard jungle. Soft damp earth, humid air, cypress trees, steamy haze coming off the stagnant water: Les was drenched in sweat within thirty seconds. They proceeded further about a hundred yards until Dave stopped a few steps ahead of him.

When Les caught up Dave pointed to a small dock with spindly supports that extended into the water. "That's how they got in and out."

"Wood shows blood better than asphalt," Les muttered, shouldering past him.

Sure enough the bleached wood clearly showed a trail of long dark stains. Les scraped out samples while Dave walked to the end of the dock.

"Careful they got gators out here." Les said.

"Here's where they got on and off. The planks are all scratched up." Les moved over and saw the deep crisscrossed marks. "Maybe these boys are some kind of bayou bigfoot. Let's go back to New Orleans. We need to find Serb—and ask him why he's the only one still alive."

+ + +

There was no sign of police activity at St. Louis Cemetery 1 and the tourists were marching through as usual.

Dave and Les searched the area where the transient was killed. Les found a casing from his own gun and held it up. "So much for police work."

"They weren't looking for a shooter," Dave reminded.

From there they walked to Jackson Square. They split up and tried to alter their appearance. Dave bought a wide brimmed plantation hat and a tote bag emblazoned with the football Saints logo. Les stayed with the baseball cap and oversized shades look. Both men were patient circling the busy tourist area slowly. However when they met at their agreed spot, they hadn't found Serb.

They wandered a few blocks then stopped in a restaurant for a late lunch. "We can't keep wandering around in costume hoping Serb will turn up," Dave said, studying a street map he had picked up earlier.

Les sipped his coffee. "What do you suggest?"

"Let's take a look at those warehouses after closing time."

"I'm in."

"Look at this…"

"What?"

"The warehouses, they're only eight blocks from the Mississippi River."

"Maybe they ship their fish directly by boat. River traffic is still a big part of the local economy."

"Maybe they ship other stuff."

"Like beast boys?"

"Or drugs."

Les signaled the waiter, "This is way beyond drugs."

+ + +

It didn't take Cozy's people very long to get a line on his missing pilot. Less than twenty-four hours after their meeting he got a call from Franny Five Angels.

"One of my girls was in a club in Lafayette. She recognized a ring the bartender is wearing. It's a custom emerald job Larry brought back from Colombia."

"You sure?"

"Yeah Larry was always flashing it at the bitches."

"Would you recognize it if you saw it?"

"Sure. He showed it to me two or three times. Very proud of the damn thing. It's a nice stone, probably worth fifty large anyway."

"Get ready to take a ride. I'll pick you up."

When Franny climbed into the big Mercedes he saw that Sal was sitting next to Cozy and one of his enforcers, a beefy guy called Bruno was at the wheel. They looked at him without expression.

"What is this a drive by?" Franny said, trying to lighten the mood.

"Something wrong?" Cozy snapped.

His steely tone alerted Franny. "Uh no. Only that I didn't bring my piece."

Sal reached across Cozy and handed Franny a .38 revolver. "Here, I got a few extra."

"Yeah good, thanks," Franny said but actually he was uncomfortable around guns. His action was strippers and sports book not muscle. He put the .38 in his pocket and kept his mouth shut.

After a few minutes Cozy looked at Franny. "The girl who spotted the ring, she'll be there right?"

"Yeah she's there now. I called her."

"That's good. I wouldn't want to go there for nothing."
Franny didn't answer.
"You go in first. When she fingers the guy you get rid of her. We'll go in after she leaves. This way she can't ID anybody."

Except me, Franny thought. "Good plan," he said. Thirty minutes later Franny walked inside the Styx Lounge and saw Lynnette sitting in a booth. He liked Lynnette. She was a young blond from some bumfuck town in Texas who thought stripping was a good career move for an actress. In truth she was a so-so stripper whose best career move would be to become a hairdresser. Sooner or later the drugs, the life or time would cut her down. He wished she'd wise up but knew she wouldn't. Like most girls these days her brain hadn't matured past fourteen.

Franny smiled. "Lynnette, my honey. Good to see you."

She didn't smile back. "You too. Must be important for you to come down here."

"Just a little business with Larry. You know him right?"

"Larry? I know he's a conceited bastard. He blew me off for some cougar he met here."

"Cougar?"

"Well,,,she wasn't young."

"Not young and luscious like you baby," Franny said, embracing her affectionately. "So where's this guy you saw with Larry's ring?"

"Over behind the bar. The big guy."

"You mean the one with the trick beard?"

Lynnette nodded.

"Let me buy you a drink sweetheart."

Franny went to the bar and ordered two Mint Juleps. As the bartender mixed the drinks Franny saw the large emerald and gold ring on his finger. It was Larry's rock alright.

He carried the Juleps to the table. "Better drink this fast baby, you have to leave now."

"But I need a lift..."

Franny passed five one hundred dollar bills under the table. "Take a cab okay?"

Lynnette plucked the money, gulped down half her drink and got up to leave. "Do you think I can get a weekend spot at your club?"

"No problem baby, you got it. Now scoot."

After a few minutes Franny left the bar and walked to the waiting Mercedes. "He's tending bar," he told Cozy, "big guy with these beads in his white beard."

"Beads? In his fucking beard? Jesus."

"Yeah, he looks like Santa on Ecstasy."

"Wait here with Bruno," Cozy said. "Sal you ready?"

From the back seat Franny watched them enter the club, hoping they weren't about to shoot the place up.

+ + +

Victor was bored. It was a slow night and Melody hadn't shown up. If he had her number he'd call. But he didn't even know where she lived. Melody was very protective of her private life.

He hardly noticed the two new customers at the bar until one of the men put a hundred on the bar.

"Two shots of your best cognac," the man said.

He was well dressed, handsome, with a scar running across one eyebrow. His companion on the other hand was large, rumpled and ugly. Victor guessed he was some sort of bodyguard. He rinsed two snifters in hot water then took a bottle of Remy Martin 1989 from the top shelf. At forty bucks a pop the Franklin would just about cover the tip.

But when he set the snifters on the bar the hundred was gone. In its place was an open wallet framing a police badge.

"I'm Detective Boyd of missing persons." The well-dressed man said," this is Detective Longo. We're looking for a man called Larry Edwards."

The name didn't register at first.

"Drives a silver Corvette."

Then he remembered. The mark.

"We get a lot of people in here," Victor said smoothly, "I know very few by name."

"Of course. Would you mind looking at some photos?"

"Sure bring them in."

"Actually they're on the computer attached to our dashboard. It will only take a few minutes."

"You mean right now? I'm…" he leaned closer and lowered his voice. "…I'm working."

"Just a few minutes. We're parked outside."

Victor thought fast. "Okay give me a few ticks to square things away."

The detective drained his snifter and smiled. "That's damned fine cognac. Take your time we'll be right outside."

Pretending to take a bottle from the shelf Victor watched them in the mirror. As soon as they left he headed for the kitchen and the back door. He needed to reach Melody somehow.

His phone rang. It was Melody.

"Where are you?" he whispered hoarsely. "The cops are here."

"Never mind where I am. Where are you?"

"The Styx. In the kitchen. The cops are waiting for me out front."

"Why are they waiting for you?"

"They're looking for the mark. They want me to see some photos on their dashboard computer. I'm ducking out the back."

"You can't be that stupid. If you duck out they'll know you're involved. Go outside, look at the pictures and if you recognize the mark say yes I've seen him in here."

She hung up.

For some reason Victor felt better.

He went back to the bar and poured a shot of Remy Martin 1989 for himself. The hundred dollar bill was a cheap cop trick,

Victor observed, letting the cognac burn away the tension in his stomach. Fortified, he went out to look at the pictures.

Boyd was waiting but his partner wasn't in sight.

"The car's right over here," Boyd said.

Then Victor saw Longo step around the corner. He'd been covering the back door. Good thing he hadn't tried to run, Victor thought. But he was nervous.

Boyd held the door open to a black Mercedes.

"This isn't a squad car," Victor said.

"Unmarked detective car," Longo said coming up behind him. "Get the fuck in."

Victor suddenly felt sick.

+ + +

Cozy hated this part.

They had taken the bartender to a garage Sal operated. At first he didn't admit to anything, claimed he bought the ring from a customer until Sal pulled out a straight razor and asked "How long since you had a shave?" He began to shave the bartender's fancy braided beard without benefit of water or soap.

That's when the bartender changed his story. He admitted taking the ring from Larry. But then he started babbling that Larry wasn't dead. That a vampire sold his body for some medical experiments.

It made Sal angry and he got creative with the razor. When he was finished the bartender's face was a crimson mass, features barely visible.. One of his ears was dangling, suspended by a thin cord of flesh. On the other side of his skull the skin had been peeled away revealing white bone.

Cozy managed to keep a cool front but Franny Five Angels looked like he was about to faint. Only Sal's boy Bruno seemed unfazed.

But in the end they got nowhere.

The bartender died of a fucking heart attack before he could tell them what really happened to Larry.

Now they had to find this bitch the bartender swore was a vampire.

Swore on his life.

Chapter 9

Dave and Les spent the rest of the evening on paperwork. They filed a report without mentioning why they needed tests the blood evidence they'd found near Nick's bar.

"It's a CYA report," Les said. He pressed 'send.'

"CYA?"

"Cover Your Ass. Find anything on Serb yet?"

They were sitting in a motel room outside Lafayette they'd rented, both working on their laptops.

"No but I have an idea. Do you remember any of the tats he was sporting?"

Les didn't look up. "Yes. SS lightning bolts, a weird crucifix. swastikas…"

"Why don't you draw what you remember? I'll do the same. Then I can check the tattoo data base."

"Long shot."

"It's all we got."

"Shit, I forgot. When I rousted Serb I got his fucking *driver's license*."

Les began going through his pockets and found his small notebook. "Here it is name Ernst Bauer, address, license number."

Dave ran the information through the Mac. The picture matched.

"Can we run his rap sheet?"

"Already on it," Dave muttered.

Serb had a long list of arrests mostly assault but only two convictions. One for misdemeanor assault pled down from felony robbery, three months. The second for felony armed robbery, got four years, served two, currently out on parole. Two arrests since, both dismissed."

"Bastard has a good lawyer or a guardian angel," Les said.

Dave shut his laptop. "Let's check that address."

Unfortunately Serb's former residence had been wiped out by Katrina along with many other homes in St Bernard parish.

As they drove back to their motel Dave kept studying the driver's license. "This was renewed in two thousand twelve," he said. "And our boy's birthday comes up in a week."

"So?"

"In Louisiana your license is valid four years. You have to renew it on your birthday."

"He'll probably give the same phantom address."

"He might go in person. I'll ask Easton to flag it for us."

Les snorted. "Do you think we can trust him?"

"Let's call it a test."

"In the meantime let's pay Detective Orsini a visit," Les suggested. "I like being a film producer."

"Okay but tomorrow night I'd like to check those warehouses again. When nobody is around."

"I'm in. How's your shoulder?"

"Sore."

"Take tomorrow morning off. We can see Orsini in the afternoon. Three to one he'll want to meet us for lunch."

It was a good bet.

Detective Orsini suggested they meet at Jolie's Louisiana Bistro and he was already there when they arrived. His huge bulk was spread across half the table and there was an open bottle of white wine in front of him. His eyes seemed small and beady inside his puffy face and disappeared into his wide grin as they sat down.

"Pleased you could join me. I hate to dine alone. And I believe you'll find Jolie's an outstanding example of Louisiana cookin.'"

"Nick's is pretty good," Dave ventured.

"Damn good bayou cookin' but Jolie here is high society. So you boys are here to shoot a movie, that right?"

"We're the advance team," Les said. "Dave is scouting locations and I'll be taking care of permits and things like street closings."

"You're talking to the right man. I can introduce you to the right people," Orsini said brusquely, as if the matter was settled. "Tell me, is this a union movie or one of them independents?"

Les understood the offhand question. Union meant more money. The detective was probably in bed with the local mob.

"Oh we're a union production," he said.

Orsini nodded approval. "Before we go any further I suggest you take a look at this menu."

He was right about the food. Les had barbecued shrimp and Jolie's special salad. Dave had crab cakes and gumbo with potato salad. Neither of them had an entrée.

Detective Orsini had everything from bacon wrapped dates and rabbit bites to seared scallops with side orders of sweet cream corn grits and smoked sweet potato. Along the way he took care of a second bottle of wine. All in all it was an impressive display of sheer gluttony.

Les and Dave both nursed their second glass of wine.

"So what's this movie about?" Orsini asked, eyes on his plate.

Dave looked at Les. "It's a horror movie."

"Plenty of ketchup right?" Orsini chuckled, pleased with his joke. "What is it, crazy slasher, vampires…?"

"Actually it's kind of a bigfoot monster, comes out of the bayou."

Orsini stopped eating and pointed at Les with his fork. "They got just such a folk tale down here. Swamp monster called *rugarou* or some such. Bayou people got they own language."

Les knew that any mention of the missing detective Ryan Morgan was pointless and might raise Orsini's suspicions. He steered the conversation back to the permits they might need.

Dave also avoided the subject. He kept the conversation light.

When the bill came Orsini checked his phone while Les paid.

"Well gentleman it's been a pleasure. You let me know anytime what I can do to help your movie along."

They watched him waddle to his waiting car.

"Even if he knew what happened to Morgan he'd never talk," Les murmured.

"But he does know they fished Delcie out of the bayou badly mutilated."

"So?"

"He didn't crack when you mentioned the bayou monster," Dave said, walking back to the car. "Where did you get that bullshit about bigfoot anyway?"

Les lifted his hands. "I had to say something. Which reminds me, did you drop the evidence we collected behind Nick's?"

"Same drop every morning. You were still asleep."

"I told you to take the morning off. Your shoulder…"

"…Is much better today. Anyway I wake up early."

"Yeah like midnight."

"Easton hasn't come back with much on the evidence we collected so far."

"A knife and a fingernail."

"Two fingernails."

Les started the motor. "Bottom line—I don't trust Easton."

"I don't trust anybody around here but he's all the forensics we got."

They went back to the motel and watched TV, planning to drive to New Orleans in the evening.

Les took a nap but Dave's thoughts kept tumbling like lottery balls as he stared blankly at the screen. This had all started with bad directions. The case was tainted before they arrived. The mole in the bureau could very well be Easton or even his boss Virgil.

Either way we are road kill Dave reflected glumly. He went to the mini bar and poured himself a scotch.

The alcohol failed to soothe his anxiety. There was some kind of contract on them and the hit men were creatures from hell. The only good news was they didn't like guns. The bad news was they would rip his heart out if he missed

Dave decided to call Jennifer.

"You sound worried," she said. He never could hide anything from her.

"Not worried—tired, exhausted from chasing bad guys on the bayou."

He heard Robin giggle. Jennifer had him on speaker.

"Daddy what's a booboo?"

"By-You honey. It's like a jungle. Has lots of animals, like the zoo."

"Can I go too?"

"When I come home we'll go to the zoo okay?"

"Okay. Bye daddy."

"Where did she go?"

"Video game of course. Are you sure you're alright?"

"Absolutely."

"Your girls miss you Dave."

"And you know I miss my girls."

"Promise you'll be careful?"

"I promise."

They talked for a while and when the call was finished Dave felt calmer. He had connected with something real and solid in the midst of a blinding typhoon.

Les prodded him awake. "Time to go to work partner."

Dave stood up, secretly pleased he actually slept.

"Shower, shave and I'm ready to roll."

"Take your time, we're on the night shift."

"The warehouses?"

"Right. Then we drive back south and recon Minny's joint."

Dave thought of Sam and went off to take a cold shower

They bought some tools along the way including a work vest for Dave to carry his flashlight, screwdriver, pliers, and a utility tool with multiple blades. He also stuffed a spare clip in one of the pockets.

Les was traveling light. Two extra clips and a small flashlight.

"Detective Orsini sure packs in the groceries," he said.

Dave kept his eyes on the highway. "I'm still recovering from lunch. He must have a steel stomach."

"Or a couch in his office. He doesn't look like he does much police work."

"It's the Big Easy out here remember?"

"Yeah what's a missing detective more or less."

Dave fell silent. He reminded himself to stay alert while they canvased the warehouses.

"I heard you on the phone with Jennifer," Les said.

"What about it?"

"It was nice is all. Must be great to have a family."

Dave grunted. "It's like riding a two-headed mule." Then he looked at Les and smiled. "Yeah it's great, but Robin's still young."

"Stay out of trouble tonight okay?"

Dave's smile faded. "Do you know something I don't?"

"Like what?"

"Like one of your 'serious hunches.' Remember Chicago?"

During a stakeout Les had a serious hunch they'd been marked. He told Dave to abort, opened the kitchen door and caught the shooter creeping up the back stairs. Fortunately Les already had his Glock ready.

"I don't need a special hunch to tell me we're targets."

Dave grunted. "That's been on my mind."

"Maybe we should pick up some Kevlar vests at the next gun store," Les suggested.

"Let me know when you spot one."

They purchased two bulletproof vests at the Alamo Guns and Ammo store outside New Orleans and threw them in the trunk of the Charger.

"Now you've got me worried." Dave said, settling behind the wheel."

"Just precaution since we happen to be on everybody's shit list."

They parked the Charger near the cemetery and walked over to the warehouse area. Both of them had strapped on the vests but the humid night air was heavy and within minutes the inside of the protective Kevlar felt like a steam bath.

Some of the warehouses had lights over their loading docks. Dave noted there were no surveillance cameras.

They moved through the darkness using their flashlights sparingly. The faint sound of human voices came from across the main access road. They paused, backs against a nearby wall.

"Do you remember where the buildings are?" Dave whispered.

"Sort of."

"Sort of where?"

"Sort of to the left of the next loading dock."

"The one that's lit up?"

"Yeah."

"Anybody there?"

"No people no cameras."

"Okay but take it slow. Do you have a cigarette?"

"They're trapped inside my vest."

Dave stepped into the dim light and ambled toward the loading dock and across the halo of light, Les close behind him.

Once in the shadows again they quickened their pace. At the corner they turned left and made their way between buildings

Dave let Les take the lead. Everything looked different in the dark.

A bright flashlight beam speared through the shadows and cut back and forth across the ground. It was attached to a man with a hoarse voice.

"What the hell you boys doing here?"

Dave didn't hesitate. "We're looking for the fish company," he said keeping his voice low.

The light slid over their vests and held. "You're late. People over there already. Keep goin.' You can't miss it."

The flashlight beam swung sideways indicating the way. Wordlessly Dave and Les followed it. The watchman moved off in the opposite direction.

"It pays to tell the truth," Dave muttered.

In a few minutes they saw a yellowish glow up ahead.

The light was coming from an open doorway. A small truck was parked in front of the door its lights dark. Dave and Les moved carefully along the opposite wall and stopped.

Two men came out of the door. A third man who had been standing on the other side of the truck stepped into view. He was carrying an automatic rifle. All three men were wearing bulletproof vests.

"No wonder," Les whispered. He grinned and patted his vest.

Dave understood. The watchman saw their vests and assumed they were there to offload a drug shipment.

As they crept closer the two unarmed men wrestled a wooden crate off the truck with some difficulty and hauled it inside.

Les lifted his hand. The Glock was in it. "Stay back."

"Are you crazy?" Dave said in a raw whisper. "This is as far as we go."

"We need to know the name. These buildings all look alike— one man job."

Before Dave could protest Les hurried closer to the open doors. The armed guard was out of sight but in the dim glow Dave could see smoke rising from the far side of the truck. Probably having a cigarette while the other two stacked the crate.

Like figures in a mechanical clock the two men came through the door, the guard appeared from behind the truck and the two men pulled another crate and carried it inside.

Through it all Les stayed in view. But when the guard ducked behind the truck again, Dave lost sight of his partner.

It was sweltering inside the vest and he resisted the urge to take it off. He also resisted the urge to go after Les.

The two men reappeared, the guard popped up and another heavy crate was hauled inside. Everything seemed normal. Then Dave caught a faint scent—the now familiar stench of the predators. Suddenly the vest felt like an oven and his mind raced between panic and survival. He pressed his back against the wall and drew his weapon, looking wildly from side to side. He wiped the sweat from his eyes and peered into the darkness. He heard feet pounding and braced himself.

Les trotted out of the shadows.

"They're here," Dave rasped, "can you smell it?"

Les kept moving past him. "Haul ass."

Both men hurried along the wall and walked quickly past the lighted area. They slowed down as a pair of car lights came toward them. The car turned and they started to trot to the street ahead.

When they reached the car they yanked off their vests and gratefully turned up the AC.

"They were there," Dave said.

"Yeah I smelled them too."

"Did you get a name?"

Les fished a pack of Camels from his shirt and shook one loose. The cigarette was limp and damp.

"Fresh Catch," he said, "your friend Nick's place."

Chapter 10

Melody had an unsettling dream.

She awoke knowing something was wrong. She tried Victor's number and got no response. But it wasn't just Victor. Someone else was in harm's way.

Someone close to her. Almost overnight a threatening cloud had begun to cluster around her and she didn't like it.

Victor had his drawbacks but he was an excellent familiar; prompt, subservient, motivated. He had even scoured the web for information about their kind.

But information is not knowledge.

Hers came from centuries of experience. And she knew when she was being stalked.

This kind of thing hadn't happened in quite a while she reflected. The last time was in London in 1865.

An overzealous pastor by the name Father Dunn had latched onto her trail after his niece mysteriously expired. He was convinced Melody was responsible.

And he was right.

However he was mistaken on one crucial point. Father Dunn believed she caused people to die by casting spells.

He didn't know what he was dealing with.

It was after she dispatched Dunn that Melody sought the more sophisticated avenues of Paris where she posed for the impressionists and learned the pleasures of absinthe.

Now someone was hunting her again.

The first possibility that came to mind was her client.

She didn't like dealing with Walther. Perhaps he was trying to back her into a corner. Without Victor she was vulnerable.

However it didn't make sense. She was Walther's sole source for the submissive patients he required.

Knowing Victor's penchant for male whores it could be a trick turned bad. Or maybe he ran off with someone for a few days.

But Melody knew better. Victor was dead. She could feel the loss deep inside her and yes, she felt a delicious tingle as her amplified instincts bristled at the challenge.

At the moment however she was hungry. She took a shower and prepared for her evening promenade.

Lafayette was a small city and she had to be discreet. Never the same neighborhood or even the same town. Always the same routine. Melody would drive to a gang area and troll for drugs on foot. Today it was a section known as the Four Corners.

In honor of Victor's demise she wore a severe black oriental sheath dress and her hair dark hair was pulled back, held in place by a scarlet silk bandanna. Dark glasses concealed her restless green eyes as she looked for the right one.

Actually she had a good supply of cocaine and hadn't even opened the bag she'd acquired from Larry. However this evening she was searching for a predator not drugs There were lots of would be killers out there.

Let them try the real thing.

Young men lounged on porches and patrolled corners, some of them armed. All eyed her, a few offered their services.

"Pretty mama you need a Man to protect you."

"Coke, weed, what you need?"

Melody ignored them. Soon she saw—and felt—what she wanted. A tall, good looking male in a lime green suit and a wide brimmed panama hat sat half reclined in the front seat of a green Mercedes convertible. He studied her through half closed lids as she neared. His evil intentions were clear behind his boyish grin. He sat up and tipped his hat.

"Evening *mamoiselle,* I believe you are looking for me."

Melody paused. "Why do you think that?"

"Because you are looking for something special, and you know it when you see it."

As he spoke he scooped up some white powder with a long black lacquered fingernail and took a hit.

He offered the bag to Melody.

"Try this and you'll never settle for less."

She reached for the bag and he pulled it away.

"Come into my living room where we can talk. I'm Cash Antoine and you are spectacular."

She smiled and got into the car. "I'm Melody. How about a taste?"

"I like your style Melody," Cash said. He lifted a fingernail under her nostril and she inhaled sharply.

It was good. Not as good as Larry's stash but passable.

"Are you in the market?"

"How about an eight ball?"

"Comin' right up." He started the car.

Where are we going?" Melody asked innocently.

Just around the corner honey. You know I can't keep stuff in my ride."

He drove two blocks and turned into a deserted alley. He stopped and when he turned he had a knife in his hand.

He pressed the tip of the knife into her throat. "Now you gonna give me your money first—and second you start taking off that dress."

"Please," Melody whispered.

Cash gave her an ugly sneer. "We can do this the hard way and I leave you nekkid and bloody on the ground —or the easy way."

"The easy way?"

"You come work for me as my number one bitch."

"I like the easy way," she said.

The knife point eased from her neck. "Then hand over the cash and get busy with the dress."

"Yes daddy," she said playfully, leaning closer.

He never knew what hit him.

In a nano-second her fangs chopped into his jugular.

With every pulsing swallow his efforts to push her off became weaker and weaker until they stopped.

It was over in minutes.

After relieving Cash of a thick roll of bills Melody carefully wiped her mouth, checked herself for bloodstains, then sauntered back to her car refreshed and ready to handle her problem. She wasn't worried out the police. Dead pimps were a low priority item.

When Victor last called he said two detectives were at the bar and wanted him to go outside and ID some computer photos. She could safely assume they weren't detectives. Then who in hell were they and what did they want with Victor?

Their last mark had hinted broadly he was a drug pilot. Maybe some cartel had issues.

But how could they connect him to Victor?

She decided to drop by the Styx and ask Kyle, the other barman if he knew anything. Although it was still relatively early Melody had a strong feeling the club was being watched. She cruised past and saw two men sitting in a black Escalade a half block from the entrance.

She decided to go through the kitchen in back. Inside it was frenetic as the cooks prepped for the late night crowd. They greeted her with familiar smiles assuming she was there to do a show. All her senses were hyper alert now as she came out the service door into the main room. There were a fair number of diners at the tables and a few drinkers at the bar. She caught Kyle's eye and he came over. "Absinthe?"

"Not tonight. What's up with Victor?"

Kyle shrugged. "Two nights ago he took a break and he never came back."

"Was he with anyone?"

"He was talking to two guys I never seen before. Are you singing tonight?"

"I don't think so."

"Dudley is here."

Dudley was the house guitar player who backed her performances. He was a consummate musician and had helped Melody develop as a singer. He saw Melody and came over to join them. Dudley had seen Victor the night he disappeared.

"He seemed pretty jacked up. Showed me this fancy ring he just bought."

"Ring?"

"Yeah like this green emerald, big as a traffic light."

Melody took a deep breath. She remembered the ring. Victor must have taken it from the pilot. *You fool*, she thought, *that's how they traced you.*

"Will you be on stage tonight?"

She shook her head sadly. "Not tonight." But she knew she could never go back now. Before leaving she scanned the room carefully and her senses zoomed in on a cheap blond making a call on her smart phone.

It was the blond the mark had been chatting up the night Melody pulled him. Melody focused. The bitch was calling the boys waiting in the Escalade.

Melody went back through the kitchen waving and smiling as if everything was normal.

When she hit the deserted delivery area she went into high gear. With blinding speed she headed for her car. Anyone watching would have glimpsed a figure seemingly darting in and out of space, vanishing and reappearing further down the street.

She was breathing heavily when she reached the car. That wouldn't have happened a hundred years ago, Melody noted. However slowly, her kind did age.

Driving home she felt slightly better. At least she knew they had traced Victor through the ring. He had always been greedy. Now she had to pay for his sins Melody brooded. Her first objective was the blond. The cheap bitch was the only one who could link her to the missing pilot.

Then there was the question of payback.

Victor's life belonged to her.

Abruptly she slowed down and made a U turn. Why put it off? she decided. The blond had crucial information.

She cruised slowly past the Styx. The Escalade was still there but it was vacant. Most likely the occupants were stationed inside with the blond in case Melody should return.

All Melody had to do was wait.

Chapter 11

"Nick? Seriously?"

"There were two attacks in his lot," Les reminded, "and that dock is behind his joint."

Dave looked skeptical. "Back in the bayou you mean" "What's with you and this guy?"

"Nothing why?"

"You're sticking up for him. Is it Sam?"

Dave took a deep breath. "There's no question we saw armed men offloading crates, but we don't know what was inside."

"It sure wasn't fresh fish."

"Could be drugs," Dave conceded.

"You think?"

"I don't know."

"What's your guess?"

Dave kept his eyes on the road.

"I *guess* I'm a lousy judge of character."

They were on their way to New Iberia and Dave was trying to process what he had seen at Nick's warehouse. He hoped Sam wasn't involved but he knew she was an integral part of Nick's bar and restaurant. Perhaps the fish business was separate he told himself.

"When we were briefed they mentioned heroin." Dave said.

"Just thinking the same thing. What I can't figure is his connection to our hairy killers."

"I did catch a whiff."

"Me too but it could have been rotten fish."

Minny's was in full swing when they got there.

Every table was occupied and the blues band on the small stage had the dance floor packed. Dave saw someone waving at him from behind the bar and recognized Sam's friend Carson.

The barman pointed to a pair of recently vacated stools. "You're back," Carson said, "how's the movie doin'?"

"This is our producer Les."

Carson dried his hand on his black jeans and solemnly shook Les' hand.

"Name's Carson. You boys gonna drink or eat?"

They decided on barbecued chicken, sweet potato fries and two cold glasses of Dixie lager. The first beer relaxed them and when the food came they ordered a second round.

Les leaned close to be heard through the music and noise. "Without back up we are royally fucked partner."

I put a rush on the blood evidence." Dave said.

"Let's hope it comes back before they find us."

Dave knew who he meant by 'they.' The hunters had become the prey. He considered ordering another beer and decided against it.

Carson seemed to read his thoughts. "So gents, everything okay here?"

Les finished his beer with a satisfied flourish. "Very good thanks."

You know," Carson leaned on the bar and flashed his perfect teeth, "I do some acting myself."

Les pretended to study him a moment. "They'll be plenty of extra work maybe a small part. You know like the first guy who gets killed."

Carson's smile widened to a grin. "Done deal. How about a shot of bourbon?"

Reluctantly Dave went along, resolving it would be his last drink of the night. "First guy killed?" he said when Carson left. "This producer stuff went to you head."

Les gave him an innocent smile. "I like this cover you came up with. It brings up fresh ideas."

"You've gone Hollywood."

"That's the idea isn't it?"

Carson came back with the drinks. When he set the down Les noticed his fingernails.

"What's with the black polish?"

"Nothin' much. My girlfriend's kind of a Goth. She wanted them black." He looked at Dave. "You ever locate Ryan?"

Dave shook his head. "Detective Morgan is still MIA. But a detective Orsini came aboard."

"Hank? You got the right guy. Knows everybody from here to Baton Rouge."

Les raised his glass. "Here's to bigger and better movies."

The bourbon was strong. Dave felt it burning through the beer and barbecue and spread hotly across his chest.

"That's good stuff," Les said, "but I think that's enough for me."

Dave was glad Les said it before he did. The long day was catching up to him and he felt tired.

They stayed for another fifteen minutes checking out the patrons, which were a mixture of Vietnamese and good old boy fisherman as well as local young people.

None of them acted suspiciously. In fact most of the customers hardly noticed they were there,

Where to?" Dave asked as they paid the bill.

"Our new motel is the safest," Les said, voice a bit slurred, "unless you want a private room."

"I can stand it if you can. But I'm driving."

Cameron grinned and waved goodbye.

"I left him a Hollywood tip," Les said as he stepped outside.

"Hold it,"

"What?"

"Our beasts seem to like parking lots." Dave reached down for his Glock."

Les did the same. "Good point. We should always remember to wear our Kevlar vests."

"Dude get real. They're too hot, not to mention a tad conspicuous."

Everyone was inside and the lot was deserted. Two spotlights on the side of the club illuminated the cars along the wall but those parked across and around the back were in darkness.

Weapons held loosely at their sides they walked slowly to the car. They had parked outside the dim splash of light cast by the spotlights and Dave scanned the shadows intently. He heard Les stumble and paused.

"You alright?"

"Bump in the road."

Dave was also feeling the effects of the beer and bourbon and moved carefully through the darkness.

He was relieved when they reached the Charger and were safely locked inside.

"Maybe we should wear the vests," Les said, holstering his weapon.

Dave didn't answer but as he drove back the adrenaline and tension flared into anger.

"This is bullshit."

Les yawned. "Got that right partner."

"We need to find out if Easton has our back. I'm going to ask for a sit down."

"He'll only tell us he knows jack shit about the bug and suggest we're exaggerating these attacks."

"What's our option?"

"We could resign, become private eyes, wind up in corporate security…"

"Or dead."

"I feel half dead right now."

Dave too, was feeling drowsy. He focused on driving, squinting to see the road signs. played good music Dave thought, listening to Ray Charles go way across town.

James Brown was chugging along on *Night Train* when they reached their motel on the outskirts of Lafayette and Dave pulled to a stop across the street.

Wearily Dave turned off the motor and stepped out of the air conditioning into the oppressive humidity.

"That bourbon must have been two hundred proof," Les said.

Before Dave could answer the night shattered into screaming fragments.

Les yelled.

An animal howled.

Dark shapes sprang from the shadows

A car screeched to a stop, horn blaring.

Something slammed him to the asphalt and a flash of agony seared his body from chest to belly

Dave heard his ribs crack as claws ripped his torso open before he was sucked into howling blackness.

Chapter 12

The blond finally left the Styx with the two men who had been sitting in the Escalade when Melody first arrived. It was nearly closing time.

These people were very patient, very professional, Melody observed putting the car in drive. Ergo they were very dangerous.

Even today, in a world that didn't believe she existed, she was vulnerable to a number of unpleasant possibilities not the least of which was extended exposure to direct sunlight. There was a reason many of her kind preferred the gloomy solitudes of Scandinavia or Seattle. Pain was a minor consideration, physical wounds would heal quickly but being held captive might become a problem. Without fresh blood she'd become weak, linger at the brink of death but she would not die.

That was not going to happen Melody assured herself. When she found out who killed Victor she would eliminate them and move on. Her sojourn in the deep south had become tainted. Perhaps she'd try Vegas which more suited her hours.

Melody followed the Escalade to a small house in a rundown area. The blond went into the house with one man while the other drove away.

Melody made a quick calculation. Now that she knew where the girl lived she would continue to follow the Escalade.

Twenty minutes later the SUV parked in the driveway of a suburban condo complex. One of those places with an Olympic pool, full gym and in-house cosmetic surgeon Melody thought derisively.

She didn't know if the man had a family, a girlfriend or a dog. Which meant she had to take him before he could enter his apartment.

He was leaving his car when she pulled up. By the time the man had pulled out his key she had crossed the street and was closing.

He never put his key in the lock.

Melody hit fast and drew deep. The first draught dissolved his resistance and she felt him sag slightly.

"Do you live alone?" she whispered."

"Yes."

"Any pets?" Dogs could be problematic and she hated their blood.

"No."

"What's your name?"

"Bruno."

"Let's go inside Bruno."

The apartment looked like a wax museum. The furniture was formal with bizarre touches like the imitation statue of Venus in the living room.

The man groaned and blinked at Melody as if trying to place her.

"Easy," she whispered and drew a bit more blood from his neck. The man shuddered with pleasure.

"Tell me the name of the girl you just drove home."

"Lynette."

"What's her last name?"

"I don't know."

"Why are you with her?"

"She's supposed to finger this chick our boss is lookin' for."

"Who's sent you?"

"Franny Five Angels."

"Who's the man with Lynette?"

"Paulie."

"Is he her boyfriend?"

"Not really."

"What do you mean?"

"After Lynette fingers the broad we're lookin' for Paulie is supposed to get rid of her."

"Franny told him to do that?"

"No. That came down from Sal."

"Very good," her tongue lightly circled the wound on his neck. He moaned softly.

"Now tell me," she whispered, "who killed the bartender Victor?"

"Sal worked him over with a razor."

"Did you help kill him?"

"I helped dump the body."

"Good."

Melody sat back and looked at him. The man was fiftyish, balding, with thick shoulders, no neck, large paunch, bulbous nose and sporting a pair of ridiculous two toned shoes. He sat in a submissive daze as Melody savored the moment.

"Now Bruno darling I want you to call Paulie and tell him we're coming to visit."

+ + +

Lynette wished she'd never said a word

She hated having to hang around with Franny's goons and now this Paulie guy was acting like her boyfriend. She should have gone to LA and taken acting lesson. Some guy at the strip club told her they were shooting a lot of TV in Atlanta but she wanted a fresh start. Far away from all this violence.

Lynette hadn't seen them do anything yet but she'd heard.

The other girls at the Zombie Club where she danced always talked about Franny's bodyguards roughing up customers who got out of line. They enjoyed breaking bones. It was kind of a game with them.

Lafayette was supposed to be a temporary stop on her way to Hollywood. She had tucked away a little money dancing. Unlike the other girls she didn't do drugs.

Except now that goon was snorting coke in her living room. He said he was there for her protection but that was bullshit. She never signed up for this.

Lynette made sure the bathroom door was locked and stared at her reflection in the mirror. It's your own stupid fault she scolded. If you hadn't been so damned bitchy about that brunette at the Styx and kept your mouth shut instead of telling Franny you wouldn't be in this. Now there was no fucking way out.

Paulie's voice muffled her regrets. He was at the door. "Hurry up baby, Bruno will be here soon. He's bringing a friend. We can party."

Party my ass Lynette thought. She let the anger leak into her voice "I'll be out when I'm ready okay?"

"Okay, okay."

She half smiled at his quick retreat. She had a natural way with men. Ever since high school. And she was competitive. Probably why she was so pissed at that older bitch walking off with Larry

Funny, at first she hated that woman and now she felt sorry for her.

Feel sorry for *yourself* while you're at it Lynette reminded. She had a sexy figure which was only partially obscured by her simple shirt and jeans. She had also washed off the makeup and combed back her hair in a gesture of defiance. She wanted to go to sleep not a fucking party.

Lynette left the bathroom and found Paulie stretched out on the couch. He seemed disappointed

"I thought you were getting ready,"

The intercom buzzed.

"Get the door," Paulie said.

"You get the door, I need something to eat."

Lynette opened the refrigerator and looked inside.

There was a jug of apple juice, swiss cheese and a loaf of bread. She popped the top off the juice and took a long swallow. Then she grabbed the cheese and bread.

She heard Paulie open the door and hurried to make her sandwich.

"Bruno what he fuck?"

Lynette turned to see what was happening and dropped the jug, splashing apple juice on her plastic floor tiles.

Paulie was slowly sliding down the wall while Bruno stood watching, his features slack.

A familiar face peeked out from behind Paulie's limp body.

Lynette's breath froze.

It was *her*, the woman with Larry.

The woman smiled, teeth stained red with blood.

Lynette ran.

Frantically she bolted for the bathroom but the woman blocked her path. When she scrambled to the back kitchen door the woman was there too… smiling calmly.

Lynette tried to scream but nothing would came out.

Sobbing, she sank to her knees and covered her face with her hands.

A soothing voice drifted into her ear. "Don't cry my darling."

She twitched as a quick pain stung her neck.

Instantly a warm sensual blanket settled over her body. The heat intensified until her senses caught fire, consumed by an alien lust. And when it died away she was powerless to resist the woman who cradled her in her arms

"What's your name?"

"Lynette Hargrove."

"Why do you want to identify me to these men?"

"I was jealous."

"What do you mean?"

"You're so beautiful you know, sophisticated. You scooped Larry and left me standing at the bar like a loser."

"And you hate me?"

Lynette pulled away." "Not any more. But they want you bad.""

Again the delicious blanket fanned the strange embers of her desire and she sank back into the woman's all-consuming presence.

"Who are these men?"

"The one on the floor is Paulie."

"Who do they work for?"

"Franny Five Angels."

"How do you know this Franny?"

"I dance at one of his clubs."

"Which one?"

"Zombie Club."

"Is that where I can find him?"

"I think he's at his main club the Tempest. In the Quarter.'"

"How much is he paying you?"

"Nothing."

"Why are you working for him then?"

"I'm saving money to take acting lessons in Hollywood." She blinked and seemed to come out of her fog. "Please don't hurt me. I don't know what this is about. Please."

"Look at me."

The silky voice wound around her will and Lynette lifted her head. The woman's green eyes searched her face.

"You're a beautiful child. How old are you?"

"Nineteen last month."

The woman leaned closer and kissed her. "Happy birthday."

The kiss set off a chain reaction at the core of her being and Lynette knew she would obey the woman forever.

+ + +

Melody had no doubt Lynette was telling the truth. The girl just didn't know very much.

"Listen to me," she said softly, "gather your things and stuff them in a small suitcase. Don't forget to take your ID."

Mutely the girl did as she was told. While she was occupied Melody searched Paulie's body. He was carrying a substantial roll of bills and a bit of coke. She put the money in her shoulder bag and snorted the coke. .

Bruno was still standing there, his eyes half closed.

Melody went through his clothes and found a .38 pistol and perhaps three thousand in cash. She also found the keys to the Escalade. Although she wasn't hungry she drained Bruno.

Lynette came out of the bedroom with her suitcase. She didn't seem to notice the two dead men in the foyer.

"Wait outside in the Escalade," Melody told her.

When she was alone Melody put a bullet in Paulie's lifeless chest. Then she shot Bruno in the temple, wiped the .38 clean and put the gun in Bruno's right hand.

Lynette was waiting in the Escalade as she'd been instructed.

"How much money did you save?" Melody asked.

"Four thousand four hundred and thirty two dollars."

Melody reached into her back and produced a stack of bills. "There's about nine thousand dollars here. Put it in your purse."

She handed Lynette the keys to the Escalade. "I want you to drive to the airport in New Orleans. Buy a ticket on the next plane heading to Los Angeles. Do you understand?"

"Yes, plane to Los Angeles."

"You will not work as a stripper. You will take acting lessons. Understand?"

"Yes, acting lessons."

Melody smiled and lightly kissed her. "Go now and never speak to anyone about this."

She watched Lynette drive off and walked slowly to her car, satisfied at her night's work. Melody recalled another girl she had helped back in the forties—a gawky foster child named Norma Jean Baker.

Of course that encounter had mixed results.

Then again Melody reflected, *no one could elude their ultimate fate.*

Not even her.

Chapter 13

It was all his fault.

He was half drunk when he got out of the car. Dave was already outside. He glimpsed the figures erupt from the rear of a parked van and lope across the street with relentless speed,

"Incoming!" he shouted.

If Dave heard it was too late. They hit him hard, knocking him to the ground and clawing at his body while one separated from the pack and leaped on top of the Charger.

Les was reaching for the weapon at his ankle. He looked up and saw a dark figure looming over him.

Surprised he hastily yanked his gun but it slipped out of his hand.

At the same time bright headlights lit up his attacker.

It was at least seven feet tall with a broad hairy chest and large bare feet with claw-like nails. His nose more closely resembled a snout protruding from his thick matted beard and his eyes blazed red as he stood pinned by the light.

Then it vanished.

Les ran into the street and saw Dave on the ground. A car was nearby, horn blaring. The female driver sat pale and open mouthed, shielded by the partially open door. Her car lights illuminated the shiny red blood spurting from Dave's ravaged torso.

"Call 911!" Les yelled to the woman. He removed his shirt and tried to stem the bleeding. By the time the ambulance got there his hands and arms were greasy with blood and the shirt was drenched. When they put Dave on the gurney Les saw one arm was partially detached at the shoulder.

The doctor at the hospital told him Dave had a ten percent chance of making it.

Waiting in the hospital corridor Les knew it was his fault. He should have been alert, checked the street, seen them coming sooner.

Instead he was fumbling for his gun like Fredo in the *Godfather*—and it probably cost Dave his life.

Shirtless he called a cab to take him to the motel where they'd been attacked. When he arrived Les took out his Glock before he exited the cab.

The taxi driver saw him. "Jesus man you gonna rob me?"

Les handed him a twenty. "Bad neighborhood."

Back in his room he took a long shower, changed clothes and lay down to rest a few minutes.

He woke up five hours later.

Groggy, Les called the hospital. They told him Dave was critical and on life support. He left his number and pulled himself together.

Still trying to sort out the events of the past few days he numbly picked at his breakfast. But by his third coffee his confusion became seething anger.

They had chosen the Fairmont Motel for its relative obscurity. They registered under false names and paid cash. There was only one way anyone could have traced them there.

Dave's call home to Jennifer.

They had a tap on Dave's home phone. Only the Bureau had that kind of juice. The bastards are treating us like terrorists Les raged.

He left the diner and headed back to his room. There he got on the computer and demanded an emergency meeting with their handler Easton. He also asked for results on all physical evidence. Then he drove the Charger back to the garage and picked up the repaired Malibu. He apologized for the scratches on the Charger's roof and paid the unhappy owner for the damage.

Easton's reply was prompt and discreet: *Sixteen hundred hours at the original place.*

After all that had happened it took Les a few minutes to remember the location of their original meeting, Shorty's Café. He filled in the remaining hours trying to check out the man he was about to meet. He used his pre-paid phone to call a deep contact in the Bureau's data division, Kelly Sand a lady he used to date.

"Kelly it's me Les. I've been thinking about you."

"Wild guess—you need a favor."

"Baby… I thought we were friends."

"We were, about a hundred years ago."

"Look this is important. I need background on the Division Director in Lafayette Louisiana, Matt Easton and I need it right away."

"Why?"

"Because my partner's on life support."

"I'm sorry."

"Yeah thanks, look believe me my request isn't frivolous."

"No but it's dangerous. If they find me hacking into classified files I could be charged. Are you on a secure phone?"

"Yes. While you're at it look up Virgil Lake, he's the state Deputy Director."

"Damn you Hensen what's in it for me?"

"Dinner and a show—if I live."

"You won't if you back out. Call me back in a couple of hours."

As Les waited his anger receded inward and depression clouded his thoughts.

He recalled his flirtation with Kelly a few years back. It had only lasted a few months before he was called to Seattle on a drug case and they never picked up the threads of their relationship. Or at least he didn't. He became involved with a woman there and stayed six months after they arrested the perps.

But Kelly was special. Red hair, blue eyes and real soul. *Problem is you were always too selfish to settle down* Les brooded. *That's why your life is a total waste.*

It went downhill from there.

Les berated himself for being half-drunk, for not paying attention when they reached the motel, for fumbling his weapon, and for getting his partner—and best friend—killed.

He went out to a liquor store and bought a bottle of Jim Beam and a pack of cigarettes. When he called Kelly a couple of hours later he had imbibed a few shots. Not enough to get drunk but on the verge. He wanted to be reasonably sober when he spoke to her.

"It's me, got anything?"

"Hello Kelly how are you?" she said, voice heavy with sarcasm, "I've got what you wanted but I'm giving it to you verbally. Best I can do."

"Wait, I'll get a pen… okay what?"

"Matt Easton is ex Special Forces like you. Joined the Bureau two years after serving in Afghanistan. Cracked two big serial killer cases, went on to break a bank robbery gang in Texas, now director Lafayette Division."

"That's it?"

"What did you expect a rap sheet?"

"Okay, okay, what about Lake?"

"That's another story. Virgil Lake is the grandson of the former governor of Alabama. Joined the Bureau after graduating from Yale law school. Very social all the right clubs. Specialist in white collar crime. Sent up a number of hedge fund managers. Busted a state wide bid-rigging fraud. Now deputy director of the State Division."

"Political."

"You think?"

"What about Easton? Where was he the two years after discharge?"

"Classified darling. I've got to go. Don't forget dinner."

Les lit a cigarette and weighed having another drink before his meeting with Easton.

He skipped the drink and changed into fresh clothes.

Shorty's was a long drive from the motel. He had made sure to take his computer and Dave's since it appeared their location was no longer a secret. He also brought the bottle. No sense losing good bourbon to a burglar he reasoned.

Arriving early Les ordered grilled redfish with rice and beans to mollify the bourbon. He almost ordered a beer but he knew Easton would use it to discredit his story.

He was right. Easton gave him a disapproving glare as if eating was somehow unprofessional.

"Okay I'm here what is it?"

"Did you bring our forensic reports?"

Easton pushed an envelope across the table. "What we have so far."

"Thanks for nothing."

Easton's bull neck reddened. "What is your problem?"

"Right now my partner Dave Chin is on life support at Lafayette Specialty Surgery."

"What happened?"

"We were attacked. And either you or Lake set us up."

"Bullshit."

With mock ceremony Les handed him a bag with the listening device. "Here's the evidence."

Easton pulled the black electronic box from the bag.

"It's a listening device. You can buy these on the internet."

"The only way anybody could have traced us to the motel where we were attacked was a call Dave made to his wife on a pre-paid phone."

"Or you were followed," Easton snapped, "I'm cutting you some slack for what happened to your partner but back off on the unfounded accusations."

Les took a deep breath and looked away. "I'd appreciate it if you'd notify Dave's wife and contact the hospital."

"Of course, as soon as you tell me what the fuck happened out there."

It was early and Shorty's Café was empty except for an elderly couple across the room but Les kept his voice low and his manner straightforward if not quite calm. Recalling the events of the past few days brought up a number of conflicting emotions all amplified by his anger.

"From day one we were targeted," he said, voice shaking, " First Dave in Nick's parking lot. Me in the cemetery. Third time at Nick's and then last night. They knew we were coming."

Easton's hard grey eyes bore into his. "Not from me Agent Hensen."

Les shrugged.

The director drummed his fingers on the checkered tablecloth. "If this is true it's a fucking nightmare."

Les slapped his hand on the table. "Ask Dave Chin if it's true. Those hairy bastards ripped his chest open. Let's get real here, something removed the hearts and livers from at least five people including your own field agents."

Easton winced and sat back. "This will be my third family call in the past two months."

"You have my sympathy," Les said as he opened the envelope. "I'm pretty sure I got one of them. We found some blood samples nearby."

"We ran DNA."

Les shuffled through the papers trying to decipher the charts and numbers.

"Any luck?"

"That blood sample belongs to our missing cop, Ryan Morgan."

Chapter 14

The news reached Cozy at his bar.
Franny came personally to tell him.
"You're not gonna believe this," he said breathlessly.
"I hope you found the woman."
"It's Bruno and Paulie."
"What about them?"
"They were watching this girl, Lynette. The one who saw the woman leave with Larry."
Cozy's eyes were on the TV above his desk. The Saints were playing the Jets.
"Get to the point."
"Bruno shot Paulie and killed himself."
It took a moment to register. Cozy turned off the TV and squinted at Franny in disbelief.
"Bruno shot Paulie?"
"And shot himself."
"Where's the girl?"
"She's disappeared. The bodies were found in her apartment," he added.
"Why would Bruno shoot Paulie? Were they fighting over this girl uh… what's her name?"
"Lynette."
"Doesn't make sense."
"There's more."
"What more?"
"The coroner said there was no blood in their bodies."
Cozy waved dismissively. "So they bled out when they got shot."
There was no blood in the apartment. I looked myself. One of the cops is on my payroll."

"Jesus." Cozy reached into a desk drawer and pulled out a bottle of Glenmorangie Scotch. "When did this happen?"

"Night before last."

"Bring those glasses on the shelf there."

Cozy poured two hefty drinks and raised his glass.

"To Bruno and Paulie they were good soldiers."

It was first-rate scotch but the warm glow in Cozy's belly was clouded by the bizarre news.

"Maybe it was drugs," he said aloud.

Franny shook his head.

"Paulie yes but not Bruno. Anyway there was nothing in the apartment and the girl Lynette I know did not use drugs."

"How do you know?"

"Kid's an amateur. Just started dancing at my Zombie club, second string."

"How many women are we looking for now?"

Franny drained his glass and leaned forward. "We should concentrate on only one. Melody."

"Why?"

"You were there."

Cozy sat upright and gave him a hard stare as if looking for a wire.

"What are you saying?"

Franny lowered his voice. "The guy said it. The woman is a vampire."

Cozy crossed himself. For some moments he was silent. Finally he heaved a sigh and refilled their glasses.

"A man in my position shouldn't have to deal with this. But it's New Orleans, we got Voodoo, all that shit right? So how do we handle a vampire?"

Fanny shifted in his chair. "I've seen movies."

"Maybe we get a priest to take her out," Cozy mused.

"Best thing, you find out where they sleep and drag them into the sunlight."

"What—you know that from the movies?"

Franny swallowed his scotch. "I go all the time. In the afternoon before the club opens. It relaxes me. Now I got the big screen TV but it ain't the same."

"Okay so her name is Melody Dawn, you got a description?"

"Sort of, from the girl Lynette."

Cozy examined his buffed fingernails. "Listen the… guy said this Melody is a singer right?"

Franny knew 'the guy' was the bartender Sal tortured, Cozy had a thing about listening devices.

"Yeah she sings at that club."

"Go lean on the musicians she sings with. See if you can get a line on where she lives."

"I'll need somebody from Sal's crew now that Bruno is down."

"Why fuck around? Take Sal."

Bringing Sal was a good idea.

The big ex-pug was six four and weighed in at three hundred pounds most of it rock solid. He had a broken nose and small hard eyes that regarded humanity with contempt.

That's what really scared people, Franny brooded, they were executioner's eyes.

He didn't like all this heavy work being dumped on him. Franny liked to think of himself as an entrepreneur, gambler and lady's man.

Muscle wasn't his department. The memory of Sal going to work on the bartender still prompted an urge to vomit.

"You gentlemen ready to order?"

Franny forced a smile. "Mint Julep for me."

Sal gave him a weird look. "Bring me a Knob Creek straight and a Dixie chaser."

"What the hell is with the Mint Julep?" Sal asked when the waitress left.

"It's refreshing," Franny said, "I'm thirsty."

Sal grunted.

A lone guitar player took the stage and began to play jazz and blues. He was good, Franny thought. He considered hiring him at his club then nixed the idea. He was already in this too deep.

Sal hot to his feet. "I'm goin' to the can. Make sure the punk stays here."

It was the opportunity Franny had been hoping for. He waved the waitress over and handed her a twenty.

"Give this to the guitar player and ask him to join us."

She went to the stage and the guitar player nodded in his direction. He put his guitar down and came to the table.

"You play good," Franny said, "sit down a minute"

"Thanks man."

He was over thirty, thin, with long blond hair and a gold cross dangling from one ear.

"Have a drink uh what do they call you?"

"Dudley Graham is my name."

"I'm Franny Pentangeli. You heard of me?"

Dudley shook his head.

"I own a club in New Orleans called The Tempest. Got one here The Zombie."

"I've heard of the Zombie."

Franny smiled and put two hundred dollar bills on the table. "Now here's how it works. In a couple of minutes my friend will be back. We're going to ask you some questions about Melody. If you answer them you get the money. You don't, my friend breaks your fingers... Here he comes now, you decide."

Dudley glanced at the huge, angry man advancing on the booth and lifted his hands.

"Melody sings here a few nights a week."

"You work with her right? Where do you rehearse?"

"We don't. She tells me the songs and I accompany. She's got a great voice."

Dudley looked stricken as Sal sat down wedging him between them.

Franny lowered his voice. "Dudley, we need to know where Melody lives."

"Nobody knows where she lives. Even her friend Victor. He mentioned it once."

"Victor who?"

"The bartender here."

Franny glanced at Sal and shrugged.

Last chance at the big bucks Dudley."

Sal gripped his arm. "Let's go somewhere we can talk better."

"Wait, wait," Dudley pleaded, "I remember something."

"Better be good," Franny said.

"One night she gave me a ride to a late night jam. She said it was on her way. After she dropped me I thought I saw her parking the car a few blocks down the street."

"That's it?" Sal glowered at Dudley. "That's bullshit."

Dudley sat up straight and set his jaw. "That's all I got so if you want to drag my ass out of here that's what you motherfuckers will have to do."

Franny chuckled. At least the kid had balls.

"Alright Dudley, tell you what, you show us exactly where she dropped you that night and everybody's happy."

The neighborhood Dudley took them to was dimly lit and secluded. The homes had weathered the worst of Katrina and there were warehouses scattered among the row houses.

A few blocks away, where she had dropped Dudley was a string of music bars and late night joints.

"You sure this is it?" Franny asked again.

Far as I know it's right down there a few blocks."

Franny handed him two hundreds. "Okay kid take a hike."

Dudley left the car and hurried towards the lights of the music bars.

Sal seemed disappointed. "I still think he's bullshitting."

"We know where to find him."

"What now, we wait for the broad?"

"We wait," Franny said, "but not now."

Again Sal seemed disappointed.

"No sense trying to find her in the dark," Franny explained as they drove back to the Zombie club for a nightcap. "Think about it. Two guys sitting in a car in the middle of the night, it's a tip off. But at *sunset*," he paused and looked at Sal triumphantly, "nobody thinks nothin' about it. It won't be dark. We can get a better look."

"I don't believe this vampire shit," Sal said, "I'll crack her fucking neck."

"What about Bruno and Paulie?"

"Bruno never liked Paulie. He thought Paulie would rat if he got busted."

"So he shot Paulie and killed himself?"

Sal shrugged. "Yeah it sounds stupid."

"Not stupid," Franny said gently, not wishing to offend Cozy's enforcer, "just not logical. Then there's the blood."

"Blood?"

"There wasn't any. I got the coroner's report."

"You're sayin' this broad drank their blood?"

"I'm sayin' I got the coroner's report."

"I sure never figured Bruno to shoot himself," Sal said morosely, "we did some nice hits together."

The next day Franny cruised the neighborhood a few times to find a good vantage point. He looked up the official time the sun would go down and made sure Sal was ready.

"From this spot here we cover two blocks either way," Franny told Sal, "I brought a couple of meatball sandwiches."

"We grab the broad when she comes out?" Sal asked between bites.

"Better we find out where she lives and catch her in the daylight."

"Vampire my ass," Sal rumbled. He gave a low burp and took another bite of his sandwich. "I'll crack her fucking neck."

As a sidekick Sal made a great fireplug Franny thought, checking his watch. The enforcer hadn't said a word for twenty minutes. Just stared straight ahead.

Franny checked the mirror. He was a few pounds overweight but he had all his hair and kept a good tan. Usually he favored colorful suits and shirts but for this job he wore black. Sal wore a black suit too but on him it looked like a large gunnysack.

He lowered his eyes from the rear-view mirror as a young woman left a two-story house less than a hundred yards away and began walking in their direction.

"I think that's her," he whispered.

Franny had to admit she was a knockout. She was wearing a simple black dress that flattered her long legs and perfect proportions. Straight black hair framed high cheekbones and perfect white skin.

She walked with slow, fluid strides that exuded sensual energy.

The woman didn't appear to notice them as she passed and they waited until she was well out of sight before leaving the car.

The name on the mailbox read M. D. Masters and an inspection of the locks showed it would be no problem to break in at the proper time.

"M.D..." Sal muttered, "...she a doctor?"

"Melody Dawn get it?"

"Oh right. We going to wait for her inside?"

"No Sal. We come back in a few hours and at sunrise you'll get your wish."

"What wish?"

"You can crack her fucking neck."

+ + +

Melody noticed the two men sitting in a black Cadillac and got a bad vibe. She contemplated killing them both right there and driving their corpses to the bayou. Too public, too early in the evening she decided and strolled past them.

Hunger wasn't a problem after gorging two nights earlier. However she had awakened to a bigger problem. A crisis in fact. And quite annoying.

They knew where she lived. And what she was. From what Bruno confessed while she had him in suspension, Victor told them everything before he died.

But now it appeared they believed it.

It was time to move her nest—always stressful—especially tonight. She was hoping for a drink somewhere quiet. The Styx was no longer an option.

Deal with it she told herself. She made a mistake when she went into business with Walther. She made another when she passed over the lawman for emotional reasons and chose the pilot as your mark.

As a result she'd lost a familiar, her anonymity, and quite possibly her wicked life.

Enough morbid self-discipline Melody reflected, time for that quiet drink.

The Voodoo Lounge was decorated with tourist grade masks and bottle candles. Black light graffiti adorned the far wall. The room was dark and the music subdued. She sat with her back to the wall at the corner of the bar. Her stool afforded her a view of the street and an exploratory trip to the ladies room located a kitchen exit.

She ordered an absinthe and tried to relax. The bartender knew next to nothing about the proper way to pour but the potent drink eased her tension.

They should be afraid of me she reminded.

However it was a bother. She had cash and ID with her but there was a passport, money, coke, a flask of burial earth, and a photo album stashed in her flat. She didn't need anything else.

There weren't many customers in the shabby bar which suited Melody as she sipped absinthe and formed a battle plan.

Tonight she would go into defensive mode and bolster her fortifications. She was extremely vulnerable during daylight hours so it was crucial to set up a secure nest.

The Totem Motel was a relic but it suited her purposes. Located on a side street the two-story building got little sunlight and at the moment was nearly vacant.

After renting the motel's only suite she started back to pick up her car and see if her house was still being watched.

There was just under a hundred thousand in cash there and her precious photo album, her sole connection to a long forgotten past.

Shortly after four a.m. she approached her neighborhood. Among her other physical attributes she had exceptional night vision. A careful scan showed the area was clear.

To make sure she used her ability to move at blurring speed. In the darkness she was virtually invisible.

Melody paused at the door until satisfied nobody was waiting up for her, then she went in.

Everything was in place, she could sense there had been no intruders. However she had a strong sense they were on their way.

She was a bit tipsy and moved slowly, collecting her essentials and putting them in her large shoulder bag. Alcohol didn't take the ravaging toll on her kind that it did on humans. But the short-term effects were similar.

Her bag was packed and as she turned to leave she remembered.

The album.

It was a large old-fashioned photo album, thick with ten thousand vanished moments. It fell open to a tintype of a dashing French youth taken during the Belle Époque. The photograph opened a torrent of memories and she was swept back in time.

For far too much time.

The combination of absinthe and mundane emotion had lulled her into an extended reverie. Even so she felt a sharp pang of anxiety coupled with the sound of a car door being closed quietly on the street and knew it was them. She glimpsed daylight creeping at the edges of her window curtains.

Instantly she scooped up her large bag and was in the kitchen. She flipped the concealed ring in the ceiling and pulled down an overhead stairway the led to her lair—a storage area converted to her needs. Comfortably padded with shelves for various toiletries and tools it served as a luxurious urban casket.

All this had taken Melody seconds. She pulled up the stairway behind her and secured it making it impossible to pull down from outside and stretched her limbs. The fact the sun was up didn't mean she automatically went to sleep. Many of her kind had insomnia.

Old blood was the best remedy.

Melody hadn't fed that night still bloated from the incident at the blonde's apartment. She had mistakenly judged her enemy by the louts they first sent. This must be the first team Melody speculated as she listened to the footsteps on the sidewalk stop in front of her house.

They knew enough to attack at sunrise but were they stupid enough to bring crosses and stakes she wondered. Among the comforts of her lair was a .45 Colt automatic. And she knew how to use it. It would be a lot simpler explaining to the Lafayette police why she blasted a pair of intruders than why she drained their blood.

By now Melody knew it was a pair. She heard them whisper at the door and begin a countdown before they burst through the door.

Actually they had to count twice. Her police lock withstood the first assault but one the second the old wood cracked. The two men stumbled in and ran from room to room. One went out the back door to the small garden. The other joined him and Melody could hear them kicking at the dirt. It amused her to think of these gangsters scuffing their expensive shoes as they tried to unearth her coffin.

It wasn't funny when they returned and started ransacking her apartment. A surge of alarm shot through her thoughts when she remembered.

The album.

She had stupidly left the album in the living room.

The intruders were angry. Like frustrated baboons they were kicking and cursing.

"Fucking bitch, where is she?"

"This is crazy Franny, there ain't no vampire here. We can wait, when she gets back we grab her."

"She's not coming back."

"How do you know?"

"Because she's a fucking Vampire. If she ain't here she's someplace out of the sunlight."

"It might rain today."

"Makes no difference. Daylight burns them."

"Yeah sure, so now what?"

"That gave me an idea. We'll torch the place. If she's here we'll flush her into the daylight."

"Finally you make some sense."

Inside her dark, padded sanctuary Melody made an effort to suppress an urge to drop down and kill them both on the spot. She had to restrain her rage for very practical reasons. Her strength had steadily waned with every moment the sun rose in the sky. And if they managed to drag her outside she'd be finished.

Melody heard a rasping click and then smelled the smoke rising to the ceiling. Fire burn would heal in time but would leave her vulnerable during that period. As a predator her beauty was a prime weapon.

She concentrated on remaining calm but the thought of the treasured photograph album rendered to ashes drove her into a frenzy. Fists clenched she rolled from side to side as the smoke began to fill the dark space. Unable to wait she unlatched the door and dropped to the kitchen floor before the descending stairway. The smoke-fogged house was empty but Melody knew her hunters were perched outside, ready to snare whatever tried to escape the spreading flames.

Using the remnants of her diminishing powers she located the album. It was on the couch where she dropped it. But now the couch was burning and he edges of the thick album were on fire.

Snatching it up Melody headed for the rear door, the still fuming album under her arm, her weakened body coiled to strike whoever was waiting there.

The garden was empty but it had one enemy she couldn't defeat.

Daylight.

Despite the overcast gray sky the heat rivaled that of the flames inside. Melody went back into the house and pulled a blanket down from her exposed sanctuary. She covered herself with the blanket and clutching the still smoldering album like a football, raced across the garden and vaulted the fence into the neighbor's driveway.

When she reached a patch of shade Melody crouched down and rummaged through her bag for the car's remote.

Not even the building's shadow prevented the sunlight from burning through the clouds, the shade, or the shelter of the blanket. She felt her skin start to blister and made one last run for her car. Sirens were screaming closer and people were about to spill onto the street any second.

Flesh seared with agony she waved the remote in front of her like a wand as she raced furiously around the corner squeezing the button to unlock the car's trunk. She got there as the trunk popped open and in one swift motion rolled inside and shut the lid over her.

A fireman seated high on an arriving truck glimpsed a hooded figure but when he looked again there was nothing there.

Chapter 15

The meeting with Easton had left Les with more questions than solutions. Either the Director was a great actor or he had really not known about the listening device.

Fine Les thought, he could accept that. But the results of the blood residue they'd collected at that remote dock were nothing less than stunning.

They had always assumed Ryan Morgan was dead.

According to FBI forensics Detective Morgan was very much alive and playing for the other side.

Rather than try to figure it out he lit a cigarette and called the hospital for an update on Dave's condition.

The head nurse, a woman called Robb, told him there was no change. "Be assured we're watching him closely. If there is any change we will call you at this number." she said curtly and hung up.

Les carefully put the pre-paid phone in his pocket. He had previously retrieved their discarded mobile phones to record his dialogue with Easton. At their meeting Les also forgot to mention his untraceable phone. Nothing the director had said gave Les reason to trust him.

While waiting for Easton to give him further instruction he was holed up at the Fairmont with a couple of take-out burgers and a half bottle of Jim Beam.

All the built-up adrenaline he manufactured since the attack had drained after his meeting with Easton leaving his body weak and his brain listless.

He ate a burger and watched TV without really registering what was being said. At some point he fell asleep.

The familiar sound of his mobile roused him from a restless doze.

"Shorty."

It was Easton using the name of the café where they had met as a prearranged code. He was a stickler for cloak and dagger procedure.

"Yeah. Did you call the customers?" Meaning did he contact Dave's wife.

"They are en route."

There was a momentary silence.

"And so are you."

Something in his voice alerted Les and he got to his feet.

"I'm not sure I got that."

"You're being placed on administrative leave."

It took Les a few seconds to grasp what he had said.

"You're serious?"

"Serious as the IRS."

"Why didn't you tell me earlier?"

"This doesn't come from me."

"The other office, is that it?"

"Affirmative."

"Any reason?"

"You no longer have an associate on this project. You're on three-week compassionate leave. After that you'll be rotated back in." Easton said in a crisp mechanical tone as if listing items on a receipt.

"This sucks. What about Dave?"

"He'll be taken care of."

"I want a sit down."

"It's a done deal. Out of my hands."

"Godamnit You can't do this"

But Easton had already clicked off.

Les threw the phone across the room. It hit the wall hard. He picked it up and saw the screen was cracked. Enraged and confused he threw it again and left it where it fell.

The bottle of Jim Beam was sitting on a small dining table. He sat down next to it.

A drink and a cigarette later he told himself that getting drunk wouldn't bring Dave back and would only justify his being yanked off the case. Still angry he had another drink anyway.

A female announcer on the TV news drew his attention.

"I'm standing in front of the landmark St. Louis Number One Cemetery," she was saying, "the site of at least three brutal murders…"

Les went over and sat on the bed. The reporter had a few facts right but nothing he didn't already know. The lady assumed it was humans killing those people he thought ruefully. He lay back on the pillow and reached for the remote.

The remote was in his hand when he woke up three hours later. He was slightly hung over and famished.

After devouring the left over hamburger Les took a shower, dressed and went out for some real food.

He anger had been swallowed by a general disbelieving numbness. Fifteen plus years on the job had taught him fairness and honesty were on the back end of the Bureau's agenda. But dumping him under the bus like this didn't make sense. Unless he had gotten too close.

Les paused, hand on the car door. *Hold that thought* he told himself.

It was his intention to eat at a local place but started driving aimlessly as if looking for something special. Although hungry he turned toward New Iberia almost an hour south.

You're too tired for this. Stop somewhere that's convenient, go back to the room and crash for the night, he kept thinking. But instead he continued south.

Without any particular destination in mind he drove directly to Nick's and parked in the dimly lit lot. Before leaving his car he put the Glock at the small of his back for faster access.

At least he'd get a good meal Les reflected, still unsure why he had driven all that way for dinner.

Sam was behind the bar and Nick was seated at the end nearest the kitchen where he could supervise the orders going in and inspect the food coming out. He left his stool when Les entered and came over to greet him.

"Good to see you suh, where's Dave tonight?"

"He came down with something. I left him back in Lafayette sleeping it off."

"Sam will be disappointed. You here to eat or drink?"

"Both."

"Our special tonight is barbecued chicken with Spanish rice and collard greens."

"I'm definitely in."

"Pick a table, What is your pleasure?"

"Cold beer."

"I'll send Sam over."

At least his intuition chose a joint where he was treated well Les thought. Now he had to remember his cover story. He sat down at a table with a good view of the bar and lit a cigarette.

Watching Sam coming around the bar Les understood why Dave was tempted. She had long legs and jean shorts topped by a Pink T shirt and it didn't stop there.

Her straight black hair framed a heart shaped face and grey blue eyes that seemed to look deep into him.

She gave him a worried pout and set his beer down.

"Is Dave sick?"

"He'll be okay, slight fever, I'll tell him you asked."

"You do that. I'll be back with your food."

Watching Sam leave was as tempting as her approach. He thought of Dave and quickly tried to wash away the guilt with cold beer. Technically he was off the case but Nick could be a key player in the attack that left Dave near death. Their warehouse surveillance was something else he neglected to mention to Easton.

You're kidding yourself Les reflected, what are he supposed to do on his own? But he knew he would try it. No way was he going back to New York and leave Dave behind in a strange hospital.

He had finished his beer when Sam came back with the food. However she had brought him another without being asked.

"Compliments of Nick," She started to leave then turned. "Do you think Dave would eat soup if I gave it to you?"

"Sure. It might be just what he needs."

Les wondered how she'd react if he told her the truth Then he thought of Dave's wife Jennifer who knew the truth by now. That managed to depress him.

At least half the customers were Vietnamese, the rest were blue collar fisherman, oil workers and tourists

Dinner was first-rate and Les wolfed it down hungrily. He felt better immediately.

Nick approached the table with a bottle and two glasses. "Enjoy the food?"

"Excellent. You should open a branch in Hollywood."

"I've got a lot on my plate right here, if you'll pardon the pun. May I join you suh?"

"My pleasure."

"It will be, I brought along a bottle of small batch hand-crafted bourbon as an after dinner libation."

Les smiled in spite of himself. The bar owner's old school formality belied his intimidating physical presence. He wondered how deeply Nick was involved in smuggling.

"To your health."

Les was a bit wary of strong bourbon after his reaction at Minny's. He was walking a tightrope between Bureau sanctions and a violent death. He needed quick wits. He raised his glass and took a discreet swallow.

The bourbon burned a smooth path through his anxieties and a glowing relaxation spread across his belly.

"Nectar of the gods," Nick proclaimed.

"Are you from these parts?" Les asked casually.

"Actually I came here from Rome about five years ago."

"You took root fast."

"If there's one thing an Italian can do it's run a restaurant. It's all about hospitality."

"I can testify to your gracious hospitality."

Nick refilled his glass. "Good bourbon clears the mind." The casual remark resonated in his brain like a trumpet.

"So how is your film progressing?"

"We've hit a stumbling block with the money people."

Nick smiled. "What's the budget if I'm not prying."

"Right now, less than three million. But that's on paper."

"You need a star."

"We need help," Les said and he meant it. "So how does a guy from Rome wind up in New Iberia?"

"It's like being on a Mediterranean island. The pace of life is slower, people take time to enjoy their food, their drink, their pleasures."

"Lots of crime in New Orleans."

"Plenty of violence down here as well. Folks here are hot tempered. Could be the spices in their diet. And the drugs of course."

He refilled their glasses. "Let's drink to peace. And if we can't have peace let's have passion."

As Nick claimed the bourbon left Les clear headed and alert.

"I've come to the conclusion that the solution to our drug problem is legalization."

"Lots of people think it's the only way to defund the criminal cartels," Les offered.

"Exactly right. We would have a medical problem of course," Nick lifted a thick finger, "but we can solve a medical problem. Nobody wins in a war."

Sam came to the table carrying a plastic bag. She gave him a shy smile

"This is some chicken soup for Dave."

"I like Dave," Nick said, "I hope it's nothing serious."

"Amen to that," Les said. He felt like a hypocrite.

"Sit down," Nick said, "we're about to solve the world's problems."

"I bet you are." Sam started to sit but her smile froze and she moved away. "I've got to get back to work," she said quickly. Les followed her gaze and jerked back as if struck.

Melody Dawn had just strolled into the bar and was heading directly to his table.

Chapter 16

Les had almost forgotten how lovely she was.
Although older than Sam she radiated a sensual vitality that was beyond age. In some ways Sam was still a girl, Melody was all woman.

Her black dress clung to a body that was as supple as a ballet dancer and could ignite senses a man never knew he possessed.

He thought he had pushed Melody to the far recesses of his consciousness but her smile of recognition skipped past his defenses and he found himself rising to meet her. .

Her voice sang in his ear when they embraced.

"I was hoping to find you here."

Les gave her a wary smile "That's odd, I was on my way somewhere else."

Nick got up. "May I get your friend something to drink?"

Melody spoke before Les could introduce her.

"Absinthe, if you please."

As Nick moved off Melody sat down drawing Les beside her. "I so happy to see you."

"How could you possibly know I'd be here?" Les asked. Her presence was both intoxicating and upsetting. He didn't need distractions from an already chaotic situation.

She noticed his distant tone. "Because we have a psychic connection."

"I don't believe in psychic connections."

She shrugged and sat back. "Ours might be stronger than your beliefs."

Her disappointed pout made Les feel guilty. There was no reason to be rude.

"Sorry," he said gently, "it's just that I'm really surprised to see you."

"I'm *happily* surprised." She took his hand. "Aren't you?"

Her fingers seemed to fuse with his and he felt a familiar stirring. She was beautiful that was certain. Her smoky green eyes met his and without realizing it he bent to kiss her. Their lips brushed and he pulled back fighting his body's urge.

"Have you had dinner?"

She half smiled. "I had something on the way over."

"And you knew I'd be here?"

"Why are you here Les?"

He looked away.

"Honestly Les, why did you drive down from Lafayette?"

"Spur of the moment thing."

"I've kind of missed you."

"Kind of?"

"Well you're not very nice. First you drop me cold, then when I reach out you push me away."

"I didn't expect to see you. You sort of caught me in the middle of a few things."

"Sorry I didn't mean to intrude."

She started to rise but Les gently took her arm."

"No I'm the one who should be sorry, please sit."

Suddenly he felt like a teenager, uncertain and awkward. The last thing he needed was a night of decadence with an alluring woman. Except his body was straining against his logic like a rare earth magnet, pulling him to her.

"You knew I'd be here?" he repeated softly.

Her smile was like moonlight breaking through dark clouds. "I had strong hopes."

Nick came back with Melody's drink. "This is a local absinthe made from an original formula. It's called Rimbaud."

"As in the poet?"

"Exactly it's refreshing to meet a lady who knows the classics. I'm Nick Casio."

"As in Nick's Café?"

"Yes."

She waved at his empty chain. "Please join us."

"I'm Melody. I believe you and Les were talking."

"Nothing serious, we were judging the qualities of this bourbon." Before Les could protest he refilled both their glasses.

"A toast to your lovely name," Nick said, "it suits you."

Melody sipped her drink and cocked her head. "The wormwood wasn't aged enough but it's quite good. My compliments to the proprietor."

Nick beamed at Les. "She should star in your movie."

"You never told me you're in the film business."

Les smiled. "We never discussed business."

Melody leaned closer. "So true."

Les was pleased with her attention having felt a twinge of jealousy at Nick's presence.

"It was indeed a pleasure Melody," Nick said, with impeccable timing "Les, please pass along our best wishes to Dave. And don't forget Sam's chicken soup."

He picked up the bottle bowed and went back to his place at the end of the bar."

"You have a sick friend?"

"More than sick."

Melody put a hand on his arm. "Tell me about it."

"Can't . Especially here."

"Drive me back to my place. We can talk there."

"What about your car?"

"It'll be fine where I left it."

She swallowed her drink and made a face. "I was just being polite about the absinthe, tastes like soda pop."

Les knew he should say no but it beat driving back alone. And he needed to be in Lafayette in case the hospital called. Weak reasons he told himself.

"Sure why not. We can talk on the way."

As Les paid the check he noticed Sam seemed angry about something. He waved goodbye to Nick who came over to escort them to the door.

"Drive careful now," he said, "Melody it was a great pleasure having you here. Come back soon."

Les had to remember his charming host probably headed a smuggling operation.

Melody noticed his overly alert manner in the parking lot. "We all should be careful these days," she whispered taking his arm.

Contrary to expectations they did very little talking for a while. Melody found some blues on the radio and curled up beside him.

Finally Les spoke. "Where am I taking you?"

"A cute little motel in Lafayette."

"What about your apartment?"

"They burned me out yesterday."

It took a moment to process the information.

"*They* burned you out? Who the fuck are *they*?"

"Local Mafia I think. Out of New Orleans. They killed my good friend Victor."

"Killed him why?"

"He stupidly stole something from them. Now they think I'm involved."

"Some friend."

"That's why I was hoping to see you."

Les shrugged. "What made you think of me?"

Melody laughed. "Because you're in the movie business."

"I don't get it."

"Very few filmmakers walk about so heavily armed."

Les thought he had concealed his gun, knife and Cobra that memorable night with Melody. Obviously he hadn't done a good job. She saved him the trouble of lying.

"Please Les, I know you're FBI. I saw your credentials while you were passed out."

"You went through my wallet you mean."

Melody straightened up and looked out the window.

"A lady likes to know what sort of man is in her bed."

"Now you know."

She glanced at him. "Not really, that's my problem."

Les sighed. "Look, I'm undercover, up to my ass in serious trouble and can't handle another problem. What I *can* do is hook you up with somebody who can help you."

"Turn off here, we're not far from my new home."

"What will you do?"

She kissed him lightly on the cheek. "You can't handle another problem, remember?"

Something in her soft tone set off pangs of guilt and he slowed down. "I understand how you must feel, but being around me is hazardous to your health. My partner is…"

He paused and shook his head in frustration.

"Les, tell me what happened."

"You wouldn't believe it."

"Come up for a drink and I'll try."

"I don't know…"

"Stop here. This is where I get off."

Les was brought up short emotionally. Despite all his objections he really couldn't leave Melody alone after what had happened to her.

"Okay, I'll come up for that drink. As long as it's not absinthe."

Despite the hot, humid night air Melody's hand was cool against his as they walked the short distance to her motel. They were silent, both of them watchful.

Melody's suite was compact but private. All the blinds and drapes were closed and silk scarves muted the lamps.

Except for a few bottles of wine and of course absinthe, the place was bare of personal touches. The refrigerator contained nothing but ice cubes and vodka.

"Don't you ever eat?" he asked, pouring a splash of water into his bourbon.

"Once a day. In the evening usually."

She moved closer and lightly caressed his shoulder. We can order in if you get hungry. But you can't stay over. Is that alright?"

Her touch sparked his pent up desire and he took her in his arms. "Then we should probably get busy."

Their embrace was an eruption of primal lust, raw need and something else.

Something much deeper.

Afterwards when they were lying exhausted with Melody nestled against his rapidly beating heart he still felt it. And he felt angry at the people who wanted to hurt her.

"These guys killed your friend?"

"You say the most romantic things," she murmured

She rolled over to look up at him. "You met Victor the night we met. The bartender."

"Heavy set, white beard?"

"Yes, poor soul. He died while being tortured. Now they think I know something about it. They came to my apartment yesterday. I saw them coming and hid. When they didn't find me they set fire to the place. I barely got out alive."

"Do you know who these guys are?"

"One of them is called Franny Five Angels, he owns a couple of strip clubs."

He reached for his phone. "I'll make a call…"

Melody gently pushed him back.

"Tell me what happened to your friend."

Les winced. "Have you heard anything about these murders in New Orleans?"

"Yes they've been all over the media. Is that what you're working on?"

He nodded. "We were supposed to be undercover but there were a series of attacks almost from the day we started.""

"Who attacked you?"

"Never got a good look until last night. They move in a group, extremely fast—and vicious. They kill, remove body parts and vanish."

Until now Les had avoided a detailed run through of last night's events. Oddly, not even Easton had requested it. However now, telling the story to Melody he was hearing it himself for the first time.

"I was very drowsy when we left Minny's," Les said, lighting a cigarette. "I thought it was the strong bourbon the bartender gave us. But I had more than one bourbon at Nick's and I'm pretty clear headed."

"You think it was drugged?"

Les sat up. "I intend to find out."

Melody's mouth brushed his ear. "Not tonight."

He gently kissed her. "I thought you wanted me to leave."

"Not yet. You still haven't told me what happened to Dave. You saw them right?"

"Just one. I had dropped my gun When I looked up he was about to jump me."

"Why didn't he?"

"A car came by. When the headlights lit them up they all disappeared... son of a bitch that's it."

He looked at Melody. "I remember seeing them come out of a van. They were on us before I even blinked."

"You said they were big and hairy."

"Big... with these clawed feet... weird red eyes. If I hadn't dropped my gun... who knows, Dave..."

"It wasn't your fault Les." Melody put her arms around him. "I can help you. We can help each other."

"How can you help?" he asked gently.

"Trust me darling, I have skills."

"I'll attest to that. But you also have bad habits."

She pouted. "Seriously? I happen to have what you need."

"Melody I'm a pro at this and right now I don't know what I need."

Her arms dropped away. "What can I do to convince you?"

His phone rang. Les answered reluctantly. The only one who had that number was the nurse at the hospital.

"This is Head Nurse Robb. Your friend David Chin has taken turn for the worse. His vital signs are down. You might want to come down to the hospital to say goodbye."

The last two words pounded at his brain, *say goodbye*.

Les had been Special Forces in the military, he had seen combat, tracked serial killers, arrested violent criminals but he wasn't prepared for this. His breathing became shallow and rapid and tears squeezed through his tightly shut eyelids.

"Les, are you alright?"

"Dave is dying."

For a few seconds there was only the sound of his muffled sobs. Then he took a deep, loud breath and lifted his head. "I've got to go."

"I'm going with you."

"No."

"Please Les let me help."

"For god's sake Melody. I saw him. His arm was practically torn off. There's no way to help."

She gripped his shoulders. Les was startled at how strong she was.

"Listen to me. I'll prove it to you. I have the power to save Dave's life. But you have to make me a promise."

Les pulled away and searched her face. "You can save his life?"

"Yes."

"What do I have to promise?"

"You'll help me with these people who are hunting me. In return I'll help you track down these beast things who attacked you. We'll be partners. Agreed?"

Les started looking for his clothes.

"Save Dave's life and you have my word."

* * *

Melody had never known a man so resistant to her charms. For two centuries she had been bending lovers to her will.

However Les managed to elude her control despite the deep connection she knew was there between them.

She had focused on finding him ever since she crawled singed and furious from the trunk of her car. She knew they belonged together. Unfortunately he knew nothing. Les was all body, brain and reflex. His psychic talents had never been developed. He was completely unaware of his great potential.

Les was also unaware of how much she cared for him. That was the factor that unsettled her. She distrusted emotions. Especially one she hadn't felt for decades.

"I'll have to be alone with him." Melody said as they drove to the hospital

"How long?"

"Less than five minutes."

"Depends on how much time Dave has."

"I can bring him back."

"What about his arm?"

"I don't do surgery. Just miracles."

Les remained silent, eyes on the road.

Melody was touched by his loyalty to his friend. It was a most desirable quality in a potential partner. She hoped that Dave was still alive. If not she would lose a star crossed lover. Destiny could be circumvented by parallel fates. And star crossed lovers transformed life from a trek to a glorious journey.

Over the past couple of hundred years she had known bleak periods Melody reflected. She needed Les on many levels. The deepest she barely understood, merely felt.

It was three a.m. when they arrived and the hospital was quiet. They went up to Intensive Care where the head nurse was waiting for them.

Nurse Robb was a tall, thin woman with a tight smile and the officious manner of an undertaker.

"His bodily signs are steadily declining," she said in hushed tones. "His wife has not yet arrived from New York."

"Can we see him?"

"I'll need you to sign a release, as well as other documents which are necessary in such cases."

Nurse Robb made Les sign a stack of papers before she would allow them into Dave's room.

Normally Melody would not have been allowed to join Les but his FBI credentials cut through Nurse Robb's reluctance. He told her that Melody was a fellow agent on the same case.

"Alright," she sighed, "ten minutes, no more."

Dave had undergone extensive surgery and he was hooked up to various tubes, drips, and sensors that monitored his heart, lungs and brain.

His skin had a ghostly grey pallor and one arm was swathed in bandages. He lay motionless, damaged arm crossed on his chest at an odd angle, silent amid the electronic beeps and pings from the machines keeping him alive.

Melody watched Les approach the side of the bed and place a tentative hand on Dave's forehead. She waited a moment in respect his feelings then glanced back at the hallway where Head Nurse Robb was prowling.

"Watch the door," Melody said.

She took his place bedside and quickly went to work. Fortunately Dave was not wearing a breathing apparatus, which could trigger the monitors when removed.

Without hesitation Melody bit deep into her wrist and placed the oozing blood against Dave's mouth. Like an infant hungry for milk his lips parted and he began to weakly suck. Within seconds she could feel him begin to aggressively draw blood from her punctured vein.

Melody allowed him a few extra pulls for good measure then pulled back well short of the amount it would take to turn him. Still, he didn't let her remove her wrist easily. If he hadn't been so weak he might even have bitten her.

"I hear footsteps," Les whispered.

Melody stepped back from the bed, hand pressed over her wrist.

"It's done."

Nurse Robb appeared a few moments later.

"There's no sense waiting here," Nurse Robb told them as she ushered them out. "I'll call you when it's over and you can make arrangements for the body's removal."

She left them with that thought and strode away, her footsteps fading down the half darkened hallway.

Les looked desolate, even disoriented.

"Are you okay to drive?"

He seemed to snap awake, "Yeah, I'm good."

They drove back in funereal silence until they arrived at her motel.

"What did you do back there?" Les said before she got out of the car.

"You didn't see?"

"I was looking for that bitch of a nurse. All I saw is you bending over him."

Even if Melody wanted to explain the punctures in her wrist had already healed. He'd never believe her.

"If my treatment works I'll tell you how it's done," she said and stepped out.

Les gave her a resigned shrug.

Melody leaned back inside. "Have a little faith. I saw you say a prayer for him."

"Prayer ?"

"You put your hand on his head and said something."

"That wasn't a prayer."

"What were you saying then?"

He gave her a sad smile.

"I said, 'I guess I was right about the Kevlar vests.'"

Chapter 17

Les was fresh out of faith.

He had lost a good chunk over twenty plus years fighting bad guys from Special Forces to the FBI.

What little of it was left he had riding on Dave.

He was disturbed at how Melody had marched back into his life and tried to take over.

He was sympathetic to her problem and definitely sexually attracted to the voluptuous brunette but he had only known Melody for a total of twenty two hours. In that time he discovered that she was deeply sensual, intense, had criminal friends and was wanted by the mafia. A volatile package wrapped in black satin. He would have to find a way to ease her out of his psyche.

Numb with grief Les barely managed to get his clothes off before collapsing on the bed. His last thoughts before dropping off were of Dave's wife Jennifer. He would have to contact her somehow.

Awakened by his phone some six hours later Les expected the worst. A nurse asked him if he would speak to Mrs. Chin.

"We don't give out phone numbers," she explained.

"I understand, please put her on."

"Les are you there?"

"Jennifer?"

"I got here about an hour ago. Everybody says it's miraculous."

"What?"

"The nurse said that at about four this morning Dave started to improve. He's conscious now and wants to see you."

"I'll be there right away."

As Les sped to the hospital conflicting emotions kept clanging against his brain like bell clappers. He was euphoric, skeptical and braced against harsh reality .

Head Nurse Madras was a wiry Indian woman with white hair and bright, intelligent eyes. She clasped her hands as she gave him the good news.

"All of Mr. Chin's vital signs have improved to near normal which is incredible considering the damage he suffered."

"Yes, it's wonderful uh can I…?"

"He was in surgery for hours."

"I'll be sure to thank the doctors. Is Jen… Mrs. Chin here?"

"She's with her husband. He's in and out," she added, lowering her voice.

When they entered Jennifer was seated next to Dave's bed holding his hand. Always an elegant and lovely woman Jennifer looked worn down and slightly disheveled. There were dark circles under her eyes and her pale skin was stretched tight over her hollow cheekbones. Les saw the suitcase standing on the floor and realized she had come directly from the airport in New Orleans.

Jennifer managed a weak smile. "Les I'm so glad you're here. He asked for you."

"When did he wake up?"

"The first time shortly before I got here. And them again when I called you. Can you tell me what happened?"

"We were jumped by three guys we were tailing," Les said. He liked Jennifer and hated to lie to her but the truth might freak her out. It did him.

"But his wounds…"

"They had machetes."

"Doctor Boudreau said they may not be able to save his arm.'

"Dave's strong. Look how fast he came back."

She nodded but she didn't believe it.

Abruptly one of the machines started piping a high, rhythmic beep and Dave's eyes fluttered open.

They moved from side to side as if he trying to get his bearings. When he saw Jennifer he smiled.

"Sweet... heart..."

"I'm here darling and so is Les."

"Les moved into Dave's view. "Hey partner."

"I'm..."

He bent closer to Dave. "You're going to be okay."

"I'm... sor... ry..."

"Sorry? Why?"

"Too... drunk..."

Les suddenly knew what he meant. "Not your fault buddy," he said softly, "not your fault. We were both drugged. They slipped us a mickey."

Dave half smiled and closed his eyes. The machine's electronic beeping slowed.

As Les and Jennifer left Dave's room a short, energetic blond nurse came up to them.

"It's nothing short of miraculous," she beamed, "I was on duty when you can to see him. No more than twenty minutes after you and your lady friend left Mr. Chin began to recover. I've never seen anything like it. Doctor Boudreau said the same thing."

"We're all very thankful for you efforts," Les said, cutting her off.

Jennifer was exhausted and Dave had slipped back into sleep so Les offered to take her to a hotel.

"You were at the hospital last night," she said as they drove, "how bad was he?"

"They were worried, so was I. When did they notify you?" he added hoping to change subjects.

"Yesterday afternoon. Dave was already in surgery. I've been out of my mind ever since. Getting my Mom over to take care of Robin, the flight, everything..."

"I'm going to give you a private number. Whatever you need Jennifer, you know I'm there."

"I heard you say somebody drugged you?"

He took a deep breath. "Maybe."

She was silent for a few minutes.

"By the way," she said finally, "who's this lady friend?"

Les groaned inwardly. Jennifer would have made an ace investigator. .

He tried to sound casual. "Fellow agent really."

"Dave never mentioned a female partner."

Les felt his neck redden. "She's not a partner. She's working the same case from a different angle."

Jennifer sniffed that something wasn't right but they arrived at the Juliet Hotel in the nick of time.

Les escorted Jennifer to the front desk, made sure she had a good room then went back to the Fairmont feeling deeply grateful for Dave's recovery.

And deeply troubled.

+ + +

Later that afternoon he decided to test Easton's loyalty. He used Dave's mobile to call the director's private number.

"Hensen here."

"Okay, what is it?" was Easton brusque reply.

"I'm requesting twenty one days of personal time before reporting for evaluation."

"Why?"

This was it. If Easton was involved he would want Les on the next plane to New York.

"My partner. I want to make sure he's got proper care."

There was a long pause. "Alright. Your request is granted." He hung up.

Les stared at Dave's phone. That's one for Easton, he reflected. Which meant the senior official who yanked him off the case was most likely state deputy director Virgil Lake.

Or perhaps Easton wanted easy access to eliminate him, Les speculated. It was no time for trust.

His prepaid phone rang. Only the hospital and Jennifer had the number.

It was Melody.

"You've been on my mind since I woke up."

"How did you get this number?"

"I told you, a lady likes to know who's in her bed."

Her throaty laughter seemed to revive him. Les took a deep breath.

"How is Dave?"

The playful question suggested she already knew the answer.

"Better actually."

"I need to see you tonight."

"Later, about ten," he said reluctantly.

"Perfect. We can have a late dinner somewhere. I'll text where to meet me."

So much for protective anonymity Les observed. He didn't want to think about the deal they'd made when Dave seemed near death. He was desperate. Head Nurse Robb was even suggesting body removal.

But it was crazy to believe Melody could prance into a dying man's room and in a matter of minutes cure him.

No more crazy than the creatures who attacked Dave and put him on life support Les reminded. It was a compelling argument.

Melody called at six thirty.

In an effort to offset drinks at dinner Les went out and ate a barbecued beef sandwich.

He took home a container of coffee and tried to watch the news on TV.

It was useless. The images melted into one another. He couldn't stop thinking about Melody. He thought he had put her at a distance and now she was right back under his skin.

At nine she texted him to meet her at the Bombay Club which proved to be a British themed restaurant with wing back overstuffed chairs and dark wood panels. He arrived early and had the pleasure of watching her enter the room.

Chin high, shadowed eyes and red lips framed by shining ebony hair, supple body sheathed in a black silk dress with a scarlet sash, Melody strode to his table followed by every eye in the room. Les had to admit the attention was flattering to his male ego.

"Have you been waiting long?" she asked, brushing her lips across his cheek.

"It was worth it."

"That's the nicest thing you've said to me lately. What are you drinking?"

"Mineral water. I'm going slow tonight."

"So am I." She smiled at the approaching waiter. "Two absinthes."

Les shook his head. "There you go again."

"Tell the truth. You like it," she said, caressing his neck. Her hand felt cool but left an electric tingling sensation on his skin. A surge of desire rippled across his instincts and he fought hard to maintain a calm, controlled demeanor.

She seemed to know it and flirted with him over drinks. He did his best to keep her at bay but every cell urged him to respond.

"Here's to Dave's recovery," she said, tapping his glass with hers.

Les lit a cigarette. "I suppose you're going to claim responsibility."

She lifted a brow and sat back. "And you believe what...?"

"Could be coincidence."

Melody took the cigarette from his hand. "There's no such thing as coincidence."

"So the night we met you were looking for me?"

She took a long drag. "No, but when we met I knew it were supposed to happen. It's called destiny."

"As you know I'm an FBI agent and before that a soldier and what I believe in are facts—hard evidence."

"I told you I would bring him back and I did, How much more evidence do you need? It says in the bible 'there are none so blind as those who will not see.'"

Les gave her a wry smile. "Never figured you for a bible girl."

"I've studied it cover to cover." She regarded him over the rim of her glass. "I've got a feeling you're trying to weasel out of your commitment to me."

He lit a fresh cigarette. "I'm just not sure."

She leaned closer. "I was there last night when that head nurse practically had you sign Dave's death certificate. You were pretty damn sure then."

She stubbed out her cigarette. "Perhaps I'm the one who should be skeptical. I thought you were a man of honor underneath that corporate wet suit."

"What happens if I crawfish?"

Her eyes narrowed.

"It means…"

"I know what it means," Melody snapped. "You intend to squirm out of our pact. What happens…?" She sat back and studied him, eyes pale green flames in the subdued light. "I saved Dave's life because I need your help. You gave me your word. I believed you and I delivered the evidence required. But I'm beginning to rethink our deal."

"Really?"

"Really. I don't need a partner with limp values."

"So what happens now?"

"I walk out of here."

"And Dave?"

Melody gathered her things. "I saved Dave and he stays saved. It's you I'd worry about. You're alone. And from this night on you are on my shit list."

Les put a hand on her wrist

"Wait… Please."

She settled back and regarded him suspiciously.

"I had to be sure Dave isn't a hostage."

His hand was still on her wrist and he felt a jolt of recognition. Melody felt it too and smiled knowing what he was about to say.

"I'll help you with your problem. You have my word."

She lifted his hand and kissed it. "I'm going to need more than that darling."

Chapter 18

Franny Five Angels didn't like Sal hanging out at his club all the time. Since they torched the bitch's house in Lafayette Sal had become his self-appointed sidekick.

It had certain benefits. The bar skim was way down and so were the number of unruly patrons. When they saw Sal sitting at the bar like a gargoyle in a rumpled suit, they became more polite.

Of course the bartenders were sure Sal was there to watch the register so the drink profits soared.

The down side was Sal himself. The hulking ex-pug put a damper on the festivities with his gloomy, lantern-jawed scowl. The girls were afraid of him and Franny knew Sal could turn from guard dog to mad dog on a dime.

Worst of all, now Cozy had a direct link to his gambling operation as well as his skin joints. Sidekick bullshit aside Sal belonged to Don Benito and Cozy.

This missing pilot thing had turned his business enterprises inside out.

Sal lumbered into the office.

Franny tried to conceal his annoyance. "Sal baby, please knock okay? Suppose I was getting a blow job?"

Sal's expression remained impassive. "Cozy just called."

Franny heaved a sigh. "Give me a few minutes."

As soon as Sal closed the door Franny pounded the desk with his pudgy fist. This shit has got to stop, he told himself.

Then he went to the mirror, ran a comb through his hair, straightened his bolo tie and walked out to meet Cozy.

Whenever the call came they knew to meet at Cana, a bar Cozy owned in the Quarter about ten minutes south of Franny's joint.

Cozy was waiting in the back room.

"One of Falconi's people spotted the Corvette," he announced.

It took Franny a moment to remember what he was talking about. The missing pilot's Corvette.

"I want you and Sal to go over and sweat the driver."

"No problem," Franny said. Then he paused as if he just recalled something. "Can I talk to you a minute? It's about this thing with the booze deliveries."

"I'll wait in the car," Sal said.

Franny was counting on Sal's departure. Everyone knew Cozy didn't like eavesdroppers at business meetings.

"What about the deliveries?" Cozy said when they were alone.

"My problem is not the deliveries Cozy. It's this new job you gave me. "Gambling, skin joints, that's what I do. I ain't used to muscle work."

Cozy pressed his fingers together as if in prayer. It was something Don Benito did while delivering a lecture.

"Manual labor is good for a man once in a while. And since we lost Bruno and Paulie at your missing stripper's apartment *you* are responsible."

Franny shifted uncomfortably in his seat. "We were running down this Vampire bitch."

Cozy slammed his palm on the desk. "Enough. Do not persist in this supernatural horror movie bullshit. This person we're looking for is an ordinary woman. You failed to get her same way this stripper got away."

Franny lifted his hands in surrender. "What am I the missing persons bureau? I'm one guy Cozy. And Sal ain't a big help."

Cozy sat back and looked at the ceiling. "Alright, alright, you are what you are. Tell you what Franny, you find whoever has the Corvette. You're good at that. Once we locate the bastard you can walk. I'll get an experienced man to work with Sal. You'll be off the hook."

Franny got up and extended his hand. "Thank you Cozy, I knew you'd understand."

Cozy gave him a limp handshake. "You make sure you find whoever is driving this Corvette… or Sal is gonna be your new partner."

Franny left the bar feeling sick at the thought of having Sal around full time. He was determined to find whoever had the god damned Corvette. It was his only way out.

"One of Falconi's dealers spotted a silver Corvette on his turf," Franny told Sal, "he hangs out in a dive in Lafayette called Aunty Mame. Ever hear of it?"

Sal grunted negative and pointed the Caddy south.

Aunty Mame was a low rent bar on the far edge of the Treme neighborhood patronized by transgenders, transvestites, cross dressers and gay hustlers.

Sal took one look and lowered his head like a stubborn bull. "I ain't goin' in there."

"Yeah fine, I'll check it out. I'll call if I'm getting raped."

Just as well Franny thought, it would be like Frankenstein walking into the Magic Kingdom.

Actually Aunty Mame's customers looked like seventies Disco Queens and big hair glam rockers. Many wore exaggerated make up including a couple of motorcycle hoods with mascara and lipstick. It was crowded inside the bar and the boys were dancing to Michael Jackson's *Beat It*, their glitter tank tops and metallic gowns stained with sweat.

Unlike Sal's Neanderthal reaction Fanny was unfazed. In his years running two strip joints he'd seen most everything.

It took a few minutes to get the bartender's attention.

He was tall and muscular with a shaved head and a gold chain that barely fit around his thick neck. A cross dangling from one ear completed the tank-topped action star look

Franny slid a fifty across the bar. "I'll have a Jack and send a drink over to Lady Darlene compliments of Mr Nathan."

The bartender scooped up the fifty and came back with Franny's drink. Then he left the bar area and plowed his way across the crowded floor. Franny momentarily lost sight of him. Then the crowd parted and he saw the bartender returning.

"Rear booth," the bartender said under his breath.

Franny picked up his drink and began threading his way through the mass of dancers, the smell of perspiration, perfume, and alcohol congealing in the hot, humid space. By the time he reached the other side his sport jacket and trousers hung damply on his plump frame.

For all his worldly experience Franny was surprised when he saw Lady Darlene. To begin with he couldn't tell if she was a he. Slim, shapely and beautiful, Lady Darlene sat almost primly in her rear booth flanked by two hefty females wearing identical sunglasses. She wore a pale blue silk blouse unbuttoned to the navel that showed off caramel breasts and a zero fat waist. She had pouty red lips and a shrewd smile that widened as Franny approached.

"How nice to see you darling. You look fabulous," she said in a deep throaty voice. "You must join us. Andre get up and make room."

Wordlessly one of the hefty females slipped out of the booth to allow Franny to sit. He noted Andre moved fast for a big girl.

Even up close Franny couldn't tell.

"I was told you'd be coming, so let's make it short and very sweet. Do you have a present for Lady Darlene?"

Franny passed a thousand dollars under the table.

She took the money and made a face like a small child. "I appreciate your generosity sweetheart but where are my goodies?"

"They'll be delivered at the proper time by the proper people, with a bonus if your tip is correct."

"Oh it's correct honey. Turns out the man who's been driving that car you want so bad has a clinic in my neighborhood. A week ago I notice he's been parking this new Corvette in his lot. Never thought he was the type for that flashy ride."

Franny sipped his drink. "How so?"

"He's very square, stuffy, always in a suit that need dry cleaning, know what I'm sayin'?"

"What's his name?"

"Walther Heck. It's right there on the sign outside his clinic."

"He's got a clinic, is he a doctor?"

Lady Darlene airily waved her hand.

"It's a dog and cat clinic sweet thing. He's a vet."

+ + +

Walther Heck had a way with animals.

He could calm a hostile dog, coax a frightened cat, or teach a chimp to respond to symbols. He also mended broken bird wings, removed thorns and retrieved objects that should not have been eaten.

In the wild or at home Walther had handled mammals and reptiles for most of his life.

It was people he distrusted intensely

His grandfather had been an eminent zoologist in Germany but his father had not inherited an affinity for animals and instead amassed a fortune in oil. Gunther was a respected figure in Louisiana politics and wielded considerable leverage in Washington. He regarded his son with bemused affection and often lamented Walther's choice of profession.

Family money had financed Walther's treks and extensive education, however these days the clinic generated a sizable income enabling Walther to operate independently. Which suited him fine.

He hated his father.

For one thing his father was an avowed hunter and had killed over a hundred rare and beautiful animals.

This for no better reason than to brag to his cronies over drinks.

For another thing he was a preening womanizer who drove his mother to an early grave. Towards the end she was confined to an institution. His father had twenty rooms in his mansion and plenty of servants but he kept his wife locked away in a sterile prison far from home where she died alone.

Walther's clinic had grown during the years. He had acquired a second building where he could pursue his experiments but was forced to keep regular hours at his primary facility to keep up appearances. Although he had also acquired a good deal of money the pursuit of knowledge was expensive and he had no wish to go to his father for funding.

Of course he could have expanded his clinic's services by hiring more people. But the idea of having them around turned his stomach. He much preferred having his one medical assistant Frieda and his receptionist Joyce. His computers fulfilled the rest of his needs.

And his laboratory of course.

It was there treating his patients that he felt most comfortable. The medical facility included a surgical unit, a testing and monitoring area replete with the latest in digital technology. And a large kennel in the rear.

But his most ambitious project was miles away, in another section of New Orleans. The product of a lifetime of dedicated research. The most radical breakthrough in the history of genetic research.

And no one knew it existed.

Chapter 19

Cozy made an executive decision
    He really didn't need any more of his crew to get whacked over this pilot thing. It was really Don Benito's old school principles that lit the fuse.
    As far as the Don was concerned nobody got over on him. It was a matter of honor.
    Except Cozy had to go out and make it right.
    So rather than risk losing more earners Cozy called in some pros from Texas. They were due to arrive sometime tomorrow. These boys worked as a team Cozy gloated, congratulating himself for the move.
    This animal doctor that Franny fingered would never see them coming.
    A knock on the office door interrupted his thoughts.
    Benny stuck his head inside. "They need you at the bar," he said and ducked back.
    Cozy knew what he meant. To avoid electronic surveillance Don Benito sent messages in code.
    This one meant the Don wanted to see him.
    Reluctantly he locked the office and went out through the bar area. The place was half filled and he paused to greet some patrons on his way outside.
    As he drove Cozy wondered what the old man wanted. That was one problem. The other was serious. Now he had to inform Don Benito of his decision to hire outside help.
    As Capo he had that right but the Don might see it as a sign of disrespect.
    The Don lived with his wife in a gated mansion that was both secluded and secure. In lieu of bodyguards who were easily bribed he had Rottweiler's patrolling the grounds. Rumor was the Don fed the dogs himself.

Two of the dogs lay just inside the vestibule when Monte the old man's driver and all around assistant let him in.

Monte was about thirty, an ex-dirt track racer and skilled mechanic who was reputed to be a black belt. About six one he had thick black hair and looked something like Elvis before the drugs. His black T-shirt stretched across his chest and biceps. He ushered Cozy in without expression and led him to the library.

Don Benito was seated in a leather chair reading a book. A decanter and two snifters were on a table beside him. He lowered his book, removed his glasses and motioned to the chair next to his.

"Come Ricardo, join me in some fine grappa from Sicily."

Cozy smiled uncertainly and sat. He watched the Don pour the clear liquid from the decanted into the snifters.

"*Salute.*" Don Benito raised his glass and drank.

Cozy knew grappa was potent but his first sniff was like inhaling kerosene and a cautious sip burned a new path to his belly. A few seconds later the base of his brain felt numb. But far from relaxed.

"I'm glad you called Don Benito," he said clearing his throat. "I made a move to call in outside help to fix a situation. I hope you understand."

"I heard what happened to Paulie and Bruno," the Don gravely. "And I understand calling outside help. You see I've done the same thing."

"Oh?" was all Cozy could say.

"They tell me this girl is supposed to be a vampire."

"I don't know about vampires Don Benito."

"Of course not. So I called Father Dunn."

"A priest?" Cozy couldn't believe what he was hearing.

"Ex-priest. He's done some special work for me. Very clean, one of the best. But you know, he's a little *strano*, you know strange. He always bragged that he hunts demons and vampires. I figured like most men in his profession he has what they call *issues*. I never paid much attention until now."

"You believe this broad is really a vampire?"

"How else do you explain Paulie and Bruno?"

"Bruno shot Paulie and…"

Don Benito waved his hand impatiently. "My people in the police tell me their bodies had no blood. We can't deny the facts." Trying to process this news Cozy sipped his drink and nodded.

"Years ago, back in the old country our people knew about such matters," the Don said gravely."*Malocchio,* the evil eye, potions, spells, fortune cards, seers, it was all there in these little towns where we come from. Even today…"

Don Benito pointed to the crucifix and *corno* on Cozy's gold neck chain. The *corno* had the shape of a gold unicorn horn. "… even today Italian men wear the *corno* to protect them from envy and betrayal."

Actually Cozy wore the chain because his mother had given it to him. But he tried to show deep interest in what the old man was rambling about.

"My grandmother, bless her memory told stories from her own childhood, we're going back a hundred fifty years, about her village with strange deaths attributed to a vampire. A group of men led by a local priest and a fortune teller found this vampire's lair and beheaded him." The Don lifted the book he had been reading.

"Do you read much Richard?"

Cozy smiled sheepishly. "Not really. You know the papers and the children's books I read to my daughter."

Don Benito gave an approving smile. "Good. You spend time with your daughter. Perhaps that's where I failed with Nadia, always thinking business."

And that lady you keep uptown Cozy thought.

"But this book here was written in eighteen ten by a Physician who had formulas and potions that can protect us against vampires and evil spirits. So if a doctor, a priest and my grandmother believe in such things I must respect them right?"

"Absolutely Don Benito," Cozy said unhappily. He got the old man's drift, fuck this up and he might end up like that headless vampire.

"When does this Father Dunn get here?"

"Tomorrow. I'm sending him to you directly. Set him up in a safe house. Take care of what he needs. You alone, nobody else understand?""

"We've located the pilot's Corvette," Cozy said lamely. He gulped too much grappa and tried not to let his pain show.

"These people you're bringing from Texas will handle that. I hope they know what they're doing. Remember we need this guy healthy enough to talk."

"I'll make it clear," Cozy said. He wondered who was feeding the Don all his information.

"And oh, Richard," the Don said as Cozy walked unsteadily to the door.

"Uh, yes?"

"Make sure you put a bible in his room."

+ + +

The three bikers had taken route 90 from Port Arthur Texas all the way to Baton Rouge. They arrived covered in dust and sweat that stained the sleeveless shirts under their leather vests. They had the hard lean bodies of hunters who spent most of their lives outdoors. Their heavy arms were tattooed and the one called Chad had a matted beard and long blond hair. They wore muddy black Tony Lama boots with pointed roach killer toes and walked with the swagger of armed men. Which they were.

The trio had dismounted in front of a ramshackle grocery and gas station outside of Baton Rouge and bought cans of cold beer, packets of beef jerky and cigarette paper. After downing the beer and jerky they rolled some weed which they smoked as they consulted a map that was torn where it folded.

Chad decided to ride straight through and get a good night's rest before they went to work the next day. They were professionals and wouldn't party until they were done and gone.

Except they were headed to The Big Enabler, New Orleans. It took another hour or so to get there. When they did they slowly cruised the streets until they came to a secluded motel. It was set back from the street and the rooms formed a U shape around the lighted pool.

Chad had never stayed there before but word was the Half Note Motel accepted cash and whatever name you cared to sign.

Chad registered as Cole Younger, Ash as Wes Hardin and Fred as John Holliday. They took two adjoining rooms, one facing the pool the other the rear, separated from the other units by a narrow walkway.

Once inside they took showers and changed into fresh jeans and shirts. They checked their weapons and made sure they were locked and loaded. Chad had a thirteen shot Glock 9 millimeter, Ash a short-barreled shotgun and Fred an Uzi converted to .45 caliber rounds. All three weapons were easily concealed under their sleeveless leather jackets or in their bikes' saddlebags.

"Let's get somethin' to eat." Ash said. He was wiry and dark with deep set eyes and high cheekbones making him look Native American. His long black hair was pulled back in a ponytail and he wore a silver and turquoise bracelet on his bony wrist.

"We could order some food delivered," Fred suggested. He was the heaviest of the three, with receding blond hair and small blue eyes that peered resentfully at the world in general.

Chad looked up from the joint he was rolling.

"And have some punk delivery boy ID three strange bikers? Maybe see our Texas plates? I don't think so. Soon as we smoke this killer green we walk real nice to that barbecue we passed a block back, pick up a bottle of tequila and hole up until showtime."

Nobody argued. They knew Chad could be snake mean when he wanted to be. And he always wanted to be.

+ + +

It had been a normal day for Doctor Walther Heck. One water spaniel and one poodle treated for worms with a potion he had developed. He was in the process of obtaining a patent. He had also stitched up a Terrier who was bitten by a small alligator.

Walther made sure the pets in his care were groomed and comfortable. Then went back to the kennels where his own personal pets were housed. He always fed Rudy and Lily with food he had prepared himself.

The two pit bulls chomped greedily, taking the meat in large chunks which was why Walther included a digestive in their diet.

He had also installed a large TV screen at the end of a long treadmill. The treadmill was always a little faster than the dogs whether the image was a cat or another pit bull. Just like life Walther reflected, stroking their taut, muscular shoulders.

It was the receptionist's night off. Usually his assistant, a sturdy woman named Frieda, walked the dogs in the evening. However he decided to do it himself while she handled the front desk.

Walther went to the console and put his assistant on screen. "You can close early Frieda, I'll take the dogs out myself."

"Alright I'll lock… Oh, I believe we have one last client."

Walther switched to his outside surveillance camera.

A tall man with a beard had parked his motorcycle next to the Corvette. He wore a sleeveless leather jacket, and held a pet carrying case in one tattooed hand.

Oddly he had lingered to examine the Corvette and set the carrying case down on one end causing his pet much discomfort.

Suspicious, Walther switched to the rear surveillance camera and saw another biker casing the back door.

"Frieda I think we have an unwelcome visitor," he said over the intercom.

"What shall I do doctor?"

"Take your purse and walk calmly out the front door. Above all do not look to your right. Do it now."

Walther watched Frieda leave the clinic and walk briskly to her left, ignoring the man still looking at the Corvette. When she reached the sidewalk he saw the third biker waiting. He was on the phone, face averted from the camera—and Frieda—who walked safely out of sight.

The damned car Walther fumed. He should have killed Melody and left her inside. However she delivered prime specimens. And docile. He always wondered how she managed; drugs, hypnosis, whatever. Something on screen cut off his thoughts.

The bearded man was on the move

Walther went into the reception area to greet him.

He paused only long enough to take a small Ruger automatic from a drawer and slip it into the side pocket of his blue smock before stepping into the front just as the bearded man entered. He was holding a battered pet cage with an equally battered cat inside

The man set the cage on the counter and opened it. The cat remained inside.

"Are you Doctor Heck?" The man said politely.

"Doctor Heck is away. I'm his assistant."

"Oh is that your car out there?"

"That belongs to Doctor Heck. He bought it last week in fact. What seems to be wrong with your cat?"

"Oh well Fifi here won't eat. I think some big cat mighta scratched her up some."

"Lets take a look shall we?"

As he gently lifted the cat Walther noticed the man was squinting at the wall behind him. Walther had forgotten about that.

"Hey, isn't that you?"

On the wall was a photograph of himself taken ten years ago that hung above the many framed degrees he'd earned from various universities.

But Walther pretended to be looking at the cat, which was indeed scratched

"No that's Doctor Heck. He's in Omaha."

The bearded man shoved a gun in his face. "Don't fuck with me. You're Heck."

"I told you h's in *Omaha!*" Walther yelled the last word.

He saw the gun start to swing against his jaw then freeze as the hissing sound of paws scrambling on polished floors abruptly stopped and the pit bulls blasted through the door like twin cannonballs.

Rudy went right for the gun hand, Lily the leg. Rudy's jaws clamped hard on the intruder's forearm and the weapon bounced on the floor. The bearded man screamed and tried to get to the door, one leg dragging Lily behind him. Rudy held on until the man sliced his jaw with a combat knife. The pit bull squealed and dropped to the floor. The man raised the knife to stab Lily but Walther shouted a command and she released his leg. The attacker stumbled back, his blade harmlessly slicing air.

Enraged by Rudy's wound Walther yanked the Ruger but managed to keep from shooting his attacker. The man was already outside hobbling to his bike. As the motor coughed to life he snapped it into gear and roared off, tires screeching and bike careening. Moments later Walther heard two motorcycle race their engines simultaneously; one in the rear and one parked in the street, their metallic rumble rising in stereo.

And then it was quiet.

Rudy whimpered and Walther picked the dog up and carried him into the surgical unit to treat his bloody jaw Lily trailing at his heels.

Later while cleaning up the reception area he found a torn fragment of faded denim Lily had torn from the man's jeans.

It was all Walther would need to exterminate him.

+ + +

The men from Texas had broken a prime rule:
Nobody parties until the job's done.

Chad wouldn't go to the emergency room knowing they would insist on painful rabies shots and ID. Instead Fred and Ash bought peroxide, antiseptic cream, bandages, dental floss and a few sewing needles of different size.

They went back to the motel where Chad downed three OxyContin pills along with what was left of the tequila. To stay alert he also took a healthy snort of cocaine. Of course Fred and Ash had to do a line as well. Then Fred went to work stitching up the worst of the gashes on Chad's forearm while Ash went out for burgers, beer and more tequila. By the time Ash returned Chad was half dozing in front of the TV and Fred was browsing his mobile for escort services.

"He seemed to know we were comin'," Fred said while they were waiting for the hookers.

"Probably has cameras," Chad mumbled from his chair. "saw me checkin' the Corvette. Won't see us comin' next time."

"When's next time?" Ash said, washing his burger down with a swig of beer.

"When I say so."

The razor edge in his tone answered all other questions.

Chad had more tequila, another oxy and another line. The oxy and alcohol overcame the coke and he fell asleep, occasionally snoring.

Ashe looked at Fred and they immediately did more lines. Then Fred called an escort service.

"You sure?" Ash said. "Chad'll be pissed."

"He'll sleep right through it. Anyway he's here in the back and we can party in the front room. We're gonna need more tequila, beer and coca cola."

"Market's ten minutes away."

"Guess you better get goin' before they close."

Fred went into the bathroom and slicked back what was left of his hair. He checked himself sideways and decided his girth was acceptable. Then he popped a Viagra.

On Ash's return they moved the party to the room facing the street. Fred had stitched Chad's arm there earlier and he hid the bloody compresses and medical gear then washed his hands. While waiting for the whores he rolled up some prime weed he scored in Acapulco.

By the time the hookers arrived Fred and Ash were feeling no pain. The girls were pretty and had short skirts and long legs. Toni was a creole and Gina a blonde from Mississippi. They enjoyed their work and were relieved their clients weren't salesmen. The girls also appreciated the coke and tequila and put on a show for the boys, undressing each other. Then they turned down the lights and partied hard.

Afterwards Toni and Gina began to gather their things. It was nearly three a.m. and they were waiting for a cab. Fred was passed out on the floor and Ash was taking care of the fee.

"You call me personally next time sugar," Toni said. "I wrote down my number."

Gina lifted her head. "What's that smell? Did somebody die?"

Toni wrinkled her nose. "Oh yeah. That's one bad stink."

There was a noise at the door, as if someone was looking for the right room.

"There's our cab." Toni said, "Just in time. Bye sugar."

She flashed a farewell smile and opened the door.

A howling tornado of pitiless fangs and raking claws flooded the room with a whirling ferocity that sprayed blood and ribbons of flesh on the walls and ceilings.

It exploded and evaporated within minutes leaving four bodies that looked like they had been churned inside a high-speed blender with the top off.

Later the medical examiner would have difficulty matching up the body parts.

Chapter 20

News of the massacre went national. Images of the cordoned-off motel kept looping through the morning news. By afternoon the victims were revealed to be two bikers from Texas. They had registered under false names but a trace on their motorcycle plates showed they were Fredrick Munson and Alfred Ashton both with long rap sheets for violent crimes. The identity of the female victims was yet to be determined.

Case closed Les thought, watching an in-depth TV report. Bikers, drugs, gangs, cartels, same old story. No mention of the cemetery murders on yesterday's news. But Les knew the gruesome executions were similar to those of the hairy creatures he had been tracking.

Correction, who were tracking him.

Les made a note to find another place to stay. For all of Melody's professed love and loyalty she refused to let him sleep over at her place.

Women.

Totally uninhibited sexually Melody was quite reserved when it came to her past or her privacy. Now that they were working together that might pose a problem. He shared this place with Dave…

Les stopped short, still unsettled by what happened to his partner.

Then he remembered. "The bartender at Minny's. The dude with the black nails, Carson. Les decided to pay him a visit.

A call to the hospital assured him that Dave was recuperating but still needed rest. Jennifer was at his side.

Right now nobody's at my side except Mrs Glock, he thought ruefully.

A new side light on the Motel Massacre as it was now known, caught his attention. The newscaster announced that a third biker had registered with the victims but had left the scene. Investigators believe he was in another room at the time of the killings.

A third biker. Les filed the information away. It was too soon to visit the crime scene. The Half Note Motel would be crawling with cops and reporters.

It was still early in the day so he checked his emails before he went out for something to eat. On impulse he went to the drop they'd set up with Director Easton and found a request to meet.

Les replied immediately and Easton chose T-Coons. It was one of Dave's favorite spots in Lafayette. He wondered if the choice had any significance.

"It's short ribs Tuesday," Easton confided as they scanned the specials on the lunch menu, "and I'm a sucker for the sausage biscuits."

"I'm a sucker period. Didn't you approve my request for personal leave?"

"Sure did. But you're still on the case aren't you?"

It wasn't a question.

"You want me to lay off right?"

"Wrong. I want to help you— unofficially of course," He slid his menu across the table. "Look underneath."

Les pulled out a large envelope and put in his lap.

"What is it?"

"I decided to have our guys find out if the Fairmont where you're staying has street surveillance cameras. Turns out they do."

"You got a video of the attack?"

"Not quite. That part was out of range. But there's a fairly decent image of that van you reported. And the driver."

Les slipped two digital photos of a van parked at the curb between the parking lot and the motel. One was a side view of the vehicle. The other picture was taken from above and looked down at the windshield. While dark, the image clearly showed the driver behind the wheel.

Rage squeezed his throat.

"Serb," he rasped, "Ernst Bauer." He glared at Easton. "We asked you to flag his name with Motor Vehicles. He license…"

"Coming up for renewal. I get all the memos Hensen. You've got to learn to trust me here."

Les sat back and took a deep breath.

"So it's Director Lake, is that it?""

Easton shrugged. "Virgil has assistants. We're narrowing the focus on that end."

"What are we looking at exactly?"

"Possible far right conspiracy. KKK hooks up with an armed militia."

"Armed is one thing, cannibalism is another. You saw the news. What I can't figure is what those bikers from Texas have to do with this."

"You figure the killers are the same boys who got our agents and assaulted your partner?"

"Not assaulted—attacked," Les corrected. "This massacre was just like the others. Same MO, same missing organs, the whole nine."

Easton narrowed his eyes. "I'll look into it. Meantime let's order some of these smothered ribs."

+ + +

Les left the restaurant feeling slightly better about Easton. But the fury ignited by the photo of Serb persisted. *I should have nailed him when I had him,* Les ranted silently, *instead I let him play me.*

He tried to remind himself that even if he had brought Serb in the bastard seemed to have a protector. He could be a government informant or he might be connected. It was easy to get connected in New Orleans Les reflected, but he still felt responsible for failing to stop Serb before the scumbag had a chance to drive that death van...

The sky turned metallic grey and lightning danced on the horizon on bright spidery legs. A sudden breeze swept a cool mist from the gulf that soon became a heavy downpour, which drenched the streets and caught Les on foot, blocks from his motel.

He took refuge in a tiny side street bar called Nanny Mojo. The bar accommodated six stools and there were four candlelit tables in the rear. It was dark inside and as his eyes adjusted to the low light Les saw the tattered Voodoo flags, the horseshoe tied with a red ribbon, the black cross with a silver nail protruding from its center, the snake and the frog floating inside separate mason jars, the mummified bat and other dusty occult artifacts decorating the walls. The shelves too held plaster statues and tiny shrines in between the bottles.

A young woman wearing a white turban and white dress was behind the bar and a grizzled African man wearing a beaded hat and a blue Moroccan shirt sat on one of the stools. The atonal chords of Middle Eastern music and drumming rain seemed to form a curtain that shut off the outside world as Les entered.

Les took a stool at the corner of the bar facing the entrance. The old man sipped beer from the bottle and followed his progress with calm detachment.

The young woman had her back to Les and when she turned his brow furrowed as if trying to recall something.

"May I help you?"

Her clear violet eyes regarded him curiously, a bemused smile at the corner of her perfect pink mouth. She had honey skin a shade darker than her dress and wispy blond hair tucked under her turban.

Her beauty glowed like candlelight in the small, dusky room

But Les was taken aback by something else, a sense of recognition. The same feeling he'd experienced when he first met Melody.

"Uh do you serve coffee?" he asked.

She half grinned. "Brewed a fresh pot five minutes ago."

"Must have known I was coming."

His joking remark landed like Katrina. The old man's head jerked up from his beer and the girl's expression clouded over.

"Why do you think that?" she said evenly.

Les smiled. "It's a joke. Actually I came in by accident, to get out of the rain."

She nodded as if she knew better. She turned to retrieve some items. Minutes later she placed a cup of fragrant black coffee and a small pitcher of cream on the bar. No sugar. The way he liked it.

Les tested the coffee. It was delicious.

"Very good thanks," he said looking around at the décor. "You have unusual stuff here."

"Tell the truth most of it's dime store voodoo paraphernalia you find everywhere in New Orleans."

"How about the rest of it?"

She paused. "You have to know what you are looking at."

Les detected a note of challenge in her lyrical southern accent. It was charming and disconcerting.

Slow down Les told himself, *you're not on vacation, and you have a girlfriend to whom you've recently sworn loyalty. Furthermore you don't even know her name.*

"Are you Nanny Mojo?"

The old man sniffed as if the idea was ludicrous. The girl too gave Les a condescending smile reserved for the ignorant and infirm.

"That would be my grandmother."

"She started this place?"

"My grandfather opened this place in forty five. He named it after his wife who is a famous healer in these parts."

"Is? She still practices?"

The old man spoke up. "Ninety two and works every day. Runs her own herb shop in New Iberia. That's her picture by the cash register."

"Papa." She said it quietly but the old man's lips pressed shut and he turned away.

The woman in the picture was perhaps thirty with the same clear eyes, oval face and proud bearing as her granddaughter. In the photo she had a dark turban and wore two thick strands of charms around her slender neck. Regal and mysterious she looked like a priestess.

"She looks like a priestess," Les said.

"In a way she is, you want more coffee?"

"Sure thanks. Still raining."

She silently refilled his cup and busied herself with paperwork, writing in a composition book while the music intensified. A woman's voice floated above an orchestra of strings, oboes, pipes and other wind instruments playing rhythmic counterpoint to the rain outside.

Les recognized the legendary voice from the years he'd spent on special ops in Iraq.

"Isn't that Oum Kalthoum?"

The girl looked up and smiled. "Yes. A great artist."

"Leda honey can I get a beer?"

Her smile turned to an icy glare as she uncapped a fresh bottle. It was clear she didn't want her name bandied about. "Here you are *Papa Ezekiel*" she said pronouncing each syllable deliberately.

Papa got the point and heaved a sad sigh

Les drank his coffee unwilling to offend the lovely Leda before he even knew her full name. *I'm definitely having early midlife crisis* Les reflected. Somehow he knew Melody would not appreciate his wandering eye—he certainly didn't. Normally he was a serial monogamist, a one-woman guy. *But there's nothing normal about this case* he noted.

No excuses. Les silently drank his coffee and watched the rain. In a few minutes, which was a bit too soon for him, the downpour slackened to occasional gusts. Unwilling to linger beyond the excuse of shelter Les dropped a five on the bar and stood up.

"Thanks for the coffee and music," he said.

"Come see us anytime," Leda said over her shoulder.

He wanted to come back in ten minutes but knew it was an adolescent fantasy. He was a serious man with serious problems. People's lives depended on him.

"Maybe the next rain will give me a reason," he said lamely.

Papa Ezekiel leaned back. "Everybody walks into Nanny's for a reason."

+ + +

Benny didn't like winter. He didn't understand what people found so great about snow. It ruined his shoes, got down behind his collar and melted over the floor as if a dog had peed there. However for reasons beyond his control he was forced to move his gaming operation to Boston.

Gaming. Benny used the term consistently in conversation. Much classier than gambling which was his specialty. Benny the bookie with a billion dollar brain. His ability to calculate odds better than the computers had built a profitable boutique operation in Louisiana. The college football take alone had made him wealthy.

He didn't mind spreading it around: the cops, commissioners, local mayor, whatever. They were all on his pad and they all had their function. It was the Big Easy and everybody got fat.

Then the mob decided to take a cut. The first year was fine but they got greedy. This Don Benito who thought he was Carlos Marcello actually wanted forty percent.

Benny came from Brooklyn and was well connected on his father's side. Rather than get involved in a war the New York head of the five families Phil Caffoni ruled that Benny could move his book to Boston with the blessing of Blackie Devlin who ran Massachusetts.

So that was it. 10 months later he was living on Beacon Hill and maintained an office jammed with computers that could process bets from Dubai to Hollywood.

The greedy Don was left with the local action in New Orleans. And Benny was left freezing his well-tailored ass up north.

In Louisiana he could wear more colorful clothes but up here he had to dress like a banker and all that flannel and tweed gave him skin rash.

It was a trade-off. Up here he was Ben Frank, respected head of a gaming company. Down there he was Benny Brains the bookie.

Right now Mr. Ben Frank was due at a political dinner for Mayor Ballard. As a major contributor to the Mayor's campaign Benny had leverage at city hall.

At sixty Benny was reasonably fit. He was tall and naturally thin with a narrow hatchet face and droopy grey eyes that viewed all humanity as *vig* on a fixed race.

The car was waiting at the curb but the slush washed over the sidewalk soaking the soles of his hand-made Italian wing tips.

"I put towels on the floor sir," the driver said as he shut the door.

Benny wiped his shoes. "I'm glad somebody knows what they're doing. They tell you the address?"

"Yes sir, the mayor's home."

Uncomfortable in his cashmere overcoat he settled back for the short ride across snow-crusted streets to Cambridge where Mayor Ballard had a modest mansion.

Along the way he made a call to a trusted associate in New Orleans.

"Hello Franny? It's me. I've got a tip on the Jets game Sunday."

"I'll call you back."

The tip was their code. Franny would call him back on a pre-paid phone that was untraceable. You never knew with the fucking feds—or Don Benito..

His phone beeped. It was Franny.

"I hope you really have a tip for me because business is way off lately."

"Problem down there?"

"Big time. Two of our top people got whacked."

"You serious? Anybody know who did it?"

"It looks like Bruno shot Paulie then off himself but… I don't know."

"Don't know what?"

"They didn't have any blood in them."

"In who?"

"The bodies, they were drained dry. Like a vampire."

"Vampire? You said they were shot."

"Yeah, but…"

"So what's this this vampire bullshit?"

"I don't know. Anyway the old man is all over this. He's got everybody lookin' for this missing pilot of his. That's how we lost Bruno and Paulie."

No big loss Benny thought, Bruno was an ape and Paulie was a weasel. "Sounds bad," he said, no wonder business is down."

"For the count. I should've gone with you when I had the chance. But you know the old man."

"My door is always open… the old man mention me?"

"I never see him. But Cozy asks here and there if I know how you're doing."

"Tell him I'm freezing my ass off."

"Speaking of Cozy I heard the old men called outside help. That's like an insult."

"Who's the new man?"

"Get this he's some kind of ex-priest. Has a rep for clean work."

"Maybe this priest can find your vampire."

"Who the fuck knows. I don't need a priest I need a sure thing. You got anything for me in that brain?"

"Yeah Buffalo plus three first half. Then take the second half odds and bet the Jets to win."

"Thanks Benny."

"Please Franny do me a favor..."

"I know, sorry, thanks *Ben*. I need to associate—like Ben Siegel in Bugsy. You see that movie?"

Benny sighed. "Listen I have to hang up. I'm having dinner with the fucking mayor."

It was the usual political dinner. Strong cocktails, mediocre food, followed by boring speeches all of which had the same point. Support us we'll support you.

Benny scanned the room. There were a number of available women there, some married others potential mistresses on the make.

He had enjoyed a brief affair with the wife of state Senator McVeigh but she seemed busy with a real estate developer. A young brunette who had possibilities was engrossed in a conversation with a priest. On hand that evening was a bishop and two priests which only served to dampen the party

Benny decided to barge right in a get the brunette off the hook. She was probably praying to get rid of the priest. He'd have a little fun at the priest's expense.

"Excuse me father could I ask you a question?"

The priest smiled patiently. "Of course."

"Have you ever performed an exorcism?" Benny smiled at the brunette. "In Louisiana they still believe in voodoo you know."

To Benny's surprise the priest waved his colleague over. "You should talk to Father Smith. He just arrived from New Orleans."

"So you're Mr. Ben Frank," Father Smith said when he introduced himself. "Just the man I've been looking for."

Father Smith was tall and athletic with a large jaw and grey eyes that beamed at him. "You were a great contributor to our athletic program in New Orleans. I was told you relocated to Boston."

How the hell would a priest know I relocated here? Benny thought, *half my family doesn't know.*

Immediately alarms went off. He remembered his conversation with Franny. Any New Orleans connection meant nothing but trouble.

"I hope now that you're in Boston you won't forget us."

"Oh I won't father, you can depend on it."

Benny looked around. The brunette had wandered off and he was stuck with Father Smith. Suddenly he needed to leave.

"Excuse me father but I'm late for another meeting," he said walking quickly to the improvised coat check.

He texted the driver to pull up to the entrance. As he pulled on his overcoat he looked back.

Father Smith was right behind him.

"I wanted to give you my card," the priest said.

Benny snatched it. "Yes thank you father. Goodnight."

He practically ran to the waiting town car spooked by the priest's familiarity with him and his whereabouts. True he had donated money to build a kid's gym after Katrina. But how would the priest know that offhand?

Gratefully he saw his driver holding open the door. Climbing inside the warm interior he saw the driver had laid fresh towels on the floor.

Benny made a note to commend the driver to the service he had hired and to give him a big tip.

Getting away from that priest was a big relief.

When they arrived at his house the driver ran around and opened his door.

As Benny got out he noticed the driver wore a narrow purple scarf around his neck.

"That scarf won't keep you very warm."

"It's a stole. It's not to keep me warm."

"What's it for then?"

"The last rites."

A moment later Benny's famous brains were spattered over the towels

Chapter 21

Les packed up and switched motels. He considered moving to New Orleans but decided to stick around Lafayette until Dave recovered.

Unfortunately he wasn't much help to Jennifer, Les reflected. He hoped Dave could explain why.

Explain why you're about to take an unarmed civilian on a potentially dangerous investigation Les asked himself.

He knew the answer. It came in three parts. The first was located between his legs, the second being he couldn't convince her otherwise and the last was that Melody was smart and motivated.

Still he knew she'd never wear the Kevlar he had in the trunk.

When she appeared in his headlights he knew why he'd agreed. She was a dark Aphrodite in in a low cut Ivory blouse almost the same shade as her smooth breasts. Her long black hair curled around green eyes that gleamed catlike in the light.

She skipped lithely to the passenger side got in and kissed him," I've missed you since I got up."

A rush of desire swept over his regrets.

"I could have picked you up at your motel."

"I like to take a walk in the evening. Stimulates my appetite."

"I'll walk with you sometime."

She gave him a sad smile. "Perhaps you will."

"Your lipstick is smudged."

Melody dove into her shoulder bag for lipstick and tissues. Les licked his lips. "Tastes funny."

"It's new," she said wiping her mouth.

"There's a pull down mirror and light above the windshield."

"Don't need it thanks," she muttered applying fresh lipstick. There how's it look now?"

"Let's see if it passes the taste test."

Les kissed her again and felt a primal surge. Melody felt it too.

"Tastes delicious," he whispered.

"Let's eat first darling I'm starved."

Les put the car in gear. "You're beginning to sound like a wife."

"God forbid," Melody said. And she meant it.

The Gulf sky was covered by black clouds tinted orange by an occasional moon. Les and Melody didn't talk much for a while, listening to music and watching the ever changing horizon. Despite the silence there was a sense that they understood each other.

"This bartender that drugged you is called Carson?"

"Yes. His fingernails are painted black and he has a black lightning tattoo on each forearm."

"Observant," she teased.

"Hard not to notice. I need to get his full name without his getting suspicious. Remember, I'm a producer down here to make a film."

"Good cover."

"Dave's idea."

"What's my role?"

"Potential star, songwriter, take your pick."

"Songwriter suits me. Attracts more curiosity than envy. Everybody thinks they can write a song."

"Have you?"

"A few. They're personal."

"I'd like to hear one sometime."

"Sometime."

A blues band consisting of a bass, two guitars and drums, was on Minny's small stage when they walked in.

Carson waved from behind the bar and Les could feel his eyes follow them. They took a table against the wall far from the dance floor and speakers.

A waitress appeared and took their drink order. Melody had an absinthe and Les a beer. The special was fresh caught grilled tuna with rice and sweet potato fries. He ordered the special for Melody and for himself grilled shrimp and salad.

Melody smiled. "Trying to lose weight?"

"Yeah, I've got a new girlfriend."

She laughed and leaned closer. "I like that. By the way was that the bartender you want to question? He's been staring since we came in."

"Probably thinks I'm going to make him a star."

"Or wondering why you're not dead."

The waitress returned with their drinks.

"Do we have a plan?" Melody asked.

"We'll have a late drink at the bar. Whatever he suggests have something else. I'll start in talking. You can help with that. I'm sure he'll be fascinated."

"What does that make you?" Melody sniffed.

"An FBI agent. This is business."

"Just kidding darling. I'll go you one better."

The arrival of their food interrupted her.

"So what's your one better?"

"After dinner. Have some of my tuna."

Melody ate with enthusiasm and when she had devoured her meal outlined her plan.

"Let's have an after-dinner drink at the bar," she suggested, wiping her mouth with a checkered napkin. .

"Think I already mentioned that."

"While we're talking to your friend leave to go to the men's room and let's see if I can get something."

"Worth a try."

Les paid the check and escorted Melody to the bar. He noticed that her passage through the dance floor left a wake of turned heads. Carson greeted them with a toothy smile from behind the bar.

"Good evening folks. Hoped you like the food."

"First rate. Melody this is Carson."

"My pleasure Miss Melody. That certainly is a beautiful name."

She flashed a magnetic smile. "Thank you Carson."

Carson straightened up. "What'll it bet folks?"

"Not that bourbon you served the other night," Les said, half joking. "Dave was so wasted he went off the road."

Carson screwed up his face in a concerned frown.

"Oh man I'm sure sorry. Dave alright?"

"He'll recover, but I'm not sure I will." Les was unable to blunt the edge in his tone.

"Why don't we have a cognac?" Melody said brightly.

Les managed a smile. "Good idea."

"Two cognacs." Carson moved off to pick a bottle from the top shelf.

"Is that how you question suspects in the FBI?" Melody whispered.

"I didn't question him."

"You weren't very subtle, you practically accused him. Now I'll have to talk him down."

Les shrugged. "Good cop, bad cop, just like the FBI."

Carson returned with two snifters and a small, cut glass bottle of Remy Martin XO Excellence.

"I hope you like this."

How could we not?" Melody purred. She examined the bottle. "You have superb taste."

Carson grinned shyly. "That's on my momma's side. She always liked the best."

Melody raised her glass. "To your mother and her good taste."

The cognac eased down his throat like warm honey and caught fire when it reached his stomach.

Les got off his stool. "Excuse me. I'll be right back."

"End of the bar and turn left," Carson said.

Les went to the restroom with new confidence in Melody's ability to pry some information from Carson.

He washed his hands and face, tried not to dwell on his reflection as he brushed back his hair and came back to the bar to find Carson engrossed in conversation with Melody. The bartender straightened up when Les appeared.

"Freshen up that cognac?"

"This is fine, I'm driving."

Carson nodded and moved off.

"Get what you need?"

"I'm meeting him when his shift is over, I'll get what we need then. "

"Correction, *we're* meeting him."

"It won't work. I'm supposed to score some coke. He's anxious to corner the coming movie crowd."

"We'll make it work, no way I'm sending you alone with that slimy horndog."

She kissed him lightly. "That's one of the sweetest things you've ever said to me."

Someone once said being in combat was hours of boredom followed by thirty seconds of sheer terror.

They waited out Melody's scheduled tryst in a ramshackle bar a few miles way. Les ordered coffee and Melody had another absinthe. Her ability to carry her liquor was close to phenomenal Les noted, and it didn't seem to affect her flawless skin.

The place was empty except for a couple slow dancing on the sawdust floor. They sat close together, talking occasionally. That was the nice thing about being with Melody, the comfortable silences. Of course she intuited what he was thinking more frequently than he would like, Les reflected.

"What do you think you can do that I can't?" Melody asked mildly.

"We don't know this guy or what kind of set up you'll be walking into."

"Carson thinks you're a movie producer."

"Is that why he slipped us a mickey the night Dave went down?"

"I know I can get more information with my methods," she sniffed.

"I'm not risking it. You don't know what we're dealing with here."

And you don't know who you're dealing with darling Melody thought sipping her absinthe.

She was due to meet Carson at two a.m. at the rear of Minny's. He told her had a place nearby.

The bar was dark and there was only a single truck in the lot when they arrived.

As they had planned, Melody parked well short of the rear, cut the headlights and Les rolled out the back door, gun in hand. He made his way along the wall, which was emblazoned with the owner's name in colors so bright he could see them clearly in the darkness. When he reached the end of building he pressed his face against the side and slowly rotated his head until he could see the rear of the bar.

There was a single light above the rear door and a line of garbage cans against the wall.

Carson was standing at the edge of the halo of light smoking a cigarette. He had changed into clean Levis and a blue short-sleeved shirt that showed off his muscles and lightning bolt tats.

He leaned into the light and squinted at his watch.

At the same time Les stepped around the corner, gun raised.

"Freeze Carson."

He kept his voice low but Carson got the message. He half lifted his arms.

"Listen man, this was her idea. I didn't know it was like that."

"Why the drugged bourbon Carson? Who are you working for?"

Before he got an answer hard steel smacked the back of his skull and he fell to his knees.

"He's working for me," somebody said.

Chapter 22

Father Clarence Dunn found his roman collar gained him favored treatment at the airport, as well as a certain measure of anonymity. With his black hat, tinted glasses and dark, non-descript clothes he faded out of people's radar. Most of them were engrossed in the tiny screen in their hands anyway Clarence mused settling back in his window seat on the red eye to New Orleans.

He allowed himself a scotch when the stewardess came along. It had been a long haul from Los Angeles where he had dispatched the gay son of a Chicago boss. Clarence understood. For the boss it was a matter of honor. For Father Dunn it was a matter of money

And moral duty.

He had been defrocked, cast from the church by a deviant faction within which he had threatened to expose.

Lies, false evidence, slander, calumny: any number of sins short of murder had been used against him.

Clarence supplied the murder when he took his revenge. Three priests died violently and a fourth fled to Argentina.

After the third he turned professional.

As a priest he had heard hundreds of confession and knew most humans were vain, weak, despicable creatures. And the men he killed were the worst of them.

So he was truly doing God's work.

Father Dunn was looking forward to seeing Don Benito again. He respected the Don's old school sense of blood justice. He shared these same values.

He had been pleased to act as the Don's emissary but after Boston he needed a bit of warm weather.

On landing at Louis Armstrong Airport he went directly to the men's room. When he emerged he was wearing an open collared black shirt, black cap and dark glasses. His fedora and jacket were in his bag.

The priest was now an anonymous tourist.

As instructed he took a cab to a safe house in the French Quarter provided by Cozy Costanza

He didn't have much in the way of belongings and in the morning he needed to acquire a suitable wardrobe.

The apartment was compact but comfortable with a large kitchen that overlooked a small garden that belonged to the house next door. The shower worked and the bed was comfortable. It was do fine for his brief stay.

He rose early as he did each day and knelt on the floor to say his prayers. Then he went for a walk.

He was angered at what he saw. Every block harbored new evidence of a depraved Sodom be it strip clubs, Voodoo shops, fortune tellers or harlots with insomnia. In the course of an hour he was solicited for drugs or sex at least a half dozen times.

He sought refuge in a church on Rampart Street called the Center of Jesus the Lord. A priest was saying early mass for a handful of worshippers.

Clarence took communion then lingered after mass to ask the priest for the best place to buy clerical clothing. Still too early to go shopping he bought a newspaper and found a café that was open for breakfast.

The news was full of the recent motel massacre and the mutilated bodies being found in the area. Obviously some psychotic serial killer Clarence speculated, professionals like himself did quick, clean work.

After breakfast he visited the store recommended by the priest and walked back to his flat carrying a large black athletic bag full of new equipment.

He took a nap, a shower and changed into fresh clothes. Then he strolled over to the Cana bar to have a chat with his handler.

+ + +

Cozy was in his office when the day man came to tell him a priest wanted to see him.

"Another charity right? Okay send him in."

An emaciated looking man wearing an ivory panama hat a sand colored linen suit and a black shirt with a roman collar sauntered in. His sharp, narrow face was partially obscured by rose tinted glasses. He took off his hat freeing a shock of thick white hair. It was when he removed his glasses that Cozy saw his deep set yellow eyes the color of old mustard. There was no light, no spark of humanity, only a flat, accusing stare.

"I'm Father Dunn. I was told you might help our cause." As he spoke he scanned the room as if trying to spot any cameras or recording devices.

"I'll do everything I can Father. Would you like any refreshment? Coffee, a drink…?"

"I take it the name of this establishment is based on the New Testament?"

"Yeah Cana like the wedding where Jesus changed water into wine…"

"I consider it blasphemy to pervert the meaning of the holy book to promote drunkenness and licentious behavior."

"Wait a minute now, we have real priests come in here and they all…"

"I *am* a real priest."

His voice crackled like an electric shock sending alarms blaring in Cozy's brain. He glanced at the man's hands half expecting to see a weapon

"Sure, right, I meant church affiliated. No offense."

"None taken sir. Now to business. There's the matter of your contribution."

The tension in the room subsided a notch but Cozy was on full alert. *This dude is fucking loony tunes*, he thought. *And extremely dangerous.* The barely repressed malevolence in Dunn's scrawny body radiated like a black sun.

Cozy took a thick envelope from a drawer and carefully pushed it across the desk. "I trust it will meet your needs."

Father Dunn put the envelope in his jacket without opening it.

"Now then, tell me everything you know about this harlot you're looking for."

When Father Dunn left Cozy helped himself to a large scotch. He had encountered all kinds of violent criminals and killers but his guy was out of *Dante's Inferno*.

For some reason he was completely disinterested in the missing pilot. He was focused on finding this girl Melody. Cozy reminded him that they needed her alive and Father Dunn had assured him he understood.

However Cozy was unconvinced.

He sensed the priest had an agenda all his own. Which made him very nervous. He was already on the hook with the Don over this. He didn't need a loose cannon making things worse.

So it was with enormous relief that Cozy received a call from Falconi telling him that one of his runners had located the girl Melody in New Iberia. He was sending three experienced hitters to pick her up and deliver her in handcuffs.

Cozy silently thanked his saints. The sooner he wrapped this up the sooner he could send Father Dunn back to planet Wacko.

Chapter 23

The man with the gun frisked Les efficiently and relieved him of his Glock and his knife. He missed the Cobra at the small if his back.

"Where's the fucking girl?"

A slap with the man's gun punctuated the question.

"Check the parking lot," the man barked not waiting for Les to answer.

Les heard the sound of feet scrambling over gravel and pecan shells. He hoped Melody had the sense to drive away and call 911.

"I'm leaving okay?" Carson said.

"Get the fuck out of here."

Les heard Carson shuffle off.

The man found his wallet and read off the information on his ID.

"Lester Hensen F fucking BI. What is this a drug sting? Cause there ain't more than an eight ball to find, if that. This bitch Melody is playing you."

His gun smacked Les again. Stunned Les staggered forward and fell. He heard the man call on his phone. "Arnie? Talk to me... Go find out where he is," he said to someone.

Up on one knee Les turned slowly, one hand fumbling for the spring loaded blackjack in his waistband until something slammed him down again.

Instinctively he rolled and tried to scramble to a defensive position but this time it took longer to react.

He heard a shot, then two more.

By the time he managed to sit up and push himself to his feet it was over.

Two men lay on the ground. They were dead. One man's hand still gripped a gun. Les checked but it wasn't his.

He found his Glock nearby and hurried around the corner to find Melody. She was standing in the darkened parking lot talking to Carson. When Les came near he heard Melody questioning him. Carson's responses were wooden as if he was drugged.

"I called Falconi."

"Why?"

"The money. Five thousand dollar bounty to anyone who finds you."

"Are these his men?"

"Yes."

"Did this Falconi tell you to drug us?" Les said.

Carson didn't seem to hear him.

Melody looked at Les and lifted a finger. "Did Falconi tell you to drug this man?" she repeated.

"No."

"Who did?" Melody persisted.

"Serb."

"Ask him where we can find Serb," Les said, excited now.

"Where can we find Serb?"

"Bar Noir in New Orleans," Carson said as if reciting a forgotten name.

"How do you know Serb?" Melody persisted.

"The Golden Circle. Doctor Heck."

"What's the Golden Circle?"

Carson extended his arms and pointed to his lightning bolt tattoos. "White brotherhood."

"Who's Doctor Heck?" Les said.

The distant whine of a siren pierced the quiet

"We'd better go," Melody said.

"What about Carson?"

"He won't remember anything."

"Ask him about Doctor Heck."

"I know who he is—move."

Half running to the car Les saw another man lying on the ground.

"What happened back there?" Les said as he gunned the car out of the lot with the headlights off.

"They would have killed us."

"You killed them?"

"Of course." Les could hear the siren coming closer and he saw lights sweeping the tips of the dark trees ahead. He pulled off the road onto the shoulder and waited until the police cruiser flashed past.

"You shot all three?" he asked quietly.

"Not exactly." She shifted away from him, face averted.

"How exactly?"

For a long moment the question hung in the air. Then she leaned close, green eyes shining in the darkness.

"I'm a vampire."

+ + +

"You don't know what happened? Sal rip his face off."

Carson's hands were bound but his feet scrambled to push his chair back from the brutal hulk reaching for his throat.

"Wait, wait, I'll tell you what I remember. Just wait."

"Sal, let him talk."

Carson took a deep breath. "This is how it went down. The girl was supposed to meet me in back of Minny's to score some blow. I recognize her from the description and call you Mr. Falconi. You send three guys out and they stake the place out. Only this movie producer shows up instead of the girl.

"One of your boys slaps a gun upside the guy's head and tells me to walk. Next thing I know I'm standing in the parking lot with three dead bodies on the ground and police lights in my face."

"My question is why are *you* still alive?"

"That's what the cop Orsini kept asking me. I still don't know."

Falconi lit a cigarette. "Do you know who got you out of jail?"

Carson blinked and tried to smile. "You did Mr. Falconi. And I appreciate…"

"The only reason you lived this long is because you didn't mention my name."

"Mr. Falconi I would never rat anybody out. Ask anybody,"

"There's no record of your being booked," Falconi went on, "No fingerprints, no mug shots, so when you disappear…"

A man entered the room and whispered something in Falconi's ear. Falconi seemed annoyed but resigned.

"You're going to meet somebody special," he said, "lie to him and he prays at your funeral."

Carson began to whimper his innocence until Falconi cut him off.

"We're done here. Let's go Sal."

Carson took short breaths trying to control his nausea and his bladder. "Why didn't I keep my mouth shut? he thought. Got myself jammed for a lousy five grand. He heard the door open and looked up, half hopeful half terrified.

He couldn't believe it.

A tall, thin priest with white hair and intense yellow eyes walked into the room. His narrow face was the color of dry white wallpaper that had wrinkled and cracked. Carson wailed softly when he saw the purple stole over the man's black jacket. He had been an altar boy and knew the stole was used for Extreme Unction, the last rites.

The priest regarded Carson with a manic smile reminiscent of a scrawny vulture eyeing a corpse.

He lifted one hand and showed Carson the Bible. "I have the power to absolve you of this." His smile grew narrow and he lifted the other hand. It held a Ruger 45 automatic fitted with a silencer.

"I also have the power to administer severe penance if you reuse to repent."

His voice lowered to a whisper.

"Now my son I want you to confess the truth. What happened last night?"

Voice shuddering and belly heaving Carson blurted the same thing he had told Falconi. With the same result.

"Ah, my son, my foolish son." The priest put the Bible down on a nearby stool and produced a vial of liquid. Carson knew what it was. He strained to avoid the priest's fingers as he moistened his forehead with oil.

"Do you repent your sins my son?"

"Yes, I do, I do ,Father really," Carson sobbed, "I swear I don't remember anything…"

He heard the priest murmur something in Latin. Then he saw the Ruger pointing at him like God's accusing finger and twisted his head away.

"Oh, Jesus," he cried, eyes squeezed shut.

Someone must have been listening.

Seconds passed.

Finding himself alive with his skull still intact Carson opened his eyes.

The priest was bent close to him peering at his neck.

"Where did you get that bite?" he rasped, licking his lips. His breath was stale.

"Bite? I don't know, last night in jail maybe."

"Maybe not," the priest said almost to himself. "Now tell me son—and this is very important do you understand?"

"Yes, Father."

"What is the very last thing you can remember?

Carson shut his eyes, desperately probing his tattered memory.

"The guy with the gun tells me to walk so I go around to where I parked my truck. And I see Melody talking to this guy Arnie. Then she looks at me funny and comes towards me. And I… I… that's it. I wake up and the cops are all over me."

Eyes closed, Carson could feel the priest pull away from him. He felt the rope around his wrists loosen and heard the words... "*et te absolvo.*"

Carson looked up. The priest was walking out of the room.

Weeping softly Carson sat in the chair until he was certain no one was outside waiting to kill him.

Chapter 24

Les found it difficult to wrap his mind around the concept.

"Vampire you say. As in Dracula."

"As in Melody. I am neither a cheap novel nor a mindless film."

"But you drink blood."

"Not always. Certainly not your blood."

They were in her new motel room, a suite with blankets over the bedroom windows. Melody was lying on the bed her black hair spread over the pillow and her narrowed eyes regarding him like a cat regards cream. .

"What about crosses, garlic, stakes through the heart?"

"The stake thing is nasty," she said with a small smile, "but it can be survived. The crosses and garlic are a myth."

"Can you turn into a bat?"

"No but I move pretty damn fast. Fast enough to keep you from getting shot."

"I told you it was a set up."

"Who was setting who up? Don't you get it darling? I can survive the odd bullet, they can't survive me."

"Then what am I doing here?" Les said quietly. "You can take care of the entire mob yourself."

"Not really. Tonight we had the element of surprise. I'm not invincible darling. Bullets don't kill but they definitely slow me down—and then I'm vulnerable to a long messy death."

When Les didn't answer she added, "One thing I can promise you. my victims die happy."

"Hey that's really comforting," Les said, "I think I need a drink."

"Pour me one too."

Of course there was nothing but absinthe. Les dispensed with the ritual sugar cube but added extra water to his glass.

"You said you know this Doctor Heck that Carson mentioned." He handed her a drink.

"Yes."

"How?"

"I provided some necessary supplies for certain experiments he's been conducting."

"You still do business with him?"

"No. However I believe I can resume my affiliation."

"What kind of supplies are we talking about, drugs?"

She took a long swallow of the potent green liquid.

"Submissive males."

"What is it a sex thing?"

"Nothing that interesting. I thing he performs medical experiments."

"You don't know?"

She shrugged. "I just delivered the product."

Sensing his displeasure she added, "The word was out in certain quarters. Carson is probably a supplier as well."

"Carson, Serb, Heck," Les recited, "We're finally getting somewhere on my side. "He lifted his glass. "And you've done some damage on your side."

She lifted a smooth white arm and beckoned him to the bed.

Les looked down at his glass. "Maybe we should call it a night."

Melody sat up. "Why darling are you afraid of me?" she teased.

He glanced at her, eyes level. "How did you know?"

"Tell me, do you ever have flashes of intuition, hunches, that sort of thing?"

"Actually I do."

"Ever thought about it?"

"What are you getting at?"

"You're unusually gifted psychically," she smiled, "as well as physically. I felt it as soon as I saw you."

"Which part?"

"You felt something special too. You can't deny that."
He lit a cigarette. "I felt a strong attraction but…"
"And something more admit it."
Les lifted his hands in mock surrender. "I had strong feelings yes and still do. But psychic? I'm a soldier Melody not a magician."
"Well I do have psychic powers but when it comes to you I keep them locked away in a safe. You carry your weapons openly. Don't you see? I would never harm you. We have a bond that goes deeper than love."
He took a deep breath. "That scares me too. But I have a hunch you're telling the truth."
"Well hold on to those hunches my darling, "she whispered coming closer, "they'll keep you alive."
After making love they lay close and discussed the next day's agenda. They decided to go to the Bar Noir together. Les would check the motel where the bikers had been massacred.
Abruptly, as Les started dozing off Melody started pushing him out of bed."
"Time to go darling. I need my beauty sleep."
"Why can't I stay?"
She kissed him. "I might devour you in my sleep. Now go. A lady vampire needs privacy."
"Where's the coffin?" he said searching for his trousers.
"Now you're being gauche. I'll explain the rules some other time. It's nearly sunrise."

+ + +

Driving back to his motel Les felt numb, still unable to process what had gone down in the past six hours.
When he reached his room he fell asleep immediately.
He got up at noon and out of habit opened the laptop. He was surprised to see a curt message from Easton waiting in his dummy Draft box.
Contact Detective Hank Orsini Lafayette PD.

Les stared at the words for a few moments then dragged himself into the bathroom.

Somewhat revived by a cold shower he took his time. Odds were Orsini was probably gorging at an expensive table.

His own odds were bleak Let reflected. He was emotionally entangled with a beautiful woman who was either a vampire or a lunatic serial killer.

Both of them were being hunted by the local Mafia and a pack of rabid beasts led by a scumbag known as Serb and a mad doctor. Not to mention that a local dick had just blown his cover.

It was a radical departure from life as he knew it.

He called the hospital. Jennifer was there and sounded upbeat.

"He's improving by the day," she said lightly, "and been asking for you."

"Tell him I'm okay but I'll be out of town."

"What's up Les?"

Her tone alerted him that Dave hadn't told her anything.

"Business as usual," he said casually."

Whatever this is it sure ain't business as usual Les thought. He walked to a barbecue joint that still served breakfast. Along the way he bought a newspaper.

Small white clouds salted the sky and a light breeze brought the scent of still water and tropical flowers until he neared his destination.

The aroma of meat being smoked and grilled in the small back yard of Little Mac's wafted onto the sidewalk before he entered. Inside was a hot grill and a counter with the menu chalked on an overhead blackboard, Les was tempted to try the grilled Catfish and sweet potatoes but decided to keep it simple with a cheese omelet, bacon, grits and coffee.

The motel massacre had dropped to the third page in favor of the three dead hoods found in New Iberia.

There was a sidebar on the mystery third biker who had registered as Cole Younger.

The front page proclaimed *Mafia Shoot Out* and the story identified the three men as known mobsters with rap sheets in Florida and Louisiana. The police conclusion was they shot each other in a drug deal gone wrong or a turf war.

No connection between the two was suggested.

The short order cook served his breakfast on a heavy white plate and he poked at his food. The thick slices of bacon reminded him too much of the mutilated bodies he'd seen including Dave's. He drank three cups of coffee and ate his grits and omelet. Despite a generous tip the short order cook seemed to take the uneaten bacon personally.

It was still early so Les walked back to the motel and opened his laptop. There was another message from Easton.

Keep Orsini on need to know. Cite national security.

Obviously Easton knew Orsini was dirty.

Still wondering how Orsini found out he was FBI Les drove to Lafayette Police headquarters. On arrival he passed through security. It was then Les realized how Orsini had found out.

His wallet was gone.

He had left it behind in Minny's parking lot.

It took about fifteen minutes before he was cleared to go to Orsini's office. By then he had come up with a plausible explanation. Unfortunately his cover was blown to smithereens Les realized. From now on he was everybody's target—especially the mole inside the bureau itself.

Orsini was seated behind a desk cluttered with stacked paper files, empty coffee containers, a paper plate crusted with tomato sauce, newspapers and the remnants of a glazed doughnut.

His wide, mirthless smile made him resemble a pasty white pumpkin.

"Well hello sir. Please sit down. Would you like some iced tea or something stronger?"

"Thank you Detective Orsini but I'm fine."

"Mighty fine acting job you boys pulled off. Had me goin' myself."

"Part of the job, you know how its is."

Orsini pursed his lips and nodded solemnly. "Course *I* do. Some better than others though."

"Guess I'm not very good or I wouldn't be here," Les said smoothly, "How did you find out?"

"You don't know?"

"All I know is somebody contacted my boss. My cover is exposed and here I am."

"What exactly were you boys working on?"

"Actually your two missing detectives Delcie and Morgan were involved. We believe they're connected to two dead FBI agents in New Orleans."

Despite the heat Orsini was wearing an eggshell colored linen suit that matched his pallor. He leaned away, his immense bulk filling the chair like an octopus backing into a cave.

"Wished you'd shared the information with us poor local detectives," Orsini said. He wasn't smiling.

Les shrugged. "When our guys were murdered looking for your missing detectives the Bureau figured there could be a mole in the Lafayette PD."

Orsini's eyes were slits in his jowly face. "Could very well be. I'll have to look into it. But these days I'm real busy. Just caught me a triple homicide."

"Saw that in the papers. Minny's, I was just there."

Orsini reached into his desk and produced the wallet.

"I know you were Les. Matter of fact we found this at the crime scene. How do you think that happened?"

Les shook his head. "I used my credit card when I paid the dinner tab. I must have left it at the bar… or dropped it."

"And you didn't notice your wallet and badge were missin' 'till now? You expect me to believe that?"

Les reached into his pocket and took out a wad of cash.

"You know how it is Detective Orsini. When you're undercover you don't want to leave a paper trial."

"Until last night."

"I was with a friend."

"Lady friend."

"Yes."

"Lots of people seemed interested in that lady."

"That depends on who you know."

Orsini's features hardened into a pugnacious scowl.

"What's that mean agent Hensen?"

"It means the only people looking for her are local mafia. That's why she's under witness protection."

Les knew Orsini would think it was official.

He was right. The paunchy detective tossed the wallet across the desk.

"I would appreciate your keeping me informed of your operations in this area. You might even be surprised to find we can be of help."

Les left Orsini's office feeling he'd dodged a bullet. However from now on he would have to keep dodging the local police Les noted. Officially he was on personal leave. There was only so much Easton could do to cover his ass. Provided Easton was really on his side.

He decided to have a late lunch and took the four lane highway to New Orleans.

He drove to the quarter for a po' boy and a beer then took a stroll. The flowered courtyards and laconic pace of the town relaxed him a bit. However he knew that New Orleans was like a poisonous flower, brightly colored and sweetly scented. Seductive and lethal. At any moment he could be taken out by the mob, the police, the beasts or the bureau.

The thought prodded him alert. Most likely Carson had told his handlers that Melody was hooked up with an FBI agent. Every snitch in the city would be looking for that bounty. And Melody stood out no matter where she went.

There were still a few hours before sunset so Les drove to the Half-Note motel. The police and media presence was gone but a cleanup crew was working on one of the rooms facing the pool.

Les noticed there were a few motorcycles in the small lot as he walked to the manager's office.

The desk clerk studied the badge Les showed him then nodded.

"I checked them in but I was off duty when the tragedy occurred."

The manager was a burly man with round glasses and a wispy grey beard. His wide denim jeans were held up by red suspenders and his faded blue T shirt was coffee stained.

A heavy silver key chain looped from one pocket. The metal Harley Davidson logo dangling on the chain gave Les an idea.

"Did you happen to notice the bikes they rode in on?"

"Oh yeah, sure did. All three had Texas plates but one bike kind of stood out."

"How so?"

"It was a custom job, twelve hundred CC engine with an oversize gas tank. Special cams, supercharger, special seats and shocks for long rides, all flat black except for a red German cross on the tank."

"Who was riding that bike?"

"The dude that haul assed out of here."

"Can you describe him?"

The manager scratched his T shirt. "Tall, blond beard, tats, you know... biker type."

"Anything else you remember?"

"Just the bike. I forgot to tell the other FBI guy who was here this morning."

"FBI? He show you ID?"

"Oh yeah. Just same as you."

"You remember his name by any chance?"

The manager stroked his beard. "Virgil somethin'," he said finally. "I remember thinkin' it was a funny name for an FBI agent."

Not funny if you're the state deputy director Les thought returning to his car.

+ + +

Les hit traffic on his way back and it was late afternoon when he reached Lafayette. He had a couple of hours before Melody called and decided to get some coffee. Half thinking about his plans for the night Les drove across town to Nanny Mojo's café. *It's damned good coffee* he told himself. But that wasn't it. When he saw Leda he knew why.

The turban was gone and in its place a pale blue headband that held back rivulets of curly blond hair from her glistening face. The blue headband framed her violet eyes and pink mouth. Tiny silver crosses studded her small ears. When she saw Les she half smiled and turned away.

The old man called Papa Ezekiel was at a table reading the newspaper. The high, stretched out strains that introduce *Sketches of Spain* accompanied his entrance. Les always considered the album by Miles Davis and Gil Evans a masterpiece but in the confines of the small café it was ominous.

As he sat at the counter Leda put a cup of coffee and pitcher of cream on the counter.

Les gave her a quizzical look. "How did you know?"

"It's not raining today so I guessed you liked the coffee."

"You're a good guesser."

She shrugged. "Would you like some beignets?"

"What do you think?"

A faint smile broke her cool expression. "I think you do."

She was correct. Fresh and warm they were delicious. Restraining himself he lingered, taking small bites and sipping his coffee slowly.

"Waiting for someone?" she asked finally as she refreshed his coffee cup.

"Enjoying the music and the atmosphere."

Papa Ezekiel spoke up. "Leda can I get a beer?"

Leda floated around the counter her white apron cinched tight around her lithe waist, hips swaying gently to the rising tempo of the music.

Les had to stop himself from staring but she seemed to sense his gaze and shot him an annoyed glance as if she'd caught him in a lewd act.

Papa Ezekiel looked up from his paper. "'I tol' you everybody comes to Nanny Mojo for a reason."

Les grinned. "The coffee was reason enough but the beignets are..." he was about to say seductive than caught himself... uh. incredible."

"Thank you," she said shyly.

He pressed his luck.

"What else do you do besides create incredible beignets?"

"Tell your fortune," the old man muttered. ""just like her gramma."

Leda pressed her eyes and lips shut as if trying to stop up her anger. It still managed to leak through he quiet, measured tones.

"Papa you know better than to tell stuff around strangers. I know you know because you're the one who taught me. Now you have had way too much beer for one day. Understand me?"

He ducked his head and buried himself in the news.

"I'd like my fortune told," Les said impulsively, surprising himself. .

In the silence the orchestra started to build to the crescendo.

Leda put her hands on her hips and looked at him, her head cocked as if examining a fish in a tank. Finally she sighed and came around the counter. She went to the door, locked it, and pulled down the shade.

The dim light and pulsing music made the room seem much smaller. For a moment Les regretted asking.

The Leda took his hand and he didn't regret a thing.

Her long slender fingers were cool as they passed over the skin on his palm.

"Give me a silver coin," she said softly.

"I don't believe I have one."

"Give me twenty dollars."

Reluctantly Les removed his hand from hers. He took a twenty from his pocket and gave it to her. In turn she gave him a vintage silver dollar, blackened with age and use, and pressed it into his palm.

"Hold tight for a few moments then pass it to me."

He did as instructed.

The hair on his forearms bristled as she lightly traced the contours of his palm with one finger.

"I see you are loyal, an honest man. But you are surrounded by enemies. Right now you have an evil presence at your shoulder like a winged predator. You must be very careful this presence doesn't steal your soul."

Les looked up. Her eyes were half closed as if in a trance. The trumpet solo was soaring over the relentless rhythm section.

Leda released his hand and opened her eyes. "That's all I can see now." She said breathlessly.

Les was hoarse. "That's quite a lot."

She went to the door and pulled up the shade.

"Usually you make an appointment. If you come around tomorrow I'll have something to protect you."

"Protect me?"

"From the winged predator. Not to mention your many enemies. You're not very popular."

"You saw this winged predator?"

"Yes. It's like a powerful hooded falcon. It can be an ally. But once the hood is removed it will revert to its predatory nature, beyond any control."

The music had stopped. In the dense quiet their eyes met. And Les glimpsed the depth of her power.

+ + +

Les had just stepped out of the shower when Melody called. He changed into fresh clothes before he picked her up. However it didn't help elude Melody's acutely tuned senses.

"You've been with another woman," she said sharply as he bent to kiss her. Her eyes flashed with sudden ferocity.

He leaned back, astonished by her acute sense of smell, right through the shower and new clothes.

"Matter of fact I just had my fortune told."

She took a deep breath and glanced away. "Look at me, acting like a schoolgirl. What did this witch tell you?"

"Basically, watch my back."

"Wise lady, I'm jealous of her even though I have no right to be."

"Right now my back is your back. I need to find Serb and sweat him."

"You find him I'll do the rest," Melody said. "What can we do about the bounty on my head?"

"Three things: leave town, wait for them to attack, attack them and wipe them out or,,, make a deal."

"I believe that's four things."

Les laughed sheepishly. "Used to do that with Dave. He would bust me every time."

"Do you miss him?" she asked softly.

He started the car. "I'm concerned, yes. He's a real friend. I'm concerned and grateful."

Melody moved closer and kissed him. "You don't have to thank me. We made a deal."

"And you kept it. So far all I've done is join you on the mob's most wanted. But if it's a hit man you want I don't think I'm up to it. I'll protect you sure but..."

She put a scented finger to his lips. "I understand darling. Let's play it by ear. Where tonight?"

"Bar Noir."

"Fine. We can have dinner in New Orleans." She fished a phone from her shoulder bag. "Shall I make reservations?"

+ + +

Melody chose Café Degas in the Esplanade district. It was an unpretentious bistro named after one of Melody's favorite artists. The food was excellent and the tin roofed cottage an intimate setting for a late dinner. She wore a dark green and black dress with a slanted neckline that left one smooth white shoulder exposed. Her eyes glinted in the low light and her husky voice drifted across his senses.

"Tell me about your fortune."

Les shrugged. "Believe it or not I have enemies."

Her cool fingers caressed his hand. "I'm sure she—it was a she wasn't it—told you something more specific."

He sipped his wine. Never lie to your partner he thought, especially if she's a vampire. Reluctantly, feeling as if he was violating a confidence, he told her.

"She said there was a dark presence hovering over my shoulder.

She lowered her eyes and studied his hand for a moment.

"Did she say anything else about this presence?"

"Only that It might steal my soul. And you know what?"

"What?"

"You do sound jealous."

She half smiled and pulled her hand away. "Perhaps I am. You're right darling. It's unprofessional and has nothing to do with our deal."

Les leaned closer and covered her hand with his.

"For somebody who's lived a long time you move very fast. I mean it would be hard enough if you were merely a mysterious and beautiful woman on the wrong side of the mob. I would still need a some time to adjust before I committed. Like six months at least. But you're... special."

"A vampire." She freed her hand and searched for a cigarette.

Les gave her a light. "Okay, a vampire. And you expect me to swallow that whole? Make love to you all night and go home in the morning no questions asked?"

"You have to admit it's convenient."

"It's a few flowers short of a relationship."

"I had no idea you were so sentimental."

"You're the one who's jealous."

Melody took a long drag on her cigarette. "Guilty as charged. Yes, darling I have lived a long time and I know that only once in a long, long while does a love like ours connect. Perhaps that's why I'm afraid to lose you."

"You afraid?"

"Underneath the armor I'm a lonely woman."

"We're all lonely. Come's from living on a planet with no neighbors."

She laughed. "You're so strong and brave."

"Speaking of brave. Did you say you know this Doctor Heck?"

"Yes, Walther Heck. I dealt with him—why?"

"Dealt how?"

She hesitated and looked away. "I supplied healthy submissive males."

"For what purpose?"

"Porn films for all I know. Look I'm not proud of it. I did it to help Victor. He's the one who made the contact."

"How much was your fee?"

"Twenty for me, five for Victor."

"Thousand."

"Yes, it's not cheap living off the grid."

When he didn't answer she added, "Believe me Les all of my victims dead or alive *deserved* it."

Les downed his cognac. "Sort of a moral vacuum cleaner."

"You bastard."

He ignored her. "Tonight we need to hunt down Serb. He's our link to the creatures who attacked us."

She pouted. "When do we hunt down our Mafia friends?"

He smiled and dropped some money on the table. "We don't have to. They're hunting us right now."

Chapter 25

Bar Noir was in the French Quarter on the waterfront.

The only sign that they were open for business was a blue neon glow in the grimy plate glass window.

The crowd was a mix of scowling bikers, stone faced pimps, punk girls with orange hair and red sneers, Goth girls with black hair and purple sneers. Only the few working girls in tight short skirts, their breasts edging out of their tank tops, were smiling—as were the college boys they were working.

A knot of skinheads stood at the pool table at the far end of a long bar, pasty white and grim.

The lights were dim, the room crowded, but everyone seemed to notice when they walked in. Les headed for an open space at the bar. He stood and let Melody take the leather barstool giving him an opportunity to scan the room.

He might have saved himself the trouble. Melanie ordered an absinthe and when the bartender departed she motioned her head at the mirror behind the bar.

Les looked and saw Carson seated at a table against the wall. He was in deep conversation with a skinny man in a black T-shirt.

Serb still had a bandage on the nose Dave damaged. Instinctively Les stepped in their direction.

Serb glanced up.

The sound system erupted with Tina Turner's voice and people began to dance, obscuring his view of the table. When he looked again both Carson and Serb were gone.

He turned back to Melody. Her drink was there but she wasn't.

Where is everybody? Les thought as he peered through the tangle of bodies writhing to the pulsing beat of Ike's big band.

Les sat in Melody's empty seat. He considered plunging through the dance floor like a linebacker then decided to wait until the big wheel stopped turning. He doubted that Melody was in the ladies room. In fact he had a hunch she had gone after their quarry.

The music segued to a ballad by Lucinda Williams giving him a chance to move across the room in search of possible exits.

For some reason he was calm, operating under the assumption that Melody was on the case. *Assumption is like trying to fill an inside straight* he told himself, *just find where the scumbag went.*

Around the corner of the long bar were three doors.

Two were restrooms. He moved past them and tried the third door. It opened onto a small parking lot and loading area.

Melody was standing there waiting for him. Both Carson and Serb were seated on the ground, their backs propped against the wall.

"You knew I'd be out here didn't you?" Melody said playfully.

Les took a deep breath. "What happened?"

"I saw them head for the exit and got there ahead of them. Then I subdued them."

"Subdued?"

"Rendered them submissive. Ask them anything you like."

"Is this the way you rendered subjects for Doctor Heck?"

"More or less. You're supposed to question Serb darling-not me."

Les sighed and turned his attention to Serb.

"Who told you to drive the van to the Fairmont Hotel and attack us?"

Serb's usual sneering cockiness was gone, replaced by a wooden demeanor. As if he had been drugged or hypnotized.

"Our leader."

"Who's your leader?"

"Odin, master of the Knights of the Golden Circle."

"Are you a knight?"

"Not yet."

"Where did you get the van?"

"Doctor Heck."

"What was inside?"

"Heck's wolf pack."

"What are they?"

"Mutants, part human part some kind of animal. Heck calls them the new breed. "

"Where are they now?"

"I don't know. Heck has a secret lab somewhere in the warehouse district."

"Near the cemetery?"

"Yes I think so."

Melody stood by calmly while Les continued to question Serb. Her patience wore thin when Les methodically starting taking down lists like names, numbers, places, times of meetings, especially concerning the Knights of the Golden Circle. Oddly enough she knew the name from her time in New Orleans following the Civil War.

"We've been here too long." she said, "I feel heat."

"What about them?"

"They'll be alright in a few hours."

"Will they remember?"

"Not if we don't want them to."

"Take care of it."

She smiled. "You're getting pretty comfortable with my skill set."

+ + +

As Les drove back to Lafayette, Melody kept shifting in her seat.

He glanced at her. "Why so nervous? That was actually easy back there."

"We're being followed."

Les slowed down and scanned the rearview and side mirrors.

"Can't see anybody."

"I know something's stalking us."

"They may be driving with headlights off," Les said, "let's find out."

Les stepped on the pedal and turned off the four-lane at the next exit. They swung onto a wide boulevard and a hundred feet later Les made a screeching U turn.

Sure enough a rental Ford with its headlights dark came off the exit ramp.

Les switched on his brights. The Ford accelerated past but not before he glimpsed a thin white male wearing a black fedora at the wheel. Les thought he had a black shirt with a white collar.

"Damn them," Melody said ruefully.

"Damn who?"

"That man —he's a priest."

"Which means…?"

"They hired a professional to kill me."

"A priest?"

"A vampire hunter."

"You know this from one quick look at the guy?"

"I know he's a priest. Why else would a priest be tailing us with his headlights dark?"

It was a good question. Les stepped on the accelerator and got back on the four-lane, his eyes checking the rear view all the way to Lafayette.

Before they reached Melody's place Les stopped at a small convenience store for a bottle of Jim Beam, a bottle of Patron tequila and a bottle of Hennessy cognac, as well as an array of snacks. He was tired of the stark absinthe and cocaine diet at her motel and his adrenaline was still pumping.

"Shopping, how domestic," she said as he put the bag in the rear seat.

Les sat behind the wheel for a moment peering into his side and rear view mirrors for any sign of a tail.

"I don't feel a predator out there anymore," Melody said softly.

"Yeah well, we've got more than one to worry about. Including this priest of yours." He turned and looked at her. "I think it's time you level with me. I want to know about your past, your present, and why this guy scares you."

"What about *your* past and present?"

"I'm an FBI agent. My life is in a file box."

"That's not all you are."

"What I am is confused and paranoid. I'm about to go up against your friend Walther's mutants and now a killer priest so I need to know who the fuck I'm dealing with."

Melody slumped in resignation. "Can we have a drink first?"

Chapter 26

"My father was one of the first settlers in New Orleans. After the revolution he returned to France and married my mother. They lived in Paris where I was born and educated. It was a wonderfully innocent time for me. My father was a wealthy merchant and my mother was a dazzling beauty with a taste for art.

Some of the leading intellectuals of the time sat at our dinner table including one memorable evening with Benjamin Franklin himself."

Melody paused, green eyes misted with memory. The room was lit by red dinner candles that threw long shadows across the draped windows. The only sound was the low hum of the AC. She took a sip of her absinthe and went on.

"France at that time was in turmoil. The revolutionary Robespierre brothers and Napoleon were stirring things up everywhere in Europe. So my father boarded up our Paris flat and took us back to New Orleans. I was seventeen.

New Orleans society was quite different than what I was used to. Much less... restrictive. I had gone to convent schools and the ladies in Paris were extremely conservative compared to the Southern belles.

Although very shy I was courted by a number of beaus. Life was a whirl of debutante parties and balls."

Melody lit a cigarette and seemed to search the smoke for images of a lost era.

"My parents were very concerned that I make a proper marriage and watched over me carefully."

But I was a bit headstrong and set on finding the prince of my fairy tale. When I was twenty my mother tried to convince me to marry a young lawyer from a prominent political family. I refused. My heart was set on an older man, a dashing count from Vienna, Philip Borgia. Like my father he was a shipping merchant. Unlike my father he was a man about town, a gambler. And unlike most of the men in New Orleans he was well educated, well-traveled and conversant with literature and fine art. I was entranced." Melody took a long thoughtful sip of her drink.

"I was a fool of course. Everyone warned me about him but I was headstrong. Count Borgia seemed to share my infatuation and began courting me secretly.

It was all so romantic. Letters passed by servants, secluded meeting places, always the rush of being together despite all opposition. One magical evening Philip deflowered me in a gazebo hung with scented flowers under the stars. After that we became bolder. People started to whisper.

"But at that same time people started to die suddenly as if a plague had swept into New Orleans. Young people, healthy people would just… expire. Their lifeless bodies would be found in the morning, some in their beds, others in the streets. Everyone shuttered their windows and sought remedies from physicians. They flocked to the church. There was talk of evil spirits, especially among the slaves.

"One day Count Borgia's housemaid Melissa delivered a message to me. It was a note of apology in his hand. Business would take him away for a few days. I was crestfallen. Melissa, who was no older than I, saw my disappointment and took my hand in solace. She pressed a black cotton pouch into me palm and told me to put it under my pillow and it would protect me from the angel of death. I naively followed her instructions not realizing her true intentions.

"You see, although scarcely my age Melissa was wise beyond my romantic delusions. That night I put the pouch under my pillow and went to sleep dreaming of Count Borgia.

"A chill breeze woke me up and I saw the window to the veranda was partially open. I went to close it and saw a dark figure standing near the drapes. He was almost completely hidden until he emerged from the shadows and took me in his cold embrace.

"I thought I was still dreaming and Philip had come for me. My heart was beating violently until he kissed me.

"A warm luxuriant calm wrapped me like a shawl. I felt the sharp prick of his teeth at my neck, then a long sensual ripple of naked lust... then nothing.

"When I woke again it was to the sound of stone grating against stone. It was terribly dank and cold. The darkness was musty and thick with scents. Feeling around I realized I was in a padded box of some sort, lined with satin. Then it dawned."

Melody shuddered and took a long, last drag on her cigarette.

"I was actually in a casket. Terrified, I screamed over and over but a soft voice told me to stay calm. It was almost as if he was in the casket with me. I remained silent more from terror as reassurance.

"Time seemed to stand still. My entire world was reduced to the regular rocking of stone overhead. Like a doomsday clock.

"Petrified with the belief that this was God's punishment for my sins with Philip and I was about to be ushered into hell I lay still in my satin prison listening to the monotonous sawing of stone on stone.

"After what seemed like hours a puff of multi scented air entered the cramped space followed by a brilliant flash of light and I could breath.

"Suddenly I was free. In my hysteria I imagined Philip had come to rescue me. I sat up and almost fell back, overwhelmed by an assault on my senses. A mixture of sharp scents filled my nostrils, even the dim candle flame seemed like a spotlight to my amplified eyesight. At the same time a ravenous hunger drew me erect. I was aware of a sweet dank scent like overripe fruit. Like an animal mad with hunger I hurried to the smell. Then he appeared out of the shadows as he had in my bedroom. Tall, slender, young, with long blond hair and pale blue eyes that seemed to stare into my deepest need. He was holding a white dove against his breast.

"Without a word he lifted the dove to his mouth and bit its neck. Mouth smeared with blood he handed me the bird. Still alive it fluttered weakly in my hands.

"Driven by a hunger beyond heaven's control I drove my teeth into the poor creature and drained its blood right there.

"When I lifted my head my hunger was sated—and I was very calm. For the first time I took stock of my surroundings

"I was inside a crypt which I recognized as belonging to my family. My rescuer watched me with a strange smile as I recovered my composure. And then he began to speak to me.

"His voice seemed inside my brain. He told me that his name was Rober and he had been drawn by the pouch Melissa had given me. Melissa had been Count Borgia's mistress and was insanely jealous of me. To get rid of me she had prepared a poultice of herbs which would attract Rober—the vampire responsible for all the recent deaths in New Orleans.

"But when Rober saw me he recognized something familiar in me. He fell in love—and turned me into a creature of the night.

"I became Rober's consort and he taught me the ways of the vampire. We returned to Europe. It wouldn't do for a recently deceased young lady to be seen walking the streets after dark.

"Paris, Vienna, Budapest, Prague. Berlin, Barcelona; we toured the world unencumbered by anything except our own pleasure... unencumbered by time itself.

"But then, as it will, things took a nasty turn."

She paused to refill her glass. "Why does everything take a nasty turn?"

Les shrugged. "If it wasn't for nasty turns the world would not be round."

He lit a cigarette and waited.

"For the next sixty years or so Rober and I traveled together, loved together, fed together. Then on Christmas Eve it happened. We were in Barcelona and all the churches and cathedrals were full of holiday worshippers. We strolled the festive streets selecting potential victims. Rober had a strong sense of honor and sought out criminals and human predators.

"We sat in a café that had a view of an unsavory alley. Through the window we saw a young girl walking hand in hand with a tall man in black who had a cane decorated with red ribbons. The girl too wore Christmas ribbons in her hair and was laughing at something the man said. I watched them walk into the darkened alley out of sight. A few moments later the little girl appeared from the alley. She looked wild eyed and she was screaming that her father had been attacked.

Rober told me to stay put and bounded outside.

"I waited for what seemed an hour but was merely moments.

"Suddenly I was seized by a violent shudder as if an icy blade had been thrust into my skull. Blindly I ran outside to find Rober.

"Halfway down the alley I saw the tall man crouched on the ground.. With a maniacal smile he lifted a sack in the air. As I came closer his yellow eyes gleamed in triumph. He stood and lifted the sack higher. But it wasn't a sack.

"It was Rober's head.

"Then I saw the man's gaily festooned cane was actually a sword. Our eyes met and I knew he knew.

"Coward that I am I ran. I remained hidden for days mourning Rober's death and frightened for my own life. For I had seen what was written in those mad eyes. He intended to hunt me down as he had Rober."

Melody leaned back as if exhausted. "These memories are depressing. I need something to lift my spirits." She rummaged through her bag and produced a glass vial containing a small amount of white powder.

Les sipped his drink and watched her tap out lines on the glass-topped coffee table.

"Would you like some?" she asked, bending over the table with a short straw.

"Not tonight."

She snorted both lines and looked at him with a quizzical smile. "You're not getting judgmental on me are you?"

"Maybe."

"Look I'm telling you all this so there'll be no secrets between us. But it is painful. So spare me the righteous disapproval. A week ago you were doing lines right alongside me."

Les lifted his hands in surrender. "I'm listening."

Melody wiped her nose and lit another cigarette.

"I fled to France and lived among the bohemian artists and prostitutes that inhabited the Montmartre quarter in Paris. Actually it was perfect for me, anonymous and yet brilliant and exciting. Toulouse Lautrec taught me the joys of absinthe, I modeled for Modigliani and Degas, I smoked hash with Baudelaire and discussed philosophy with Verlaine. We were all young, unknown, free and burning with creative fire.

"I had lovers and never found love but it didn't seem to matter during that age of enlightenment. America was locked in a Civil War and Napoleon was about to embark on another disastrous campaign.

"Did you know that a Southern sea raider battled a Northern ship right off the coast of Cherbourg? Some of my friends actually had a picnic and watched the Union ship USS Kearsarge sink the CSS Alabama outside the harbor. They said it was quite a show with the two ships circling each other firing their cannons.

"Unfortunately I couldn't be there that afternoon, or any other for that matter. It was about that time I suddenly became aware of a pervading sense of dread.

"One evening I entered a cafe and an artist friend motioned me over to his table. He told me a tall thin man who walked with a stick had been inquiring about me. He thought he might be a detective and put him off track.

"I knew immediately who it was. Even before my friend described the man's strange yellow eyes

"The next evening I departed for Marseilles. From there I sailed to New Orleans. The Civil War had changed this once gracious city into a teeming brothel filled with thieves and killers of every stripe. I had a wide choice of victims.

"One night I saw an old negro woman tending an herb stand on lower Bourbon Street. Despite her years she was still slim and graceful with long silver hair that framed the strong contours of her face. Something about her was familiar and drew me closer.

"It was Melissa, the servant girl who betrayed me for the love of Count Borgia.

"When Melissa recognized me her dark skin paled to grey. In sixty years I had not aged. She stood stock still petrified with fright, eyes bulging and mouth moving soundlessly.

"I laughed and moved away so quickly she could not have been certain I was actually there in the flesh—or was an apparition born of fearsome guilt.

"Oddly I had thought little of Philip since my metamorphous, having been obsessed with Rober.

Restless, I sailed west to San Francisco by clipper ship. The gold rush had created a rich lawless city populated by scoundrels and dreamers. For the next decade or so it suited me fine except I had yet to find anyone who could replace Rober in my soul.

"I lived in New York in the years leading to the great war. And afterwards took a leading part in the roaring twenties. The poet William Blake said the road of excess leads to the palace of wisdom.

"However it also leads to an early death unless… one is a vampire. Our kind is able to regenerate cells and organs in a short time.

"Air travel proved to a boon. Previously the longer the voyage the more crewman succumbed. I had to plan very carefully. Now I just have to make sure my plane lands long before sunrise.

"I became bicoastal spending more time in Hollywood during the thirties. I dated Errol Flynn, Doug Fairbanks and Gary Cooper. Cary Grant sent me a roomful of flowers. But I was still terribly lonely. I wandered from city to city searching for the one I was destined to love."

Melody stubbed out her cigarette and reached for the glass vial. It was empty. She got up and returned with a large plastic bag packed with white powder.

"That's serious weight you have there," Les said pouring scotch in his glass.

"A couple of ounces, not even a quarter pound."

Melody refilled her vial and put the bag away.

"But if it will make you feel better I won't do anymore."

"Any more might keep you awake way past sunrise."

"Don't worry darling I sleep like a baby... most of the time."

"And other times?"

"Lately I've had disturbing dreams. Now I know why. They're alarms warning about the man hunting me."

"Hunting *us*," Les reminded.

"I glad you said that. Most people would try to distance themselves." Melody refreshed her drink.

"Which brings me to the point. During the last few years I felt a need to circle back to this part of the world. In an effort to stay low key I settled in Lafayette rather than New Orleans. And one night—after an absence of over two hundred years—I reconnected with my long lost soul mate."

She gave Les a lazy smile. "I'm talking about *you* my darling. Whether you like it or not we were destined to be together."

Chapter 27

Les got home at dawn but couldn't sleep.

I'm already keeping vampire hours he brooded pouring a nightcap. The problem was he felt the same deep connection to Melody. It was the destiny part that worried him.

After four restless hours he woke up, took a long shower then arranged to meet Easton before going out for breakfast.

Daylight did nothing to dispel his dark speculations.

Eye on the ball Les told himself, *this is business*. He'd turn over Serb's address, phone number and his statement that Doctor Heck was conducting human experiments connected to the murder of two agents and near death of another. Not to mention the slaughter of a dozen civilians.

"Heck calls them his wolf pack," Les told Easton over lunch. "They're some sort of animal human hybrid. It's connected to a group called the Knights of the Golden Circle. I understand it's been around since the Civil War."

Easton swallowed an oyster and washed it down with a beer. "That's right. Jesse James, John Wilkes Booth, they were members. They worked out of Canada during the Civil War. Booth was a Confederate spy and it's said Jesse James robbed banks to finance the Knights. After the war they morphed into the KKK."

"You seem to know a lot about them."

"They're on our radar. Nobody's gotten this close."

"You have Serb driving the van the night Dave was attacked," Les said, "You have his address. Pick him up and sweat him. Serb and his pal Carson work for the Circle and help Heck find victims. Oh yeah before I forget there's one other thing."

"What's that?"

"An FBI agent named Virgil something was at the Half Note Motel nosing around."

"How do you know?"

"I went nosing around there myself. Those killings are definitely connected to Heck. Which means Virgil is connected somehow."

Easton drummed his fingers on the table.

"Yeah okay, I've got it."

Les was starting to trust him, but barely.

After leaving Easton he called the hospital and was surprised when Dave answered.

"Jen went out for a walk," Dave said. His voice was stronger.

"You sound good. How's it going?"

"The doctors are surprised at how well I'm recovering, except…"

"Except what?"

"They still don't know if they can save my arm."

Les felt his anger rising. It wasn't just Heck. It was Virgil Lake degrading the Bureau, the racists degrading America, the mob and the human corruption that allowed them to flourish. They were all responsible for his partner's terrible injuries.

"The doctors were wrong before," Les said, "they don't know what a tough son of bitch you are."

"I hope so. A side effect of all this is I have to stay in a dark room. Sunlight makes me very uncomfortable, headaches, nausea…"

"Probably a reaction to the medication," Les said. In a way it was true.

Les remained angry long after he hung up.

He found an address for a Dr. Walther Heck, Veterinarian then drove out to case the place.

It was large enough to house a wolf pack. The building was in the shape of a post WWII Quonset Hut with a parking lot on the side and front. Doctor Heck's name was on a sign above the door. On impulse he decided to go inside.

An older blond woman with large breasts and wide shoulders packed into a starched white uniform was behind the desk in the lobby. On the wall behind her hung an impressive array of diplomas and certifications.

"Can we help you?" the nurse said with a slight accent.

Les was ready. "I hope so. I need a good kennel for my dogs when I leave town next week."

She gave him a toothy smile. "Of course. Be sure Doctor Heck will return your friends in better condition then when they come."

As she spoke Les scanned the lobby for cameras and found two. "Uh great… do you have a pamphlet or something with your rates?"

"What breed of dogs you have?"

"Pit Bulls, but they're very well behaved."

The smile grew toothier. "Doctor Heck has two himself. I love to walk with them."

Les smiled back. "Maybe you can show me your kennels. That's if you house the dogs right here."

"Yes, of course right here. Doctor Heck and myself will take care of your friends personally."

"I thought perhaps you had another-uh larger facility."

The smile faded, replaced by a defiant expression. "Our kennels very comfortable and very clean. Come I show you." She pressed a buzzer and a wide door slid open. Les followed her inside taking note of the security console and interior cameras. Doctor Heck had a sophisticated set up.

The nurse was right, the kennels were large, clean and comfortable despite the number of dogs, cats, rabbits and birds living in the interior of Heck's building. There was a surgery area, an X-ray section with lead drapes, and post-surgery cells with computerized monitoring devices. Les noticed two machines that looked like airport moving sidewalks and realized they were treadmills for dogs.

"You can see yourself this is a first class home for your friends. What are their names?"

"Uh… Virgil and Homer."

"Two boys, Doctor Heck has one of each. Rudy and Lily."

Les nodded and looked around. "You're right this will be a fine home for the guys. But uh… do you have a back yard or something? You know, just to run around a bit."

"Yes, yes, I show you."

As they walked to the rear entrance Les tried to memorize the position of the security cameras. Along the way they passed a wide, padded cage that housed two enormous pit bulls. They gave Les a heavy lidded stare and growled softly as he passed.

The rear door had cameras inside as well as the parking area outside.

"This is it?" Les said.

"Of course not, come."

She waved her hand and led him to a garden area on the side of the lot. Les saw that the garden was a path to a grassy, well-tended park shaded by oak trees and fenced by brilliant red hyacinths.

"Doctor Heck keeps this park for the animals."

"Beautiful," Les said. He kept scanning for cameras and found three. "Well that settles it. I'll bring Virgil and Homer in this Friday."

The nurse eyed him suspiciously. "It is Friday."

"Of course. I mean next Friday."

"Of course."

Les got a full look at the back exit to the clinic. When he passed the pit bulls they got up and followed him the length of their cage, growling ominously.

After giving the nurse a hundred dollar reservation deposit and a phony address Les drove away with more questions than answers. He knew how to get into the clinic if need be. However he saw no sign of human experiments.

He had to locate the doctor's secret lab and he had a vague idea of where it might be.

Without thinking about his destination he drove aimlessly until he found himself near Nanny Mojo's café. He decided to have coffee and beignets.

"Well look who's here," Papa Ezekiel said when Les entered the small, bizarrely decorated café.

Leda was behind the counter, her back to the door.

"I was just making fresh beignets," she said as if he was expected. Her next remark refreshed his memory. "The pouch you need is ready."

Les was reminded of the pouch that drew the vampire Rober to Melody.

"And it's supposed to protect me?"

"Not *supposed* to protect you, it *will* protect you. If you believe," she said with a trace of impatience.

Lately Les had been forced to accept lots of things he wouldn't ordinarily believe.

"Just wanted to make sure," he said quietly, "you're the expert."

Lightning Hopkins spare, penetrating voice was singing *Mojo Hand* over the speakers.

Without asking Leda served him a cup of coffee and a plate of warm beignets.

Les smiled. "Thanks, you're very thoughtful. So uh—if I'm not being too forward—can I see the pouch?"

She put a hand over her mouth in embarrassment.

"Actually it's still at Gramma's herb store in New Iberia. I can have it here tomorrow."

Les nodded. "Sounds good. He drank his coffee and enjoyed the warm, sweet beignets listening to Tracy Chapman singing *Gimme One Good Reason*.

As Leda refilled his cup Les was aware of the way her slim body moved with womanly grace.

"Where is your Gramma's store?"

She paused, violet eyes searching his as if looking for a sinister intent.

Papa Ezekiel spoke up. "It's just off the Old Spanish Trail, 'bout a half hour from here."

Leda shook her head. "You listen to him you'll wind up in the bayou. He's talking about Highway 182 that goes to Spanish Lake."

"Why don't you show me where?" Les said without thinking. "I'll drive you there and back."

"We got to go there anyway," Papa Ezekiel said.

"Hush you old mule," Leda exploded, "you think I'm going to get in a car with a stranger. Especially one with his kind of trouble around him."

"I'd be with you," the old man protested.

"Big help you'd be," Leda said, her tone softer.

Les lifted his hands. "Hey I was just being neighborly."

Leda turned her ire on him. "Neighborly? You're not even from around here."

He grinned sheepishly. "I guess I wanted a chance to get to know you a little better."

Papa Ezekiel laughed. "That ain't gonna happen on a car ride."

Les knew he shouldn't pursue it. Melody would catch her scent no matter how many miles he drove with the windows open. But the truth was, he really did want a chance to be with Leda.

You are looking for trouble, Les told himself. He was ready to let the matter drop until Leda challenged him.

"Do you have ID?"

What the hell, my cover's already been blown, Les reflected. He passed his wallet across the counter.

Leda's eyes widened when she saw his FBI credentials but she didn't comment.

"I suppose you're reliable enough. Alright Papa close it up for an hour. I'll call Gramma and tell her we're comin.'"

+ + +

Papa Ezekiel had been right.

Leda sat primly in the back seat while Papa took shotgun. She spoke only when spoken to and then kept her answers short and to the point as if wary of saying too much to an FBI agent. On the other hand Papa Ezekiel kept up an amiable commentary on the history of the area.

"Some say the pirate Jean Lafitte buried some treasure around Spanish Lake," he said as he gazed out the window. "Round the Civil War they was Union troops here too. My own gramma tol' me stories.

"There you see Ol' Spanish Trail" he said, half-turning to Leda as they neared a roadway exit sign.

"That's for tourists and you know it." Leda said. She caught Les looking in the rear view. "Turn off onto 31, the store is just a few miles."

From time to time Les had been stealing looks in the rear view mirror. Leda silently watched the scenery with an expression of deep contemplation as if seeing into the heart of the earth.

They turned off the highway onto a narrow dirt road. Nanny Mojo's herb shop was located a mile off the highway on a rise that afforded a partial view of the lake through the oak trees. Steely grey rain clouds hovered in the distance.

"You get lots of showers out here," Led said, straining to make conversation.

She gave him a sideways glance. "That's good isn't it? For the land I mean."

"As I recall that's how we met."

Her shy smile arced like a brief rainbow above her solemn demeanor.

The shop was a stout wooden building with a stone foundation and a peaked roof. A neat white sign had the name Nanny Mojo printed in faded blue. Along one side extending into the back of the shop was a large cultivated garden and at the far end a greenhouse.

"Gramma grows her herbs and makes her cures herself," Leda said proudly.

There were two women in the store when they entered. One was an overweight black woman in a yellow dress and pink flip flops. The other a blond woman wearing designer sunglasses, tight jeans and red high heeled shoes.

She probably belongs to the Mercedes in the parking lot Les thought, looking around. Like Leda's café it seemed cluttered. However it was a *neat* clutter. Bunches of dried plants hung from the ceiling. There were bins filled with roots and dried animal paws in the display cases. Behind the long counter was a ten-foot high wooden cabinet with what seemed like a hundred drawers of the type favored by old fashioned pharmacists. A spicy scent floated through the shop stirred by two slowly rotating ceiling fans.

A tall woman with white hair was waiting on the woman in the yellow dress. It was clear the blond woman was restless. She shifted from foot to foot, sighed, checked her iPhone, and sighed again.

The white haired woman appeared not to notice and continued waiting on her customer. Leda made a small face and walked away. Les followed and began to peruse the objects in the glass display case. There was snake skins, dried bats, dried insects. animal body parts, teeth, rolls of colored ribbon, strings of colored beads, crystals and Tarot cards.

The blond woman looked at her watch, tapped her foot and sighed.

Les looked around for Papa Ezekiel but he had disappeared somewhere in the back of the shop

"I don't have much time," the blond said.

The white haired woman did not look up.

"I said…"

The whitehaired woman looked up.

"Heard what you said. This lady was here first." Her turquoise eyes fixed on the blond. "So you either come back when you have more time or hush up and let me take care of this lady." The exchange lasted only a minute but when Les drifted closer the white-haired woman gave him a hard look that pushed him back a step.

Obviously she's Melissa's gramma Les thought, *and she's in full charge.*

Leda beckoned him over. "Bet it's a love potion," she whispered, "gramma's famous for it."

Les glanced out the window and saw the heavy set woman in the yellow dress putting her shopping bags in the trunk of her Mercedes.

"The woman loading her car is Sister Mamba the healer and pastor of the Afro-Christian Church," Leda said quietly.

So much for my powers of deduction Les thought.

"Hello my sweet thing, come give your gramma a kiss."

As they embraced Les saw how closely Leda favored her grandmother. The same honey skin, regal posture and natural grace. Leda's eyes were shaded purple rather than turquoise blue but the resemblance was unmistakable.

"Gramma this is Lester, he drove us here. Lester wants to pick up that little pouch I asked you to fix up."

For a moment it didn't register. No one had called him Lester for years. Not since his mm's death.

He smiled but it was too late.

Gramma gave him a disapproving nod as if she knew all his sins. "Be sure you know this is powerful protection," she said without preamble.

Les looked at Leda then back at Gramma. "I'm grateful to you for preparing it but it was really Leda who thought it was necessary."

"If Leda thinks it's necessary then it's so." When she smiled at her granddaughter the years melted from her face and she looked like a young girl.

Gramma went to one of the drawers behind her and took out a white cotton bag stitched with red thread.

She handed it to Les.

"You keep this bag in your pocket and it will absorb bad energy like a sponge."

"Thanks for your trouble on my behalf."

"Really on Leda's behalf," Gramma said.

"I *knew* it, I knew he looked like somebody."

Gramma pursed her lips in disapproval as Papa Ezekiel came from the back waving something in the air. "Take a look at this and tell me it ain't so."

Smiling broadly the old man put a square wooden object on the counter and opened it like a book.

It was a carved double frame containing two old daguerreotype photographs.

One was a picture of a young couple. The man stood erect the woman beside him smiled easily at the camera. The man was tall with blond hair and chiseled features. The young woman's radiant beauty was evident, even in the time-yellowed image.

The other was a portrait of a light-skinned Afro-American girl with fair hair and pale searching eyes who looked exactly like Leda.

"Who is she?" Les asked, his throat suddenly dry.

That's Leda's double great gramma Melissa," Papa Ezekiel said, "she the original Nanny Mojo. Her knowledge got passed down through family. But look there at the man. I kept thinkin' I seen you before, then it come up on me… You look just like the man in that ol' pitcha.'"

"Hate to admit it but he's right," Gramma said. "real close resemblance."

"Who is he?" Les asked through a haze of confusion.

"Name is Count Philip Borgia."

Les didn't have to ask the girl's name.

It was Melody.

Chapter 28

Melody was fuming.

"Front seat, back seat, don't try to parse this. The point is that woman has been in this car again—as in twice in two days."

Les knew this might be coming but he wasn't prepared for the intensity of Melody's anger. It was palpable. His body stiffened behind the wheel as it dawned she might harm Leda.

"Are you saying I'm forbidden to engage other women, even professionally?"

"I'm saying I'm sick of the smell of her."

He pulled the car over and turned off the motor.

"I'll level with you—only if you promise you will not harm her."

"So it's like that is it?"

Les shook his head. "Think about it Melody. How many women do I know who are capable of that?"

"I'm certain you've met a few in your line of work."

"But none that I'm connected to."

"Connected but not committed," Melody sniffed.

Les lifted his hands. "I'm not ready for your lifestyle. The drinking alone would kill me."

"I could turn you," she whispered, voice husky. "We could live forever without fear of time or death."

Les gave her a rueful smile. "I'd make a lousy vampire. I'd lose my job, my life, my…"

His voice trailed off and Melody filled the silence.

"…Your soul?"

"Maybe. Look, we agreed, this is supposed to be a professional arrangement. Drama won't help us do what we need to do. So if you want to pull out do it now."

Melody folded her arms and looked away. "You are the only man who's able to resist me. Why is that?"

Then she turned and kissed him. "You're right. I promise I'll behave darling. No more drama."

Les started the engine. "Then let's do it the way we planned."

"Not so fast." Melody put a hand on the wheel.

"What now?"

He green eyes gleamed in the darkness. "You haven't told me who this bitch is that I'm not supposed to harm."

Les sighed. "Her name is Leda. She runs a small café here in Lafayette and tells fortunes on the side. Her grandmother is some kind of herbal healer, has a shop in New Iberia. Leda has an elderly grandfather. So I drove them both to her grandmother's shop."

"The last boy scout."

"No. She's very pretty. And yeah, I suppose I was flirting. But she sat in the back and didn't talk."

She laughed. "Finally a woman who can resist you."

Les decided not to mention the photographs. It would pull them all into deeper water and they were in over their heads already.

"One of my many faculties is my ability to spot a lie."

She leaned close and nuzzled his ear. "You passed admirably."

He grunted. "Fasten your seat belt..."

"...it's going to be a bumpy night. Bette Davis, All About Eve. I've only seen it two hundred times."

Les didn't answer, his mind on their task ahead.

+ + +

Doctor Heck's clinic was open until seven thirty p.m.

Their plan was simple enough, Melody would incapacitate Heck the way she had rendered Serb submissive and question him. Melody was vague about her methods but Les had observed the bite marks on her subjects.

Knowing the clinic was loaded with cameras Les parked on the street and turned out the lights.

"You ready for this?" he said.

Melody took a vial of white powder from her bag.

Les threw up his hands in exasperation. "Really? What the hell are you doing?"

"Just a tiny bump darling." She tapped a bit of the powder on the dash and snorted it with a rolled bill.

"See? No big thing. Now I'm ready."

She patted her nose with a silk hanky and stepped outside.

She managed two wobbly steps before she fell back against the car.

Les slid over the hood to reach her.

"What's wrong?"

"Wasn't cocaine…"

Melody collapsed in his arms.

Desperately trying to suppress his emotions Les used a basic fireman's carry to lift her onto his shoulders and haul her insert body into the clinic.

The nurse rose to meet him.

"Emergency. Please call the doctor."

"Of course."

The nurse hurried into the back and returned with Doctor Heck in tow. He was pushing a movable table.

"Put her on here," he said briskly, "careful now."

Les carefully transferred Melody to the table and followed Doctor Heck through the door.

Heck rolled her into the surgical area and stopped.

"I have something to bring her around, nurse please the stimulant."

The nurse hurriedly prepared a hypodermic and gave it to the doctor.

"Please sir, steady her shoulders."

As Les bent to brace Melody's shoulders something stung his neck. He jerked his head up and saw the doctor holding a needle and smiling.

Then the smile melted into oblivion.

+ + +

Les awoke with a monster headache. Very slowly he sat up and gathered his shattered senses.

The light was dim, there was a slight earthy smell in the conditioned air...

...and he was in a cage.

"Are you awake finally?"

"Melody?"

"Over here."

"Where?"

"Directly across from you."

Les peered through the gloom and saw Melody standing across the floor. Like him, she was in a cage.

His memory came into focus. "You passed out."

"Yes. Like a fool I assumed I was using cocaine. It proved to be heroin which is dangerous for my kind. It can render us helpless for days. Fortunately you stopped me from doing too much."

"Bully for me. Now what?"

"There's a nurse here who's making sort of preparations. Did you meet Doctor Heck?"

"Oh yeah. He suckered me with a needle."

"If I'm still in here at dawn..." Melody's voice trailed off.

"Did you say preparations? For what?"

"To move us I think. I saw her wheeling some sort of Frankenstein table with restraints for arms and legs."

"I'm thirsty."

"So am I—thirsty for that damned nurse," Melody said vehemently.

Something occurred to Les. "How did they know?"

"Know?"

"We were coming... Jesus."

"Are you alright?"

"My brain feels like oatmeal."

Holding the bars Les managed to get his feet. He tested the door and found it solidly locked.

"He's got dog cages bigger than this."

"Easier to transport I suppose."

"You would know."

"Please don't play the guilt card now darling. I'm a reformed woman since we committed…"

The lights went on.

"I see you two are awake," the nurse announced cheerfully. As Melody had reported she was wheeling a table with built-in restraints.

She was also holding a Beretta 9mm.

The nurse put on a pair of Latex gloves that were on the table. Les saw there were two hypodermic needles on there as well.

"Now let us see. Which one wants to go first?"

Les felt his anger rising. "Where's Doctor Heck?"

"Don't worry, you will meet him very soon."

Adrenaline revived his groggy brain and he began to take deep breaths. But alert or not he was still in a steel cage.

"I think you first brave man," she said with a small smile. She lifted the hypodermic to the light and squirted some liquid through the needle.

The room exploded.

Short bursts of automatic gunfire sent Les to the floor as bullets tore into the ceiling and walls.

"Get down!" he yelled.

Everybody was way ahead of him. Melody flat in a corner, the nurse crouched behind the table, gun ready.

"Omaha!" The nurse yelled.

Les heard claws sliding across the polished floor and half expected hairy creatures to appear. Instead two muscular pit bulls streaked past his cage like linebackers.

Over a sustained burst of automatic fire Les could hear their death squeals. Then he heard the click of a spent magazine. He visualized the shooter drop the empty clip and reload.

"No!"

The nurse stood up and began firing.

"No!" she repeated.

Les had misjudged. So had the nurse. The shooter carried a spare weapon. From the blast and impact it seemed to be a shotgun.

A giant red rose blossomed on the nurse's white smock as she was lifted off her feet and blown backward by the blast.

Silently, a fog of gun smoke and acrid cordite filled the room. Then a tall, bearded man with long blond hair stepped through the haze.

He wore a sleeveless black leather vest, stained jeans, and black leather cowboy boots. He held a short-barreled shotgun in one hand and an Uzi in the other.

"What the fuck is this?" the man said when he saw the cages.

"Doctor Heck kidnapped us," Melody said. "Get us out."

"Where is Heck?"

"I don't know. I think the nurse was taking us to him."

The man studied her. After a moment he strode to the nurse's crumpled body and went through her pockets. He found a ring of keys and began to test each one on Melody's cage. Finally he unlocked the door and gestured at her with the still fuming shotgun.

"Come with me bitch," he said hoarsely, "we are going to party."

"Leave the keys bro," Les said.

The man snorted. "Go fuck yourself," he said over his shoulder, prodding Melody with the shotgun.

Les watched them go.

He squatted, leaned back against the bars, closed his eyes and waited.

A slight breeze parted the smoke.

Melody appeared. She lifted her hand, jingling a ring of keys like a Christmas bell.

Wearily Les looked up.

"What the hell took you so long?"

Chapter 29

The man lay sprawled on the ground next to his motorcycle. Les recognized the machine from the description given him by the manager of the Half-Note Motel.

It was the third biker. The one who had escaped the creatures who mutilated his friends, He had returned, blasted open the rear doors, killed the dogs and murdered the nurse.

"He told me everything," Melody said calmly. "He was hired by a mobster named Cozy Costanza to find Doctor Heck and recover fifty thousand dollars and two ounces of pure heroin."

"That would be the heroin you snorted."

"Probably. It was taken from a pilot named Larry Edwards. Now missing"

"By you."

"Yes, I found it when I was readying him for consignment."

"Consignment? Is that what you call delivering a live body to a mad doctor?"

"It's a living. I choose all my victims carefully. The pilot was a drug courier who liked to use women. I evened the score a bit."

"Who wrote your Bible—Jack the Ripper?" Les started back inside

"Don't be crude. Where are you going?"

"To find out how they knew we were coming."

"The police might arrive."

"You can go. I need to work on their computer."

"You stay, I stay."

Les sat down at the security console. "That's encouraging."

Heck had a number of cameras inside and out and four screens on his console. Les concentrated on the camera at the front entrance and ran the recorded images backwards until he saw himself staggering to the entrance carrying a blurred figure on his shoulders.

"Is that me?" Melody said softly.

Les didn't answer he ran it back a bit more and then pressed forward. Sure enough as soon as his face appeared clearly it was framed by a red square. That along with a series of short beeps alerted those inside that Lester Hensen FBI was entering the building. It was all there inside the red square.

Facial recognition at its best.

Working from that point Les found the links from Heck's computer to the FBI data base.

This is when I find out if Matt Easton is real or I'm dead Les thought. He sent all the links to Easton's computer then started to delete his own image from the security camera.

"They're coming," Melody said.

"I don't hear anything."

"You will."

Deletion was almost complete when he heard a siren.

He left the computer on and hurried to the front lobby. Melody darted ahead and opened the door. But when Les got outside he heard the sirens wailing louder and realized they'd be pulling into the parking lot by the time he reached the sidewalk. Instead he pulled out his badge and lifted it high to greet the rotating lights approaching the lot.

"FBI!" he yelled as the uniformed cops left their vehicle.

"Keep those hands up suh," one man said his gun pointed at Les.

The other policeman was overweight and had trouble getting out.

"Stay there and cover me Jake."

The cop approached and took the wallet from Les. He backed up and examined the ID with his flashlight. Satisfied, he lowered his Glock.

"All clear Jake," he called to his partner who slowly emerged from the passenger seat.

"I'm officer Holly," the man said, "we got a call there was a shooting."

"Yes. Around the rear. I'm calling for back up right now."

Holly started jogging to the back door, Jake lumbering behind him, shirt stained with sweat.

Les pulled out his phone and pretended to speak while edging away from the policemen. When they rounded the corner he looked for Melody. She was gone.

He ran to his car and found her waiting.

She smiled. "You're slow."

"I couldn't find you," he said starting the car.

"I was there. As soon as you eluded the law I left. You didn't notice. Don't fret darling," she added as they pulled away, "you'll get used to it."

"Really? I don't think so.".

"Now what's your problem?"

"You left a dead witness back there."

"He was a contract killer who slaughtered that Nurse and two dogs right in front of you. If I was an ordinary woman he would have raped and murdered me and you'd still be in a cage. So cut me some goddamn slack."

Les was silent for long minutes.

"Let's get something to eat and figure this out," he said finally.

+ + +

Cozy's well-ordered world was crumbling.

The hit men he'd hired to retrieve the Don's heroin were dead—two of them horribly mutilated and Chad, the third, found drained of blood after shooting his way into an animal clinic. What the fuck was that about?

And that priest the Don called in gave him serious creeps.

Cozy considered making Father Dunn disappear but knew it wouldn't redeem him in the Don's stern eyes even if he managed to pull it off—which he doubted.

The tall priest seemed to have a special sense, like a coral snake with yellow eyes. Once in a while his tongue would dart out between his thin bloodless lips as if seeking prey.

Good news was that Father Dunn remained stashed in the safe house and Cozy rarely saw him. However his local sources told him the priest slept half the day and stayed out all night.

Forget the vampire, the joker in this deck was the fucking vet. What was a dog doctor going to do with two ounces of smack? Falconi's drug network hadn't reported any unusual activity.

Maybe this vet was working with the woman, Cozy speculated. He remembered the bearded bartender's tortured confession the night Sal killed him. At the time Cozy thought the poor bastard was crazy with pain. Not any more.

Or maybe this vet has a habit, Cozy thought. Two ounces of pure would keep him off the street for a long time. And junkies would do anything for a score that big. Problem was Doctor Heck had disappeared since Chad assaulted the clinic.

Cozy tried to remember everything Chad had told him about Heck before he got himself killed. It really wasn't much, just that the vet had the Corvette and a pair of trained pit bulls. Chad was also certain that Heck was responsible for what happened to his crew.

Right now it was Heck three, crew zero, Cozy noted. Chad had told him how Heck's dogs had fended off his first attempt and he'd be ready the second time.

At least he'd succeeded in killing the pit bulls.

Suddenly Cozy had an idea.

People loved their dogs more than humans, he reasoned. A man who lost his bodyguards would feel vulnerable.

He called Jason, his computer man and told him what he needed. As usual the young tech wizard was unfazed by Cozy's odd requests.

Feeling like a genius, Cozy took a stroll through the quarter. As usual the local vendors and hustlers put the bite on him for a buck or two. In exchange they gave him the word on the street.

This day the word wasn't good.

It started with Zab, at the news stand who handled a little action for Franny's book

"Mornin' Mister Coz', got your Times Picoon, want the form too?"

"Not today. How the football cards running?"

"Nice an' steady thank you. You hear about that girl down by Bennville?"

"No. What happened?"

"Working girl, Vanessa. Used to stroll by here. Always nice and polite. Pretty too. Somebody strangle her in her apartment."

"Risky business." Cozy gave him a ten, "keep the change."

"Yes suh. Funny thing though."

"How so?"

"Cop told me they found rosy beads 'round Vanessa's neck.

"Rosary beads?"

"What the man said."

Shaking his head Cozy walked away. Coincidence he told himself, the quarter was a magnet for all sorts of freaks. He would make discreet inquiries. He walked a few blocks to his favorite café and settled down to read the newspaper in peace.

After breakfast he started to leave some cash on the table but Louie the proprietor waved him off.

"No charge Mister Costanza, he said with a slight Italian accent. Louie also handled a bit of Franny's book.

"You make the best coffee in the quarter. Croissant was perfect."

"*Grazie.* Thank you. But I'm very sad today."

"Oh why?"

"This very nice girl, worked here once in a while until she started, you know," he lowered his voice, "hooking. And a few nights ago somebody killed her."

Cozy nodded gravely. "I heard. She was strangled right?"

"Strangled yes, with rosary beads. Poor April, she was so young."

"Did you say April? I heard her name was Vanessa."

"April. She lived on Royal somewhere. That's where they found her."

Vanessa lived on Bennville. That's two… with rosary beads. Cozy couldn't help making the association.

The priest was free lancing on the side. But not for money. He wasn't a professional, he was a fucking serial killer

Bad for business Cozy thought as he punched the Don's emergency number. Maybe now the old man will let me whack this maniac and things can go back to normal.

+ + +

Aware of the bounty on Melody's head they brought take-out food back to her place.

"I'm tired of this motel," she said, pouring herself an absinthe, "I think I've located a proper house to rent."

"How did you find it?"

"Craig's List. I told the landlord I'd pay six months in cash. That seemed to do it."

Les didn't answer.

"You're still moody I see."

"Moody? We just left three dead bodies back there and Doctor Heck is still on the loose."

"You mentioned you had some idea of where he might be."

"Maybe. But it definitely will take more than the two of us."

"You'd be surprised at my skills."

"You'd be surprised at Heck's resources. I scoped out his clinic carefully and if you recall he still managed to cage us despite your skills."

"That was an anomaly, I wasn't myself."

"Heck has help from on high."

"So do I."

"Political or spiritual?"

"Spiritual of course. How else can you explain my existence?"

"How do you explain it?"

She took a long swallow of her drink.

"I can't really. How do explain your existence darling? It was more of a plea than a challenge.

Les felt the loneliness behind her question. He drew her close and kissed her.

"Let's take a break and let the universe run itself for a while."

At dawn, driving back to his place, Les marveled at how much intensity a little brush with death could inject into their intimacy.

As soon as he awoke Les contacted Easton. The FBI director scheduled a meeting immediately.

Over lunch he sat without touching his food, listening to Les describe the events at Heck's clinic.

"We got a report some guy was Impersonating an FBI agent at a murder scene." Easton said.

"Heck saw me coming all the way—thanks to Virgil Lake."

Easton put his fork down. "We analyzed the correspondence from Heck's computer. Lake had previously sent files and photographs of our murdered agents, Ken Larkin and Sid Fairman."

"I've got some idea of where Heck might keep his secret lab but I need back up."

Easton stabbed a shrimp and dipped it in hot sauce.

"Once I call for back up Director Lake will be alerted. But if you need an extra gun I'm ready."

"Which reminds me. Heck must have taken my Glock. I need to rearm."

"I've got a spare Glock 45 in my trunk you can use."

"Ammo?"

"Full clip."

"Can't go wrong, let's go take a look."

They walked to Easton's car and he gave Les the weapon.

"It's a G21 .45 caliber with a thirteen shot clip," Easton said, "slightly heavy but it will stop almost anything."

That's good. My nine-millimeter didn't seem to slow anybody down. But Heck's wolf pack does have a weakness. They get spooked by gunfire."

Les thanked Easton but he still needed a holster, a combat knife and an ankle weapon. He'd also lost his Cobra along the way. He recalled a gun shop on the way to New Iberia and decided to do a bit of shopping. Fleeman's Firearms and Fishing Center was located on the side of the highway along with a gas station and grocery store. Les found an ankle holster for the Glock he had just acquired and a snub nosed .38 to replace the spring loaded blackjack he usually carried at the small of his back. He also purchased a serrated fishing knife with an ankle scabbard as well as a box of .45 ammo. Leaving the store he didn't feel as vulnerable until he remembered he was well armed when Doctor Heck took him down without a shot fired.

He considered another visit to Nanny Mojo's place as long as he was in the neighborhood.

Use your head he told himself, do not risk involving Leda and her family in your mess. Anyway he had business elsewhere and it couldn't wait.

It was still early when he pulled into the parking lot in front of Nick's Lounge. When he walked into the bar the aroma of barbecued ribs wafted through the humid air.

Sam the bartender was chatting with a couple of patrons while Nick sat at the end of the bar doing paperwork.

The bald man looked up as Les approached but he didn't smile. Neither did Sam.

"How is Dave doing?" Nick asked, voice flat.

"He seems to be out of danger."

Les sat across from him. "I guess you know by now we're not movie producers."

"Most everybody knows. News flies fast around here."

Les took a deep breath. He didn't have time to be cagey. "Look we have no beef with what you're doing…"

"*Doing* exactly what suh?"

Nick's muscular body seemed to expand with indignation and he looked very angry. At that moment Les was glad he was armed.

"Okay here it is," Les said calmly, "A few nights back Dave and I were nosing around the warehouse in New Orleans on another matter and saw your men offloading cases."

Nick snorted in disgust. "Cases of *what suh*?"

"Whatever it was Nick, your guys were guarding it with Uzis."

Nick lifted his hand and began counting on his fingers. "*Number one*, it's New Orleans, warehouses get invaded all the time. Fish, furniture, meat, doesn't matter—everybody knows that. *Two,* guns are legal out here. *Three*, it might have been whiskey in those cases, also legal. *And four*, the warehouse might belong to Minny."

"As I said I have no beef with you."

"Then tell me what were you doing nosing around there at night?"

Les hesitated. "We were trying to get a line on a certain Doctor Heck."

"Why?"

"We think he's responsible for a rash of killing including the pack that attacked Dave."

"So why are you here?"

"I thought you might know where Heck keeps his animals."

"You mean those nasty, smelly things that keep running around my parking lot?"

"I mean exactly that."

Nick's scowl broke into a slow smile. "Are you hungry Les?"

They took a corner table and Nick served the food and drink himself. "She's still pissed off about Dave," Nick said, tilting his head in Sam's direction.

Les shrugged. "They all seem to be pissed off at me lately. Man this smells good."

"Slow cooked ribs with my own special sauce with Vietnamese fried rice and grilled vegetables," Nick said, setting the plates down with a flourish. "What are you drinking wine or beer?"

"Beer is great."

As Nick went to the bar Les noted he was very agile for a big man. He returned with a pitcher of beer and two frosted glasses. Les raised his glass in a toast. "I apologize for our deception. Goes with the territory."

"Believe me suh I understand," Nick said clinking glasses. "*C'est la guerre* and all that. Now let's eat and you can tell me what brought you to our little corner of the devil's paradise."

Between mouthfuls Les told him how they'd been assigned to cover the murders of two FBI agents and were targeted by Heck and his cohort Serb. "They're somehow connected to a right wing group called the Knights of the Golden Circle. Ever hear of it?"

"I happen to know all about it."

Les stopped eating. "Okay, you've got my complete attention."

Nick refilled their glasses.

"The Knights were a secret Confederate society that was formed a few years before the Civil War. Their original intention was to annex Mexico and set up a series of slave states throughout Central America. When war broke out between the states they set up a spy network headquartered in Montreal Canada because England was partial to the South. Jesse James was a member as was John Wilkes Booth. It's generally believed Jesse James tried to fund a second Civil War by robbing banks. Another of their alumni Albert Pike, distinguished himself by starting the Klu Klux Klan. And of course you know all about Booth."

Nick tossed a rib onto his plate and wiped his hands with a napkin.

"Thing is, they never went away. And now they're gaining strength thanks to someone high up. There's even rumors they plan to assassinate the President."

"That's hard to believe."

"Don't forget Lee Harvey Oswald came from Louisiana. Matter of fact Lee and Dave Ferry would enjoy weekends at Carlos Marcello's farm."

"You think the KGC is connected to the mafia?"

"I *know* they are affiliated with various neo-Nazi militias. They are well funded by the drug trade and protected from on high right up to Washington."

"And you're a liberal whistle blower."

"More than that. I'm Mossad."

Les let it sink in for a few seconds.

"What is Israeli intelligence doing down here in the bayou?"

Nick shrugged. "As you might imagine these people have no love for Jews. And as I said they are heavily, no—*massively*—funded by everything from heroin to human trafficking. This money supports anti-Semitic cells from Dallas to Paris. And a great deal of it is flowing right through the bayou to the KGC in New Orleans. And yes those crates we unloaded contained weapons. These people are heavily armed."

"Actually I know the time and place of their next meeting," Les said.

The bald man sat back and tugged at his earring.

"Very well done *suh*."

"It's tonight."

"I see."

"Would you like to join us?"

"Us?"

"You've already met her."

"It's your party."

"Depending on what happens I'd like to move the party to your warehouse so I can search the area."

"Not a problem."

"Tell me what you know about Doctor Heck?"

"His grandfather was Hitler's zoologist. Under Goering's personal protection Heck performed genetic experiments on animals trying to revert them to their primitive—or purer—state. Yes, lately we've heard rumors of strange, foul, creatures seen around the bayou. Like the ones that attacked you. But nothing connected to Heck. Despite what we know of his background Heck is very low key, way under the radar. But we do think he has a space in our warehouse area. One of my informants spotted him there. He noticed because Heck was driving a Corvette. He said Heck had a companion who seemed to be drunk."

"Did he mention where he went?"

"No. My informant didn't think anything of it. He's a dog owner and Heck had treated his pet. He knows we pay for information on Heck and called it in."

"Called you?"

Nick shook his head. "Not directly. I have a small network. You saw some of them."

Les grinned. "They never spotted me."

"Bravo," Nick said, "so—did you like the rice, how about a few more ribs?"

"I'm done eating for the week. That was dynamite."

"So when do we drive to New Orleans?"

"I'm going ahead. You can meet me at a bar nearby and I'll give you the exact location."

"Why the secrecy?"

"You of all people should know."

"How about a drink for the road?"

"I love Louisiana hospitality. Thanks but have to roll. Give me your number, I'll text you the address."

Sam lifted her nose skyward as Les passed the bar on his way to the door. He reminded himself to ask Dave about that the next time he visited the hospital.

Driving back to Lafayette Les felt optimistic. He now had a bit of back-up at the KGC meeting and a guide though the maze of warehouses in New Orleans. His main problem was keeping Melody under control—and undercover.

Neither of them could risk having her true identity known. She would have to take a night flight to Rio. Under the circumstances it might not be a bad move he speculated.

Les was surprised by the emotions stirred by the possibility of Melody's sudden departure. I'm in deeper than I thought, he told himself.

The realization troubled him but he didn't have time for fucking *issues*. Right now he needed to find Heck's secret kennel and destroy rabid wolf pack that chewed up his partner.

Chapter 30

Melody was not pleased "That bar owner? He'll turn me over for the bounty as soon as he recognizes me. They spread my description in every juke joint in the area. I can't ever go back to the Styx." Her tone softened. "That's where we met."

"I remember. And don't worry about Nick. He's not a bounty hunter he's a Nazi hunter."

"Seriously?"

"The Knights of the Golden Circle share their racist politics. We'll be crashing their meeting tonight. You don't need to come if you think…"

"I wouldn't miss it. You know I heard of this group shortly after the Civil War. Then they disappeared. Or so I thought. Anyway, you're going to need me."

"Nick is trustworthy to a point you can't…"

"Trust me he won't know. I've had years of experience."

They had time for dinner before the meeting but Melody couldn't dine openly. "Why don't you take a nap darling?" she suggested, "I'll go out for burgers or pizza."

Les didn't argue A little time alone would help center himself for the coming encounter.

"Make it pizza," he yawned. As soon as she left he fell asleep.

His rest was disturbed by vivid dreams. A dark winged creature snatched up a striped serpent while a shadowy hunter stretched his bow and launched a flaming arrow. In the flaring light he saw Leda…

He was awakened by the rattle of the key unlocking the door. Melody came in bearing a large pizza box aloft.

"Did you miss me?"

"I fell out." Les checked his watch. "I was asleep for over an hour."

"I walked until I found a place that smelled good. Let's eat, I'm famished for solid food."

Melody was right, the pizza was delicious. However Les was dismayed to see her follow it up with absinthe. At least she's not doing drugs he noted. Last night's heroin scare had dialed her way down.

Les texted Nick the address of a small bar in the Treme district. Along the way Les stopped at a costume and novelty shop called Fat Tuesday where he purchased a fake moustache, eyebrow liner and a longshoreman's cap. Lake had already made him a public figure and Serb would certainly spot him.

Melody also decided to do some shopping. She bought a sleeveless motorcycle jacket, which she wore over a black lace tank top and black jeans. To this she added a motorcycle cap, slanted sunglasses and high heel black boots. She put one foot on a chain and her hands on her hips.

"How do I look?"

"Like a neo-Nazi wet dream."

Melody kissed him on the cheek. You look awful by the way. But nobody will know it's you."

"On the other hand everybody will be looking at you."

"I can handle it, I hope you can."

"Try not to stir up the psychos. I can't use any side trips on this run."

Les had chosen a rundown bar called Homer's that he had seen in passing days earlier. When they arrived Nick was already there. He squinted through the low light when they entered then turned back to his drink.

There were a few other men at the bar none younger than sixty. Les guessed they were holdovers from Katrina. The water damage on the walls was still visible.

"Two shots of Jim Beam," Les told the bartender.

When Melody started to protest he took her arm and whispered in her ear. "No absinthe in here please. Keep it simple."

"I love it when you take charge."

"Keep your head in the game."

"Just how do you mean that darling?"

Les ignored her and sat one stool away from Nick. The ancient jukebox was playing Elvis Presley's *Heartbreak Hotel* and all six customers seemed to know what he was singing about.

"Excuse me," Les said, "are you waiting for someone or is this seat available?"

Surprise flickered across Nick's stoic expression then vanished.

"Seat's not taken," he said flatly.

The bartender wiped the bar, set down two tumblers of bourbon and moved back to the cash register.

Melody sat down.

"Cheers," she said, lifting her glass.

+ + +

Cozy couldn't wait to tell the old man about this.

After Chad fucked up the hit Doctor Heck had gone into hiding.

Except Cozy figured an angle.

He had Jason find him a rare—and expensive—breed of dog that was available right away.

At the same time Jason placed an ad in Craig's List. It said that because the owner was called away suddenly he was forced to give away his beloved Czech Vzak to a responsible party. It also stated the new owner must prove they can provide a suitable home for "Vladamir."

It worked like a charm.

Doctor Heck was among the first to respond. He provided an impressive professional resume and assured them Vladamir would enjoy a safe, healthy environment.

Under the pretense of inspecting Vladamir's new home Cozy arranged to meet Heck and show him the dog. Heck seemed quite eager on the phone.

The only drawback was he had to bring Sal along to make sure the large dog behaved. And to help him torture Heck.

"You stay in the car," Cozy reminded, "I'll go inside with the dog. You come in five minutes later."

"What if it's locked?"

"Break it."

"Okay. Uh listen Cozy…"

"Yeah."

"After we're finished can I keep the dog?"

Cozy had to admit it was a beautiful animal with its silver tipped coat, alert ears, intelligent eyes and compact, muscular body. It also cost him four grand.

But it wasn't a good idea to refuse Sal a favor.

"Sure, you can have him."

The address Doctor Heck provided was in the warehouse district near the old cemetery. As he had assured over the phone he was there waiting at the entrance to the complex

The rumpled figure that stood beside his Mercedes SUV hardly looked dangerous. I could have handled this by myself Cozy speculated. Except for the torture part. That was Sal's specialty.

Doctor Heck smiled and waved them closer. "I'll lead the way. It's not far."

"Okay Sal, this is it," Cozy said under his breath, "you remember the plan?"

"Sure, we take care of the guy and I keep the dog."

Cozy sighed. "I get out first with the dog and take him inside. You wait five minutes and come in behind me."

"Yeah right. But then…"

"…you keep the dog Sal."

Doctor Heck led them to a building near a cluster of fish suppliers, one of which—Clete's—Cozy recognized. It was part of Falconi's network.

They parked behind Heck's SUV. Cozy got out of his Cadillac and opened the back door. The dog lay on the seat and seemed reluctant to leave the car.

Cozy tugged at his leash and Vladamir finally jumped out. He yawned and stretched displaying his lean, muscular flanks.

Doctor Heck beamed when he saw Vladamir. "Such a magnificent animal. Come inside Mr. Cozanza, I want to show you my special kennel."

"We can't wait."

For the first time in years Cozy carried a piece, a Beretta 9mm. He felt Vladamir dragging at the leash and pulled him inside. There was a loading area in front but beyond that the interior of the industrial building looked like a modern medical clinic.

"Come, come," Heck said, bustling ahead of him. As he went further inside Cozy became aware of a dank, unpleasant odor.

"What's that smell?"

"Oh that's coming from the place next door. Rotten fish."

It smelled more like rotting meat. When they passed the hospital area they entered a room with four large cages. Each cage had a large mat on the floor and oddly, a toilet.

"Do you toilet train your animals?" Cozy said.

Heck turned. He had a gun in his hand.

"No Mr. Costanza the toilet is for you."

"What is this—I bring you a prize dog as a gift and you threaten me?"

"Please do not insult my intelligence. When I saw the post on Craig's List it seemed too good to be true. I made a few inquiries via computer and *voila* I discover that you purchased Vladamir only two days previous to making him a gift to me. Very clever Mr Costanza, you calculated I would not be able to resist and I am embarrassed to say you were right. I coveted this very rare Czech Vzak. And do you know why?"

"Educate me please."

"Because he is part wolf. Now turn around."

Heck patted him down and found the Beretta. Cozy remained calm knowing that Sal was about to come in heavy.

"Well well, you are armed."

"Yeah well, this is New Orleans and this is a valuable dog. Now please lower your weapon and I'll be on my way."

"Not until you people call off this absurd vendetta. You don't seem to realize my associates are more powerful than your Don Benito. Oh yes I know who he is. What I don't know is why you people wish to kill me."

"We don't want to kill you. Don Benito wants to know what happened to his pilot, his fifty K and his heroin."

"Step inside this protective cage and I'll tell you.'

"Protective? Protect against what?

"You'll see."

Cozy entered the cage and saw the TV screen above the bars. Heck locked the door and crossed his arms.

"I know nothing of the money and drugs. You'll have to discuss those matters with a lady called Melody.However I do have your missing pilot. Would you like to see him?"

"Uh sure."

Heck went to a console and flicked a switch.

The wall at the far end slowly began to rise. Behind it was another wall made of glass. Pressed against the other side of the wall was a group of foul, snarling creatures, their bared teeth jutting from drooling red jaws matted with thick hair. Their reddened eyes bulged with aggression when they spotted Cozy and they began pounding their clawed fists against the glass.

"That's him at the left," Doctor Heck said, "the one with the blond mane."

Except for his humanoid posture the creature Heck pointed out was unrecognizable as the former daredevil drug courier and playboy Cozy had known his dirty, tangled hair hung to his furry back and his nose had broadened to a snout. His eyes rolled madly as he clawed at the glass, trying to get to Cozy.

"That's not Larry," Cozy said, voice cracking.

"Not any more. Now he's number four in my wolfpack. Perhaps I'll make you number five."

"You're crazy. I'm a made man."

"That means nothing to me."

"It'll mean something trust me," Cozy said. His eyes darted to his watch. Where the fuck was Sal?

An electronic buzzer sounded.

"Now Mr Cozanza you will understand why your threats are meaningless."

The TV screen above Cozy's head winked on and he saw Sal slowly entering the building. His Colt Python .357 magnum pointing the way.

Sal's big gun against doctor bug brain's Glock, Cozy speculated. Counting experience and pure natural meanness his money was on Sal.

"Would you like to watch my pets at play?"

With growing horror Cozy saw what Heck meant.

The glass wall slowly slid to one side and the creatures scrambled over each other to get through. At the same time a putrid stench reached his nostrils and he nearly retched. But his senses froze with naked fear as the creatures poured through the opening, their rabid jaws gnashing hungrily.

And then they were gone.

Cozy heard a screech and looked up at the TV.

Shock drove him to his knees. The creatures were literally eating Sal alive, tearing open his ribs and devouring his organs.

A gunshot boomed, then it was quiet.

Cozy crawled to the toilet and threw up his guts.

He lay on the floor for some time until he heard the rattle of a key in the lock. He turned and saw Doctor Heck smiling down at him.

"I going to release you now. I want you to go to your Don and assure him I did not steal from him. Do you understand?"

"Yes," Cozy managed, "I understand,"

He got to his feet and moved towards the exit.

Abruptly he stopped, propping himself up against the wall. Sal's mangled remains lay between him and fresh air.

Fighting an urge to collapse he edged around the mound of torn, bloody flesh and entrails.

"One more thing Mr Costanza."

Cozy paused, eyes pressed shut.

"Yeah what?"

"Thank you for the dog."

Chapter 31

Melody checked her reflection in the rear view mirror. These days, car mirrors were not backed with silver. It was the antique mirrors she had to avoid. "Do you really think we'll be able to waltz right in there without some form of ID?"

Les glanced at Nick who was standing next to the car. "She has a point."

The bald man slapped the top of the Malibu in frustration. Les had parked a half block in front of Nick's truck and from that point they could see the building where the meeting was being housed.

"So what do you suggest?"

Melody leaned over and smiled. "Let me go there alone and reconnoiter. Sit in the car. I'll be back before you know it."

Nick got in and watched Melody walk toward the building her stride both sensual and determined.

"She is some lady… FBI?"

Les lowered his voice.

"Classified."

"I understand. Are you armed?"

"Yes. I assume you are."

Nick smiled "PK 380. You?"

"Glock .45."

Nick's smile faded. "Where did she go?"

"Who Melody?" Les said, trying to sound casual, "I thought I saw her turn the corner."

Thankfully Nick didn't question the fact there was no corner between the car and Melody's destination. Les had glimpsed her dart forward with incredible speed and vanish into the shadows. He still didn't know all the powers at her disposal.

Probably better that way Les thought.

"That moustache really changes your looks. I almost didn't recognize you back there."

"That's good."

They fell silent for a few minutes.

"Cigarette?" Les said finally.

"I don't usually smoke but I'll join you."

Les passed him the pack, his eyes on the building ahead. As they smoked Nick tapped his foot impatiently.

"You nervous Nick?"

Nick gave him a wry smile. "Perhaps. You see with me, these people… it's personal."

"It's personal with me too. They nearly killed my partner."

"I admire your attitude Les."

"Have you boys had time to bond?"

Melody was standing beside the car. She leaned into the open window and kissed Les.

"There are two goons at the door. You need a password to enter."

"Please tell me you have it."

"Of course. It's 'blitzkrieg.'"

"Bastards," Nick said under his breath.

"Anything else I should know?"

"You were right. I do look like a neo-Nazi wet dream.They practically made me homecoming queen. A wealthy admirer told me about the hospitality suite on the second floor for their most elite members. There's a password for that too."

"Which is?"

"Lebensraum, which means…"

"…room to grow," Nick said, "it was Hitler's rationale for ravaging Europe."

"Well then that's settled, we're ready to join the party. I'll go first and mingle."

Before Les could say anything she was gone. He looked at Nick. The stocky Mossad agent was checking his weapon.

Les and Nick walked slowly to the building at the end of the street. It was a former hotel converted to a ballroom that housed various events. The pair of blond giants at the door sneered as they approached.

Les saw Nick bristle and stepped ahead of him.

"Blitzkrieg," he said quietly.

The sneers stayed but the guards let them enter.

Inside it looked like a meeting of the Aryan Brotherhood. Prison tats and Mohawks abounded, along with biker vests, beer bellies, scruffy beards, leather pants, studded belts, confederate caps and cowboy boots. The crowd was mainly male and the occasional females were beefy and militant. Most wore tank tops that showed off their tattooed bosoms.

Two of the walls were decorated with Confederate flags and a third banner hung from the ceiling. It was black, with a gold circle in the center. A pair of crossed swords arched over the circle.

The ballroom inside the former hotel had been renovated and looked quite elegant in stark contrast to the low rent white supremacists drinking beer and swapping macho bullshit. With his longshoreman's cap and fake moustache Les looked almost civilized.

Nick too, seemed cleaned and pressed in his Hawaiian shirt and gold chain around his neck.

Les grabbed a beer and edged through the throng. Food was being served at two tables both of which were well attended. He looked for Melody but she didn't seem to be there.

Les spotted Serb and nudged Nick. "The skinny guy with the bruised nose. His name is Serb. Friend of Carson at Minny's."

Nick nodded. "I know Carson."

"They're connected."

"What happened to Melody?"

Les shrugged. "My guess is she's upstairs with the elite. That's her style."

"Shall we?"

The ballroom had a wide stairway that curved up to an upstairs balcony. Beyond that were two rooms on either side of a center door. Each room had a picture window looking out over the ballroom.

There were two men guarding the stairway and Les could see two more on the balcony. Obviously that's where the party is Les thought as he moved to the stairway followed by Nick.

"Lebensraum." Les said to the guards who blocked their path. The guards parted and let them pass.

They repeated the process at the head of the stairs.

The guests in the rooms off the balcony were decidedly upscale. Eschewing the beer kegs below, both of the rooms had a hospitality bar and tables laden with fine food. The men had smooth florid skin and sleek suits and the women had hard bodies and lots of jewelry. The conversations were muted and laughter was at a minimum. In fact what little merriment there was came from the corner of the bar where Melody was holding court surrounded by a coterie of admirers, one of which was wearing her motorcycle cap.

No sense breaking her concentration Les thought. He moved into the facing room to get a drink then paused at the doorway.

Virgil Lake was standing in a corner, deep in conversation with Doctor Heck.

Nick stood behind Les.

"Melody's doing good work."

"I wish I had a camera." Les said.

"Why?"

"Those two guys in the far corner, the short one with the wrinkled suit is Doctor Heck. The tall elegant man is his protector."

"It happens Mossad is always prepared for these occasions."

Nick adjusted his large wristwatch and edged through the knots of people. Les stood aside and observed the bald man got into position and lift his hand to scratch is head. Then he looked at his watch and put it to his ear as if making sure it was ticking. He lifted his hand and scratched his bald dome again.

Nick smiled as he edged his way back to Les.

"Two shots. Where do you want me to send them?"

Les gave him his Email address which Nick recorded on his smart watch.

"Actually we can leave," Les said, "one picture's worth a thousand words."

"Wait a few ticks. I think I see some of our leading citizens. There's the county sheriff talking to the councilwoman." He waved. They waved back.

"No doubt I've picked up a few new customers," Nick said with a gleeful smile, "and new sources of information."

The sound of a dinner bell drew everyone's attention. People from the other room drifted inside including Melody's fan club. One of them was still wearing her cap. The bell rang again and the room fell silent.

A tall, sleek man dressed in a grey suit, pale blue shirt and yellow tie stepped forward and lifted his arms. As he ran a hand through his long silver hair Les noticed the diamond ring on his finger.

"Members and supporters of the Golden Circle, My name is Wellington Swan and I am here to thank you for your loyalty to our sacred cause. I am also the bearer of good news. In a short time our plan will be implemented and all of you will be rewarded with the knowledge that you helped bring about a new era in American history. An era that will witness the rebirth of true southern ideals and the supremacy of our kind over the lesser races that now threaten the very foundation on which this great nation was built."

There was a healthy round of applause.

Les looked over at where he had last seen Lake but the FBI director was gone, as was Doctor Heck.

Wellington Swan kept speaking but the content was predictable. Les had the nagging feeling he had heard the name before.

"Let's split before they get to asking for donations," Les said quietly.

Nick nodded and they moved slowly to the exit. Les caught Melody's eye and she gracefully edged to the door. One of her admirers stopped her.

"Not leaving?"

She put a finger to her lips. "Ladies…"

He leered and let her pass.

From the balcony Les saw that the crowd had congealed around a speaker who was literally standing on a box. Les was reminded of the old Nazi beer hall rallies.

Melody was first down the stair and her exit attracted a ripple of interest, drawing attention from the speaker who was approaching a fever pitch. Les saw one burly biker type follow her outside and hurried to join her. But when he reached the sidewalk there was no one but the biker in sight. Scratching his head the biker returned to the festivities inside.

"Where is she?" Nick said.

Les started walking.

"She'll be waiting in the car."

I'm beginning to get used to some of her talents, he thought.

"I recognized four local politicians back there including a judge and a sheriff," Nick said.

"I spotted the top dog of them all. And you took his picture."

"Who is he anyway?"

"Happens to be state assistant director of the FBI. The other guy was Doctor Heck."

"Now we have the smoking gun."

"We still don't have Heck. If we can squeeze him…"

"I wouldn't count on it, he is after all third generation Nazi. No—I expect he has a cyanide capsule handy."

"Maybe you're right. But it's worth a try. Either way we get rid of him. Bad news is Lake will be a lot more difficult to pin down without Heck."

"Lake?"

"Virgil Lake, our FBI defector."

Les knew he was sharing information freely on short acquaintance. However exposing the Knights of the Golden Circle for what they were required publicity.

As he expected Melody was waiting for them with a satisfied smile. "I've got the names and numbers of some of our state's most prominent citizens," she said proudly.

Les got behind the wheel. "We'll compare notes later. Right now we're going to flush out Heck's secret lab."

Nick led the way in his truck, a black Ford 150.

Les followed, still unsettled by what he'd seen and heard at the meeting. Virgil Lake was a powerful man to go up against. If they failed to nail Heck they'd be targets of a full frontal assault by the Federal Bureau of Investigation. They'd be road kill within forty-eight hours.

"Are you sure you can trust Nick?"

Melody's question echoed his thoughts.

"I'm about to find out. Right now he's all I've got."

"You've got me."

Les glanced at her. "Thanks. I'm going to need back up."

"You mean you want me to wait in the car."

"It means I still remember the cage you were in. You were powerless remember?"

Melody pretended to fan herself. "I've always depended on the kindness of strangers."

"This could be a trap. If something happens you're my secret weapon."

"You're so romantic darling. But you're perfectly right. You go with Nick and I'll lurk in the shadows."

"I didn't mean…"

He was cut short when Nick's truck turned into the warehouse area. Les slowed down and followed him.

A wide drive cut through the middle of the complex and smaller roads sliced between the large buildings.

What little light there was came from the loading ramps.

Nick' stopped and turned off his headlights.

Les did the same.

Nick walked back to the car. "Best we proceed with the lights off. I know the way but it's a bit of a maze back there. So stay close."

He was right. Once they turned off the main drive the darkened buildings all looked alike. Minutes later Les saw Nick tap his red brake lights twice and he stopped. Nick got out of the truck.

"What's that?" Melody whispered. She sounded nervous.

As Nick approached Les saw he had a dog with him.

"It's just…"

"…a dog. I know. We don't get along well with them."

As she spoke Les saw the animal's neck hair rise. With an angry snarl the dog bared his teeth and lunged at Melody's window.

"Whoa Jonah," Nick said pulling back on the dog's leash. "Sorry, he's usually friendly."

Les took a flashlight and some tools from the glove compartment and stepped out of the car. Jonah ignored him and kept growling at Melody

"What's up with the dog?"

"Jonah is an excellent hunting dog. He's familiar with the foul stench that lingered in my parking lot on occasion. We'll need him to locate Heck's zoo."

Les glanced at Melody and put his palms up in a gesture of helplessness.

She folded her arms and looked straight ahead.

The two men continued on foot leaving Melody to sulk. For a few minutes Jonah meandered along the sides of the darkened buildings. Then the animal paused, body tensed and ears cocked forward.

A second later Jonah strained at the leash, pulling Nick past one of the larger fish warehouses. The sign read Clete's Sea Feast, the operation owned by Minny Free. Across a narrow gap was a larger warehouse. When Les saw the sign it all came together in his brain.

Knight Fisheries, owned by Wellington Swan, the man who just spoke at the executive meeting of the Knights of the Golden Circle. . Jonah led them to the rear of the building which was effectively obscured by a wall. Nick produced a pencil flashlight and in the brief flare Les saw a set of double steel doors.

Jonah stiffened and began to growl. "Easy Jonah, good boy," Nick murmured. He turned to Les. "That's it, any ideas?"

"Heck likes security cameras. You own one of these buildings Nick. Is there any way to knock out the power?"

Nick snapped his fingers. "These old warehouses all have an outside fuse box. I know mine does."

He moved back and began flashing his light along the buildings side."

"Here it is. Or is it? This box is new. And it's locked."

Les stepped closer. "Let me try. I have some experience with security hardware."

Nick held the light while Les pried the box open with his screwdriver. Instead of fuses there were five colored wires: red, blue, green, yellow and white. Using his combat knife Les cut the green and blue wires

"That should take care of the alarm and the cameras," he said.

As they approached the rear doors Jonah growled softly.

"Easy," Nick said. He glanced at Les. "Something is in there all right. Jonah knows."

"Let's see what it is."

Along with his flashlight and screwdriver Les had brought a set of burglar's picks. It was one of the skills he'd acquired over the years.

The steels doors were heavy but the double locks were fairly ordinary. It took him about seven minutes to open them.

Inside it was very dark and the two flashlights revealed an inner door. Straining at his leash Jonah paused at a large dark stain on the floor that seemed to be oil but on closer inspection proved to be blood.

The two men looked at each other and drew their weapons. The inner locks were less difficult. When Les entered the huge space he saw that it was an industrial sized version of the playpen that served as Doctor Heck's animal clinic. Cages, electronic equipment, computers, surgical tables, instrument trays, X ray machines, drug cabinets, Intravenous equipment: all clean, white and antiseptic, unlike the building's grimy exterior.

"He's got a hospital in here," Nick said.

"That's strange."

"What?"

"The cages. They have toilets."

"Yeah so?"

"Animals don't flush."

Les found a control panel and computer. He'd cut the alarms and cameras but the electrical power was still available. He found the computer and switched it on.

Suddenly the room was flooded with light.

Nick blinked. "Why did you do that?"

"Negative. We've been made."

Guns sweeping the area they moved to the door.

Before they got there they heard an electronic hum behind them.

Jonah started barking in alarm. Les saw the rear wall slide open revealing a large glass panel.

Cold sweat froze his limbs.

Pounding and clawing at the glass was a pack of madly yowling beasts, jaws drooling with rabid hunger.

They fought each other to squeeze through as the glass panel slid open.

Chapter 32

"In here!" Les yelled as the creatures clawed though the sliding wall panel.

He yanked open a cage door, pulled Nick inside and slammed the door shut. Jonah hadn't needed guidance having dived in the moment Les opened the barred door. Les felt the lock click and hoped the cage could hold back the shrieking creatures who were shaking the door and thrusting their long arms between the steel bars, their clawed hands like hungry jaws. .

Les drew his weapon.

"Don't shoot Mr. Hensen," an electronic voice boomed over a loudspeaker.

Too late. Les fired a round into the ceiling and the pack scuttled back.

"Fortunate you didn't wound one of my pets," the voice said

"Call them off or we' kill them all." Les shouted.

"*Think* Mr. Hensen. You're in no position for a firefight. You're locked in a *cage*."

Nick glanced at Les. "He's got a point."

"Fuck him. Look at those things. If we don't kill them they'll tear us apart."

After scurrying away at the gunshot the creatures circled back. They slowly advanced on all fours, carefully creeping nearer. Their foul stench was stifling. They stared with angry red eyes, snarling and snapping their jaws.

"Call them off Heck." Les. said, raising his Glock.

Nick did the same, pointing his pistol at the leader of the pack, a beast with dirty blond hair.

"You may get us but your pets will be gone."

"You wound one and you'll suffer before you become like them."

The blond-maned beast lunged at the cage thrusting his clawed hand inside. Instinctively Nick stepped back

Les fired. A third red eye appeared above the beast's snout and it dropped heavily to the floor.

With blurring speed the other beasts in the pack scrambled behind the panel.

"You have made a serious mistake Mr. Hensen. You and your friend are going to join my little wolf pack."

Les glanced at the door. Melody was due to arrive soon. Her powers would alter the odds considerably.

+ + +

Melody was frustrated.

Usually she could steer her men into the warm harbor of seeing things her way.

Les was more difficult. Despite destiny and her most seductive wiles honed over centuries, he stubbornly went his own way forcing her to follow.

However he could be incredibly sweet and charming and… *accepting,* despite his previous belief system.

And a devastating lover. That, neither of them could deny.

Unfortunately he had this maddening tendency to treat her like an ordinary female.

But he'd learn.

Melody's amplified senses sliced through her thoughts. She heard a shuffle and her vampire eyes picked out three figures moving along the side of the darkened warehouse.

Silently she slipped out of the car and melted into the shadows.

As Melody followed the three men a bolt of fear flickered through her body and she knew Les was in danger.

Then she heard the dog barking.

However the men she was following had yet to reach the warehouse Les and Nick had entered. In fact the trio seemed a bit uncertain of their destination. Meanwhile the threat was already inside and imminent.

She was at the entrance to the warehouse long before the three men even located the right building in the dark.

Melody found the outer door unlocked. Inside the area reeked of fresh blood. Someone had been killed there recently. She was also uncomfortably aware of a foul stench seeping from somewhere beyond d the inner door. The barking had stopped but she could hear a cacophony of howls, grunts and snarls. And she felt her lover's terror.

As Melody started to rush inside she heard an odd sound.

A large shadow leaped through the door with incredible speed. Nearly overcome by its fetid odor she managed to wrench herself aside to avoid a direct blow. Even so a claw raked her shoulder slashing open her skin.

The scent of her own blood acted as a stimulant raising her physical powers to their hieght. The creature's distorted face loomed up close, its rancid breath burning into her nostrils like acid.

She struck without hesitation, sinking her fangs into its filthy throat but it failed to achieve the usual hypnotic effect. Instead the creature thrashed violently from side to side in an effort to dislodge her.

And its thick blood tasted like rotted flesh.

As the creature weakened her grip tightened but it took all her will to keep absorbing its abominable essence.

Finally it was dead.

Melody staggered back from the body and retched violently, spraying the walls with stinking black vomit.

She felt unusually weak, as if she'd been poisoned.

Lungs heaving, Melody lurched outside for fresh air and collapsed.

Chapter 33

Franny Five Angels had never seen Cozy like this. Usually the Capo was cool and collected. Tonight he looked half crazy. His tie was loose, his suit wrinkled and his tan shoes were spattered with crap.

But it was understandable. Nothing like this had ever happened before. Three top guys whacked. Franny still couldn't believe Sal was gone. He'd always thought the huge enforcer was indestructible.

Most of all Franny couldn't believe he was going out on a hit. Cozy had called him and Falconi to a bowling alley for a meeting and informed them they were on the clock. In the parking lot he popped his trunk and showed them a buffet of heavy weapons to choose from. Ak47's, shotguns, grenades, even a Tommy gun

"We're going to need serious firepower," Cozy said as they drove. "Those things ain't human."

"You mean the vampire?" Franny ventured.

Cozy shot him an annoyed look. "I mean those fucking things that ripped Sal apart like a paper bag."

"Jesus," Falconi said, "exactly what kind of *things* are we up against?"

Cozy shifted nervously behind the wheel. "They're like... part human part wolf... or bear or something. And they're fast... they opened up Sal in sixty seconds flat."

"Jesus," Falconi said again. .

"Maybe they're werewolves," Franny suggested, "you know, like in the movies."

"They ain't werewolves and this ain't the fucking movies Franny. It's some kind of mad scientist shit and we're gonna blast Heck and his freak show back to hell. You got that?"

Franny hesitated. "Yeah I got that."

"You sure the three of us will be enough?" Falconi demanded. "I mean if these things are as fast as you say."
Cozy nodded. "I called in three zips, experienced boys. They're meeting us at the cemetery."
The cemetery. Franny shrank back into the corner of the rear seat. Cozy was wrong. It *was* a fucking horror movie and to Franny's personal horror he'd been chosen to play a major role.

He had selected a shotgun as his weapon of choice but now he wished he had that Tommy gun with a fifty round clip.

He was reassured when he saw the zips waiting in a black Maserati. The three men were dressed in dark suits and wore shades despite it being night. They looked like pros unlike Cozy, Falconi and him.

Franny noticed that Falconi was sweating which didn't make him feel any better. *I shouldn't even be here,* he brooded *I never even roughed up my broads at the club.*

Cozy led the way into a maze of darkened warehouses not far from the cemetery. As the car rolled slowly through the darkness Franny's heart began beating rapidly.

When Cozy switched off the lights and they got out Franny had trouble catching his breath.

"We go on foot from here. Doctor Heck has security cameras. We'll have to rush him and start blasting before he can react—old school."

Cozy said something in Italian to the zips. They fanned out and faded into the shadows

"Let's go," Cozy said.

Franny thought everyone could hear his heartbeat booming as they slowly made their way between the dark buildings.

Cozy was a yard ahead. He stopped and lifted his hand.

"Here's the plan. We blast the doors open and our button men rush inside and shoot everything in sight. Got it?"

Falconi cocked his Uzi. "What's that smell?"

Franny racked a shell in the chamber of his 12 gauge automatic. At the moment it seemed like a pellet gun.

"Let's roll," Cozy said moving forward. He lifted his Mac10 and stopped.

"What the fuck."

Franny edged to his side and looked down. A female lay unconscious a few feet from the outer door.

"Holy shit," Franny said, "that's the vampire broad we've been looking for."

"You sure?"

"Gotta be her."

"The keys are in the car. Take her back and stash her in the trunk."

"You got something I can tie her up with?"

"There's a pair of cuffs in the glove compartment. And a Taser."

Grateful to be out of the line of fire Franny hefted the shotgun over his shoulder and started dragging the girl's limp body through the darkness. She felt surprisingly light and the sudden sound of gunfire behind them pumped his adrenaline past high. He reached the car quickly, popped the trunk, found the cuffs and snapped them around the vampire's wrists before lifting her inside and shutting the trunk lid firmly.

Breathing heavily he leaned against the car, He had never moved so efficiently in his life.

It came at a price.

A giant foot pressed against his chest making it hard to breath. A surge of nausea burned his throat and the adrenaline high suddenly evaporated leaving him limp and exhausted.

The flat clatter of automatic gunfire drew him erect. Instinctively he took the shotgun from his shoulder and edged unsteadily towards the sound.

He heard footsteps and lifted the weapon.

Cozy and Falconi came hopping out of the darkness, running awkwardly in their Italian shoes.

"Don't shoot," Cozy yelled.

As they neared Franny saw their faces. Both men were pale and wild eyed as if they had seen a vision of hell. Falconi's shirt and suit were drenched and he was panting hoarsely.

"What happened?" Franny said.

"They're all dead. Get in the fucking car."

+ + +

Les kept his Glock pointed at the creatures circling the cage.

"Call them off Heck."

Suddenly the creatures charged.

But not at them.

Without warning the room erupted into a shrieking chaos of gunfire, smoke, shrapnel and blood.

Les hit the floor.

Nick covered Jonah with one arm and buried his head in the dog's neck. Les put both arms over his head and peered through the cordite smoke but screams, curses and gunshots were all he could make out.

A pair of pointed shoes ran into view then stopped.

Les heard a metallic spray of gunfire and braced himself for a bullet but someone yelled and the shoes vanished.

Then the quiet settled in.

Les looked up. Doctor Heck's sliding wall was back in place. Except for a line of bullet holes it seemed like an ordinary wall again. Heck's glass paneled DJ booth was gone—as well as Heck.

"Are you alright?" Les asked.

Nick got up slowly and checked for injuries. "I think so."

"How about Jonah?"

"He's a trouper."

Les tried the cage door. It was locked.

"You and Jonah better stand behind me."

When they were out of the way Les lifted his Glock and blew the lock apart with two well-placed shots.

To get outside they had to step around—and over—the foul remnants of Heck's wolf pack. The unknown gunmen had cut them to hairy shreds. *Fitting*, Les thought. He paused to take a few pictures of the carnage then hurried out to the moist night air.

They stood for a moment taking deep breaths. Les looked around.

"Where's Melody?"

"Probably stayed in the car if she's smart."

Les hoped he was right but knew he wasn't.

Chapter 34

Melody woke up in a dark, confined space. She was used to that.

What she wasn't used to were the handcuffs. She did have unusual strength but not enough to break steel chains.

Her ankles were bound as well. However her captor had handcuffed her hands in front so she was able to curl into a ball and free her feet.

She remained calm. If the priest had found her she'd be dead already. Humans could be dealt with provided she had mobility.

How she got here was the first question. She remembered killing the creature that attacked her. Its blood must have contained some toxic substance, possibly wolf cells which could sicken a vampire.

Perhaps even some form of opiate which rendered her unconscious.

Whatever —it put her in this ridiculous position Melody fumed. She reminded herself that she had no choice. The stinking beast was almost as fast as she was.

She wondered what had happened at Heck's warehouse. She sensed Les was alive but in what state she could not tell.

It hadn't taken her long to realize she was in the trunk of a moving car. She was trying to open the latch with her toes when she felt the car slow down.

In that moment Melody made a choice.

She could have broken free and ran the moment the trunk was opened. Bullets, knives, wouldn't stop her and she'd worry about the handcuffs later.

But Melody was curious.

She wanted to know exactly who was hunting her and why.

So she coiled and waited to see who opened the trunk.

The face that peered down at her was smooth skinned with flat cheekbones, a thick jaw and frightened eyes. A thin scar ran through one brow.

"I think she's awake," he said, and slammed the lid shut.

"What did Don Benito say?" A second voice said.

"He wants us to wait for the priest."

Melody stiffened. She could hear clearly what was said outside.

"How long do we wait?"

"I can't find the whacko son of a bitch."

"So what, we keep her in here?"

"Not in my car. We need to put her on ice for a while."

"There's a storage unit next door to my place where I keep my booze safe from the degenerates who work for me."

"That's good. You did good Franny."

Franny, Don Benito, the priest: now all Melody needed was the identity of the man with the scar and she could take her leave.

"Is she cuffed?"

"Just like you said Cozy."

Cozy. Melody readied herself to move the moment the lid opened.

"I still want to make sure there's no fuck ups this time."

The car started moving again. Melody tried the latch again. The car stopped and she waited to leap out.

Nothing happened.

Again the car started to move. Again it stopped and Melody coiled her body

The trunk opened.

She sprang.

Something punctured her calf.

Melody took a few staggering steps and dropped.

+ + +

As Les already knew, Melody wasn't waiting in the car.

Nick looked around. "Where do you think she went?"

"Whoever shot up Heck's wolf pack probably grabbed her. Unlikely as that seems."

"Why is that?"

Les caught himself. "She uh usually knows how to avoid trouble. Training."

"Do you want to search the area?"

"Sure."

It was a mandatory exercise but futile. Les knew she was gone. He could *feel it.*

They circled back to the car without finding anything that might hint at where Melody went.

"She is the girl with the bounty on her head right?" Nick said finally.

"Yes."

"Well the mob put out the bounty."

Les nodded. "You think the mob blasted Heck's operation and grabbed Melody?"

"It's a distinct possibility given the circumstances."

"Well maybe you can ask some of your contacts if they heard anything."

"What about you?"

"Melody wanted to check out a guy who owns a couple of strip clubs. Has one in the Quarter called the Tempest."

"Franny Five Angels."

"That's the guy. Do you know him?"

"Everybody knows Franny. Runs a hot club I hear. He has a little gambling operation as well. Never known to be violent *but* he is connected."

"Then the Tempest is our best bet—but not together. We'll do better if we go in separately."

Nick nodded agreement. "I can use a drink, see you there."

+ + +

Les reloaded his Glock after he parked near the Quarter. .

He caught his reflection in the rear view and saw he was still disheveled from the turkey shoot that destroyed Heck's mutants. He went into a nearby lounge and cleaned up as best he could in the men's room. After splashing cold water on his face and hair and straightening his wrinkled shirt and stained trousers he examined himself in the pock marked mirror. Barely passable. The person staring back at him was a bit too wild eyed. Anyone would make him as someone to watch.

Les took a few deep breaths. *Cool it,* he told himself, *never let them see you sweat.*

A quick scotch at the bar settled him down and he walked to the end of Bienville Street where the Tempest Club was in full swing.

Three strippers were performing on a circular stage to Ray Charles singing *What I Say*. Two of the girls were black and one a redhead.

Below the performers were three bars spaced apart to allow access to the stage by the customers who were tucking bills into what little the girls wore. A couple of large men in tight suits made sure things remained peaceful—if not quiet. Because the music was loud and the patrons louder.

Les didn't mind. In a way it was easier to get lost in the general din of the festivities. The club also had booths and scantily dressed waitresses offered a variety of services including food and drink.

He bought a drink at the bar and wandered around pretending to inspect the strippers working different parts of the stage. The music never stopped shifting genres from Disco to R&B to Vegas Pop to Hip-Hop and the ladies too kept morphing from Asian to African to Nordic. An international smorgasbord for the lonely dude.

The bouncers were placed discreetly around the large room. Les counted six, including a large man with a Mohawk guarding what appeared to be an office.

On his second trip around the bar he spotted Nick in a booth talking to a blonde girl wearing pasties and a bright smile.

Nick too was smiling but his eyes were scanning the room. He saw Les and half nodded.

Les went back to the bar. He wasn't exactly sure what he was looking for but he had a strong hunch he was in the right place. Then he saw something that got his attention.

A paunchy man came out of the office, said something to the guard and went inside again. What Les found interesting was that the paunchy man's designer suit was rumpled, his shirt wrinkled and his tie askew.

Les recalled being in the same condition when he parked the car. Whatever the reason the man definitely seemed stressed when he spoke to the granite statue guarding the door.

Keeping one eye on the office he looked for Nick.

The blond girl had departed. Les went up to the booth and pretended to be surprised at seeing an old buddy. Nick invited him to sit. Les ordered two drinks for him and his old pal from the waitress who swooped over: long legs, net stockings, silver hip spangles, big smile.

To complete the pantomime Les watched the waitress wiggle away then leaned over to make a comment. To anyone watching, cameras included, they were just two buddies who happened to bump into each other in a strip club.

Except what Les said to Nick had nothing to do with the waitress.

"Check out the office door on the left."

"I just saw Franny Five Angels pop out," Nick said.

Les nodded. "Thanks for the ID."

"You think he was there?"

"Right now he fits my profile. Let's drink our drinks and wait it out."

It was a long wait. After thirty minutes or so Fanny came out again, said something to the bodyguard and went back inside.

In the meantime the beat went on: the strippers kept grinding, the waitresses kept smiling, the liquor kept flowing and the cash registers kept ringing like it was New Years Eve.

It all stopped cold when Les saw the priest.

Chapter 35

Molly Winston was had been a prostitute for three years.
Now twenty she looked at least five years older. She had a two-year-old daughter and an Oxycodone habit to support. With the pills she didn't have to shoot up. Needles would scare her little girl Wendy.
Molly worked hard at her trade and made enough to hire a woman to care for Wendy while she was out walking the streets.
But it was past midnight and she'd barely made enough to pay the babysitter and score some Oxy. So when the minister came strolling into view Molly gave him the come on, sure he wasn't a cop.
"Hi honey, looking for some company?"
When Molly saw his strange eyes she was sorry she asked. She was relieved when the minister paused and smiled.
"I was looking for someone exactly like you," he said with exaggerated courtesy.
"Well I'm sure I can make your dreams come true."
"I'm certain you can. Shall we go someplace private and discuss it?"
"There's a little hotel down the street."
"Someplace where we don't have to deal with people." He pointed to the white collar circling his black shirt. "You understand."
"Sure honey but…"
"Perhaps that little alley over there. It's nice and dark. We won't be seen."
"Well okay," Molly said reluctantly, "but it will cost extra."
With a flourish the man took a hundred dollar bill from his pocket and showed it to her.
"Will this compensate for your discomfort?"
Eagerly she reached for the bill. "That will cover it honey."

They walked to the nearby alley and he led her away from the dim light into the shadows.

"Kneel down," he whispered hoarsely.

This won't take long, Molly thought as she knelt. A quick blowjob and she could score her pills.

To her surprise the man stepped behind her.

He dropped a beaded necklace around her neck.

There was a crucifix dangling from the necklace.

"I'm going to give you a blessing," he said pulling the necklace tight around her neck.

+ + +

When it was over Father Dunn felt tired.

He left the prostitute in the alley still wearing the rosary around her lifeless neck and walked back to his apartment. As soon as he arrived he fell on the bed. *It's always this way* he thought, slipping off his shoes. First the exhilaration of being God's avenger against the filthy tempters of Satan. Then a feeling of depletion after *His* will had been done.

Before he could remove his collar he fell asleep.

Father Dunn awoke two hours later to the electronic beeping of his phone. Only two people had the number. One was Don Benito who rarely called anyone. So it had to be that blasphemous fop Cozy. The nap hadn't helped. Too exhausted to answer he let it go to voicemail.

He showered, made coffee, but still felt empty. He was contemplating going for another walk when the phone beep roused his curiosity. Cozy never called twice. He picked it up and saw this was call four.

"Yes?"

"Where the hell were you?"

"Doing my work. What is it?"

"The girl is here with us."

Father Dunn's depression evaporated.

"Where?"

"The Tempest. In the quarter."

"I'll be there shortly."

His mood expanded like an excursion balloon and he began to dress, humming as he pulled on his socks. If they truly had her it would be a sign that he was being rewarded by God himself for executing *His* vengeance.

He was prepared for this moment. From the closet he extracted a black leather satchel already packed with the tools he must have to dispatch a vampire to the depths of Hades: a vial of holy water from Rome, a sharp wooden stake tipped with a silver point, a mallet to drive the stake and a razor edged silver and steel dagger to behead the unholy bitch to prevent her vile soul from returning.

It wasn't really heavy.

When Father Dunn arrived at the Tempest he had to suppress his revulsion at the unholy lusts of Babylon.

The doorman tried to open his satchel until he produced his cell and invoked the power.

"I'm outside, this gentleman, er what's your name sir?"

The doorman was an ex-lineman from LSU who played on the Saints' practice squad. But this dude made him nervous.

"Nathan."

"Yes Nathan wishes to examine my bag."

Father Dunn handed Nathan the phone.

Nathan listened, gave him back the phone and unhooked the velvet rope.

Inside it was deafening. However another large man met him at the door and escorted him to the office. Along the way he was disgusted by the spectacle on stage, the debased whores dancing for an audience of bestial sinners.

Thankfully the office was soundproofed. However he was disappointed to find three men in the room and no female vampire.

Father Dunn smiled at Cozy. "Where is she?" he asked gently, as if inquiring about an innocent child he intended to baptize.

"We have her on ice."

The other two men grinned, obviously an inside joke.

"I don't find this amusing. I'm a professional. Has Don Benito been informed?"

Their grins faded.

"He's in the loop," Cozy said without conviction. "You want the girl? She's right next door."

Father Dunn's expression remained grim despite his growing exultation. After all these years tracking her kills across Europe to San Francisco and now New Orleans she was finally in reach of his vengeance.

He hefted his bag and started for the door.

"Not that way," Cozy said, "too public."

Father Dunn followed him through a rear door that led outside. They were trailed by the other two men.

Two cars were parked behind the club, otherwise the area was deserted. In contrast to the electronic din inside it was quiet and their shuffling footsteps were like those of a funeral procession. *Which in effect they are* Father Dunn thought, savoring the moment.

One of the men behind, a dapper type he vaguely remembered as part of Don Benito's crew, scurried ahead to a low, square building with a metal door. The man unlocked the door and turned on an interior light.

It was cold inside, obviously refrigerated.

Father Dunn sucked in his breath.

Leaning against stacks of liquor cases, her wrists manacled, was a raven haired woman with wide green eyes and smooth white skin. Even restrained she exuded an air of fine breeding. When she saw him her sensuous lips curled into a defiant sneer but Father Dunn knew she was terrified.

The vile bitch was well aware of her grim fate.

He opened his bag and took out the tools that would ensure the eternal damnation of the devil's whore.

First the holy water to weaken her strength.

Then the stake between her breasts.

A strong blow with the mallet to drive the stake into her heart.

Finally... saw off her head to display alongside the others in his private rectory

Chapter 36

"It's going down."

Nick squinted at Les. "What is?"

"That priest. He's been hunting Melody."

"Why?"

Les didn't answer trying hard to come up with a plan.

"You want to rush the office?"

"Yes. But I'm not sure that's a good idea."

"Right. All these clubs have back doors, fire exits…"

"Fire exits… wait right here."

Les hurried to the men's room. There was only one person there washing his hands Les went inside the stall and pulled wads of toilet paper from the roller. He heard the door open and close and the man had left. Les set the toilet paper on fire and dropped it into a bin full of paper towels. Before he left he grabbed a bunch of paper towels and stuffed them under his shirt. The bin was becoming a blaze as he went back to rejoin Nick.

"Get ready to move fast," he said twisting the paper towels together.

"Where we going?"

"I'm going to try to go around back."

"Follow me. I know the way"

"Not yet." Les waited as a number of employees hurried past to the now smoking restroom. Then he lit the paper towels and left the flaming mass under the table as he slid out of the booth.

"Fire," he said loud enough to get attention.

Some people started for the exits while others turned their attention from the strippers. The dancers too, paused to see what was going on. All the while Les moved steadily after Nick who led him through an unmarked door to a kitchen area stacked with crates.

"Hey!" someone yelled.

Les turned and saw one of the bouncers coming after them. The man was huge and he looked angry. He yanked the Glock from the small of his back and met the bouncer's charge.

"I got you mother…"

As the big man lunged for him Les dropped to one side and smashed the bouncer's knee with the Glock

Howling the man stumbled and fell. Les smacked him hard behind the ear then stepped over his limp body and ran out to a parking area outside.

Men were hurrying out of a small storage building behind the Tempest Club. Les recognized one as Franny Five Angels and lifted his Glock.

"Stop. FBI." He yelled

Franny stopped short and raised his hands. The other two men behind him were outlined in the dim light coming from the open door.

One man stepped behind Franny and was momentarily out of sight. A shot boomed. Les glanced aside and saw Nick crouched behind a nearby car, his pistol smoking.

At the first blast Franny dove to the ground and lay flat. The other two started shooting and ran in different directions, firing wildly to cover their retreat.

Les hit the deck and fired three quick shots. One of the fleeing men took a few drunken steps and dropped. The other had already reached the street.

Les ignored him and rolled slowly to his feet as a wave of raw fear washed over him. Melody was in danger. Desperately he sprinted through the open door gun pointed like a direction finder. .

Melody was there.

And the priest was trying hard to kill her.

He had a sharp stake in one hand and a blade in the other and he had Melody pinned between two stacks of crates and a brick wall at her back.

She was handcuffed and her feet were bound but she managed to duck, hop and weave, eluding his fierce thrusts with incredible balance.

Les fired over his head but he only intensified his efforts, running at her with the stake extended like a lance. She sidestepped and fell against the crates which began to topple throwing her to the ground.

The priest pounced, driving his blade into her side.

"Agghh," Melody groaned, blood spurting from her wound.

The priest lifted his metal tipped stake over her exposed chest when Les hit him with a full body block.

To his surprise the priest staggered back but stayed on his feet. Momentum carried Les forward and to break his fall he grabbed at the stake.

Les hit the concrete hard still gripping the stake.

Hot pain sliced his thigh and he turned in time to see the priest's blade flash down like a silver hawk.

The knife gashed his shoulder and in desperation Les rolled, wrenching the stake free. But now he too was trapped between the crates and the wall unable to get to his feet before the priest's long knife struck. He used the stake to deflect another slash but the priest pinned his arm with his foot and brought his weight down hard. Helpless Les watched the blade swing down at his neck.

A shrieking Melody leaped onto the priest's back and hooked her handcuffs around his throat, yanking him off Les. The priest twisted, his knife flailing at Melody while she continued to throttle him with her cuffs. As the priest wildly swung his arm back Les gripped the stake with both hands and thrust upward.

He felt the sharp wooden spear punch into flesh and pushed hard.

The priest uttered a high squeal and fell back on top of Melody. Les regained his feet, kicked the knife out of the priest's hands and tried to pull the man's shuddering body off her.

"Let go of his neck," he rasped, 'it's over."

Slowly she released the pressure and unhooked herself. Blood gushed from the priest's mouth.

Les looked up and saw Nick at the door, his pistol weaving uncertainly from side to side.

"I hear sirens,: he called out.

Les used the blade to cut the cords binding Melody's ankles.

"We'll take care of the cuffs later."

The priest's thin body twisted into an agonized convulsion his hands gripping the stake buried in his abdomen. Twitching and groaning his yellow eyes rolled up and fixed on Les.

"For the love of God shoot me."

He opened and closed his mouth but a pink froth bubbled over his words.

"Let's go," Melody said.

"Shoot me..." the priest wheezed as they ran out into the parking lot.

+ + +

Outside Les saw a couple of the bouncers round the corner and start trotting towards him trailed by some curiosity seekers. He fired two shots: the first into the ground in front of them which threw up a cloud of debris, and the next over their heads

They all stopped short and scrambled back to safety.

But the sirens were louder now and there was one body on the pavement and another in the storage house.

And they had nowhere to go.

Nick called out. "Over here. Hurry."

Les followed him to the rear of the storage building where a long, narrow driveway led to the street behind the Tempest Club. However with Melody's handcuffs and his wounds they were still too visible.

As if responding to his thoughts Melody disappeared.

"Where is she?" Nick said peering down the long drive way.

"She came with us but..."

A taxi came shooting down the street and skidded to a stop. The door opened.

"Get in!" Melody said calmly.

The driver half turned.

"Emergency Room right?"

She nodded. "As fast as possible."

"Hey lady he's bleeding in my cab."

Nick gave him a hundred dollar bill. "As fast as possible."

A cacophony of sirens and whoops filled the air as fire trucks, police cars and an ambulance converged at the Tempest's entrance around the corner.

"What's goin' on?" the driver said eyes in the rear view.

Les shook his head. "Fire I think."

Nick gave Melody a hard look. "How did you find a cab so fast?"

She shrugged. "I told him It's an emergency."

"I mean… so *fast*."

"*You* sure seemed to know the ins and outs back there." Les said to divert the conversation. "Spend a lot of time watching the showgirls?"

Nick snorted. "I deliver fish there. The Tempest is one of our customers.""

The cab let them out at the Ochener Medical Center but they didn't go inside. Instead Nick helped Les pick the lock on Melody's cuffs then took a cab back to the Quarter to pick up his truck.

Les and Melody detoured to a twenty-four hour pharmacy to pick up bandages and supplies before taking a cab directly to Melody's suite.

There, Melody cleaned his shoulder wound and surveyed the damage. It wasn't pretty.

"Might need stiches," Les said.

Melody sighed. "It is deep."

"Know how to sew?"

"Perhaps I know something better. Trust me?"

"You save my life. The bastard was ready to behead me."

"Darling if you hadn't arrived I would have a stake through my heart."

"Okay agreed, we trust each other. Do what you have to do."

"This won't take long." Melody carefully stacked four gauze squares and dampened them with peroxide.

"Give me your knife."

Les took the combat knife from his ankle and handed it to her.

The stab wound in her shoulder inflicted by the priest had long since healed. With one deft slice Melody cut her wrist. As the blood poured out she swabbed it with the gauze. Then she pressed the bloody compress over his wound and bandaged it.

"Leave that on for a few hours and see if it helps."

"What about you? Now you're bleeding again."

"Not for long."

"I need a drink."

"We need more than that."

For the next few hours Melody ministered to his worn body, first with bourbon, then a long massage followed by intense passion.

As dawn neared she gently pushed Les out of bed.

He gathered his battle-soiled clothes and stumbled out into the cold, damp night to find a cab.

Chapter 37

Franny knew he had suffered a heart attack. When the first shot was fired he dove to the ground and lay still. In the confusion he managed to roll underneath a car. From there he crawled under another one, further from the shooting. He forgot that bullets have a long reach. A spray of dirt exploded in front of him and a slug punctured the metal pan above his head. Suddenly he couldn't breathe. Sweating heavily he drew air in short gasps and his heartbeat hammered his brain. More shots were fired but it didn't matter. He was a dead man anyway.

He lay on the ground until he heard the sirens come closer. Maybe the medics would find him in time he thought. Still struggling to catch his breath he crawled out from beneath the car. Revolving lights on top of the ambulance illuminated the area and Franny saw them lift Falconi onto a gurney. As they rolled his body into the waiting vehicle Franny realized he couldn't go to the medics for help without having to answer a lot of questions. He was already involved in more shit than his job description called for.

Very slowly he walked to a back entrance. The place smelled of smoke but the air was clear inside his office. Wheezing he sat heavily in his chair and took a bottle of cognac from his desk drawer. He poured a healthy shot in a water glass and drained it in one gulp. The burning liquid spread through his belly and chest opening his lungs and he took a deep breath, then another.

Jesus, Falconi dead and... he suddenly thought of something. If they searched the store room they'd find the girl's body. His heartbeat started pounding again.

Franny took a few more breaths, downed another cognac and waited for the detectives.

+ + +

"A fucking priest?"

Franny's surprise was genuine enough to convince Detective Sharon of the NOPD.

"Yeah, somebody shoved a spear through his belly. Took him a long time to croak."

"Jesus. Who could have done that?"

"Looks like a cult thing."

"Cult? In my storage shack?"

Detective Nobel Sharon was a tall black man with a permanently morose expression on his long face. The bags under his eyes made him look tired as well. Which he was.

As a homicide detective in New Orleans he had more cases than any Sherlock Holmes, James Bond or Batman could handle.

"Yeah. Could be this is the scumbag we've been looking for." Sharon drained his cognac. Franny poured him another.

"You've been looking for this priest?"

"We've been looking for somebody who's been strangling hookers in the Quarter. Nine so far. Strangles them with Rosary beads just like the ones we found in his pocket."

"Jesus."

"So you were here when the shooting took place?"

Franny looked around his office as if it could bear witness to his lie.

"Everything happened at once. Somebody yells fire. I look out the door and the place is full of smoke. Then I hear shots. I go outside and these guys are having a gunfight in my corral. So I hit the ground and crawl back inside. Ruined my suit. Meanwhile they put the fire out before the department got here."

He turned up his palms in a gesture of helplessness.

"Dead priests, gunfights, what the fuck is going on?"

Detective Sharon didn't buy Franny's bullshit but he really didn't care. The dead priest closed the book on a *big, juicy* case. The kind of case that got a homicide detective on TV. Anything else was icing on the cake.

"Do you know Anthony Falconi?"

"Tony sure, he's a regular here. Why?"

"Somebody shot him. We're picking up bullet casings all over the lot. It was a little war out there."

Franny shook his head. "This town. They're all nuts. You want a cigar? My friend just came back from Cuba"

"Maybe it was a drug war. Word on the street has it Falconi was a major dealer. Thanks, a cigar would be nice with this brandy."

"Cognac," Franny said, "the stuff is fifty years old." He lit Sharon's cigar. "What makes you think it was a cult thing? The priest I mean."

"Oh there was all this stuff a leather bag. A bottle with a cross on it filled with water, a Catholic Missal, a big wooden hammer... other things, like the spear that killed him has a silver tip."

"Weird. I still don't figure anybody doing that in my storage shack. Only thing I was worried about is somebody stealing my liquor."

Sharon examined his cigar. "Oh yeah I was meaning to ask you. Who else has the key to the shack?"

Franny was ready for that one. "My day manager, my night manager and me."

"I'm going to need names and numbers."

"No problem."

"Good."

Sharon took out his phone and examined his messages. Two texts and several emails. All from TV producers. He took a sip of cognac. Serial killer priest killed by cult. He'd probably make People Magazine and Sixty Minutes.

"So what happens now?"

The question roused Sharon from his speculations.

"I've got a press interview out front in twenty minutes. They all want to know about the Rosary Bead Strangler."

Franny relaxed a bit. This took the heat off Falconi. He weighed the odds.

The priest couldn't talk, the fucking mutants were dead, which left doctor weird and the bitch still out there. Meanwhile half their crew gone. Maybe now Cozy would listen to reason.

"How many did you say?"

Sharon looked up from his phone. "What?"

"How many broads did he kill?"

"Nine. All young hookers working the Quarter."

"Fuck."

"Yeah." Sharon drained his glass and deposited his cigar in the ashtray." "Thanks for the drink Franny, I gotta go, they're waiting. Don't forget those names and numbers."

Franny watched him leave for his moment on camera with a mixture of relief and apprehension. For now the heat was off him and Cozy. But odds were the media would start nosing around Falconi's killing. Was it connected to the priest? Was he connected to Falconi. Was he connected to the priest? Plenty of witnesses saw the priest enter the club and his office.

Franny knew Detective Sharon was on Cozy's pad but there was only so much a cop could do. He hoped the Don had enough muscle to keep the lid on this.

Otherwise they would all go down.

In the meantime he needed to see a cardiologist.

+ + +

Wellington Swan III had been born on third base and firmly believed he had hit a triple. He never questioned his family's wealth and position, accepting it as his royal due. While he considered politicians vulgar his power extended to Capitol Hill and the money he inherited increased every year no matter how much he tried to spend it.

And for years he had poured a good chunk of that cash and power into his family legacy: The Knights Of The Golden Circle.

His great grandfather, his grandfather, father and now he, served to defend the traditions and values that made America great. However that legacy was in danger.

"How in hell did you let things get so far out of hand?" He asked the question lightly as if discussing a drunken fight at a party but his guest was clearly uncomfortable.

They were in the study of Swan's mansion in New Orleans' Garden District. On two sides the walls were lined with books, many of them leather bound first editions. On the wall behind the large carved wood desk hung a portrait of Nathanial Swan who made a fortune in cotton and wisely invested in the rum business in the Caribbean before the Civil War. In one corner were two leather armchairs and a small table upon which rested two cut crystal decanters and glasses. Swan sat in one chair waiting for an answer.

"Everything was going fine until those two undercover agents arrived."

Swan shook his head. "If you consider a wave of senseless murders as 'going fine' I have to question your judgment."

Virgil Lake sighed heavily and examined the bottom of his glass. "I'd be the first to admit Doctor Heck was carried away in his zeal but..."

"I want the entire Wolfpack Project shut down."

"Be reasonable Well, I tell you Heck is on the verge of creating the perfect killing machine—unstoppable, untraceable."

"Except that a squad of armed thugs stopped your perfect killing machines cold."

Lake waved his hand. "An anomaly. This is still a work in progress and we're right there."

"Where is Doctor Heck now?"

"I've got him in a safe house."

"Good, that simplifies matters."

Lake drained his glass. He had met Swan in boarding school and by now knew when his childhood friend would not be swayed.

"Alright, have it your way. I'll pay Heck off and make sure he gets out of Dodge."

Swan shook his head. "You don't understand."

"Enlighten me."

"The moment we cut him loose he'll go straight to the CIA. I've been informed Doctor Heck has already initiated contact with elements within the Agency."

He peered at Lake. "We can't risk him revealing our existence. Think about it Virgil: if the CIA finds out what you've been doing you'll become expendable."

Lake noticed he didn't say *we*. He also saw Swan's point. Especially the part about becoming 'expendable.'

Swan's tone softened. "Look I know this project is dear to you. And to be sure Doctor Heck's credentials are impeccable. However our planet is already full of willing assassins. What's important is that our sacred cause has endured for over a century and is on the verge of breaking out. We are as you put it, right there. All one need do is watch the news. Lines are being drawn. And we control the men who control this state," he smiled at Lake and lowered his voice, "maybe very soon this country."

"I understand. You're right as usual. Be sure I'll handle it. And about Falconi?"

"A suitable replacement will be installed and it will be business as usual."

"Please inform me of the details."

"Oh you'll be the first to know dear friend. What would we do without the FBI?"

+ + +

Virgil Lake left Swan's mansion with renewed purpose. Wellington could be inspiring as well as threatening. He would clean up this matter and remove any trace of its existence.

First things first he thought, punching Heck's number.

Of course Walther demanded to meet at an outdoor café because of his damned dog. It was risky but Walther was so ordinary looking no one would remember him. Except for the dog of course.

Lake had to admit it was a magnificent animal, strong and alert. He even listened to Walther go on about the dog's pedigree with some interest.

"Czech Vzak is a very rare and special breed, also known as the wolfdog. In nineteen fifty-five German Shepherds were interbred with Carpathian wolves, I believe the ratio was seven Shepherds to four wolves. The result was a superior canine which was used by the Czech Special Forces."

He drank his Mint Julep and stared at Lake through thick glasses. "Which brings me to the point. This unfortunate setback must in no way impede our progress. Give me four months and I can rebuild a suitable site to continue my work. Six months and I'll have mutant predators superior to the ones I have already created—who will kill without hesitation."

Swan was right Lake thought, our planet is already full of assassins—who will kill without hesitation or detection.

"I'm glad you feel that way," he said to Heck, "I've arranged a transition I believe you'll find to your satisfaction."

"Transition?"

"There's a private plane waiting to take you to Mexico. There you will be free to continue our project."

Lake slid a newspaper across the table. Inside was a thick envelope.

"There's twenty five thousand to get you started.

You'll receive another hundred thousand when you arrive in Mexico City. "

"Plane waiting… you mean tonight?"

"The sooner the better."

"Vladimir."

"Who?"

"My dog."

Lake waved his hand. "Private jet, private landing field, no problem."

Heck put the envelope inside his wrinkled jacket. "It won't take me long to pack my things."

"We can go in my car."

When they got back to the safe house Heck seemed uncertain.

"Anthony can help you carry your things. I'm sure you have a lot of books and papers."

"A few hard drives," Heck confided with a smug smile.

The dog remained in the car, his head nestled in Lake's lap while they waited.

It didn't take Anthony very long.

He slid behind the wheel and started the car.

Lake picked up his phone. "I need a cleaner at 7474 Dumaine Street."

After receiving an affirmative he sat back and idly stroked Vladamir's's head.

Anthony lifted the envelope containing the cash.

"What do you want me to do with this?"

"You keep the money," Lake said, "I'll take the dog."

Chapter 38

"You're not serious."

"I'm as serious as Ebola. It's over."

Les exhaled slowly, trying to grasp what Easton was telling him.

"You got the photo of Virgil Lake with Doctor Heck. Jesus, those dead mutants at the warehouse killed two of our agents…"

Easton carefully lay down his fork and leaned back.

"About those dead mutants."

"What about them?"

"They weren't there."

"Not there? I gave you pictures. I can't fucking believe this."

"Believe it. My guys confirmed there was some kind of shootout at the warehouse. They found blood samples but no bodies. They also reported a lingering odor. Look," Easton added quietly, "Lake has resources at his disposal. Clean up crews, political clout and near full authority over our sorry asses. Speaking of which—you're being transferred."

They were having lunch at Eddie's BBQ in Lafayette and the place was full which prevented Les from venting his anger at full strength. As it was he had to restrain himself from sweeping food, plates and glasses off the table. Instead he slammed his fist on the table and when he spoke his voice was shaking.

"I'll be goddamned if I'm going anywhere. I've got a partner in the hospital and the psychoscum who put him there is still free."

Easton folded his arms and looked down at his uneaten ribs.

"Actually Doctor Heck was picked up this morning. Some fishermen found him floating in the Bayou."

Les stared in stunned silence.

"Which means the photo of Lake with Heck means nothing,"

"Which leaves me up shit's creek without a paddle." Les said.

"Something like that."

Les jabbed a finger at Easton. "Okay Heck is out, but we still have Serb. He can link Heck to Lake. And he can expose The Knights of The Golden Circle. We can publicly out the assistant state Director of the FBI as a member of a secret racist organization. That's still possible dammit."

"Give me a break Hensen. Officially my hands are tied. With you transferred I have nobody undercover. More important—nobody I can trust."

Les sat back and flexed his wounded shoulder. It was already beginning to heal.

"Where do they want to send me?"

"Hawaii."

"At least it's not Alaska. What about Dave?"

"He'll be evaluated when he gets out of rehab. Until then he's still on the payroll."

"That's something anyway." Les laughed under his breath as if he thought of something ironic. "We were patsies from the jump weren't we?"

Easton smiled. "You managed to do major damage to a mob operation, found who killed our agents and helped burn down Heck's mutant factory. I'd say whoever sent you got their money's worth."

"What about you, how do you stand now?"

Easton toyed with his food and shook his head.

"I know Lake's dirty. And it might surprise you to know that I've had Wellington Swan on my personal radar for the past two years. But Swan's connections reach to Capitol Hill. Two congressmen and one senator we know of. Not to mention a number of judges here in Louisiana. So right now I'm underwater on this."

"So?"

"So I wait for the right time, because I'll only get one shot—I miss and it's game over."

Les sighed. "I hear you."

"So when do you want to leave for paradise?"

"Meet me here tomorrow, same time. Did you bring those files I asked for?"

"Under the table, the shopping bag at your feet."

Easton looked hard at Les. "You're not planning to do something stupid with your buddy Nick are you?"

"If I do you'll be the first to know."

"You boys did a first class job. Sorry you got shafted."

"So am I."

"By the way, that guy you put down?"

"Yeah?"

"Anthony Falconi, a major drug dealer."

"He was a lousy shot. Which reminds me. You might want to check out a fish company called Clete's, belongs to Minny Free of Minny's. Also Knight's Seafood owned by our pal Wellington Swan. Both next door to Heck's hell hospital. They're probably running drugs through there."

"That's affirmative. We've had reports from our informants."

"That's about it." Les reached for the bag, "See you here tomorrow."

Easton frowned. "One more thing."

"Yeah?"

"Did you say *psychoscum?*"

+ + +

Frustration clamping his belly Les tried to walk it off but found himself circling back to his car. After making sure he wasn't being tailed he drove to his new motel. He tried to take a nap but defeat and anger clawed at his brain. Finally he got up and fitfully scanned the files he'd requested from Easton.

There were no surprises. Typical jackets on typical organized crime figures. The thinnest was the file on Francesco "Five Angels" Pentangeli . Although suspected of running a gambling and prostitution operation he had never been arrested.

One of the jackets was especially curious.

Augusto Benito, reputed to be Don of the New Orleans family. There was no record of citizenship papers, immigration papers, nothing. And yet Don Benito held a driver's license, was a prosperous businessman, and despite a conviction for felony assault twenty five years ago had never been visited by ICE. Predictably, he was associated with a number of prominent politicians.

Les stashed the files and went out for coffee. Although he thought he was driving aimlessly he eventually found himself at Nanny Mojo's.

As it happened the place was full. Which meant there were three men at the bar. Papa Ezekiel sat reading the newspaper at his usual table nearby. And there were three young people at a rear table eating beignets. The men at the bar were drinking beer from bottles. A total of seven. Eighth person who came in was on the waiting list.

That happened to be him.

Standing in the tiny kitchen behind the bar, Leda didn't acknowledge his presence. On the speakers Laura Benitez was singing *I Know You're Bad.*

Papa Ezekiel looked up from his paper and motioned to the empty chair at the table.

"Afternoon."

Les sat down. "Place is packed today."

"It's our daily double. Nanny's herb beer and beignets. Word 'a mouth. Been like this for two days. Ever since the beer been ready. You look like you could use some."

Les caught her sweet scent before she spoke.

"What can I get you?"

He looked up and collided with Leda's violet eyes.

"Uh… guess I'll try the daily double."

She seemed amused to see him flustered. "Beg your pardon Mr Hensen?"

"Herb beer and beignets. Nice to know you remembered my name."

Leda's light honey skin flushed pale pink. "I'll get your beer."

Papa Ezekiel furrowed his brow and studied the newspaper while Les listened to Muddy Waters sing *Hoochie Coochie Man*. There was low buzz of conversation punctuated by occasional laughter. All in all there was a cool, calm vibe inside the place. An oasis of peace amid the fires raging outside.

Leda put a paper napkin on the table and placed a bottle on it.

"Your beignets will be ready soon."

The first thing Les noticed was that the blue bottle had no label. The herbal beer inside tasted of juniper mixed with sweet black tea. It was smooth and relaxed him immediately. The beverage was definitely alcoholic but the herbal infusions gave it a soothing edge.

"Very nice," Les said.

Papa Ezekiel leaned close. "Nanny put some Kava in the brew."

"Old man you think you're whispering but I can hear you back in the kitchen," Leda said, setting a plate of beignets in front of Les.

Papa Ezekiel glanced around the room. "Now don't be tellin' fibs. We just passin' the time."

"We're *all* passin the time Papa but you got to watch what you say to some people."

"Did I do something to offend you? Les asked. "Last I remember I gave you a ride and was polite to your gramma."

She flushed again. "I'm sorry it's just that... Papa go see to the customers a minute while we talk."

Grumbling he did as Leda asked. She sat in his chair and looked at Les. "Forgive me if I seem impolite. It's just that you're carrying a lot of baggage right now."

"Baggage?"

"Whatever you've been involved in has affected you in a deep way."

"Well yes, that's true."

"Might even change your life."

"That's been on my mind."

"Do you still have the pouch Nanny gave you?"

Les checked his pockets. "I changed clothes," he said sheepishly.

"Keep it on you. It will absorb evil energy."

"I'll remember."

"How do you like Nanny's beer?"

He grinned. "I like it a lot."

"Good for the soul."

She started to get up.

"Hold on, I wanted to ask…"

Leda's hazy violet eyes seemed to see inside him.

"Some things you just have to ask yourself."

She smiled sadly and stood.

"I'll bring your beignets."

When Les returned to his room he searched through the clothes he'd tossed on the floor. Finally he found it in his shirt pocket. The shirt stank of sweat and fear and the pure white cotton pouch Nanny Mojo had given him had turned almost black.

+ + +

"Why do you need these files?"

"Isn't it obvious?" Melody said. "These are the men who are still hunting me. Eventually they'll find another priest."

"You can always go someplace else."

"Where would you like to go darling?"

Les refreshed his scotch. "Actually I'm being transferred to Hawaii."

Melody made a face. "Too sunny. How about Seattle?" Then she sat upright. "Seriously? You're not really going?"

"I'm thinking about it."

"What about us?"

Les looked at her and shook his head. "That's a big question."

"Massive actually."

"Haven't found an answer yet."

She lit a cigarette." At least you're working on it."

He moved closer and kissed her. "Can't help it. That's my problem."

"Your problem is you think you can outrun fate."

Again Les had no answer.

As if in reproach Melody prepared an absinthe and rolled a joint. Les had convinced her to ease up on the cocaine or so he thought.

She fell silent and began poring over the files she had demanded. Les knew she intended to go after them. Melody was what she was and these men were determined to destroy her.

Morally Les had no trouble justifying Melody's intentions. Realistically he had no illusions. For every Mafia captain she removed, another would pop up in his place. The significant difference being she would no longer be on their America's Most Wanted.

Which brought him back to his own dilemma. If he accepted the transfer Dave would be here alone—and vulnerable.

Les had no illusions. Men like Virgil Lake and Wellington Swan didn't like loose ends. Perhaps it would cast less suspicion if he should have a surfing accident in Hawaii. Or maybe trip and fall into a volcano.

Perhaps it was the joint he was sharing with Melody but his suspicions took shape. This was far from over.

While Melody continued to study the files Les saw an old fashioned photo album under the coffee table. He reached down and began to idly glance through. The cloth edges of the album were charred as if burned, but the photographs were undamaged.

The pictures in the front of the album were mainly daguerreotypes yellowed with age. The people were stiffly posed and dressed in the ornate clothing worn in Paris during the era. Then the photographs changed venues. There were pictures of grand mansions and the New Orleans waterfront. The people wore more Americanized fashions, from men in hunting clothes to ladies in ball gowns.

Suddenly Les stiffened.

It was a photograph of a woman who looked exactly like Melody standing beside a man who looked a lot like him.

The same photograph he had seen in Nanny Mojo's shop.

"What is it darling?"

Then she saw the album. "Oh—where did you find that?"

Les showed her the photograph. "Why didn't you say something?"

"I tried to tell you. Kept trying as a matter of fact."

"One picture is worth a thousand words."

"You're right. I'm sorry. I just didn't know what you'd think. I didn't want to scare you."

"Scare me? Of course I don't know what to think. The lady in that photograph—*you*—are still alive while the gentleman—who closely resembles *me* —has been dead two hundred years. I'm not scared but I am rattled as hell."

"Funny *I'm* ecstatic. After two hundred years I'm finally reunited with the love of my long, lonely life."

Les put the album aside still open to the photograph.

"It's hard to wrap my brain around the concept."

"And it's easy just to wrap your arms around the reality. Relax darling and enjoy us.'

Melody kissed him softly, "We're all we have." She said, voice like warm honey. "The FBI wants you out of town and the Mafia still wants my scalp."

She kissed him again, deeper this time, and his objections faded into dark bliss.

Chapter 40

Easton looked disappointed. "You'll lose your gun privileges." The average civilian in Louisiana has more gun privileges than a New York City cop."

"That's *before* you shoot. After you pull the trigger they're quick to convict. And you've made serious enemies."

"So have they."

"Whoa Wyatt Earp this ain't Tombstone."

"Do you seriously think they'll forget about me in Hawaii?"

Easton shrugged. "Not really."

"So I'll make sure they don't forget me and stay."

"Here in Lafayette?"

"New Orleans. How about your recommendation on my Private Investigator license?"

"Lake won't like it."

"He probably doesn't like you already."

"There is a buzz around the office."

"Where there's a buzz there's a sting."

"What the hell. We closed the book on our murdered agents. Heck was named but I didn't mention the Knights of The Golden Circle. If Lake is suspicious he won't find anything in my report. Sure I'll vouch for you."

"Thanks Matt."

"Easton didn't smile." I give you a sixty second life expectancy. Why the hell are you doing this?"

"Like I said. I'm a target either way." He shook his head and lit a cigarette. "There's another reason. I served in Special Forces in Afghanistan and Iraq because I believed that bullshit about Democracy, equality and the rights of man. And you know what—I still fucking believe it.

"Did you know that an asshole member of the Knights named Albert Pike started the *KKK*? And here they still are.

Seriously—FBI agents, murdered by their own superior? These people are as dangerous as any Taliban terrorist. And they're already entrenched on Capitol Hill. Somebody needs to keep tabs on these bastards."
    Les stubbed out his cigarette after a few puffs. "I've got to stop smoking. Anyway a private eye in New Orleans gets to eat well."
    "After a while things get tough to digest."
    "Things already have. That's why I'm quitting the Bureau." Easton snorted. "We're back where we started."
    "Not quite. You pick up the check."

+ + +

    Melody took her time getting dressed.
    Les had helped her rent a quiet house on St Charles however they still lived apart. At the moment the arrangement suited her plans nicely.
    At the moment...
    She studied herself in the mirror. How absurd that old wives tale about not having a reflection she mused.
    For tonight she'd chosen a sheer red silk blouse with black bra beneath. Black stretch mini and black Jimmy Choo pumps with red stiletto heels. Bold but tasteful.
    For the past week she had been trying to find a way to get close to Don Benito.
    It was useless. Even if she managed to get inside the gates his guard dogs—there were four—would be on her. She could kill the dogs but by then his crew would be alerted.
    She could kill the bodyguards but stray bullets might hit her in vulnerable places like an eye, or the base of her skull. Although she would recover from these serious injuries it would take at least a month during which she would be relatively helpless.
    Anyway she could only drink so much blood in an evening. No, she had to devise something more subtle.

Think Lucrezia Borgia she told herself putting together some goodies: four Oxys, two blackbirds, two capsules of ecstasy, an eight ball of coke and a bit of heroin. A buffet of temptation for her intended target.

The new house afforded her a comfortable measure of security. There was a garage attached with a door that went directly inside so curious neighbors would rarely see her.

For the same reason she had purchased a used Escalade with tinted windows. In the back seat was a motorcycle helmet with a dark polarized visor (she had gotten the idea from a sleazy horror film) to protect her from any chance encounter with the sun.

As well as a shotgun to defend her honor.

Good to go.

It was still early for her tryst so she decided to have a snack.

As Melody cruised the evening streets she felt a twinge of unease. She missed Les terribly. However they had agreed to give each other some space. Despite her strong emotional bond Melody knew that her lover could not be part of what had to be done. New Orleans was a rich pond to troll. Predators prowled every parish: pimps, dealers, whores pickpockets, purse snatchers, gang punks with automatic weapons, psychos with razors— it was her kind of town.

Even if she picked off two a night the pond would still be stacked. To be sure New Orleans had been that way when she was a proper young lady some two hundred years ago.

And tonight it suited her mood.

Melody had no problem choosing. She spotted a burly white male standing in front of a two story house on a corner lot set off from the other few dwellings on the block. The man was wearing a cut off shirt which showed off his thick tattooed arms. He had long blond hair and a chubby face that looked almost innocent as he passed drugs to two boys no older than fourteen. The boys glanced at each other, obviously their first time.

The man put his arm around one boy and offered him a drink from a pint bottle. As the boy drank the man kept rubbing his shoulder. The bottle passed to the other boy and the older man kept touching them.

A classic creep Melody thought, parking her Escalade.

She despised pedophiles.

The creep actually patted one of the boys on the ass and directed both of them inside the house as she approached. Like any good predator he was aware of her immediately and Melody could see him rapidly assessing categories as she neared: cop, customer, freak, fool. He still hadn't made up his mind when she stopped and smiled at him.

His tiny pig eyes glared at her. "Hep' you?"

"I'm looking for party favors."

He leered, beady eyes taking in her long shapely legs and confident hips.

"I ain't doin' favors 'less I get a favor."

An equal opportunity pervert she thought, pretending to think it over.

"What do you have in mind?"

"Nothin' much, blow job."

"What's my favor?"

"Coke, meth, smack, cash, got it all only…"

"Only what?"

He produced an iPhone from a pocket hidden beneath the fold of his belly.

"I got to take a selfie while you're doin' it."

Another sign of a pathetically narcissistic society Melody noted, giving him a *whatever* shrug. "That your truck?"

"Yeah."

"Let's get in and negotiate."

He grinned revealing missing teeth. "Now that's what I'm talkin' 'bout."

Inside the cab of the truck the man lifted his phone.

"Now we get close you 'n me."

He never had a chance to take the photo.

In four minutes it was over.

Melody paused long enough to take a picture of the dead man slumped behind the wheel. She scanned his gallery and found numerous shots of underage boys in sexual poses. Leaving the phone under his body where the police would find it Melody walked back to her Escalade and drove off.

Never go hungry to a party she reminded. And tonight was an A-List affair.

Chapter 41

Caligula was ostensibly a club featuring male strippers for a female audience. It was also a hunting ground for women seeking women.

Melody had done her due diligence and rather than risk going up against Don Benito directly she had turned her attention to his daughter.

Nadia Benito was a dedicated playgirl. Educated at a private Catholic school in Rome she had remained after graduation to complete her education in sex and drugs. For her rock and roll experience she spent a year in London before returning to the States. For a few years Nadia was a fixture on the Hollywood club scene along with Kim, Paris and Lindsay. A brush with the law involving a DUI and a small amount of coke sent Nadia to rehab then back to the family estate in New Orleans.

Now a hard thirty she made the rounds of the juke joints by night and by day recovered at the New Orleans Country Club.

Caligula was far from a juke joint.

Normally a high-end strip club for men it converted one night a week to a strip club for women. Many of the local soccer moms used the occasion to cover a hook up with other bored housewives or naughty girls like Nadia.

Melody made her entrance before eleven since most of the suburban ladies had to get up early. Not Nadia of course. For her Caligula was just an appetizer on her way down the food chain.

Melody's appearance caused a noticeable stir. She was oblivious to the attention as she scanned the room and spotted her target.

The speakers were pumping Bob Marley's *I Shot The Sheriff* as she strode to the bar and took a stool a few feet away from where Nadia sat watching a near naked cowboy twirl a lasso.

It wasn't long before Nadia glanced her way.

She looked Melody up and down, smiled and raised her glass. After that it was easy.

+ + +

Don Benito was surprised to see his daughter at dinner

"Hi daddy." Nadia kissed the top of his head and sat down beside him at the long dining table.

"It's been a long time."

She nodded. "I've been busy."

"Doing what?"

Nadia was quite aware of his acid tone. She was used to it. Her father often lamented she hadn't been a boy.

"I'm planning to open a fashion boutique in the Quarter," she said sweetly.

"I see. You need money that it?"

"Oh no daddy. All I need is your blessing."

The Don's granite expression relaxed a notch.

"I'll give you my blessing when you open your doors."

"I understand."

They ate in silence, the meal was cooked and served by an ancient Sicilian woman who had been with the Don for decades. Her ravioli were a bit heavy for Nadia's rarified diet but she ate a few without comment. When coffee was served she took a box from the bag at her feet.

"I brought you a present."

Without any noticeable change of expression Don Benito opened the box. Inside were two cannoli. The pastry shells stuffed with sweet ricotta cheese and cream were an Italian dessert specialty.

"I got them at Minucci," Nadia said. The small bakery was known for their authentic pastries.

"They make good cakes," he said grudgingly.

If he was pleased with the gift he didn't show it. Instead he stirred his coffee and eyes half closed listened to the opera

Carmina Burana. Then he picked up one of the cannoli and waved it like a baton before taking a big bite.

+ + +

Don Benito died in his sleep.

The funeral was lavish even by Mafia standards. The governor was there, as was the mayor.

Les made it his business to attend.

He remained in the background, standing on a hill that overlooked the swell of mourners seated around the grave site. A few faces were familiar including Wellington Swan, Minny Free and Nick Casio. He also recognized Cozy Costanza. Hanging on the Mafia captain's arm was a slim young woman draped in black. Although her face was veiled she appeared to be weeping heavily.

A gaudy tsunami of floral wreaths cascaded at one end of the site. Standing at a podium in front of the wreaths a bishop delivered the eulogy which lauded the Don as a philanthropist and pious family man. His words were amplified by two speakers buried somewhere inside the flowers.

All in all a pretty good show.

He noticed that after the service a line of well-dressed men wearing shades made a point of speaking to Costanza. Even without the traditional hand kissing it was clear Cozy was the new boss.

As Les slowly joined the retreating crowd a large shadow loomed in the corner of his eye' He turned and saw Detective Orsini of the Lafayette PD laboring to catch up. Despite the cool weather he was sweating inside his rumpled black suit.

"Mistuh Hensen. Made any movies lately?"

Les paused. "Sorry about that Detective. Just business. You know how it is."

"Oh sure." He lowered his voice. "Isn't that why we're all here on this tragic occasion?"

"Certainly there are persons of interest here."

"You may be one of 'em. A lot of people been winding up dead since you hit town."

Les caught the threat.

"They were winding up dead long before I came," he said, voice steely. "In fact that's the reason I came. Two of your own detectives remember?"

Deep inside his jowly scowl Orsini's beady eyes blinked. "I hear you turned in your badge for a PI license," he countered.

"News travels fast around here."

"That's the truth." Orsini switched gears and his tone became confidential. "So you here on a case?"

"Why Detective Orsini, you know that's privileged information."

Orsini gave him a shrewd smile. "Might get cold out there alone."

"Just like undercover work."

"Can't argue that. Well you take care now heah?"

Orsini turned and waddled off to his waiting car.

As Les watched him go he had the feeling he'd been marked. He glanced back. Cozy and the veiled woman in black were walking slowly to a limo, arms linked.

+ + +

Cozy couldn't believe his luck.

When the Don croaked his daughter turned to him for support. And Nadia was a sexy woman.

Don Benito's wake lasted three days By the second day they were sleeping together.

It was perfect. The heiress and the captain of the guard. It wasn't lost on Cozy that Nadia was enormously wealthy. But they had to be careful. If people found out it wouldn't look right.

Right now Cozy had to maintain the traditions. He needed to rebuild his crew fast. With Falconi gone their drug profits were shrinking. And with Sal gone he needed enforcers he could trust. Filling Don Benito's shoes would be difficult at best.

He would have to meet with the old man's political connections. Maybe Nadia could help him with that. Cozy had a brief image of a perfect Mafia couple entertaining governors and judges at their mansion.

He had to admit Nadia had gotten under his skin. After their first time together he had set up a little love nest at one of safe houses. Actually it was the place he'd set up for the priest.

Good riddance to that fucking weirdo Cozy thought.

When they hauled Father Dunn to the morgue he had the place cleaned top to bottom.

The flat was private and romantic, looking out over a flower garden and furnished comfortably with an oversized four-poster bed ideal for fun and games.

The sudden halt in rosary murders was a bonus. That kind of thing was bad for business.

As befitting his new station Cozy had moved his base of operations to a two story mansion on Charles Street. The bottom floor featured a large library with a floor to ceiling window overlooking the courtyard a few feet below. Cozy made it his new sanctuary, complete with a panic room and secret exit.

He installed Jason as his new assistant and intel expert and had no body guards. As Frank Costello used to say, "*The bodyguards are he first ones they bribe.*"

So Cozy kept a Beretta handy in his desk and a small Glock in his pocket. Both legal. He used the upper floor as his private suite and only saw his daughter three nights a week. She seemed content with the arrangement and he was just a half hour away.

Right now he had it all.

+ + +

Except for the corny pony tail he sported Nadia found Cozy attractive. He was smart, in good shape and an enthusiastic lover. She might have done worse Nadia mused, considering the draft pool. Most of her late father's cronies were cro-magnons. Cozy was right up there with the early Romans.

And she needed Cozy to help her keep control of her father's empire. Nadia liked being head of the family. It gave her a sense of purpose and put all her vices to good use.

At Cozy's insistence she had a driver who was also her bodyguard. Daniello was a martial arts and small arms expert who had served in the military. His manner was very correct and Nadia was confident he could be trusted.

However the first sit down she had with Cozy and the new crew did not go well. They were polite but decidedly cold. The boys weren't used to taking orders from a woman no matter what her claim to the throne.

'Black' Jack Calello who had taken over Falconi's drug distribution network was openly dubious.

"You got to make your bones before you can be boss, ain't that right?"

The others shrugged in agreement.

Nadia wanted to tell them she poisoned her father but that would really make them nervous. Instead she looked at Calello and smiled.

"This is a business Jack. Of course Don Costanza will continue to run the day to day but I'll be exploring legitimate havens for our profits."

Cozy glanced at Nadia grateful for her tact. "Nothing will change gentleman," he said, adopting a somber tone befitting his title. "If anything Miss Benito will maximize our financial position."

Nobody argued. The Don had left her at least one hundred million. They all could respect that.

For the next month things went very well. Cozy brought in extra muscle from Italy and Calello's drug franchise was doing better than ever. Don Benito had set it up so he controlled the product and Cozy already knew the distributors. Their romance was heating up but Nadia had enough experience to see it would go down a predictable path

And she wasn't interested in settling down.

After all, she just got here.

But she knew that Cozy, once spurned, would become a vicious enemy. He hadn't been her father' Capo for nothing.

Nadia's ace was Melody. They saw each other on the nights Cozy was with his daughter. More than anyone she had ever known, Nadia worshipped Melody.

Their relationship wasn't sexual, which was certainly a new level for Nadia, however Melody embodied everything she admired. If she had been interested she would have made a powerful Don.

Melody was definitely not interested.

Instead she gave Nadia the means to take that position for herself including the poison for her father's cannoli. But her new plan had Nadia worried.

"Don't you think it's too soon?"

Melody sipped her drink. "Actually that's your problem. What I propose solves mine."

"That leaves me in a very vulnerable position."

"The moment you killed your father you became a target. Just like he was my dear. It's an occupational hazard. Now you hold the scepter. Or do you?"

Melody paused to light a cigarette.

"How long do you think Don Costanza will keep you around once he cools off? Power is the ultimate mistress. You do know there were some questions about his wife's death?"

"We never…"

Melody took a folder from her shoulder bag and tossed it on the table. "Take a look at this, if you can find the time."

"This is an FBI dossier," Nadia said when she had finished reading the folder's contents.

"I have assets."

"Cozy told me his wife had a heart condition."

"Yes—she had a bullet in it."

"The police report says she was shot during a carjack."

Melody blew a dismissive puff of smoke. "They later found the shooter dead in her car. Very neat wouldn't you say?"

Nadia reached for one of Melody's cigarettes. After a few thoughtful moments she sighed deeply.

"As usual you are absolutely right. When do you want to do this?"

+ + +

When Nadia made the suggestion Cozy snapped it up like a hungry gator.

"Yeah sure, yeah, that would be hot," he said, voice husky. "But we don't need publicity. It can't just be any bimbo."

Nadia pushed him back on the pillow and kissed his chest. "Don't worry *amore*. I have the perfect choice. She's a high end call girl from DC and she owes me a favor."

"After this I'll owe you one."

"We'll see."

"When does this happen?"

"Sometime around Valentine's Day or perhaps Mardi Gras, what do you think?"

"Well Valentine's is more private. And maybe we can come up with something else for Mardi Gras."

"I like the way you think. I'll arrange for someplace anonymous."

Nadia took care of everything. Using Cozy's credit card she rented a suite at an out of the way motel, ordered champagne and made sure there was absinthe and cocaine on hand for Melody.

She booked a table at the Pelican Club and Cozy seemed hyper all through dinner. Like a kid trying to suppress his anticipation at Christmas, Nadia thought.

It made her like him a little more. But it wouldn't change anything.

When they arrived at the motel Cozy seemed disappointed. "Where is she?"

"Honey relax, it's not even dark yet. She'll be here in an hour or so. Meanwhile you have me to play with."

Cozy smiled. "My favorite toy."

Nadia lit the candles, popped the champagne and put a Sinatra CD on the player. After two drinks she unknotted Cozy's tie, took off his shirt and then slipped off her dress revealing a black lacy bra and panties.

Cozy was steaming and congratulated himself on taking two Viagra when they arrived. He pulled away for a moment and had a glass of wine.

"I hope I can wait until she gets here," he said, voice hoarse. "You're very hot tonight."

Nadia moved closer and unzipped his fly. "It'll be worth it honey, you'll see."

Cozy's skin was damp. He was considering a third Viagra when he heard a knock.

"I'll get it," Nadia said.

The female who entered was everything Nadia promised. She had long blonde hair and wore a simple black dress, black stiletto heels and a hat with a black veil that partially concealed her face. All he could see was her sensuous red lips.

The veil lent an air of elegant mystery that heightened Cozy's anticipation.

Nadia gave him a wicked smile. "Here's your valentine present lover. Her name is Dawn."

Cozy took a deep breath.

"Tell Dawn to take off her dress."

Frank swung into *Come Fly With Me* and the tension in the room heightened.

The blond unzipped her black sheath, shrugged and let the garment fall to the floor. She stepped out of the dress and stood there swaying to Count Basie's band. Cozy drank in her full breasts, narrow waist and long legs. A black thong set off her perfect hips.

By this time the Viagra was pounding through Cozy's bloodstream.

"Take off the thong," he said, voice ragged.

Dawn's lip's curled into a lustful challenge. She stepped closer.

"Why don't you take it off for me?"

Hands shaky Cozy reached out. Her skin was as cool as white marble. As she bent over him her breasts brushed his face. His fingers hooked the thong and he felt her breath hot against his ear.

A needle-like pain stabbed his neck. An instant later a voluptuous euphoria swept over him. He basked in the warm wave of pleasure as it rose higher, reached a peak and collapsed into blackness....

Melody lifted her head. Red streaks of blood stained her lips and teeth. For some reason Nadia felt aroused.

Cozy lay dead, eyes wide in a surprised expression.

Nadia tilted her head at Cozy's prominent erection.

"At least he died happy," she said, voice low and suggestive.

Melody took off her blond wig and shook out her black hair. "I need a drink and a bump."

"The coke is next to the absinthe on the liquor table," Nadia said. She sat on the couch and watched Melody walk across the room, lust in motion.

Two lines later she came back with her drink and sat close to Nadia.

"I hope the cops don't connect me to this," Nadia said.

Melody caressed her naked shoulder.

"I wouldn't worry about that."

Still aroused Nadia kissed her.

She too died happy.

Afterwards Melody felt bloated. *Two feedings are one too many she observed.* She resolved to diet.

Despite the advantage of having a Mafia boss under her complete control, the discovery of two prominent naked bodies in a love tryst that included alcohol and coke would completely obscure the fact that both corpses were drained of blood. The news reports would probably go viral. And she would finally be free of bounty hunters.

She would take care of Franny Five Angels after she digested this feast. The way she felt now she could sleep for two days.

Chapter 42

Les still hadn't told Dave he had retired from the Bureau. He had been visiting often, especially since Dave had recovered sufficiently to start rehab. Today Les carried a stack of magazines and newspapers with him.

The staff had gotten to know Les by now and waved him into Dave's private room.

"What's up partner?"

Dave looked up from his book. Having still not recovered the full use of his damaged arm he put the book aside with some difficulty.

Les sat down and dropped the magazines on the table. "What are you reading?"

"*Jolie Blon's Bounce* by James Lee Burke. Takes place right around here. But you know my mind keeps going over what happened."

"To you?"

Dave made a face. "No to *you* dude. You were in a cage face to face with those…"

"Mutants. The smell was enough to kill me."

"And this lunatic Doctor Heck."

"Assassinated."

"This business about…" he lowered his voice. "…Lake being dirty, setting up those agents, it's hard to believe."

"Believe it. He's in bed with some powerful fanatics. Most likely had Heck whacked to sever their connection."

"Not much you can do in Hawaii."

"Oh that, Actually I'm not going to Hawaii."

"But…"

"I turned in my badge. I've decided to stick around and see this through."

"How? I mean what will you do?"

"I'm opening a private investigation firm."

"Seriously?"

"As serious as suicide."

"That should be your office motto. You'll be alone out here-a sitting duck."

Les took a deep, patient breath.

"In Hawaii I'd be alone. Easy target. Here I have limited support. What about you? Did the Bureau take any official stand?"

"Beyond paying my salary and the hospital bills there's no change in my status. Doctors say I'm at least a month away from walking out of here. My left arm is near useless and sunlight seems to trigger migraines so Director Easton suggested a transfer to a desk job in Seattle or Portland where it rains a lot. Alaska was an option but I'd rather risk the headaches."

"Easton came to see you?"

"A few times. I had to revise my original opinion about him."

"He's one of the last of the stand-up guys."

"That reminds me. Have you seen Nick?"

Les grinned. "You sure you don't mean Sam?"

"Back up. Jennifer spent weeks here while I was critical.'

Les lifted his hands in surrender. "My bad."

"Always is," Dave grumbled. "Anyway Sam paid a visit yesterday." He nodded at a bouquet of tulips in a nearby vase. "Brought those."

"She's a nice kid," Les said. He left it at that. Judging from Dave's reaction it was a sensitive issue."

"To answer your question," he said to change the subject, "I see Nick a few times a week. The food is great and Nick is a great source of information. A bar owner gets to hear everything."

"Any clients yet?"

Les nodded. "Very first one. Missing teenager. I think I've got a line on her,"

"Jennifer says she's looking forward to living in a real house and having me keep regular hours."

"How about you, looking forward to it?""

"I've got to think of Robin. At least her daddy can make sure she goes to college."

"I hear Portland is a nice city."

"Rains more in Seattle."

Les nodded. "I'm starting to get used to the Big Easy. I rented a two story place near the quarter. Office on the ground floor sunny apartment above. Drop in anytime."

"I will when I'm mobile."

Les started to go. "One more thing."

"Yeah?"

"Should you decide to get an honest job the door's always open. Full partner, Hensen and Chin. What do you think?"

"I think my wife would divorce me."

+ + +

Linda Gold was a fifteen-year-old runaway.

A student at Isidore Newman a high end private school, Linda maintained top grades and had a few close friends.

Both her teachers and classmates described Linda as conservative. When Les questioned her girlfriends they had a slightly different view.

"Yeah sure, she studies a lot," a girl named Dale Fitch told Les. "And she is pretty talented."

Dale ran a nervous hand through her long black hair. A black designer jacket, blue eye shadow and dark lipstick completed the Preppie/Goth look.

The kid would freak if she met real Goth Les thought.

Instead he said, "How is she talented?"

Dale shrugged as if it was obvious. "You know she plays piano. Practices every day. Used to anyway."

"Used to? Why did she stop?"

"She got into electric keyboard. Cyber rap. Not my thing."

"Is there someplace she goes to hear it or play it?"

Dale sighed. "I suppose. This Club Eighty Eight. Linda has a thing for the DJ."

"Remember his name?"

She lowered her voice. "No way you tell anybody I said anything?"

"Why not?"

Her expression suggested she was about to shut down.

"Because I could seriously get in trouble. Those people at the Eighty Eight are like totally rough."

Les put his hand to his heart. "This conversation never happened."

"Cat I think."

"What?"

"His name. I think it's Cat something. Look I'm gonna be late for class."

As Les watched her shuffle away under the weight of her back pack he hoped it wasn't too late for Linda.

+ + +

Club Eighty Eight had an industrial look. Speakers and lights set on steel overhead beams, high stage with three computer banks and giant rear screen, lots of dance space and a long bar which was deserted except for the tall blond lady wiping glasses. Despite the place being empty, dance music pumped softly from the speakers.

The blond was about thirty with long tanned legs framed by denim shorts and wide shoulders that supported a pale blue tank top. The rhinestones across the tank top spelled "Beware of the Bitch" and there was room to spare across her generous bust.

She swung her hips in time to the music as she approached.

"You're way early for the action."

"Too early for a beer? "Anyway," he added as she popped a Dixie, "seems to be enough action right now."

She flashed an appraising smile.

"You a tourist honey?"

"Just moved here from New York."

She leaned on the bar revealing a stunning cleavage unimpeded by foundation garments

"Well you should feel right at home because this place doesn't get warmed up 'til after ten."

Les dropped a twenty on the bar. "When do you get warmed up?"

"You're definitely cute," she conceded, "but I don't mix business with pleasure."

"Will you be here at ten? Maybe you'll get some time off."

"Oh I'll be here somewhere honey. I'm one of the managers." She leaned a bit closer. "And there'll be lots of hot young things all warmed up and ready."

"Now that sounds like a plan."

"If anybody stops you at the door just ask for Ava."

"Like the movie star."

Ava swept up the twenty and dropped it into the ATM between her breasts

"Honey these kids don't even remember Cher."

Ava was right.

The crowd was young and energetic. The loud electronic music looped hypnotic beats for glaze eyed dancers too cool to sweat. A slim, twenty something girl with a designer hairdo slipped next to Les at the bar.

"See anything you like?"

She was perhaps eighteen with a short skirt and too much makeup.

"Do I look lonely?"

She gave him a knowing smile. "Isn't that why you're here? You don't look like a dancer."

Les put a finger to his lips. "I'm a drinker."

"For the price of a bottle you can have us both."

She pointed her perfect chin at the stairway. "The bottle club is upstairs, private booths."

"Maybe later."

She shrugged and moved off through the crowd. It dawned on Les that the bar area was heavily patronized by older men. He saw a couple of young ladies leading their 'dates' up the stairs. The males milling around the dance floor were fresh and fit. They didn't need the services of the bottle club.

The tables at the edge of the room were occupied by female hotties and a few hefty males who sported pimp bling.

Then he saw her.

Linda Gold's parents had given him a dozen recent photographs and he had hacked into her Facebook page. There was no mistaking her.

Nor was there any mistake about what was going down.

An uberblinged male with braided hair and gold teeth was practically pushing Linda towards the bar. Dragging her feet she shyly started to speak to a fifty something dude dressed in a cowboy shirt stretched tightly over a potbelly. Abruptly Linda changed her mind and went back to the table. When she got there gold teeth grabbed her arm and yanked her down.

Les started to move the Cobra already in his fist.

Gold Teeth was jawing furiously in Linda's terrified face as he reached the table.

Les didn't introduce himself.

He swung the Cobra's weighted head in a tight arc across Gold Teeth's forearm. The pain stunned him and he fell away, releasing Linda. Les took her arm and pulled her to her feet.

"I'm taking you home Linda."

Two things happened.

A bouncer started threading his way towards him and a large man at the table wearing gold chains and a savage scowl stood up.

Les shoved the table hard into the large man's belly pinning him against the wall. As the bouncer closed in Les flashed his new card identifying him as a certified private investigator.

"This girl is underage," Les said as he escorted Linda to the door. "Be cool or you lose your license."

The bouncer stopped short.

The crowd parted and Les hustled Linda outside.

Linda sat slumped in the front seat as Les drove to her parent's home. She hadn't resisted him and seemed to be on some sort of opiate.

Finally Les asked, "The guy with the gold teeth. Was that Cat?"

The question roused her from her stupor.

"No," she half whispered, "that was Royal T."

"I thought Cat was your boyfriend."

"He was. Royal T is my... trainer."

A wave of anger swept over Les and he slammed on the brakes. He was about to shout what the fuck were you thinking but then he saw that Linda was curled in a ball sobbing.

"It's okay," he said, "It's over now. You're safe."

Chapter 43

Linda's return earned Les a fat bonus and a key reference from her father, a prosperous lawyer with powerful pals. However Les was a one-man operation and could effectively handle only a limited number of clients. Which suited him just fine. After serving under a totalitarian system like the FBI for seventeen years and before that six years in Special Forces he relished the freedom to act independently-or not at all.

Out of habit, after his encounter with Royal T at the Club Eighty Eight Les met with Matt Easton and gave him a full report.

"It's a prostitution mill and lots of those girls are under age and being forced into it."

Easton swallowed a piece of crab cake and nodded.

"It's already on our surveillance priority list. But we'll squeeze this guy Royal T and see if he gives us something."

"How are things otherwise?"

"Real quiet ever since the mysterious deaths of some of our top organized crime figures. Don Benito, his daughter Nadia, Cozy Costanza… the last two had no blood in their bodies."

Easton drummed his fingers on the table. "Funny—they were all in those files you requested. Is there anything you want to tell me about that?"

Les had an idea but in truth he didn't know. He hadn't seen Melody for weeks.

He lifted his beer. "Drinking blood is way above my pay grade."

Easton pressed it. "Before he died Don Benito had a bounty out on a girl who was rumored to be a vampire."

"Only in New Orleans do you hear this stuff. Maybe the next Don will be a voodoo priest."

"Well whoever it was disabled the mob all the way to Baton Rouge. Political connections broken. Hijacking, extortion, even drugs are down. But we hear a Mexican cartel is inching their way in."

"If they try to inch past the Vietnamese connection you'll have an ugly gang war."

"Unless the Mafia plugs those gaps right away. We have intel New York might even send in their own."

"And?"

Easton sighed. "Personally I hope the New York boys settle it. They already have a deal with the Vietnamese." He leaned closer. "And your friend Minny Free. Thanks for the tip by the way. We've had her wired since."

He leaned back and regarded Les with steely admiration. "You're assignment was to find out who was murdering our agents and you sure as hell did that and more. Cost you your job—figure that out."

Les met his eyes. "Cost me a damned fine partner. And as for my job? Inside, your boss Virgil Lake, the murdering son of a bitch who sent those agents to die, would dispose of me like a fly. Only difference is, outside the Bureau I'm harder to swat."

Easton looked away. "And inside I've got leverage."

Les sipped his beer. "Is that a promise?"

Easton grunted. "Last time I did you a favor half the parish wound up DOA."

Later, driving back to New Orleans Les thought about Melody. In fact he had thought of her hourly the entire week.

He was attracted to Leda but Melody was deep under his skin. However it made no difference. Les hadn't seen either of them since he left the Bureau and opened up his own agency.

His first case, finding Linda Gold proved to be the most exciting so far. He soon discovered that PI's do a lot of computer searching, take depositions for law firms, and tail fraud suspects which requires hours of waiting. Paid hours of course but hours he might have spent on his own private project.

Bringing Virgil Lake down.

Les also found that a one-man agency had to work overtime to keep up with invoices, receipts, emails, and bills. After putting it off for weeks Les nailed himself to his desk and caught up on it all. When he finished it was nearly ten p.m.

Maybe it's time to hire a secretary Les thought. He moved from the desk and went upstairs. Along the way he shut the ground floor lights.

The second floor had a kitchen and dining area, a comfortable living room and two bedrooms separated by a large bathroom. . During the day sunlight flooded in the wide widows. At night it was quiet.

Les fixed himself a drink and eased onto the couch.

As he sipped his bourbon Les wondered what Melody was doing. She had already disposed of her enemies. He missed her as a matter of course, an empty throb that had become a companion... but tonight she loomed in his thoughts.

He slipped a CD of Sketches of Spain by Miles Davis into his player and freshened his drink.

Melody always liked this album Les brooded.

An odd noise interrupted his reverie.

Les put the drink aside and went to the stairway that led to his office.

Again he heard a shuffling sound.

Thinking it might someone at the door Les went downstairs. There were no lights except for the glow leaking from the upper apartment. At the bottom of the stairs he saw the front door was slightly open. He slipped the Cobra from the small of his back and reached for the light switch.

Something hard pressed into his temple. He heard—and felt—the loud click and realized it was a gun.

"Drop the blackjack bitch or I smoke you now."

Les let the Cobra fall to the floor.

"Step away."

Les half turned and saw a man scoop up the weapon, his gun trained on him.

The man stood and circled back. Eyes adjusting to the light Les saw the man was hefting the Cobra in one hand.

"Might just whup you upside the head with this shit before I blow your candy ass away."

As the man spoke Les saw the metallic reflection of gold teeth in the dim light.

It was the scumbag known as Royal T.

Les knew he was moments away from a stupid way to die.

"The door was open so I came in."

Both their heads swiveled sharply.

Les recognized the shapely brunette standing in the doorway. Royal T didn't.

"Who is this cunt—your woman?" Royal T smiled, revealing his ornate gold bridgework. "I'm gonna show her what a real man is like."

Melody came closer. "Ouuu now that sounds like fun,"

She slipped one arm around his shoulder. "And who are you?"

"Move aside bitch while I shoot this chump."

He tried to shrug her off but it was too late. In the dim light Les saw her head buried in his neck and Royal T's rigid grin of surprise.

Les reached for the wall switch but she lifted her head.

"Not yet darling. I want to spare you the details."

He turned the lights on anyway.

Royal T was cradled in Melody's arms his features contorted in a golden death grimace. Melody's lips were shiny with blood.

She shook her head in exasperation. "You're so damned stubborn."

Les was in mild shock. He had never seen Melody at work before. On the other hand the scumbag was about to kill him.

"Get me a blanket."

He blinked. "What?"

"Get me a blanket. To wrap the body."

Melody lowered Royal T to the floor. "Fortunately, there's no bleeding."

"Not so fortunate for him."

"You're sorry?"

He looked at her. "I'm grateful."

Her bloody smile was like an embrace.

"Get me that blanket," she said, her voice low and husky, "let's get this over with so we can catch up."

Les fetched the blanket and was struck by how efficiently she wrapped the corpse and hefted it over her shoulder.

"Need help with that?"

Melody licked her lips. "I'm very strong for a woman."

+ + +

An hour later Melody was back. She looked like she just returned from the beauty spa where nothing unusual had happened. She kissed him softly.

"I trust you have absinthe."

Perhaps it was the separation or the warm, primal scent of her breath but their bodies ignited and they never made it upstairs to the bar.

Much later while lying in bed eyes half-closed, sipping his bourbon and listening to Lightning Hopkins, Les felt Melody nudge him.

"Are you awake darling?"

"Yeah. Something on your mind?"

"I think you need a partner."

Les uncoiled himself from the pillow and sat up.

He knew what was coming but didn't know how to handle —or more precisely—dodge the issue

"Uh, I don't know. I already have access to the local FBI."

"The head of which wants you dead."

Les couldn't deny her logic.

"So what do you propose?"

"I propose—such a charming term— I propose we resume our relationship on a more stable basis and I join you as a silent partner."

"You a PI?"

She gently pulled him close to her naked skin

"After dark there's no one better."

He was in no position to argue.

I would like to gratefully acknowledge Christine Roth, Rob Cohen, and Richie Dueñez at Rothco Press for their creative enthusiasm. I would also like to thank Ellen Smith for her love and support, and Larry Townsend for his legal brilliance.

Made in the USA
Middletown, DE
06 October 2022

11814508R00209